TALES FROM SHAKESPEARE

Tales from
SHAKESPEARE

retold by

Roger Lancelyn Green

foreword by Christopher Fry

illustrated by Richard Beer

Atheneum   1967   New York

Copyright © Roger Lancelyn Green 1964
Illustrations © Richard Beer 1964
All rights reserved
Library of Congress catalog card number 65–21725
Published simultaneously in Canada by McClelland & Stewart Ltd.
Manufactured in the United States of America
Printed by The Murray Printing Company, Forge Village, Massachusetts
Bound by H. Wolff, New York
First Printing September 1966
Second Printing February 1967

To

NEVILL COGHILL

with affection and gratitude
and in memory of
many O.U.D.S. productions

'You played once i' th' University, you say?'
'That did I, my lord; and was accounted a good actor.'
Hamlet, III. ii.

FOREWORD

by *Christopher Fry*

AMONG ALL THE celebrations of the four hundredth anniversary of Shakespeare's birth—among the productions of his plays, the lectures, the readings, the essays, the biographies, and all manner of junketings—here is a quiet one which is very much to be welcomed: the re-telling of the plays in story form. It is about a hundred and fifty years since Charles and Mary Lamb did their versions. They gave us a minor classic which has pleased children ever since; but, just as we gain from seeing different productions of the plays, and different actors acting them, so it is good to hear these stories told again. And I can think of no one better to tell them than Roger Lancelyn Green. He has four excellent qualifications: a love for literature, for the theatre, and for children, and personal experience of acting in the plays.

I met him when I went to direct some productions at the Oxford Playhouse at the end of the war. I remember that he played one of the Barrett sons in a production I did of *The Barretts of Wimpole Street*. He also acted in *Hamlet*, and *Macbeth*, and before that, with the O.U.D.S., played Biondello in *The Shrew*, Peter Quince in *The Dream*, Elbow in *Measure for Measure*—and once did an unusual 'double', being Oliver and le Beau in the same production of *As You Like It*.

Now he has brought both his experience of the theatre, and the humour and charm of his personality, to the telling of these stories, and the result is a vivid preparation for seeing the plays performed, or for reading after a visit to the theatre, so that our thoughts about the production can be clarified, and we can sit in our memories watching the actors again. For so much happens on the stage, and the words are so abundant, that we can't hope to take it in all at one sitting; these tales increase our pleasure in the theatre, and prolong it.

Roger Lancelyn Green is not only a clear, swift story-teller. He produces, as it were, and acts the stories, too. They are not just stories; they are the plays we see in the theatre. In the Lambs' *Tales* we miss many of the minor characters, particularly the comic ones, but here they are to the life, presented to us by a man who has acted many of them himself. He keeps an admirable balance between the simple language of story-telling and the words of Shakespeare, so that we pass from one to the other with perfect ease, and are guided adroitly through the ramifications of the plots. There is one line of Shakespeare's that I hanker after (which couldn't be included without holding up the story). It is a line which I used to chuckle over when I was a boy, from *The Taming of the Shrew*. Hortensio tries to play his lute; Bianca cries 'O fie! the treble jars.' And then Lucentio says: 'Spit in the hole, man, and tune again.'

I add that line to this book for old time's sake. But for the rest, as Banquo almost says, I will 'shut up: in measureless content.'

C. F.

FEBRUARY 1964

CONTENTS

PART I

THE COMEDIES

THE COMEDY OF ERRORS

THERE WAS ONCE a merchant of Syracuse, called Aegeon, who went on business to Illyria. While he was staying with his wife at an inn at Epidamnus she gave birth to twin sons so exactly alike that nobody could tell which was which. By an extraordinary coincidence, a poor peasant woman also gave birth to twin boys in that same inn, on the very same night. As was customary in ancient times, Aegeon had no difficulty in buying the peasant-woman's children to be brought up with his own sons to become their personal servants.

The four boys were still babies when the time came for Aegeon and his wife Aemilia to return home to Syracuse. They had sailed as far as the south-east corner of Italy when a terrible storm arose. It became so strong that the sailors despaired of saving the ship, and departed selfishly in the only small boat, leaving Aegeon and his family to perish.

Aegeon did the best he could. He took two spars, fastened one of his sons and one of their servants at the end of each, and himself to the middle of one spar, and his wife to the other. He was just in time, for the ship split on some rocks and sank. But the two spars drifted away, and Aegeon saw the one to which Aemilia was fastened picked up by fishermen from Corinth.

He himself was rescued a little later by another ship, which took him and the two babies who were with him safely home to Syracuse. But he had no news of Aemilia and his other son, and enquiries in Corinth failed to reveal what had become of them.

When Antipholus, the son who was saved with him, was grown up, he set out with his servant Dromio to seek his mother and brother. But neither returned to Syracuse: and at last old Aegeon set out to look for them. For five years he sailed from port to port in Greece and Asia Minor, but with no success; and at last he landed at Ephesus, which was almost the only place he had not visited.

Here he was promptly arrested and brought before Solinus, the Duke. For a state of war existed between Ephesus and Syracuse, and a native of either was liable to instant execution if he landed in enemy territory—unless he could pay a fine of a thousand pieces of gold.

Aegeon had no hope of raising this money. But when he told his sad story, Solinus was so sorry for him that he would have let him go if he could have done so. But he could not alter the law so he stretched it as far as he could by allowing Aegeon the whole day in which to find the money to pay his ransom.

Now it happened that on this very day his son Antipholus with his servant Dromio had also arrived at Ephesus, unknown to Aegeon. They were more fortunate than he, for a merchant warned them what would happen to any Syracusans found in Ephesus, so they pretended to be citizens of Epidamnus instead. Antipholus sent Dromio to their inn, 'The Centaur', with the luggage and most of their money, telling him to wait there; then he went for a stroll round Ephesus, intending to join Dromio in time for midday dinner.

Having dismissed his servant and arranged to meet his merchant friend that evening in the market, Antipholus felt free to go sight-seeing. But he had not been thus engaged for many minutes, when to his amazement and annoyance he saw Dromio coming towards him, no longer carrying the luggage.

'Well, you're soon back!' he exclaimed.

'Soon!' answered Dromio. 'Why, it's you who are late! The dinner's over-cooked, my mistress has boxed my ears, and it's well after twelve. . . . Come home, I beg you sir, unless you want a cold dinner and a colder welcome!'

'Stop all this nonsense!' exclaimed Antipholus, 'and tell me what you have done with the money I gave you?'

'Money?' said Dromio, looking puzzled. 'Oh, sixpence last Wednesday! I gave that to the saddler who mended the mistress's crupper. He has it, not I!'

'I'm not in the mood for your jokes just now,' said Antipholus. 'Tell me where that money is. We're strangers here, and it's a great mistake to leave it around!'

'Please master, keep your jokes until we are at home!' begged Dromio. 'You know how annoyed the mistress gets if you're late for dinner.'

'What mistress is this you're talking about?' asked Antipholus angrily.

'Why, your worship's wife, of course,' answered Dromio. 'She and her sister can't start their dinner until you come and join them.'

'If you're quite determined to make these ridiculous jokes when I tell you not to, you must take the consequences!' shouted Antipholus, getting angry; and he began to beat Dromio.

'What do you mean, sir?' cried Dromio. 'Please stop! Oh, if you won't, I'll use my heels!' and so saying he turned and dashed away.

'He's been robbed of the money,' thought Antipholus, 'and he daren't own up to it. Instead he's making these fatuous excuses . . . I've heard that Ephesus is full of clever thieves and jugglers— even sorcerers. I'd better go at once to "The Centaur" and see what has really happened.'

It took Antipholus some time to find his way. But when he got there, he found all his money and luggage quite safe, though there was no sign of Dromio. So he set out to seek him and met him hurrying across the market-place.

'Hallo!' he exclaimed. 'Have you got over your mad jokes about knowing nothing of the money at "The Centaur", and being sent by some mistress to hurry me home to dinner?'

'When did I make such a foolish joke?' asked Dromio, looking bewildered. 'As soon as you gave me the money and the luggage, I took them straight to "The Centaur" and saw to it that they were in safe keeping. Then I came out to look for you, and have only just found you.'

'This is too much!' exclaimed Antipholus angrily. 'Because I let you play the fool and speak to me with more freedom than most slaves are allowed, you must not presume on my kindness.'

'But I swear I never spoke with you after you sent me to "The Centaur", and never said anything about a mistress!' insisted Dromio.

While they were still arguing, they were suddenly approached by two finely dressed ladies, one of whom exclaimed:

'Antipholus, you may well look confused and ashamed! I know what the trouble is: you're getting tired of me! Of me, your own wife Adriana, and you've deserted me for some other woman. And yet not long ago you used to say that you could not bear to be out of my sight, and that my voice was music in your ears. Please come home; do not leave me!'

'Are you pleading with me, fair lady?' asked Antipholus, looking behind him to see if she was talking to someone over his shoulder. 'I don't even know who you are. Indeed I have only been in Ephesus for two hours.'

'Shame on you, brother!' exclaimed the other lady. 'You used not to torment my sister like this. She sent Dromio to tell you it was dinner-time.'

'Dromio!' exclaimed Antipholus.

'Me?' cried Dromio.

'Yes, you!' cried Adriana. 'And you came back and said that he'd beaten you, and sworn he'd never heard of me!'

'Did you meet this lady and make some plot with her?' asked Antipholus.

'I, sir!' cried Dromio, much hurt. 'Why, I've never seen her before!'

'Villain, you lie!' shouted Antipholus. 'When you met me in the market you gave me her message exactly.'

'I never spoke with her, nor met you in the market,' insisted Dromio.

'Then how does she know our names?' asked Antipholus helplessly. 'It must be by magic.'

'Yes, master, and this is fairyland,' agreed Dromio. 'Let's not annoy these goblins, or they'll pinch us black and blue.'

'Enough of this nonsense!' exclaimed Adriana imperiously. 'Come along in: dinner is waiting. Dromio, shut the door after us, and lock it, and stay on guard—inside. Don't let anyone in. I want a long private talk with my husband.'

'Am I on earth or in Heaven—or in Hell?' thought Antipholus. 'Am I asleep or awake? Am I mad or dreaming? Well, I'll smile .and nod and agree with everything they say, and see how this adventure will end!'

So Antipholus followed Adriana and her sister Luciana into one of the finest houses in the market square, where he was treated to a magnificent meal, while Dromio fared almost as well: he locked the door and found his way to the kitchen—where the fat cook, Dowsabel, greeted him as her husband and gave him the best of everything.

Although neither Antipholus nor Dromio could make head nor tail of their strange experiences, the explanation was simple. When Aegeon's ship had been wrecked, the spar to which Aemilia was tied had indeed been salvaged by fishermen from Corinth; but the two children had been separated from her and sold as slaves. They were fortunate, however, in being bought and brought up by Duke Menaphon, uncle of Solinus the present Duke of Ephesus. Not knowing that their brothers were alive, they took the names of Antipholus and Dromio, and when they grew up served Menaphon so well that, after Antipholus had saved the Duke's life in battle, he was not only given his liberty, but also a large fortune and a rich lady of good family to be his wife. So this Antipholus and his wife Adriana, with her sister Luciana and his servant Dromio, settled in Ephesus.

While Antipholus of Syracuse and his servant Dromio were being mistaken for their brothers by Adriana and the entire household, the real householder, Antipholus of Ephesus, had been delayed in the shop of a wealthy goldsmith called Angelo, in company with the merchant Balthazar. After a while he invited both his friends home to dinner, mentioning that his wife was inclined to be jealous and a bit of a scold. He suggested that Angelo should explain why they were late—they had been discussing a necklace Antipholus had asked him to make for Adriana.

As they reached the house, Antipholus was still berating his servant Dromio who had complained of being beaten by his master that morning.

'Hallo!' he exclaimed, breaking off suddenly. 'The door's locked! Very odd! Hammer at it, Dromio.'

Dromio did as he was told, and was answered from inside by Dromio of Syracuse, who told him to go away. When Antipholus of Ephesus shouted angrily to be let into his own house, Adriana shouted back that her husband was already in; that he must be a very impudent rascal to come and knock on somebody else's door and pretend that it was his own house.

Then Antipholus lost his temper, and hammered louder than ever, and Angelo and Balthazar joined him, while Dromio of Syracuse, inside, shouted to them saying that they must be some street-gang, and they'd better go away quickly.

'Go and fetch me a crowbar!' shouted Antipholus to Dromio of Ephesus. 'I'll break down the door.'

But Balthazar managed to persuade him that if he did so, it would cause a dreadful scandal. 'Never mind about dinner,' he ended, 'let's all go and have a meal at "The Tiger" instead.'

'You're right,' agreed Antipholus of Ephesus. 'But we'll go and dine at "The Porcupine". There's a very pretty girl there who talks well and has a good sense of humor. My wife will be terribly jealous and it will serve her right for locking us out just because I'm late. And Angelo, you could call in at your shop and get that chain you were making me for her: it should be ready by now, and I'll give it to the girl at "The Porcupine"—just to spite Adriana.'

Meanwhile, things were not going too happily inside the house. Antipholus of Syracuse took an instant dislike to Adriana—but he took just as instant a liking to her sister Luciana, and after dinner, finding her alone, began to profess his love for her.

Luciana was shocked and horrified; for of course she thought it was her sister's husband who was declaring his love, and it was in

vain that Antipholus protested he was not married. At last she
broke away from him and went to look for her sister, while
Antipholus talked with his Dromio, who had been having a
difficult time in the kitchen with the fat Dowsabel.

'This town is full of sorcerers and witches,' said Antipholus. 'It's
high time we got away from it. So go off immediately to the

harbor and see if there's any ship scheduled to set sail this evening. I'll walk about in the market-place until you come back.'

Off went Dromio, and Antipholus strolled up and down outside
the house, thinking over his strange adventures, and regretting
having to leave Luciana with whom he was fast falling seriously
in love.

Suddenly as he walked, Angelo the jeweller came up to him,
and said:

'Master Antipholus, here's the chain; it took longer than I
expected to get it ready. Did you get tired of waiting at "The
Porcupine"?'

'What am I to do with this chain?' asked Antipholus blankly.

'Anything you like!' smiled Angelo. 'I made it for you. Take it to your wife and make your peace with her. I'll call this evening about supper-time, and you can pay me for it then.'

'You'd better let me pay you now,' said Antipholus. 'Otherwise you may never see the chain or the money again.'

'That's a good joke!' laughed Angelo. 'See you later!' And off he went.

'Well, if they offer me chains, why shouldn't I keep them?' thought Antipholus, and pondering still more on the amazing adventures of that day, he walked on into the middle of the market.

Meanwhile Angelo had scarcely handed over the chain, when another merchant pounced on him for a debt and would have arrested him for failing to pay it if Angelo had not explained that Antipholus owed him just that sum of money.

They were saved the trouble of going to collect it, for almost immediately Antipholus himself met them.

'Ah, there you are!' he cried when he saw Angelo. 'You're a nice one! I expected you at "The Porcupine".'

'This is no time for wit,' said Angelo. 'This gentleman is about to put to sea and wants a sum of money I owe him which is exactly the amount you owe me for the chain. I should like it now since I haven't any ready money at the moment. He's in such a hurry, he'll arrest me if I don't pay my debt immediately.'

'I haven't the money on me,' said Antipholus. 'But go to my wife and give her the chain and ask her to pay for it out of the cash-box in my desk.'

'Certainly,' said Angelo. 'Let me have the chain, and I'll take it to her.'

'It seems to me it's you that's letting his sense of humor run away with him,' said Antipholus severely. 'I haven't got the chain; you must have it—if not you'll get no money!'

'I cannot wait while you argue!' interrupted the merchant. 'Either pay the money, or I'll arrest Angelo for debt immediately.'

'I owe nothing until he gives me the chain!' cried Antipholus angrily.

'You know I gave it to you in the market-place less than half an hour ago,' insisted Angelo.

'You did not!' shouted Antipholus getting more and more annoyed, 'and I haven't seen you since this morning!'

'I've had enough of this!' exclaimed the merchant. 'Officer, arrest him at once!'

'Angelo, I arrest you for debt!' said the police officer whom the merchant had brought with him.

'And, officer, arrest Antipholus on the same charge!' cried Angelo furiously.

'Antipholus, I arrest you for debt!' said the officer clapping him on the shoulder with his other hand.

'I'll obey until I give you bail,' said Antipholus. 'And then I'll see to it that Angelo suffers for this insolent nonsense.'

The officer was just moving away with his two prisoners, when Dromio appeared, and was hailed eagerly by Antipholus.

'Master, there's a ship sailing for Epidamnus this evening!' cried Dromio. 'I've booked our passages, and taken our luggage on board as you commanded.'

'Is everybody mad today?' cried Antipholus. 'I told you, block-head, to fetch a piece of rope so that I could beat my wife and the servants for locking me out at dinner-time today—and you come and tell me about ships to Epidamnus! But never mind about that now. Take this key to Adriana immediately and ask her to give you the purse full of money which she'll find in the desk in my room. Tell her I'm arrested on a false charge, and need the money for bail. Hurry! Now officer, lead on!'

'Adriana,' said Dromio to himself when the prisoners had gone. 'That's where we dined—where that fat Dowsabel claimed me as her husband. Well, I suppose I must do as I'm told,' and off he went.

He arrived at the house in time to interrupt a violent quarrel between the jealous Adriana and her sister Luciana, to whom Antipholus (of Syracuse) had declared his love after dinner.

The news that Antipholus (of Ephesus) was in prison stopped the quarrel for the moment, and Adriana readily gave the money to Dromio (of Syracuse) who hastened in the direction of the prison.

He was surprised to meet Antipholus walking at liberty near 'The Porcupine', and ran up to him exclaiming:

'Here's the gold you sent me for, master. I'm glad to see you've gotten away from that police officer.'

'You idiot!' exclaimed Antipholus. 'I sent you to see if there was a ship leaving Ephesus tonight.'

'Why sir, I came to tell you less than an hour ago that *The Expedition* of Epidamnus was sailing with the tide this evening. But you had just been arrested, and sent me for money to bail you out!'

'The fellow's crazy—and so am I!' said Antipholus. 'I only wish we could get away from here. Everywhere I go, people greet me by name. It's a city of sorcerers!'

Scarcely had he spoken when the door of 'The Porcupine' flew open, and out came a beautiful girl.

'Ah, my dear Antipholus, I'm delighted to find you here!' she cried. 'Is that the chain you promised me today?'

'Sorceress, leave me alone!' cried Antipholus.

'Then give me back the ring I gave you at dinner,' she said, 'or else give me the gold chain as you promised.'

'She's a witch, Dromio!' exclaimed Antipholus. 'Run!' and he set off at full speed, followed by his servant.

'Now I understand it all,' thought the girl. 'Antipholus suffers from fits of madness. That story he told at dinner about being shut out of his own house—he must have been mad then, and his wife shut him out. . . . I'll go and tell her that he stole a valuable diamond ring. . . .'

She had no difficulty in persuading Adriana of the truth of her story. The two of them set out with Luciana to look for Antipholus, accompanied by a doctor called Dr. Pinch who professed to be able to cure the sort of mental illness from which Antipholus seemed to be suffering.

They found Antipholus still being held by the police officer, but engaged in beating Dromio with the rope's end which he had brought instead of the money for which he had sent the other Dromio.

'There you are!' exclaimed the girl from 'The Porcupine'. 'Could a man be madder than that?'

'He certainly seems to be out of his mind,' agreed Adriana. 'Good Dr. Pinch, see what you can do to bring him to his senses.'

Dr. Pinch began accordingly with the correct kind of jargon. But Antipholus interrupted him angrily:

'Shut up, you foolish charlatan. I'm perfectly sane. And as for you, wife, if this is the sort of fraud you give lunch parties for and shut me out of the house as you did today, you deserve more than I intended for you!' and he flourished the rope's end with which he had been beating Dromio.

'Dearest husband!' protested Adriana. 'I swear before God that you dined at home today. I wish you had stayed there, and saved us all this trouble.'

'Dined at home?' cried Antipholus. 'Dromio, you can bear me witness in this. Weren't the doors barred against us? And did not your mistress and Dowsabel both shout abuse at us?'

'All these things are true,' said Dromio.

'Should I pretend to believe all these false statements?' Adriana asked Pinch.

'Yes, soothe him,' was the answer. 'The more he talks, the easier it will be to discover what complex he's suffering from.'

'You've bribed the goldsmith to have me arrested,' went on Antipholus.

'On the contrary!' cried Adriana, quite forgetting Dr. Pinch's advice. 'I sent money to bail you out. Dromio came for it.'

'I came for it?' exclaimed Dromio. 'Never! All I went for was a rope's end!'

'He came to me, and I gave him the money,' insisted Adriana.

'I can bear witness to that,' said Luciana. 'I saw her give it to Dromio.'

'Madam,' said Dr. Pinch aside to Adriana. 'Both your husband and his servant are possessed by devils; I know the symptoms well, their pale and deathly looks. They must be bound and laid in a dark room.'

'This is a plot against me!' cried Antipholus. 'You wretched woman!' and he rushed at Adriana with the rope's end at the ready.

'Help! Bind him quickly!' she shrieked.

'Hold him!' cried Dr. Pinch to the bystanders who had gathered. 'He is frantic!'

In spite of all he could say and do, Antipholus soon found himself tied hand and foot—and Dromio fared no better.

'Officer!' cried Antipholus, 'surely you won't allow this? I'm your prisoner.'

'I'll pay his bail,' said Adriana quickly. 'Dr. Pinch, see that my husband and Dromio are carried home carefully to my house.'

As soon as she and Luciana were left with the officer, Adriana asked:

'Who had him arrested?'

'Angelo the goldsmith,' answered the man. 'Your husband owes him two hundred pieces of gold for a necklace.'

'He ordered the chain for me,' she said, 'but he never had it.'

'Soon after your husband took my ring, I saw him wearing a chain,' said the girl from 'The Porcupine'.

'I know nothing about that,' said Adriana shortly. 'But come, officer, let's go to the goldsmith and find out the truth.'

They were just leaving the market-place, when round the corner they met Antipholus of Syracuse with a drawn sword in his hand, followed by his proper Dromio.

'God save us!' shrieked Luciana. 'They've broken loose!'

'Run for help, and have them bound again!' cried Adriana, taking to her heels.

'They'll kill us all!' echoed the officer, dashing off also.

'Witches are always afraid of cold steel,' said Antipholus sheathing his sword. 'Come along, Dromio, let's go to "The Centaur", and collect our luggage. Then we'll go on board *The Expedition*—and we'll be down the river with the tide before morning.'

But it was not to be; as they came round a corner just outside the Temple of Diana of the Ephesians, they met Angelo, the goldsmith, and the merchant to whom he owed the two hundred pieces of gold.

'Why!' exclaimed Angelo, 'here is Master Antipholus, with my gold chain round his neck! I wonder, sir, that you put me to so

much shame and trouble on account of it! You received that chain from me today; can you deny it?'

'I certainly received it from you,' answered Antipholus, 'and I wouldn't dream of denying it.'

'You not only denied receiving it, but swore you'd never seen it!' cried Angelo.

'Who ever heard me say any such thing?' asked Antipholus in amazement.

'I did,' said the merchant promptly. 'A thief and liar like you should not be at liberty in a decent city like Ephesus!'

'Villain!' cried Antipholus, drawing his sword. 'Take back those words, or prove them in fair fight!'

'That I will!' replied the merchant, drawing his weapon too. But before they could fight, Adriana and Luciana appeared round the corner with a large party of friends and servants.

'Do not hurt him!' cried Adriana. 'He is mad! Catch him and Dromio and bind them!'

'Run, master!' shouted Dromio. 'Quick, into the Temple! We shall be safe there!'

Scarcely were they inside, when the High Priestess came out on to the steps and sternly bade the crowd be gone.

'But I want my husband!' cried Adriana. 'He's mad, and he's just run into the Temple with his servant.'

'How long has he been mad?' asked the Priestess.

'He's been very odd all this week,' answered Adriana, 'but only this afternoon did he really break out.'

'Has he something on his mind?' asked the Priestess. 'Some loss of fortune? Or the death of a dear friend? Or does he feel guilty; has he been neglecting you for some other woman?'

'I think there was a girl at "The Porcupine" . . .'

'Did you reproach him?' asked the Priestess.

'I did indeed,' replied Adriana. 'Day and night I kept at him!'

'That's the cause of his trouble,' declared the Priestess. 'The continuous nagging of a jealous woman is more poisonous than a mad dog's tooth.'

'She only reproached him mildly!' cried Luciana indignantly.

'Friends, please bring my husband out,' begged Adriana.

'No one enters here,' declared the Priestess. 'Your husband took sanctuary with me, and here he remains until he is cured— both with the aid of prayer, and with wholesome medicines of which I have many. Therefore go away, and leave him with me.'

'I won't go away!' cried Adriana. 'You cannot separate husband and wife like this!'

'Be quiet, and go,' said the Priestess firmly. 'You shall not have him.' So saying, she retired into the Temple.

'Complain to the Duke,' suggested Luciana.

'I will,' cried Adriana. 'Let's go to the palace at once!'

'It is just the hour of sunset,' said the merchant, 'and the Duke will be here at any moment. A Syracusan merchant is to have his head cut off unless he can pay the fine by sunset.'

'You're right,' said Angelo. 'Here they come!'

When the procession arrived at the place of execution in front of the Temple, Duke Solinus said:

'Let it be proclaimed once more that if anyone will pay this merchant's fine, he shall not die.'

Immediately Adriana flung herself at the Duke's feet, crying:

'Justice, most gracious Duke, against the Priestess! My husband Antipholus has gone mad. We bound him, but he escaped and fled into the Temple with his servant Dromio, who is as mad as he. And the Priestess will not let us go and fetch him out!'

'I am sorry to hear this,' said the Duke. 'Your husband served me faithfully in the wars, and I promised to help him all I could when I gave you to him in marriage. Go, someone, into the Temple, and ask the Priestess to come out and speak with me.'

The words had hardly passed his lips, when one of Adriana's servants came dashing up to his mistress, gasping:

'Save yourselves! Run! My master and Dromio have broken loose! They've thrashed the servants and tied up Dr. Pinch, singed off his hair and beard and quenched the blaze with dirty water. My master preaches patience to him, while his servant nicks at him with a scissors.'

'Be quiet, you idiot!' cried Adriana. 'My husband and Dromio are here, in the Temple!'

'On my life, I swear what I say is true!' gasped the servant. 'Look out! he's coming!'

'Woe is me, it *is* my husband!' shrieked Adriana—and this time she was right.

'Justice, most gracious Duke!' cried Antipholus of Ephesus, rushing forward and falling on his knees before Solinus. 'Justice against that woman there whom you gave me as wife! She has abused and dishonored me; she shut me out of my own house while she feasted with her low friends.'

'No, my lord,' exclaimed Adriana indignantly, 'Antipholus, my sister and I dined together today. I swear this is so!'

'It is just as she says,' agreed Luciana. 'Kill me if it is not.'

'Wicked, lying woman!' cried Angelo the goldsmith. 'Antipholus dined with me, and what he says is true.'

'It's all a plot!' declared Antipholus. 'This woman locked me out, and I dined at "The Porcupine" with Angelo the goldsmith. But he is a liar too, since he swears he gave me the chain I ordered from him—which I have never received. He tried to arrest me on this false charge, but my wicked wife and her sister, aided by their disreputable friends, seized me, bound me, and handed me over to a foul-minded doctor called Pinch who declared that I was possessed by all sorts of devils. He had Dromio and me tied up and put in a dark cellar—from which we have only just escaped by chewing through the ropes with which we were bound.'

'It is certainly true that he was locked out at home, and so dined with me at "The Porcupine",' said Angelo.

'But did you give him the chain he mentions?' asked the Duke.

'I certainly did,' answered Angelo. 'And when he ran into the Temple a little while ago, he was wearing it. Everyone who was here can bear witness to my words.'

'Not only did I see the chain round his neck,' said the merchant, 'but I heard him admit to receiving it from Angelo—after swearing he hadn't when we met him earlier in the market. It was because he was trying to double-cross us over it that I drew my sword on him just before he fled into the Temple.'

'I never went near the Temple, nor drew my sword on you, nor received any chain from you!' shouted Antipholus. 'And Heaven be my witness.'

'I cannot make head nor tail of all this,' said Solinus. 'He's certainly not mad, or he could not speak so clearly. Dromio, did your master dine at home as Adriana says he did, or with the goldsmith?'

'We were locked out,' said Dromio. 'He dined with that young woman at "The Porcupine".'

'That's perfectly correct,' agreed the girl. 'And it was then that he took my ring which you see on his finger.'

'And did you see him go into the Temple?' asked the Duke.

'As sure as I see you here!' she answered.

'This is most extraordinary,' repeated the Duke. 'Someone go and tell the Priestess to hurry! Either you are all mad, or there's a spell on us!'

'My lord,' said old Aegeon during the pause while the messenger went for the Priestess. 'May I speak? I think I see a friend who can save my life.'

'Certainly, Syracusan, you may say what you please,' answered Solinus.

'Your name is Antipholus, and your servant is called Dromio?' asked Aegeon. They nodded, and he went on: 'Then you know me. Or you will when I tell you who I am, for my seven sad years spent in seeking you may have altered me out of recognition. I am your father, Antipholus! I am Aegeon!'

'I never saw my father in all my life,' confessed Antipholus.

'But it was only seven years ago that you left me in Syracuse!' exclaimed Aegeon.

'The Duke, and all who know me in the city can bear witness that I have never been to Syracuse,' said Antipholus.

'He speaks the truth,' declared Solinus. 'I have known Antipholus for twenty years, during which time he has never left Ephesus except in my company—and I have never been anywhere near Sicily. I'm afraid that your age and danger have interfered with your reason.'

Everything now seemed completely at sixes and sevens; but

at this moment the Priestess came out of the Temple leading
Antipholus of Syracuse and his own Dromio.

'Most gracious Duke, here is a man who has suffered much
wrong!' she cried.

'I see two husbands!' shrieked Adriana.

'One of these men is the other's wraith!' gasped the Duke.
'Which is the living man, and which is the spirit?'

'*I'm* Dromio, send *him* away!' shouted both Dromios in one
breath.

'Aegeon! My dear father!' cried Antipholus of Syracuse.

'My dear old master! Who has bound you like this?' cried his
Dromio.

'Whoever bound him, I will loose his bonds!' declared the
Priestess in a great voice. 'And by so doing, I will gain a husband!
Speak, old Aegeon, if you are indeed he, and say if you once had
a wife called Aemilia who bore you twins?'

'Unless I'm dreaming, you are Aemilia!' said Aegeon. 'Tell me
what happened to the son who floated away with you on the
spar.'

'We were rescued by fishermen of Corinth,' she replied,
'but what they did with our son Antipholus, I do not know.
He and Dromio were taken from me, and I was sent as a priestess
here to Ephesus. But ask him how he comes to be here—for this
is he!'

'Dromio and I were brought here from Corinth by Duke
Menaphon,' said Antipholus of Ephesus.

'Which of you two dined with me today?' asked Adriana
helplessly.

'I, gentle lady.'

'And you are not my husband?'

'No, indeed I'm not!' said Antipholus of Syracuse. 'And now I
can repeat what I said to your sister Luciana—for I meant every
word.'

'That's the chain I gave you,' said Angelo.

'It is,' agreed Antipholus of Syracuse.

'And you arrested me because I denied receiving it,' said
Antipholus of Ephesus.

'I suppose I did, sir,' agreed Angelo.

'I sent you money by Dromio——' began Adriana, but she pointed to the wrong Dromio, who shook his head violently.

'This bag of gold I received from you,' said Antipholus of Syracuse. 'And my own Dromio brought it to me. But I see that we kept mistaking each other's servants. However the money will pay the fine to redeem our father's life.'

'It is not needed,' said the Duke. 'His life is safe; he is the father of an Ephesian citizen.'

'But I must have my diamond ring back!' cried the girl from 'The Porcupine'.

'There, take it,' said Antipholus of Ephesus. 'And many thanks for my good dinner!'

'Then this comedy of errors ends happily,' said the Priestess. 'Come, let us go into the Temple and give thanks for our wonderful reunion. Then we will feast together and rejoice, and tell each other what has happened during all these years of separation.'

'With all my heart,' said the Duke, 'I look forward to hearing everything at this feast.'

'Master,' said Dromio of Syracuse, 'shall I first go and fetch your luggage from on board *The Expedition*?'

'What luggage of mine is on board ship?' asked Antipholus of Ephesus, looking puzzled.

'Why, all the goods that the host of "The Centaur" was looking after!' cried Dromio in surprise.

'He's speaking to me!' said Antipholus of Syracuse. 'Dromio—*that* Dromio!—I'm your master Antipholus—not *that* Antipholus!

And so, still mistaking each other, the two Dromios and both Antipholuses followed the Duke, Adriana, Luciana and their parents into the Temple, laughing heartily.

THE TWO GENTLEMEN OF VERONA

IN THE FAIR city of Verona there once lived two young gentlemen, Valentine and Proteus, who were cousins and close friends.
They had no secrets from one another, and were happiest when
they were together; indeed their friendship was already becoming
as famous as that of David and Jonathan or Damon and Pythias,
when for the first time a shadow came between them.

As usual this shadow was a woman; Proteus fell in love with a
girl called Julia. He began to sigh and look pale as a lover should,
to weary his hearers with praises of his lady's beauties and virtues,
and to spend his time mooning about, writing verses and love-
letters to her. Julia loved him with all the strength of her intense
nature; her love was of the finest—she would dedicate her whole
life and her every thought to him. So strong was this emotion
that she felt that she might play with it a little, and pretend that
she did not really care for him; then her final surrender would be
more utter and absolute than if she had shown her love from the
start. She may also have realized that Proteus had a much shallower
character than she had, and felt that he would value her more if
she were harder to win.

So the love-affair dragged a little, and Proteus spent more and
more of his time wooing Julia. Meanwhile Valentine decided
that he ought to see some of the other cities of Italy. He hoped
that Proteus would come on his travels with him; but his love-
sick friend could not tear himself away from Verona where his

beloved Julia lived, so he tried to persuade Valentine not to go.

But Valentine was not to be turned from his purpose:

'It's no use trying to make me change my mind,' he said. 'It's high time I saw something of the world: "Home-keeping youth have ever homely wits", as the saying goes. I had hoped for your company and could wish that Love had waited, to clap you on the shoulder, until after we had made our Grand Tour. But since you love, you are quite right to set your lady first—as I shall do when my turn comes to love.'

'At least write to me often and tell me all that you are seeing and doing,' said Proteus. 'And I'll reply—I'll probably bore you with news of Julia.'

So the two friends bade farewell to one another, and Valentine prepared to set out for Milan, while Proteus remained marvelling at the power of love which could separate him from his friend, keep him from his studies, and make him care nothing for the amusements in which he had once taken delight.

He was interrupted in his thoughts by the hasty arrival of Valentine's servant, Speed, whom he had asked to carry a letter to Julia.

'Sir Proteus, have you seen my master?' he began.

'He has probably set sail for Milan by now,' answered Proteus.

'What a silly sheep I am to have got left behind,' said Speed glumly.

'You're certainly woolly-headed enough to need a shepherd,' said Proteus with a smile.

'I'll prove that I'm not a sheep,' exclaimed Speed promptly. 'The shepherd hunts for the sheep, not the sheep for the shepherd; but I'm hunting for my master and not he for me!'

'But the sheep follow the shepherd for food just as you follow your master for wages, and not the other way round,' countered Proteus.

'Oh, I cry "baa!" to such proofs!' was the best Speed could do.

'And I bar such jokes,' said Proteus. 'So tell me now, did you give my letter to Julia? What happened?'

'I gave her your letter,' said Speed. 'But you'll get no change out of her.'

'What makes you think so?' asked Proteus anxiously.

'Well, I didn't,' said Speed. 'Not a single coin for all my trouble!'

'Didn't she say anything when she received my letter?' repeated Proteus.

'Not even "Here's a ducat for your trouble",' said Speed sadly.

'Oh, run after your master before the ship sails!' exclaimed Proteus, laughing against his will. 'He'll need you to save it from sinking; it can't sink while you're on board; you're obviously born to be hanged, not drowned!'

'I must find a better messenger,' thought Proteus, and he set to work on a fresh love-letter which he entrusted to Julia's maid, Lucetta.

Now although Julia pretended that she cared nothing for Proteus, Lucetta knew perfectly well that she loved him—and so she took every opportunity to tease her mistress. On this occasion she led the conversation round to Proteus, and praised him until Julia declared she was not interested, before producing his letter.

'Take it back unopened, and give it to him!' directed Julia— and, to her consternation, Lucetta immediately took her at her word and left the room, taking the letter with her.

'Oh, I wish she'd left the letter!' thought Julia. 'She ought to know perfectly well that when I say "No" it means "Yes!". That I must pretend to be shocked at receiving love-letters from a young man—but that it *is* only pretense. Now I shall have to humble myself and call her back. . . . Lucetta!'

'Did you call, madam?' asked Lucetta reappearing with suspicious speed, but looking so knowing that Julia hastily said:

'Is it nearly dinner-time?'

'I wish it were,' said Lucetta, ostentatiously dropping the letter, and then picking it up again. 'Then you'd have something better to do than plague your poor maid!'

'What was that you picked up?' asked Julia.

'Nothing to do with me!' said Lucetta.

'Then leave it where it is for whoever it belongs to,' said Julia.

'That's not where it ought to be,' said Lucetta, handing it to Julia. 'It concerns you, neither me nor the floor! And it's Proteus who is concerned with you.'

'Well, I'm not concerned with him!' cried Julia, and so saying she tore the letter and dropped it on the floor. 'Now go—and leave the bits where they are!'

'It's only waste paper,' said Lucetta pertly as she went out. 'Though I'm sure there's nothing you'd like so much as some more of the same sort to be angry about!'

As soon as she was alone, Julia gathered up the pieces of the letter, kissing them and apologising to them for her cruelty, while she read eagerly all she could reconstruct that 'love-wounded Proteus' had written 'to the sweet Julia'.

What she read touched her heart so deeply that she could keep up the pretense of coldness no longer, but wrote at once to Proteus confessing her love.

When Proteus read this letter, he became almost delirious with happiness: 'Dearest love! Loveliest lines! Oh, the glory of life!' he thought. 'She loves me! Here is her oath of love written with her own sweet hand. Now if only our fathers would give their consent to our marriage, my happiness would be complete. . . . Adorable, heavenly Julia!'

Proteus had good reason to worry over his father's consent, for old Antonio was accustomed to getting his own way in everything, and flew into the most violent rages if contradicted. Moreover he was apt to be prejudiced in advance against any idea which he had not thought of himself—but when he had once decided on anything he insisted on it being done immediately, and no arguments were allowed.

Proteus was still dreaming happily over Julia's letter when his father came sweeping in, full of his latest idea. Proteus hastily put away the letter, but Antonio had seen it, and exclaimed:

'Hallo! What letter's that you were reading?'

'Just a few lines from Valentine,' said Proteus readily. 'A friend brought it to me from Milan.'

'Let me see it,' said Antonio.

'Oh, there's nothing worth reading in it,' Proteus made haste to assure him. 'He merely says how much he is enjoying Milan, how kind the Duke is to him—and how much he wishes I was with him.'

'His wishes shall be gratified,' declared Antonio. 'I have just decided that it's high time you set out on your travels too. So be ready to leave first thing tomorrow morning. I've determined that you should spend some months in Milan—and Valentine will be able to help you by introducing you to the Duke.'

'I cannot be ready so soon!' exclaimed Proteus desperately. 'At least give me a few days to prepare for my journey.'

'What you haven't got can be sent after you!' cried Antonio. 'You leave first thing tomorrow! I will go and give orders to the servants to prepare for your immediate departure.'

'How like an April day my love is,' thought Proteus, when his father had gone. 'One moment the sun shines and shows spring in all its glory, and the next a cloud hides the sun and all is shrouded in grey mist and rain.'

However, Proteus had just time to pay one fleeting visit to Julia, and managed to get a few minutes alone with her in the garden.

'I will come back as soon as I can. Please wait patiently, sweet Julia,' he said.

'As soon as you can!' begged Julia. 'Will you wear this ring for me?'

'And you wear mine,' said Proteus as they exchanged rings.

'I'll seal our bargain with a holy kiss,' sobbed Julia.

'And I pledge myself as devoutly,' answered Proteus kissing her. 'And vow myself yours, and yours only for ever. And now I must go, to catch the tide—farewell, sweet Julia!'

Proteus was almost chased on to the ship by his father's steward, Panthino, who then had to hunt for Proteus's servant, Launce, who was bidding farewell to his whole family.

'I need an hour for weeping!' he protested. 'All the Launces are famous for their tears, and I have been receiving my full proportion like the Prodigious Son in the parable! Everybody has been weeping over me—except my dog, Crab, who is the sourest-natured animal that ever lived! There was my mother weeping, my father wailing, my sister crying, my blind old granny so tearful that she couldn't see a thing, our maid howling, our cat wringing her paws—and yet Crab remained dry-eyed: he's a cruel-hearted cur; he has no more pity in him than a dog!'

'Hurry, you fool!' interrupted Panthino. 'You'll miss the tide!'

'The tied doesn't miss me!' said Launce shaking his head sadly. 'It's the cruellest tied ever!'

'What's the cruellest tide?' asked Panthino blankly.

'Why, he that's tied here!' answered Launce. 'Crab, my dog!'

And with that he set out at full speed, and joined Proteus on his ship just as the ropes were being cast off.

Meanwhile in Milan things were going both well and ill for Valentine. The Duke had made him welcome and shown him much kindness; he had also introduced him to his daughter Silvia, with whom Valentine had fallen truly and deeply in love, and she with him. But here his good fortune ended, for the Duke had promised his daughter in marriage to a rich lord called Thurio—in spite of the fact that Silvia cared nothing for him and realized that he was conceited, a coward, and capable of loving no one but himself.

On account of Thurio, Valentine and Silvia had to keep their love a secret, with Speed to carry their letters. At first Silvia pretended to have another love, and when Valentine vowed to do anything she might command, she told him to write a love-letter for her. Very unwillingly he did this, and gave her the letter—which she at once returned to him, telling him to write another, even more passionate.

'And when you have written it, read it over for my sake,' she said. 'And if it pleases you, all's well. You may have it in reward for your labor!'

Silvia left Valentine with the letter in his hand, wondering what to make of her words.

'She said she was not moved by my letters,' he murmured.

'Yet she wrote to you often enough!' laughed Speed.

'She never wrote to me at all!' cried Valentine.

'Why does she need to?' asked Speed. 'You write the letters for her!' The truth slowly dawned on Valentine, and he stood enraptured.

'What are you thinking about, sir?' said Speed at length. 'It's dinner-time.'

'I've had my dinner,' answered Valentine absently.

'But listen, sir,' begged Speed. 'Love may feed on air like the chameleon, but I'm only an ordinary man; I want meat and drink. So please don't be like your mistress: be moved, sir—in the direction of the dining-room!'

After this, Valentine's wooing went well in all respects, except for the Duke's consent. Finally Silvia agreed to run away with him if he could smuggle a rope ladder to her so that she could escape at night from her room. Just as everything was arranged, news came that Proteus was on his way to Milan—and Valentine's happiness was complete.

It was the Duke himself who brought the news—he had received a letter from Antonio.

'Do you know this Proteus well?' he asked.

'As well as I know myself,' answered Valentine, and went on to sing the praises of Proteus until the Duke laughed and said:

'This paragon of yours is already here in Milan. I'll send him to you so that you can make him welcome and introduce him to my daughter Silvia and to Thurio.'

'Proteus is the friend of whom I told you,' said Valentine to Silvia when the Duke had gone. 'The one who would have come here with me if he had not been held in Verona by the love of his Julia.'

When Proteus arrived, Valentine had only a few minutes in which to introduce him to Silvia before the Duke sent for her, and she and Thurio left the two friends together.

'And how is your lady Julia?' asked Valentine, after greeting his friend and learning that all was well at Verona.

'My tales of love used to bore you,' answered Proteus. 'You can care nothing for what a lover can say.'

'True, Proteus,' answered Valentine, 'but my life is altered now I have done penance for scorning love—with nightly tears, daily sighs, fasts and a penitent's groans. Love has so humbled me that I now enjoy no conversation that is not about love. Now, like you, I can breakfast, dine, sup, and go to bed feeding on nothing but thoughts of love.'

'I thought that I had read your looks aright,' smiled Proteus. 'And Silvia is the idol that you worship so?'

'Yes, she is the perfect saint of my devotion,' sighed Valentine. And he went on to tell Proteus of his wooing, and of how he had won Silvia, and of how wonderful she was.

'But my foolish rival has gone with her,' he ended. 'Her father favors him only because of his great wealth. I know she cares nothing for him; but I must go after them, for love cannot help being jealous.'

'And she loves you?' asked Proteus.

'We are already betrothed,' answered Valentine, 'and our marriage-hour is fixed, together with cunning plans for our flight. I'll tell you about it later on.'

Off went Valentine after Silvia, but Proteus stood as if in a daze. For Silvia's beauty had worked on him like a charm, and had sent the sudden madness of desire coursing through his veins. Julia and his love for her, honor and his friendship with Valentine, were all drowned in the surging flood of this wild passion. Like his father, what he wanted he must have. Silvia had suddenly become an obsession; nothing could be too mean or too treacherous if it helped to win her—even though Julia and Valentine were the victims.

The means of removing Valentine, his only serious rival, were all too easy. For Valentine was as open, honest and true a lover as the saint after whom he was named, and, trusting Proteus absolutely, told him every detail of the scheme for elopement. Valentine could not imagine anyone being treacherous or changeable, nor dream that his friend might be rightly named Proteus like the Old Man of the Sea in Greek legend, who could change in a moment from one shape into another.

Once the madness of desire was upon him, and he had given way to its temptations, Proteus found no difficulty in persuading himself that to love Silvia, to desert Julia, and to betray Valentine were all right and proper actions. 'Love comes first,' he told his conscience. 'What love bids me do, I should do. Everything must give way to my love for Silvia; it would be quite wrong to repress my natural instincts. So there's no harm in breaking my promise to Julia and getting Valentine out of the way—in fact I'm proving what a devoted lover I am.'

Having smothered his conscience with false reasoning, Proteus went to the Duke.

'My gracious lord,' said Proteus, 'I have something to tell you which the law of friendship bids me hide. But honor and loyalty should be above friendship, and your kindness to me reinforces my duty; it makes me tell you what nothing else in the world would draw from me. My friend Valentine intends to steal away your daughter this very night. Any moment now he will be here; he will have, under his cloak, the rope ladder by which your daughter is to climb down from her bedroom window. When you uncover his plot, do not, I beg you, let him know that it was I who gave him away; for it is love of you, not hate of my friend, that has made me tell of his deceitfulness.'

'Proteus, I am deeply grateful,' said the Duke. 'I suspected their love, but had no idea it had gone as far as this. I am determined that Silvia shall marry Thurio, so I'll see to it that Valentine is banished immediately from my land—and without knowing that you had anything to do with it.'

Scarcely was Proteus out of sight, when Valentine appeared walking fast with his cloak wrapped round him.

'Why Valentine!' exclaimed the Duke. 'Where are you going in such a hurry? Stay and talk for a little; there's a matter on which I want your advice. . . . You know how anxious I am for my daughter to marry Sir Thurio?'

'I know it well, my lord,' said Valentine. 'And from the point of view of position and wealth he seems an excellent match. Haven't you yet been able to persuade her to accept him?'

'She's a disobedient, peevish, stubborn and undutiful daughter!' cried the Duke. 'If she were not my only child, I'd wash my hands of her. And I will too! That's why I want your advice. I'm determined to marry again, and the moment I have another child, out goes Silvia.'

'What do you want me to do or advise in all this?' asked Valentine cautiously.

'There is a lady in Verona whom I love,' said the Duke. 'But she is promised to a rich man far younger than I am. It seems that I am out of date in my methods of wooing; you are young, and you know the customs of Verona: instruct me how to proceed.'

Valentine accordingly advised the Duke as to what letters he should write and what gifts he should send.

'But she is kept in her room, and no man is allowed to visit her alone except the one whom her parents have chosen,' said the Duke.

'Then you must visit her by night,' answered Valentine.

'But her room is much too high up for me to climb to her window,' objected the Duke.

'Then you must use a rope ladder,' said Valentine.

'How can I get it to her?' asked the Duke.

'You may hide it under a cloak,' Valentine explained. 'Then you can carry it by day without anyone knowing about it. And if you cannot actually take it to her, you can leave it where she can find it in her house.'

'A cloak such as yours would do,' said the Duke. 'Lend it to me!'

So saying, he caught suddenly at Valentine's cloak, and from it there fell a rope ladder and a letter.

'This is just what I needed,' cried the Duke, putting his foot on the bundle of rope. 'And this letter: "To Silvia!" I'll make so bold as to read it: "Silvia, this very night I'll come to you and set you free." And a poem. . . . Hmm . . . "My thoughts do harbor with my Silvia nightly", and so on. . . . Valentine, you are a villain, and I've caught you just in time! You think that you can reach the stars because they shine on you, do you? Go, this very day—and thank my patience rather than any virtues you may possess for your escape. If you are within my territories tomorrow,

you shall suffer the worst punishment I can devise. Go at once:
I do not wish to hear your vain excuses: if you love your life,
fly—and quickly.'

When he was alone, Valentine gave way to despair. 'I fly to
save my life,' he thought. 'But life for me is where Silvia dwells—
without her I fly but to death, for I cannot live without her.'

Presently Proteus found him and tried to comfort him with
false words.

'Go, since you must, to save your life,' he urged. 'Even if you
could stay in Milan, you would not be allowed to see Silvia. So
return to Verona, and wait for better fortune. Meanwhile, write
to Silvia as often as you wish—but send the letters to me, and I'll
make sure she gets them: if you address them directly to her, the
Duke is certain to intercept them.'

So Valentine set out sadly and alone on the road to Verona,
trusting in his false friend to help him keep in touch with
Silvia. He never reached home, however, for on the way he and
Speed were captured by a band of outlaws who intended to
rob them. But when Valentine showed that he had no money,
and told a feigned tale of how he himself had been outlawed
for killing a man in a duel, they asked him if he would be their
leader.

'I will accept your offer,' said Valentine at length, 'if you will
promise to obey me in everything, and to do no harm to any
woman, or to poor travellers. If you agree I'll make a virtue of
necessity, and captain you as Robin Hood of England did his
merry thieves.'

The outlaws agreed readily to this, and led Valentine away
to their hiding place in the forest. There he dwelt with them for
several months, finding that in spite of their wild manner of
making a living, they were decent men at heart. Before long
he grew to love the simple life in the open and almost to prefer
the song of the birds and the loneliness of the woods to the
noise and bustle of the city. Yet this new-found contentment
did nothing to lessen the pain at his heart for the loss of his
beloved Silvia.

But she was lost to him only by distance. Never for a moment did she waver in her faith and love, in spite of all that Proteus and Thurio could do to make her forget Valentine.

Pretending to have only the Duke's will in mind, Proteus suggested that the best way to make Silvia forget Valentine was to slander him.

'Make her believe that he was a liar, a coward, and a penniless adventurer—not the gentleman he pretended to be,' said Proteus. 'These are the three things a woman hates most in a man.'

'But she'll think they are all lies, spoken by someone who hates Valentine,' objected the Duke.

'Someone whom she knows to be his friend must tell her,' said Proteus.

'That must be you,' declared the Duke. 'Since no good words can help him, bad ones won't do him any harm. And as you unravel her love from Valentine, you must weave it round Thurio, by saying how wonderfully he reveals all the virtues which Valentine lacks. For as she falls out of love with the one, she must fall into love with the other. . . . And we trust you, Proteus, since we know you are promised to a certain lady of Verona called Julia, and are famed for the depth and constancy of your love.'

'I will do all that I can,' said Proteus. 'And to words must be added music: songs of love sung at night under her window will help in Thurio's wooing. . . . I myself will engage the musicians and write the songs.'

So Proteus set to work to double-cross Thurio while slandering Valentine and betraying Julia—for he had given himself up to his unholy passion so completely now that there was no longer any room in his heart for even a crumb of honor or decent feeling.

It was on the very night that Proteus first brought the musicians beneath Silvia's window that he gained a new servant: a young man who said his name was Sebastian.

Proteus and Thurio stood beneath Silvia's window, with Sebastian behind them, while the musicians sang:

'Who is Silvia? What is she,
   That all our swains commend her?
Holy, fair and wise is she;
   The heaven such grace did lend her,
That she might admired be.'

When the song was ended, Proteus stayed behind to plead Thurio's suit. Sebastian remained in the shadows.

'What is it you want?' asked Silvia, looking out of her window.

'To grant whatever you may ask——' began Proteus. But Silvia interrupted him contemptuously:

'All I ask is that you go away and never let me see you again— you cunning, lying, false, disloyal villain. You must think me very foolish to be deceived by your lies and flatteries. I despise you. Go back to the lady whom you have wronged so sorely, and beg her forgiveness on your knees.'

'I confess, sweet love, that I did once love another lady,' said Proteus. 'But Julia is dead.'

'*That* I know to be a lie,' muttered Sebastian under his breath. 'Or else I could not be here to contradict it.'

'Even if you speak the truth,' continued Silvia, 'there is still your friend Valentine, to whom I am betrothed.'

'I have just heard that Valentine also is dead,' declared Proteus.

'It may be so,' said Silvia sadly, 'then is my heart buried in his grave.'

Proteus went on trying to persuade Silvia to retrieve her heart from Valentine's grave, and bestow it upon him; but Silvia bade him to weep beside Julia's grave and not trouble her again.

Nevertheless Proteus sent his new servant Sebastian to Silvia next day to beg for her picture and to give her a ring. He also sent a letter which Silvia tore up unread—and she refused to accept the ring:

'Shame on Proteus for sending it!' she exclaimed. 'I have heard him say a thousand times that his Julia gave it to him when he left Verona. Even though his false finger has profaned the ring, mine shall not do such wrong to Julia.'

'She would thank you for those words, if she were here,' said Sebastian.

'Do you know her?' asked Silvia. 'What is she like?'

'I know her almost as well as I know myself,' answered Sebastian. 'And she is just my height and size—for I once wore her gown in a pageant in which I played the part of deserted Ariadne, and everyone said that the dress might have been made specially for me.'

'I weep to think of her in her desolation,' said Silvia. 'Here, take this purse—I give it you for her sake. But bring me no more messages from the false Proteus.'

Sebastian had no chance to do so, for that very night Silvia fled from Milan, aided and accompanied by a kind old knight of her father's called Sir Eglamour.

The Duke discovered her disappearance next morning, and set out to scour the country for her, bidding Proteus and Thurio spread out on either side of the road to Verona by which he felt sure she must have fled in search of Valentine.

Meanwhile Silvia was captured by those very outlaws over whom Valentine was king. Eglamour escaped into the wood and, for a while longer, was pursued by all but one of the outlaws.

'Come with me, lady,' said Silvia's captor. 'I must bring you to our chief. Do not be afraid: he is a man of honor, and will allow no harm to come to any lady.'

Before they reached Valentine, however, Proteus and Sebastian came upon them, and the outlaw fled, leaving Silvia. She tried to escape, but Proteus soon caught up with her in the glade of the forest just in front of Valentine's cave.

'Madam,' exclaimed Proteus. 'I deserve at least some gratitude for saving you from this wicked outlaw.'

'I would rather have been caught and eaten by a hungry lion than rescued by Proteus!' cried Silvia. 'Heaven be my witness to my love for Valentine—and my hate for Proteus! So leave me— and do not trouble me more.'

'I'd do anything to win you!' cried Proteus excitedly. 'Oh, what a curse love is when a woman will not love the man who loves her!'

'When the man cannot love the woman who loves him,' corrected Silvia. 'Think of Julia, your first and truest love, you faithless, perjured man! You false friend!'

'In love, who troubles about friends?' demanded Proteus.

'All decent men. Not you,' answered Silvia with spirit.

'So, gentle words will not move you!' cried Proteus. 'Then I shall have to use force!'

'Oh, Heaven help me!' shrieked Silvia.

Now Valentine stepped forward from the cave where he had stood watching this unexpected scene.

'Ruffian, take your hands from her!' he cried.

'Valentine!' gasped Proteus, staggering back.

'Unless I had seen and heard, I could not believe your vileness,' said Valentine sternly. 'You give me no choice: I have no longer a friend called Proteus. Woe's me that my dearest friend should prove my worst foe.'

'My shame and guilt are more than I can bear,' sobbed Proteus. 'Forgive me, Valentine. If such sorrow as I now feel is sufficient ransom for such an offense as mine—I tender it freely. I swear that I suffer at this moment enough punishment for all I have done.'

'Then I forgive you, and once again count you as honest,' said Valentine, the true goodness of his heart welling up to receive the repentant sinner whom he still loved. 'He who is not satisfied by true repentance, is fit neither for Heaven nor Earth. We have God's example before us and—since true friendship is nearer to Him even than the love of man and woman, I release Silvia from all her vows to me if she wishes to turn to you.'

'Oh me unhappy!' gasped Sebastian suddenly, and sank to the ground in a faint.

Proteus bent over him anxiously. Soon the dazed Sebastian sat up and turned to Valentine who knelt on his other side asking what was wrong:

'My master told me to give a ring to Madam Silvia,' he said. 'But I have not done so. Here it is.'

'Why, this is the ring I gave to Julia!' cried Proteus.

'Oh I'm sorry, it's the wrong ring! This is it,' whispered Sebastian.

'But how did you get this ring?' asked Proteus. 'It is the one I gave to Julia when I left Verona.'

'Julia gave it to me,' answered Sebastian. 'And—now Julia gives it to you!'

'Julia!' cried Proteus, slowly beginning to understand.

'Yes, I am Julia,' was the answer. 'Let this disguise make you blush, Proteus—you have so often wounded me to the heart. Be ashamed that I needed such immodest raiment to come and seek you—if indeed there can be shame in a disguise dictated by love. At least it is better for a woman to change her shape than a man his mind!'

'Than a man his mind,' echoed Proteus. 'Yes, there's man's great imperfection. Why have I behaved like this? What is there in Silvia's face to draw me from Julia—whom now I see to be the one true choice of my heart?'

'Enough. Now give me each a hand,' said Valentine. 'Allow me the blessing of joining your hands thus. So. Now, Proteus, we are fully friends again.'

'And may Heaven be my witness that I have my wish for ever,' said Proteus fervently as he drew Julia towards him.

'And I mine!' she answered with a sigh of happiness.

At this moment the outlaws burst into the glade leading the Duke and Thurio and crying: 'A prize! A prize!'

'Stop! Release them!' cried Valentine. 'It is my lord the Duke! Your grace is welcome, and I beg pardon for these rough followers of mine.'

'Banished Valentine!' exclaimed the Duke.

'There's Silvia, and she's mine!' cried Thurio.

'You have first to reckon with me,' said Valentine, drawing his sword. 'There's Silvia—take her, if you dare fight for her!'

'I don't want her!' exclaimed Thurio hastily. 'A man's a fool who runs into any danger for a girl—particularly one who doesn't love him. I make no claim—she's yours if you want her.'

'I'm disgusted with you, Thurio,' cried the Duke angrily. 'You made such efforts to win Silvia, and now you give her up out of mere cowardice. . . . Sir Valentine, I applaud your spirit, and I take back all that I have said against you. You are a gentleman, and worthy of Silvia: she is yours, for you have well deserved her.'

'I thank your grace for the gift which has made me happy for ever,' said Valentine. 'But I must beg one further boon.'

'I grant it, whatever it may be,' said the Duke.

'These banished men deserve to be recalled from exile and taken into your service,' said Valentine. 'I have lived as one of them, and I know that they are all now reformed characters.'

'I pardon them as I pardon you,' declared the Duke. 'Now let us hasten back to Milan, there to celebrate your wedding to my daughter.'

So they all set out happily for Milan. And when the Duke realized that the boy Sebastian was none other than Julia, and that she had won back the love of her erring Proteus, he insisted that they must also be married at the same time as Valentine and Silvia.

LOVE'S LABOR'S LOST

FERDINAND, KING OF NAVARRE, was an earnest and romantic young man. His little kingdom enjoyed peace and prosperity, and did not need much direction from him, so he decided to spend three years in study. But instead of going to the University, he created a university of his own—of a select and novel kind— and drew up the statutes of his new organization to be signed by himself and his three friends Berowne, Longaville and Dumaine.

'Navarre shall be the wonder of the world,' he said. 'It will become as famous as that first Academy in ancient Greece founded by Plato. You, my three disciples, have sworn to dwell with me here for three years, and during that time to abide by the rules which I have drawn up. So now it remains only for you to sign—and to keep your solemn oaths.'

'I am resolved,' said Longaville. 'It is only a three-years fast. The mind shall banquet although the body may pine.'

'I also,' agreed Dumaine. 'And I here forswore the ordinary delights of life such as love, wealth and wordly shows, and dedicate myself to philosophy.'

'As for me,' said Berowne, who was the gayest and most vivacious of the three, 'I can only repeat what they have said and what I have already sworn—to live and study with you here for three years. But there are other conditions in your statutes which I hope you are not going to enforce: one is not to see a woman during all that time; and to fast one day in seven, and eat only one meal a day for the rest of the week. Then there is something about spending only three hours a night in sleep—and not to be seen yawning and blinking by day. I am certainly used to being up most of the night—but only if I can stay in bed all the next morning!'

'The conditions are all there,' said the king sternly, 'and you have sworn to obey them. Surely you do not think them wrong?'

'Oh, I can give you a very good argument to prove that each one is a grave mistake!' cried Berowne; and he proceeded to do so at length, until the king exclaimed:

'Enough! Enough! You have proved that you are not a suitable member of our fellowship. So off home you go!'

'No, my good lord,' said Berowne, suddenly serious. 'I have sworn to stay with you, and I will. And although I have argued against all your rules, I feel sure that I shall be able to keep them for these three years. Give me the document, and I will sign each rule.'

Berowne read it through carefully; when he had signed, he said:

'Here is a rule that if any man be seen to talk with a woman during these three years, he shall endure such public shame as his colleagues can devise. Now this rule you yourself must break, for as you know the daughter of the aged King of France is on her way to visit you and discuss the question of giving up Aquitaine.'

'What do you all think?' asked the King, looking worried. 'I hadn't thought of that.'

'This is what happens,' said Berowne. 'The more you study, the less practical you become!'

'We will have to cut out this rule,' said the King. 'The Princess must be received—even if it is only out in the park. That is simple necessity.'

'Necessity will make us all break our oaths three thousand times in the next three years,' smiled Berowne. 'So here I sign my name to all these rules—and if I break any of them, well—I do it through bare necessity! But none the less, I have a feeling that I shall be the last of the four of us to break my oath. Now tell me is no entertainment allowed at all?'

'Certainly it is,' answered the King. 'There is a Spanish knight, Don Adriano de Armado, who will give us plenty of amusement. He is an expert in the new fashion of using as many complicated words as possible to say the simplest thing. He adores listening to his own voice, and is always inventing fresh and ridiculous phrases. I assure you we shall have plenty of entertainment listening to him.'

'There is also Costard the country bumpkin,' said Longaville. 'He'll be a splendid contrast to Don Armado: the natural fool opposed to the artificial one.'

Costard had already got himself into trouble; and while the four young men were still discussing him, he arrived in their midst in custody of the local policeman, Constable Dull.

'Which is the King's own person?' demanded that worthy, gazing stupidly about him.

'Here,' said Berowne, pointing to the King. 'What do you want with him?'

'I reprehend him very well,' said Dull, 'because I am his grace's constable. Senior Arma—Armadillo commands himself to you. There's villainy going on: this letter will tell you all.'

'Sir,' said Costard, 'the contempts of it are about me.'

The King opened Don Armado's letter, which ran to several pages, and read it out, to the great amusement of his friends and the bewilderment of Dull and Costard. The point of it turned out to be that Costard had "Sorted and consorted, contrary to thy established, proclaimed edict and continent canon, with—with,— oh, with—but with this I passion to say where with—"'

'With a girl,' interrupted Costard.

' "—With a child of our grandmother Eve," ' went on the King, ' "a female; or, for thy more sweet understanding, a woman . . ." '

'I confess the woman,' said Costard. 'She is Jaquenetta.'

'Did you hear the proclamation?' asked the King.

'I confess to hearing it,' answered Costard, 'but not taking in what it said.'

'I condemn you to fast for a week,' said the King severely, 'with nothing but bran and water. Don Armado shall be your keeper: take him, Lord Berowne, while the rest of us go and enter upon the new lives to which we have sworn ourselves so firmly.'

'I'll bet my head against any man's hat that these oaths will prove no more than empty words!' remarked Berowne as he set out with Costard and Dull.

In the end it was Constable Dull who delivered Costard to Don Armado who was holding forth in his usual lofty and fantastical way to his page boy, Moth (who was keeping a very solemn face, but laughing at him inside).

'Sir,' said Dull, 'the King's pleasure is that you keep Costard safe; and you must not let him enjoy himself, nor do penance, nor eat more than three days a week. As for Jaquenetta, she must come along with me. She can stay here in the King's park and work as a daily-woman.'

'Villain, thou shalt fast for thy offences ere thou be pardoned,' said Don Armado.

'Well sir, I hope that when I do, you'll let me have a really good meal first,' replied Costard.

'Take away this villain, and shut him up!' said Don Armado to Moth; and when he was alone, he thought to himself how useful Costard might prove to carry letters. For in spite of the proclamation and the oath which he too had sworn, Don Armado had fallen in love with Jaquenetta.

Soon after Costard's arrest, the Princess of France arrived at the King of Navarre's palace, accompanied by her chamberlain, Lord Boyet, and her three ladies-in-waiting, Rosaline, Katharine and Maria. They were not strangers to the King and his friends, for already these ladies had met Berowne, Longaville and Dumaine and knew quite a lot about them.

The Princess had also heard of the Academy which the King had formed, and she and her ladies were ready to make fun of it if the chance arose. The more so when Boyet, who had been sent to inform the King of their arrival, returned saying:

'The King is coming to meet you here. And it seems that rather than break his oath he intends to lodge you in tents and pavilions out here in the park; he will allow no woman to enter his palace.'

Sure enough, the King of Navarre appeared a moment later, followed by his three lords, and greeted the Princess courteously:

'Fair Princess, welcome to the court of Navarre.'

' "Fair" I give you back again,' said she with spirit, 'and "welcome" I have not yet heard. The roof of this court,' she added, gazing up at the sky, 'is too high for it to be yours; and a welcome to your fields is unworthy of my rank.'

'Madam, you shall be welcome to my court,' said the King.

'I will? Then lead me into it,' answered the Princess promptly.

But the King hastened to explain about his oath, which the Princess treated with polite amusement. Then having discussed the proposed settlement of the dispute over Aquitaine—the reason for her visit—the Princess announced that she must stay in Navarre until further letters came from her father.

'I have made arrangements for your visit,' said the King. 'Although, for my oath's sake, I cannot invite you to enter the palace you shall be entertained in my park so royally that you shall deem yourself lodged in my heart.'

With which delicate compliment the King took his leave, promising to visit the Princess again next day.

While the King and the Princess had been discussing affairs of state, Berowne, Dumaine and Longaville had renewed acquaintance with Rosaline, Katharine and Maria.

'Unless I am very much mistaken, which I seldom am,' said Boyet when they had gone, 'the King and his lords are all infected!'

'With what?' asked the Princess.

'With the disease called love!' said Boyet. 'If you noticed, he couldn't take his eyes from your face; his tongue stumbled when he spoke, and matters of foreign policy did not seem to interest him at all. Depend upon it, you will soon be able to buy Aquitaine for a kiss!'

'You speak wisely, old love-monger!' cried Rosaline.

'He is Cupid's grandfather!' teased Maria, 'and his grandson has been telling tales!'

Certainly Cupid, the god of love, was at work in that park; and his arrows had pierced the hearts of more than its royal master and his three lords. Already Don Armado was wooing the country girl Jaquenetta, in his own cumbrous fashion, and he had written her a letter which she could not possibly have understood—even if she had been able to read. He needed a messenger to deliver this ridiculous epistle, so Don Armado sent for his prisoner, Costard the bumpkin.

'Sirrah Costard,' he said, 'I will enfranchize thee!'

'Eh?' said Costard, 'marry me to Frances? Frances who?'

'I mean,' explained the Spaniard grandly, 'that I will set thee at liberty, enfreedoming thy person; thou wert immured, restrained, captivated, bound——'

'Oh, and you'll let me off?' interrupted Costard.

'Yea, I give thee thy liberty, set thee free from durance,' said Don Armado, 'and in lieu thereof impose on thee no greater penalty than this: that thou bear this letter to the country maid Jaquenetta. Here is remuneration for thee!'

So saying, Don Armado handed the letter to Costard, pressed some coins into his hand, and strode away.

As Costard stood puzzling over what the Spaniard had been saying, Berowne appeared out of a nearby thicket, and seeing him exclaimed:

'Ah, my good fellow, Costard! I am delighted to see you.'

'Please sir,' said Costard, 'how much carnation colored ribbon can one buy for a remuneration?'

'How much is a remuneration?' asked Berowne, with a smile.

'Why sir, it is a halfpenny and a farthing,' answered Costard.

'Then you can buy three farthings' worth of ribbon!' answered Berowne.

'Thank you, sir!' cried Costard, and was hastening away when Berowne stopped him.

'Will you do something for me?' he asked. 'I'll make it worth your while.'

'When do you want it done?' asked Costard cautiously.

'This afternoon.'

'Right, sir, I'll do it. Goodbye for now!'

'But you don't yet know what it is!'

'I shall know, sir, when I've done it,' said Costard brightly.

'But, you villain, you must know first!' laughed Berowne.

'Then I'll come and ask your worship what it was tomorrow morning,' said Costard.

'It must be done *this* afternoon,' repeated Berowne. 'Listen, you rogue. The Princess of France is coming to hunt here in the park, and in her train there is a beautiful lady called Rosaline. Give her this letter. Here's recompense for your trouble. Hurry now!'

'Recompense!' exclaimed Costard gazing lovingly at the shilling which Berowne had given him. 'Oh, sweet recompense! Better than remuneration: elevenpence-farthing better: most sweet recompense! I will do it sir, without fail. Recompense!' and he kissed the silver shilling. 'Remuneration—pah!' he spat as he looked at the three farthings, and hastened away on his errand.

Berowne stood and watched him go, saying to himself: 'Oh, that I should be in love! I that have often mocked others for giving way to what seemed so foolish a passion! And with a dark lady who may well prove false! To think that I must serve this black-haired, white-browed witch—to sigh for her, to watch for her, to pray for her. . . . This is Cupid's revenge for my light words about love! . . . Well, I will love, write, sigh, pray, beg, groan and do everything that becomes a lover. And may Cupid speed my wooing.'

But the god of love was not prepared to let Berowne off easily. For his messenger, Costard, who could not read, muddled the letters and, in spite of the great difference between remuneration and recompense delivered Don Armado's lengthy epistle to Rosaline, and Berowne's elegant verses to Jaquenetta.

Rosaline realized at once that the letter was not meant for her; but the Princess bade Boyet open it and read it to them none the less. It was in Don Armado's best style, and began:

'By Heaven, that thou art fair, is most infallible; true that thou art beauteous; truth itself that thou art lovely. More fairer than fair, beautiful than beauteous, truer than truth itself, have commiseration on thy heroical vassal!' And it continued in the same lofty and ridiculous style for several pages—much to the delight of the Princess and her ladies.

Meanwhile Jaquenetta, not being able to read any more than Costard could, took the letter which she had received to the local parson, Sir Nathaniel. She found him discussing a deer, which the Princess had shot, with Holofernes the village schoolmaster and Dull the constable.

'Good Master Parson,' said Jaquenetta curtseying, 'will you be so good as to read me this letter. It was given me by Costard, and sent me by Don Armado.'

'*Lege, Domine,*' said Holofernes, who always used Latin words whenever he could think of them; and Sir Nathaniel proceeded to read Berowne's elegant sonnet on the beauteous Rosaline.

'How, maiden, was this sent to you?' asked Holofernes.

'Yes, sir,' answered Jaquenetta, 'from Don Armado.'

'Let me look at the address,' said Holofernes. 'Ha! "To the snow-white hand of the most beauteous Lady Rosaline"; and it is signed: "Berowne". Sir Nathaniel, this Berowne is one of the students in the King's monastery of learning, and here he has written a letter to one of the ladies attending upon the Princess of France. Take the letter, my dear, and give it into the very hand of the King—it may be of great importance. Hurry!'

Off went Jaquenetta and Costard, while Holofernes invited Sir Nathaniel and Dull to dinner, promising to prove over the meal that Berowne's sonnet was badly written, unlearned, and showed neither poetry, wit nor invention.

While his verses were being subjected to the criticism of the pedantic schoolmaster, Berowne was wandering in the wood near the palace composing more poems in praise of his beloved Rosaline.

'She has one of my sonnets already,' he mused. 'I would not mind being in love, if the other three were, too!... Hallo, here is one of them, and carrying a sheet of paper. Oh, if I might only hear him groan!'

Hiding in the thicket, Berowne saw the King pacing slowly by. As he drew near, he heaved a deep sigh: 'Ah me!'

'Hit, by heaven!' thought Berowne gleefully. 'Cupid's arrow is in his heart. Ah-ha, secrets!'

Thinking himself alone, the King proceeded to read out loud

the sonnet he had written to the Princess of France; he had fallen as deeply in love with her as Berowne with Rosaline. Scarcely had he finished, when there was the sound of someone moving among the bushes, and the King had just time to hide before Longaville appeared, also with a paper.

'Here comes another fool!' thought Berowne.

'I hope he's in love too!' thought the King.

'Alas!' exclaimed Longaville out loud, 'I fear these verses will never move the heart of sweet Maria, empress of my love. Yet

I will see how they sound,' And he too proceeded to rehearse a passionate sonnet.

It needed but one more to complete the foursome of foresworn woman-haters; and sure enough, to Berowne's delight, Dumaine came into sight with his eyes cast on the ground: Longaville slipped hastily behind a tree.

'Oh most divine Kate!' sighed Dumaine; and Berowne thought: 'Ah: he's transformed too. Now we are like four wood-cocks on the same dish!'

'I'll read my ode once more,' murmured Dumaine.

'I'll listen once more to see how the same things can be said in different ways!' thought Berowne; and Dumaine proceeded to recite his ode with the most melancholy fervor.

'I'll send this to her,' he murmured. 'But oh how I wish that the King, Berowne and Longaville were in love too. There would be no offence if we all offended!'

'Dumaine, your love is most uncharitable,' said Longaville, stepping from behind his tree. 'You may well look pale. But I know that I should be blushing if anyone had heard *me* make such a shameful admission.'

'Then blush now!' cried the King, leaving his hiding place. 'You blame him—but you are twice as much to blame yourself! How about "the sweet Maria, empress of your love"? Did you never write sonnets to her? Ah, what will Berowne say when he hears how you have broken your oaths? You know what a gift he has for words, and how sarcastic he can be. I'm glad that I am not in your position!'

'Now it is for me to punish hypocrisy!' exclaimed Berowne, coming forward. 'How, my lord King, can you possibly reprove these two for being in love, when you yourself are more in love than either of them? You scorn to break your oath, do you? How about a certain Princess to whom you write sonnets?'

'You jest unkindly,' said the King. 'But are we three really betrayed?'

'It is I who am betrayed by the three of you,' cried Berowne. 'I that am honest and hold it a sin to break my oaths! When are you likely to hear *me* praising any woman's beauty—and in such ridiculous verses? As if there were any difference between one woman and another, or any sense in writing odes and sonnets in praise of particular hand, foot, face, eye, breast, waist, leg, or——'

'Silence a moment!' interrupted the King. 'We have company!'

It was Costard and Jaquenetta who came hastening through the wood hand in hand, and paused in front of the four men.

'God bless the King!' exclaimed Jaquenetta.

'Here is some treason for you!' said Costard, holding out the letter.

'I beg you sir, have this letter read,' added Jaquenetta, 'our parson says he thinks it's wicked!'

'Read it to us, Berowne,' said the King.

Berowne took the letter, looked at it, flushed red, and tore it up hastily.

'What are you doing? Why do you tear it?' cried the King.

'It's of no importance,' said Berowne, trying to shrug it off. 'There's nothing to worry about.'

'It's in Berowne's writing!' exclaimed Dumaine, picking up one of the pieces.

'He was upset by it!' agreed Longaville. 'Look at his face! Let us collect the bits!'

'Guilty, my lord! I plead guilty,' cried Berowne. 'I am in love too, as deeply as any of you. Send these two turtle-doves away, and I'll tell you all.'

When Costard and Jaquenetta had gone, Berowne confessed his passion for the disdainful Rosaline—the dark lady of his sonnets. The King tried to make fun of him for falling in love with a girl who had black hair and black eyes, but Berowne defended himself—and his lady—with all his usual wit and skill.

'Well, have your way,' said the King at length. 'And as you can argue that black is white so well, tell us how we may persuade ourselves that we are not foresworn and false to our oath by falling in love with these girls from France.'

'There is no difficulty in that!' declared Berowne confidently. 'Consider first what we swore to do: to fast, to study, and to see no women. To begin with, this is treason against the state of youth! We are too young to fast; if we do, it will only lead to some illness or other. And as for study, what can any of us understand without seeking it in a woman's face? Women are the books, the arts, the academies that hold, reveal and nourish all the world: without them nothing can be truly well done. We were fools to foreswear women. So, for wisdom's sake—and wisdom is the true goal of study—we must at once forget our oaths, and find our true selves—and our true loves!'

Thus Berowne encouraged the King and the other two academicians to forget their oaths and strive only to win their ladies. And he succeeded so well—for they were ready to be convinced—that very soon all four were planning how to woo and win the French Princess and her companions.

'First of all,' said Berowne, 'let us meet them as they return from hunting, and conduct them back to their tents. . . . This will allow each of us to take his beloved by the hand. And this afternoon, let us think of some novel entertainment to amuse them.'

It was during the afternoon that the ladies received love-poems from the King and his companions, and discussed them together with some amusement. Presents of jewels accompanied the letters, and although they professed to mock at the bad verses, and to wish that the poems had been shorter and the necklaces longer, it was only Rosaline whose mockery was mixed with any bitterness.

While they were still discussing their suitors, old Lord Boyet arrived, almost speechless with laughter.

'Madam, prepare!' he cried. 'Ladies, arm for the battle! Love is coming to invade you, in disguise!'

'St. Cupid protect us!' exclaimed the Princess in mock terror. 'Against what must we guard ourselves? Tell us, you good scout.'

'As I was sitting in the park,' said Boyet, 'I saw the King and his three lords coming in my direction. I hid in a nearby thicket, and overheard all their plans. First of all they were instructing Don Armado's page, Moth, how to be their herald and recite a speech which they have written. Moth has been rehearsed in every detail, and the four suitors are full of merriment over the whole entertainment—so you need not scruple to play whatever tricks on them you may devise.'

'What disguise are they coming in?' asked the Princess.

'As Muscovites, from the farthest steppes of Russia,' answered Boyet. 'They are imitating the embassy sent lately by the Muscovite King to find him a wife among the ladies of England to be Queen of Russia. *They* also come to find themselves wives, and mean each to woo the lady of his choice—whom they will know, even if you receive them masked, by the jewelery which they sent you recently.'

'Then let us play a trick on them!' laughed the Princess. 'We shall, of course, be masked. But let us exchange the love-tokens which they sent us. Here, Rosaline, you wear mine and I'll wear yours. Then Berowne will take me for you, and you shall exchange him for a royal lover. Then, when next we meet, unmasked, we can tease them thoroughly for having made love to the wrong ladies. But now we'll be so cold and distant to them— pretending we think they really are Russians—that their joke will be turned against themselves. . . . Sssh! Here they come! Quickly, masks everyone, and you, Katharine and Maria, change love-tokens.'

They were scarcely ready when the embassy from unknown Russia arrived, properly booted and bearded, with blackamoors in attendance carrying musical instruments. Moth stalked proudly in front of them, to speak his prologue.

'All hail, the richest beauties on the earth!
A holy party of the fairest dames—'

he began. The Princess and her ladies promptly turned their backs on him, and he went on:

'That ever turned their—backs—to mortal view!'

'Their *eyes*, villain!' hissed Berowne.

'That ever turned their eyes to mortal view,'

continued Moth desperately,

> 'Out of your favors, heavenly sprites, vouchsafe
> Not to behold with your sun-beamish eyes—'

'Once to behold!' prompted Berowne.

'They pay no attention to what I say, and that puts me off!' explained Moth.

'I'll put you off!' muttered Berowne. 'Away with you!'

When Moth had gone, Rosaline who was pretending to be the Princess, bade Boyet speak to the Russian strangers and ask what they wanted.

'No more than to visit you in peace and friendship,' said Boyet, after a word with the King.

'Well, they have done so,' said Rosaline. 'So tell them they can now depart.'

'Fair Princess,' said the King, pretending to speak with a strong Russian accent, 'we have come a very long way for the honor of dancing with you.'

'You dance for us, and we will watch,' said Rosaline; and the King and his friends had no choice but to obey her.

'And now, since you are strangers and have far to go, you may kiss our hands and depart,' said Rosaline when the dance was over.

'If you will not dance with us,' said the King, 'at least allow me to speak with you in private.'

Rosaline agreed and drew aside with the King, while Berowne chatted with the Princess, and Longaville and Dumaine with the two ladies who were wearing their love-tokens.

Very soon each of them was wearing a second love-token; and as soon as she saw this, Rosaline cried suddenly:

'Not one word more, my maids! Farewell now, my frozen Muscovites!' and she waved to Boyet, who solemnly ushered the four visitors out of the clearing by the royal tents and away on the path towards the palace.

When he returned, the Princess and her ladies had taken off their masks and retrieved their original love-tokens.

'The King is my sworn love!' laughed Rosaline.

'And Berowne has plighted his troth to me!' cried the Princess.

'Longaville swears he was born to serve me alone,' said Katharine.

'And Dumaine can never love anyone but me,' added Maria.

'They'll be back soon, undisguised,' said Rosaline. 'Let us continue to mock them. We'll tell them about the fools who were here dressed up as Russians, and about the shockingly bad verses they gave us.'

Sure enough, the King and his three friends re-appeared a few minutes later in their ordinary clothes and immediately apologised for leaving them so long unvisited and unentertained.

'Oh, we have had very good entertainment,' answered the Princess. 'Not long ago a party of Russians was here—all the way from their strange, foreign land.'

'Russians?' said the King, pretending to be surprised.

'Four,' nodded the Princess, 'oddly clad, but most courtly.'

'Madame, speak the truth!' cried Rosaline. 'You are only being polite! There were indeed four men here, dressed as Russians. They stayed for quite a time, and talked a great deal. But more arrant nonsense none of us has ever heard!'

They were not able to keep the joke up for long before the King was driven to confess who the Russians were, and to endure more raillery.

'Well, we'll forgive you your deception,' said the Princess at last. 'Now at least we know why the Russians made love to us so ardently, and swore such solemn oaths of faith. . . . My lord, when you were here in disguise, what did you whisper in your lady's ear?'

'That I held her dearer than the very sight of my eyes,' said the King, 'that I valued her above all the world, and that if she would not wed me, I would die a bachelor.'

'When she asks you to fulfil these promises, you'll reject her, I'm sure,' said the Princess.

'Madam, I swear by my honor, I'll do no such thing,' declared the King.

'You have broken one oath already,' murmured the Princess, 'you can hardly expect us to trust your word!'

'Despise me if ever I break this oath!' cried the King.

'I will: so make sure you keep it!' said the Princess. 'Rosaline, what did the Russian whisper in your ear?'

'That he held me dearer than the very sight of his eyes,' answered Rosaline promptly. 'That he valued me above all the world, and that if I would not wed him he would die a bachelor.'

'Then may you both be happy!' cried the Princess. 'His Majesty is famous for the way he keeps his oaths!'

'What do you mean by this?' asked the King anxiously. 'By my life, I never swore such an oath to *this* lady.'

'By Heaven you did,' protested Rosaline, 'and you gave me this jewel as a token of the truth of your love.'

'I gave this jewel, and swore this oath of eternal love to the Princess!' cried the King. 'I knew her by that other jewel on her sleeve, which is the one I gave her before.'

'You are wrong, my lord,' said the Princess demurely. 'Rosaline was wearing this jewel on her sleeve. And see, this token was given me by Lord Berowne who swore that he loved no one else in the whole world.'

'I see the trick!' cried Berowne. 'Someone gave away our plot, and these ladies changed love-tokens to make fools of us . . . I suspect it was Lord Boyet who stands grinning at us there!'

So peace was made and they all laughed at the trick the Princess had played on them.

The next entertainment, a Pageant of the Nine Worthies, was to be given by Don Armado, with the aid of Sir Nathaniel, Costard, Moth, and Holofernes who had devised it. First came Costard:

'I Pompey am, Pompey surnamed the Big!' he declared.

'The Great! The Great! Pompey the Great!' cried Dumaine.

'The Great it should be,' said Costard, and continued with his speech. Then he stood aside while Sir Nathaniel strode forward as Alexander the Great, with a speech beginning: 'While in the world I lived, I was the world's commander,' but he was not allowed to finish, and so he departed in a huff.

Then Holofernes appeared dressed as Judas Maccabaeus, and leading little Moth as Hercules.

The schoolmaster was thoroughly enjoying himself, and began declaiming in the grandest manner:

'Great Hercules is presented by this imp,
    Whose club killed Cerberus, that three-headed *canis*;
And when he was a babe, a child, a shrimp,
    Thus did he strangle serpents in his *manus*!'

When Moth had taken his bow, and gone off with great applause, strangling snakes valiantly with both hands, Holofernes drew himself up still more grandly, and began his own part:

'Judas I am!'

'Ah Judas! A Judas!' cried Dumaine.

'Not Iscariot, sir!' explained Holofernes hastily, and began again. But he was given no chance to say more and was interrupted so often and teased by Berowne, Boyet and Dumaine, that he too went stamping off after Sir Nathaniel.

Don Armado was treated very little better when he made a pompous appearance as Hector of Troy; and before he had been allowed to finish his speech, Costard suddenly interrupted him and threatened to beat him for making love to Jaquenetta.

'Hurrah!' shouted Dumaine. 'A duel between Hector of Troy and Pompey the Great!'

'Good for Pompey!' cried Berowne. 'We'll change his name and call him Pompey the very Great! Pompey the Huge!'

The two angry Worthies were just about to fight, when an unexpected messenger arrived to tell the Princess that her father, the old King of France, had died suddenly.

And so the happiness of the four pairs of lovers was clouded, and the Princess made ready to return to her kingdom, of which she would now be Queen.

'Lady, before you go,' said the King of Navarre, grown grave too, 'you must answer my question—and your three ladies must answer that which Berowne, Longaville and Dumaine have asked them. Though we have joked and played and made fools of ourselves in the happy Spring season of love, now that sober Winter has suddenly been forced upon us all, it is only right that you should answer us soberly. For what we swore with smiling lips, we meant with sober hearts. Briefly, we love you, and ask you to be our wives.'

'This is too short a time in which to make such a world-without-end bargain,' said the Princess. 'And you know how often each of you has proved to be an oath-breaker. But if you truly love me, ask my hand in a year's time—and in the meanwhile, to prove that your words are not empty, you must become a hermit, live alone in a cell on bread and water, and fast and pray as a hermit should. If you can endure this, and still love me, I shall know that your love is true. Then, when you come to ask my hand again, I swear to place it in yours, and to be yours for ever.'

Katharine and Maria laid the same commands on Dumaine and Longaville; but cruel Rosaline was less kind to Berowne.

'I have often heard,' she said, 'and now I know from experience, that you are a man full of jests and quips and sarcastic jokes. Your penance shall be to visit the sick each day, and make them laugh. No hermitage for you, but the wards of a hospital; no solitude, but the constant companionship of the ill and the dying.'

'To move wild laughter in the throat of death?' gasped Berowne. 'It cannot be, it is impossible. Mirth cannot move one who is in agony.'

'Yet you must try,' insisted Rosaline. 'A jest's prosperity lies in the ear of whoever hears it, and never in the tongue of him that makes it. I do not think sick people will laugh at your idle, scornful jokes at other people's expense. You must learn a deeper, kinder sort of humor, and give up making jokes full of unkindness and sarcasm. In a year's time, if you are cured, I'll marry you.'

'Twelve months in a hospital, making kindly jests!' cried Berowne, 'well, to win you, I'll endure even that!'

And so the Princess of France and her three ladies set off for home. But none of them had any doubt that in a year's time there would be a great wedding feast that would unite France and Navarre in four-fold bonds of true love and unending happiness.

A MIDSUMMER NIGHT'S DREAM

DUKE THESEUS CAME home to Athens, after one of his foreign wars, bringing with him the beautiful Hippolyta, Queen of the Amazons, to be his wife. Soon Athens was full of preparations for the wedding, and of plans for great feasts and entertainments to celebrate the important occasion. All the people from the highest to the lowest, were determined to do something to show their loyalty to Duke Theseus and their joy at his marriage to so famous a queen. And not the least among them was a poor Athenian carpenter called Peter Quince.

Several days before the wedding he gathered some of his friends together and suggested that they should put on a play as part of the entertainments.

'What are we to act?' asked Nick Bottom, the weaver.

'We will act the story of Pyramus and Thisbe,' said Quince.

'An excellent idea, and a fine play!' cried Bottom, who had never heard of it. 'What part am I to have?'

'You are to be Pyramus,' said Quince.

'What sort of part is that?' asked Bottom. 'A lover? Or a tyrant?'

'Pyramus was a lover, who killed himself most gallantly for love!'

'Ah, a tragic part!' cried Bottom. 'The audience must have their handkerchiefs ready when I'm playing it. I'll wager there won't be a dry eye amongst them! But who's next?'

'Francis Flute, the bellows-mender,' announced Quince, referring to his list. 'You, Flute, are to play Thisbe."

'What is Thisbe?' asked Flute, in his squeaky voice. 'I hope he is a wandering knight.'

'Thisbe is the lady Pyramus loves,' said Quince.

Everyone roared with laughter at this, and Flute became quite upset.

'I don't want to play a woman,' he objected. 'Anyhow, my beard's beginning to grow.'

'Well, you could wear a mask——' said Quince. 'And you must speak in a small high voice.'

'A mask?' interrupted Bottom. 'Let *me* play Thisbe too! I'll hide my face in a mask, and I'll speak in a monstrous little voice. Like this!' He began at once to shriek in a ghastly treble: 'Oh Pyramus, my dear, dear love! I am thy lady dear, thy Thisbe!'

'No, no!' exclaimed Quince firmly. 'You Bottom, must play Pyramus; and Flute will be just the right person for Thisbe.'

'All right,' agreed Bottom rather sulkily. 'Well, what are the rest to play?'

'Snug the Joiner: you must be the lion who frightens Thisbe away and makes Pyramus think that he has killed and eaten her.'

'Good,' said Snug, nodding slowly and solemnly. 'But look here, Peter Quince, I hope you have the lion's part all written out for me now, because I'm very slow at learning.'

'No need to bother about that,' Quince said reassuring him. 'You can make up the lion's part as you go along—for it's nothing but roaring!'

At this Bottom could contain himself no longer.

'Let *me* play the lion's part too!' he cried. 'I will roar so well and so terribly that the Duke himself will ask me to do it again!'

'Our lion mustn't roar too fiercely,' said Quince anxiously, 'or it will frighten the ladies. And if the Duchess were to faint, the Duke might hang us all!'

'Certainly if we frightened them out of their senses, they'd not have sense enough to do anything else,' agreed Bottom. 'But I'll roar as gently as a dove; I'll roar as sweetly as a nightingale!'

'No, no!' cried Quince firmly. 'You must play no part but Pyramus!'

At this Bottom began to sulk; so Quince had to flatter him, saying how good a part it was, and that no one else could possibly play it.

'And now,' said he finally, 'here are your parts. We'll meet and rehearse tomorrow night in the wood a mile outside Athens. The moon is full, so we shall have plenty of light to see by. If we rehearse in the city someone is sure to find out what we are doing —and our play must be a surprise for the Duke and Duchess. By tomorrow night I'll have found parts for the rest of us. But be sure, Bottom and Flute, that you know your lines perfectly!'

'We'll not fail you!' cried Bottom. 'See you at the Duke's Oak tomorrow night!'

Quince and his friends were not the only Athenians who arranged to meet in the wood that night. There was also a girl called Hermia, the daughter of Egeus, one of the Duke's chief councillors, who had decided to run away and marry Lysander, with whom she was in love. Egeus, an obstinate, bad-tempered old man, was determined that she should marry Demetrius, another young Athenian noble, whom he had chosen to be her husband.

According to the laws of Athens, no girl could marry without her father's consent. If she refused to obey him, she had to become a nun—or in extreme cases could even be put to death.

Hermia refused to marry Demetrius, particularly as her best friend Helena was in love with him; he had seemed to be in love with her, too—until Egeus offered him Hermia, a very good match since she was the only child of the rich old noble.

Nobody knew that Hermia was going to run away and meet Lysander in the wood near Athens, except Helena; and she was foolish enough to tell Demetrius, hoping that he would then give up all thought of marrying Hermia, and perhaps turn to her again.

Demetrius, however, set out at once in pursuit of Hermia, and

Helena followed him, for she loved him so much that she could not bear to let him out of her sight—particularly when he was looking for Hermia.

Now although none of the Athenians who were venturing into the wood so carelessly this night seemed to realize it, this wood near Athens was filled with magic and enchantment. It was a favorite haunt of Oberon, King of the Fairies, and of his wife, Queen Titania, with all their court—including Oberon's hob-goblin servant Puck whose greatest delight was in playing tricks on humans.

At this time there was a great quarrel going on. After the fairy custom, Titania had brought a human child, a changeling, to the Magic Wood, to be her servant; but Oberon was jealous, and wanted the little boy to become one of his own fairy knights. Whenever Oberon and Titania met, they quarrelled so violently that their smaller elves would run and hide in acorn cups—for they knew what great powers of enchantment both the Fairy King and the Fairy Queen possessed.

On this very night, as Hermia and Lysander were running away from Athens, and Quince and his friends were starting out to meet at the Duke's Oak to rehearse their play, the fairy quarrel came to a head.

Oberon and Titania, with their attendants, met by chance in the woods. After a bitter quarrel, Titania, refused to obey Oberon or even speak to him again, and swept away in a rage.

'Well, go where you like!' cried Oberon. 'This time you have overstepped yourself, and must be punished. Am I not your lord, and the King of all the Fairies?'

Then he called Puck to him and bade the mischief-maker set out in search of a magic flower called Love-in-idleness. The juice of this flower if laid on anyone's eyelids while asleep would make that person fall madly in love with the first live creature he saw on waking.

'I'll go right round the earth, if need be, and be back with it in less than an hour!' cried Puck; and he was gone in a flash.

As he stood waiting for Puck's return, Oberon saw Demetrius

coming through the Wood, followed by Helena, and at once made himself invisible so as to hear the two of them without being seen.

'I do not love you, so leave me in peace!' Demetrius said angrily. 'Go away, I tell you! The only person I want is Hermia—she's breaking my heart by running away like this. If only I can catch Lysander, I'll kill him! You told me they had come into the wood, and I'm grateful to you for telling me. But I can look for them by myself!'

'Wherever you go, I cannot help following you,' sobbed Helena. 'I love you so much that I can't bear to lose you. It's as if you were a magnet and I was a piece of iron—you draw me to you, just as a magnet does!'

'This is too much!' shouted Demetrius in exasperation. 'I tell you plainly that I do not and I cannot love you, and yet you still follow me about. I'll run and hide deeper in the wood, and leave you for the wild beasts to catch!'

'The wildest beast is not as cruel and hard-hearted as you are,' sobbed Helena.

'I will not have any more of this nonsense!' cried Demetrius. 'If you follow me, I'll strike you!' And so saying he dashed away into the shadows, Helena still following and calling desperately: 'Demetrius! I'd rather die by your beloved hand than live without you!'

'Well,' said Oberon to himself when they had gone, and he had become visible once more, 'I'll see to it that before they leave the wood, that cruel young man is pursuing the maiden and begging *her* to marry *him*!'

At that moment Puck appeared and knelt before Oberon.

'Have you the flowers?' exclaimed the Fairy King eagerly. Puck nodded and held up a little bunch. 'Give them to me!' said Oberon. 'I know a bank on which the wild thyme grows; oxlips and violets too. The woodbine and the musk roses twine over it to make a canopy, and there Titania will lie down to sleep away part of the night after being lulled to rest with songs and dances by her fairies. There I'll steal upon her unseen and squeeze some of the magic juice on to her eyes, and when she wakes she will fall in love with some monster—a lion, a bear, a wolf, a bull, a stupid, meddling monkey or whatever she first sees. Then she will know that I am indeed King of the Fairies and she will have to give me her changeling boy before I take the charm from off her eyes. And do you, Puck, take some of these flowers and seek through the wood for a hard-hearted Athenian youth, and the lady who loves him. Pour some of the juice in his eyes, and make sure that she is the first thing he sees when he wakes. . . . You may recognise him easily by his Athenian garments.'

'Fear not, my lord, I shall do just as you command me!' cried Puck; and he sped away while Oberon went in search of Titania.

He found her under the Duke's Oak preparing to sleep on the bank of wild thyme; she was just giving her orders to the fairies who attended on her:

'Dance a roundel for me!' she said, 'and sing me one song. Then away all of you while I sleep. Some go in search of bats whose leathern wings will make coats for my elves; and some drive away the owls so that they may not disturb me. But first sing me to sleep—a charm to keep away snakes and spiders and all such creatures; and instead of them beg sweet Philomel, the nightingale, to join in your song and lull me to sleep.'

So the troops of tiny elves and fairies danced in the moonlight for their Queen, and sang sweetly and soothingly:

'You spotted snakes with double tongue,
　Thorny hedgehogs, be not seen;
Newts and blind-worms, do no wrong,
　Come not near our Fairy Queen.

Weaving spiders come not here;
　Hence, you long-legged spinners, hence!
Beetles black, approach not near;
　Worm nor snail do no offence.'

And then they all went dancing away among the flowers, singing to the nightingale as they went:

'Philomel, with melody
Sing in our sweet lullaby;
Lulla, lulla, lullaby; lulla, lulla, lullaby:
Never harm,
Nor spell nor charm
Come our lovely lady nigh;
So, goodnight, with lullaby.'

But their spells were not strong enough to keep Oberon from her. As soon as they were out of sight, and Titania well asleep, he became visible and squeezed the magic juice into her eyes as he whispered a charm. Then he stole quietly away, smiling to himself, and wondering what vile monster Titania would fall in love with when she woke up.

Meanwhile Hermia and Lysander were wandering together in the wood, trying in vain to find the way out on the side farthest from Athens. But they were lost, and when at last they came to the open glade not far from the Duke's Oak, Hermia confessed that she was too tired to go any further.

'Then let us sleep here for the rest of the night,' said Lysander, 'and in the morning we shall be able to find our way.'

So he kissed her goodnight, wrapped a cloak round her, and then settled himself to sleep in the warm summer air on the other side of the same hawthorn-bush which sheltered her.

By and by Puck came flitting through the trees, still looking for Demetrius to put the magic juice into his eyes as Oberon had commanded. As soon as he saw Lysander, he danced with delight:

'This must be the man!' he exclaimed. 'Yes, my master told me I would know him by his Athenian garments, and sure enough, this young man is wearing them. And there's the pretty lady who loves him, asleep on the other side of the bush. Well, my fine fellow, when you wake up, you'll love her even more desperately than she loves you!'

Having squeezed the juice into Lysander's eyes, Puck went scampering away to look for Oberon and tell him how faithfully he had obeyed his orders.

But scarcely had he gone when Demetrius came striding through the wood, with poor Helena panting behind him.

'I can't go any further?' she sobbed. 'Surely, Demetrius, you won't leave me alone here, all alone?'

But nothing would stop Demetrius, who strode on, looking neither to right nor left. He soon disappeared in the darkness.

Helena could follow him no further. But as she was looking for a place to rest, she came upon Lysander asleep under the hawthorn bush.

'Lysander!' she exclaimed in surprise. 'Lysander, lying on the ground! Perhaps he's been killed by a wild animal—but I see no blood, no wound. Lysander! If you are only asleep, wake up!'

'Wake!' cried Lysander, sitting up and gazing at Helena. 'I've never been awake until this moment! Helena, beautiful Helena! I'd run through fire for your sweet sake! Where's that villain Demetrius! He deserves to perish by my sword!'

'Oh no, no!' begged Helena anxiously. 'Don't hurt Demetrius. Forget that he loves your Hermia—she loves you, and you should be content with that.'

'Content with Hermia?' cried Lysander in scorn. 'Never! How could I have wasted so much time over her? No, it is not Hermia I love, but Helena! Who would choose a raven if he could have a dove? You are more beautiful than she could ever be, and I love you and you alone.'

Helena, sure that Lysander was making fun of her, was furious. 'How dare you insult me like this!' she cried. 'Isn't it bad enough that I could never win a kind word from Demetrius; but now you mock and tease me by pretending to be in love with me—when everyone knows that it's Hermia whom you really love!'

In anger she turned and rushed away after Demetrius.

'Thank goodness she didn't see Hermia,' thought Lysander. 'What a fool I've been—and how strange it is that I hate the very sight of Hermia. Well, let her sleep on there. I must find Helena! Helena, I love you so! Helena!' And away he dashed in pursuit.

A moment later poor Hermia woke to find herself deserted.

In a terrible fright she rushed off further into the wood calling desperately for Lysander.

Titania was still sleeping peacefully when Peter Quince and his friends arrived in the open glade by the Duke's Oak for their midnight rehearsal of *Pyramus and Thisbe*. Bottom as usual was laying down the law:

'I tell you, Peter Quince, that there are things about this play which will offend the Duchess and the other ladies. First of all, Pyramus has to kill himself, and that will frighten them terribly. What do you say to that?'

'I'm afraid we shall have to leave the killing out,' said Robin Starveling, the tailor, shaking his head sadly.

'Not a bit!' cried Bottom, looking round first to be sure they were all properly worried, 'I know just what to do! You must write a prologue, Peter Quince, and say in it that we will do no harm with our swords, and that I'm not really killed. And if you like, you can tell them that I'm not Pyramus at all, but only Nick Bottom the weaver. I'm sure that will comfort them!'

'Won't the ladies be frightened of the lion?' asked Tom Snout the tinker anxiously.

'I'm certainly afraid of lions!' said Starveling.

'To bring a lion among ladies is a dreadful thing to do!' Bottom agreed.

'What about another prologue, to say that he's not really a lion, but only Snug the joiner?' suggested Snout. Bottom agreed and immediately began to tell them just how this prologue should be written, until Quince cut in:

'That's easily done. But we have two much harder things to decide. How can we bring the moonlight into the great hall at the palace? For the old story says very clearly that Pyramus and Thisbe met by moonlight! And then Pyramus and Thisbe begin by speaking to each other through a tiny hole in the wall which divides their fathers' houses.'

'You can never bring in a wall!' said Snug sadly.

'Oh yes you can!' cried Bottom. 'Someone must come in dressed up as a wall and tell the audience just who and what he is.

There's a part for you, Snout! And just the same with the moonlight. Starveling must come in dressed as the Man in the Moon, with a dog and a bundle of thorns; and he must hold up a lantern and tell them that he is the moon!'

This seemed an excellent idea to everyone. And with these difficulties out of the way the rehearsal began—but not unobserved as the actors thought. Instead they had an unexpected audience; for Puck happened along just as Bottom was starting to pose and posture as Pyramus.

'Ha-ha!' said Puck to himself. 'A play, indeed! I'll watch it—and take part in it too, if I can see my chance of playing a trick on these foolish mortals!'

The chance came soon enough. When Bottom went off after his first speech and disappeared behind a tree, Puck skipped after him and gave him a great big donkey's head instead of his own.

'Now then, Bottom!' shouted Quince. 'You ought to be on by now! When Flute says "never tire", that's your cue!'

'If I were fair, Thisbe, I were only thine!' declared Bottom-Pyramus striding out of the shadows into the clear moonlight.

Quince and the rest of them took one look, saw a hideous monster with a donkey's head and a man's body, and went dashing away towards Athens, shouting in terror.

Bottom did not realise what had happened to him; he stood and watched in great surprise, and then grew angry.

'They're playing a trick on me!' he exclaimed. 'They want to frighten me! Well, I'm not such a silly ass as they think. To show I'm not frightened, I'll walk up and down and sing.'

He proceeded to do this, although his song sounded far more like a donkey braying than a man singing—and the noise he made woke Titania.

'What angel is this that wakes me from my bed of flowers?' she asked, rising slowly and stretching out her arms.

Bottom, who had not noticed her before, was frightened; but he went on singing.

'Sing again, gentle mortal,' begged Titania when he paused. 'You have a lovely voice. I could quite fall in love with it. But you are so handsome that I would love you even if you did not sing so divinely. And I am sure you are as clever as you are beautiful.'

At this Bottom's fear got the better of him.

'I—I'd be as clever as I want to be if only I could find my way out of this wood,' he stammered.

'Do not wish to leave the wood—and me!' cried Titania. 'Indeed, I will not let you go. And I can prevent you, for I have great powers, and many fairies who will hold you back. But I am sure you will not try to go when I tell you that I love you dearly, and you shall come with me, and have fairies to attend on you and do whatever you wish.'

Then Titania called to her four fairies whose names were Peasblossom, Cobweb, Moth and Mustard-seed, and gave them special orders to look after her love:

'Be kind and courteous to this gentleman,' she said. 'Dance for him and amuse him. Bring him apricots and dewberries to eat, also purple grapes, green figs, and mulberries. Lead him to my secret bower, and light him to bed with fairy tapers of bees' wax; and when he is asleep, fan the moonbeams from his eyes with the bright wings of butterflies——'

Bottom hearing this, let out an enormous 'Eee-ore!' like any donkey, and Titania added hastily: 'Tie up my love's tongue! Bring him silently!'

So the fairies twined garlands of flowers round his ass's head and led Bottom away to Titania's bower, while Puck, watching, laughed so heartily that he nearly fell out of the tree in which he was hiding.

When Titania and her new love were gone, Puck sped away to Oberon and told him what had happened.

'This is better than anything I could have thought of!' cried the Fairy King in delight. 'You have done well. But tell me: did you obey my command and pour the magic juice into the eyes of the Athenian who scorned the beautiful lady?'

'Yes, I've done that too!' cried Puck gleefully. 'I did it so cleverly! He can't help seeing the lady first thing as soon as he wakes!'

At that moment Hermia appeared among the trees, with Demetrius following her and begging her in vain to be kind to him.

'Here is the man himself!' whispered Oberon.

'It is certainly the same woman!' gasped Puck. 'But it's a different man!'

Standing invisible, Oberon and Puck heard Hermia accuse Demetrius of killing Lysander out of jealousy. And even when he persuaded her that he had not seen Lysander at all that night, Hermia had nothing but bitter words for him, and finally left him with the hope that she would never see him again.

There seemed to be no point in following her further when she was in such a mood, so Demetrius settled himself down to sleep, rather miserably, under a nearby tree.

'What have you done?' asked Oberon angrily. 'You have made some dreadful mistake and laid the charm on some true lover's eyes! Go quickly through the wood and find Helena of Athens. Bring her here at once!'

'I go, I go!' cried Puck, desperately anxious to show that he had not disobeyed on purpose. 'Look! I go as swiftly as an arrow from the bow!'

He was only away for a few minutes. Oberon just had time to pour some of the magic juice into the sleeping eyes of Demetrius; then Puck was with him again:

'Captain of our fairy band!' he cried, fairly bubbling over with excitement. 'Here comes Helena! And with her is the Athenian in whose eyes I poured the juice by mistake.'

'Stand out of sight!' commanded Oberon. 'The noise they make will rouse Hermia.'

'Oh what fun!' laughed Puck. 'Then both of them will fall in love with Helena and beg her to marry them. That's just the sort of joke I like best!'

Sure enough, the moment Helena reached him, Demetrius woke up and caught hold of the edge of her dress:

'Helena! Oh goddess! Oh divine beauty!' he cried, on his knees before her. 'How can I tell you how beautiful you are, how devotedly I love you? Let me but kiss your hand, and I shall be in Heaven!'

Helena turned on him furiously. 'It's all a plot!' she cried. 'You are doing this as a cruel joke. First of all, Demetrius, you say you hate me. And then both you and Lysander suddenly begin to pretend that you're madly in love with me. It's shameful of you!'

In vain they both protested that their love was no pretense. Helena would not accept their pleas. And when Hermia arrived on the scene a few minutes later, and Lysander told her to go away because he hated her, Helena was even more certain that it was all a trick. At last Lysander and Demetrius grew so angry with each other, and so jealous because they both loved Helena, that they drew their swords and set off to find a quiet glade where they could fight.

Then Hermia lost her temper completely. 'All this is your doing, Helena!' she shrieked, running at her friend.

'You may have sharper claws than I have!' cried Helena, 'but I've got longer legs!' And with that she was away into the wood, with Hermia after her.

'This is all *your* doing!' said Oberon sternly to Puck. 'I think you have done it on purpose!'

'Believe me, great king of the fairies, it was a mistake,' Puck answered hastily. 'After all, you told me I should know the man by his Athenian garments—and at least I made no mistake about that!'

'We must put this right,' said Oberon. 'You see that the two men have gone to find a place where they can fight. Prevent it! Fill the wood with thick mist so that they shall both get lost— and the women too. Then lead them here one by one, without seeing each other, and put them to sleep in pairs. . . . The *right* pairs, mind you!'

Away went Puck in high delight; this was a job he knew he could do well. Imitating first Demetrius's voice to Lysander, and then Lysander's to Demetrius, he soon had them both exactly where he wanted them. When they were in a magic sleep, he found Hermia and Helena, and led them, too, through the white mist to fall asleep, each beside the man she really loved. And when they were all there, Puck took another magic herb which Oberon had given him and squeezed the juice into Lysander's eyes, saying:

'Gentle lover, when you wake, love your true love again. Then all shall be well, and you will live happily ever afterwards, all four of you.'

When this was done, Puck raced away to look for Oberon, and the magic mist thinned and faded until the moon shone out once more through the wood.

With the moonlight came Titania leading Bottom; and before very long they too were fast asleep on the enchanted ground. There Puck and Oberon found them, as the moon was going down and the night was drawing to a close.

'What a sweet sight!' smiled Oberon. 'Poor Titania, I pity her. And now I will release her from the spell. For a little while ago when I met her gathering sweet-smelling flowers to make necklaces for this hateful creature, I scolded her for her folly. But she begged me to be patient with her, and willingly gave me her changeling boy to be my follower. And now that I have him safe in Fairyland, all this enchantment can come to an end. Puck, you must take the donkey's head off this Athenian workman so that when he gets back to Athens he will think, like these lovers, that all the events of this night have been no more than a midsummer night's dream.'

Puck did as he was told, and Oberon touched Titania's eyes with the juice of the herb that undid the spell of Love-in-idleness. When Titania woke, and took Oberon's outstretched hand, she came to him with a happy smile, too pleased to be released from the charm to bother about the trick he had played on her.

So the two of them set off for Fairyland, with Puck prancing gaily along behind them, and the great fairy quarrel was at an end.

Hardly had the fairies gone, when the lark began to sing high up in the morning sky, and the daylight to steal among the trees, bringing with its golden beams the promise of a glorious summer morning.

Then Duke Theseus and the beautiful Hippolyta came riding through the wood, with old Egeus and a whole band of lords and ladies, hunting the deer. They were surprised to find Hermia and Lysander, Helena and Demetrius asleep there. The company was more surprised still after the four had been awakened by the hunting horns, and had told the strange tale of their night in the woods. For whether it was a dream or not, it was certain that now Demetrius loved Helena as much as she loved him, and Lysander and Hermia loved one another even better than they had before.

'Egeus, you must agree to your daughter's marriage with Lysander,' said Theseus when he had heard all. 'And then both these couples can be married at the same time as Hippolyta and myself. No more words, let us go back to Athens!' So the two pairs of lovers followed hand in hand, full of peace and happiness.

When he woke up, Bottom went tearing home as fast as he could to tell Peter Quince and the rest about his wonderful dream. He found them very much upset at what had happened and afraid that they would not be able to act the play without him. But he arrived just in time, and the whole troop set off for the palace to find that the three couples were now married and had just finished dinner.

The actors were led into the great hall to give their entertainment. Peter Quince delivered a wonderful prologue, though he was so nervous that he got tied up in it more than once. Snout dressed up as a wall held up two fingers to make the chink through which Pyramus and Thisbe could talk to one another and arrange to run away and meet outside the city. When the lovers and wall had gone, the Lion appeared and explained to the ladies that he was really only Snug the joiner, and would do them no harm. With him came Starveling with his lantern.

Theseus, and all the audience were, by now, holding their sides with laughter.

'The man should be put inside the lantern!' Theseus gasped.

'And the dog and bundle of thorns too! Then he would indeed be the Man in the Moon!'

Now Thisbe came again, and was chased away by the fierce Lion. She dropped her mantle, which was all that the Lion caught. But when Pyramus came and found his beloved's mantle all stained with blood—to everyone's delight, there was no sign of blood until Bottom hastily took the mantle over to Quince to paint the stain on it—he thought that the Lion had eaten Thisbe. So he made a noble speech of farewell, drew his sword and stabbed himself. By now the audience was laughing so much that they could hardly hear Thisbe's thin screams of woe when she found Pyramus dead; and they were nearly as exhausted by their mirth as the actors were when Thisbe, after a frantic search for the sword which Pyramus at last handed to her since he was lying on it, stabbed herself too; and the play ended.

Theseus congratulated Quince and his friends and gave them a generous reward.

They went away greatly pleased and quite certain that audiences always laughed at a real tragedy.

By now it was midnight, and all the happy couples went off to bed, while Oberon and Titania, attended by Puck and the Fairies, came to dance through the sleeping palace and bring good luck and happiness to all who dwelt in it.

THE TAMING OF THE SHREW

THERE ONCE LIVED at Padua, in Italy, a rich gentleman called Baptista Minola. He had no son to succeed him, but had two daughters, Katharina and Bianca. The second daughter was a pretty, gentle, rather spoilt girl whom everyone adored; but her elder sister was of quite a different temper. Indeed it was her temper that everybody feared, and she was so peevish and violent that in time she became known as Katharina the Shrew.

Naturally many young men, and old ones as well, wanted to marry Bianca; and it was equally obvious that no one was likely to fall in love with the shrewish Katharina. But Baptista did not intend to be left with his elder daughter on his hands; so, one day, he issued an ultimatum to the two suitors for Bianca's hand whom he favored most. These were an oldish man called Gremio, who was exceedingly rich, and one somewhat younger, but also very wealthy, called Hortensio. They had both called at the same time to ask Bianca's hand in marriage, and Baptista was seeing them off in front of his house, with his two daughters beside him.

'Gentlemen, it's useless to urge me further!' he was saying. 'My firm resolution is that my younger daughter shall not be married until I have a husband for the elder. So if either of you wishes to marry Katharina, you may woo her—and if you win her, the other shall have Bianca.'

'Court Katharina?' jeered Gremio. 'I'd rather cart her through the streets as an example to others! Will you have her, Hortensio?'

Hortensio was even more offensive, and Katharina burst out in a fury:

'If I married either of you two fools, I'd begin by combing your hair with a three-legged stool to let in a little sense!'

'Signior Baptista,' said Gremio, 'you are surely being cruel and unfair to poor Bianca.'

'Sir,' murmured Bianca to her father, 'I will obey you. My only companions shall be my books and my music. I'll learn and practise all by myself.'

'Why do you shut this poor girl up?' burst out Hortensio. 'It's too harsh a penance to be lashed by the sharp tongue of her fiendish sister.'

'You cannot make me change my mind,' said Baptista firmly. 'Go into the house now, Bianca. Gentlemen, since I know she takes delight in music and poetry, I'll hire tutors to instruct her—and her sister. So if you two know of any such, send them to me; I'll treat them kindly and employ them to teach my daughters.'

When Baptista and Katharina had followed Bianca into the house, Gremio said to Hortensio:

'Although we are rivals for Bianca, let us be friends until we have a husband for Katharina—and tutors for both of them.'

'The tutors will not be hard to find,' said Hortensio, 'but a husband for that hell-cat will be impossible!'

'Well, there are men who would marry even such a devil as that for her money, and she will have enough to make it worth somebody's while,' remarked Gremio. 'Let's go and see what we can do.'

Now it chanced that all this had been overheard by a young gentleman from Pisa called Lucentio who had just arrived in Padua to pursue his studies—and also to seek his fortune.

Lucentio fell in love with Bianca the moment he saw her; and as soon as Gremio and Hortensio had gone, he began to make plans with his servant Tranio, a clever and intelligent youth of about his own age.

'We cannot find a husband for Katharina,' said Lucentio sadly, 'but her father asked for tutors for his daughters as well——'

'Ah master, I see what you would be at!' chuckled Tranio. 'You'll turn tutor and instruct this lady-love of your's yourself!'

'Exactly,' agreed Lucentio. 'Do you think it a possible plan?'

'Quite out of the question,' said Tranio, suddenly looking glum. 'Who'll play your part in Padua while you follow your new profession? Many people will come to visit Vincentio's son—and who will there be to welcome them and entertain them?'

'That's easy!' cried Lucentio. 'No one has yet seen us in Padua, nor knows us by sight. We'll change garments: you shall be Lucentio, son of Vincentio of Pisa, and I'll be Tranio—while I turn into a tutor and go to instruct Bianca.'

And so, very soon the supposed Lucentio was introducing a young scholar called Cambio to Gremio, having heard that he was anxious to find a tutor for two young ladies.

Meanwhile Hortensio had been even more fortunate than his rival Gremio. Scarcely had he returned home, when he was visited by an old friend, Petruchio, from Verona.

'My dear fellow!' exclaimed Hortensio. 'What good wind blows you hither?'

'Such a wind as scatters young men through the world to seek their fortunes,' answered Petruchio. 'To tell you briefly, my father is dead; I have a good house of my own now, though not enough money to keep it as I could wish. I have come to see the world—and if possible to find a rich wife!'

'I can help you to a wife rich enough for any man!' exclaimed Hortensio eagerly. 'But you are too dear a friend for me to wish you married to her. She is intolerably cursed with a shrewish disposition.'

'Be she as ugly as sin and as old as the Sibyl, I'd marry her, if she had money enough!' cried Petruchio. 'I've come to seek a fortune in Padua, and for a fortune I am ready to take any wife.'

'I was but jesting,' said Hortensio. 'Yet, if you speak even partly in earnest, I'll help you to a rich wife, who is young and beautiful, and brought up in all ways as a gentlewoman. She has this one fault, which cancels out all else: she is a violent, vicious, disobedient girl! And however hard-up I was, I would not marry her for a goldmine!'

'Tell me her father's name, and if he is of suitable rank, I'll begin my wooing at once!' cried Petruchio, clapping his hat on his head.

'She is Katharina, eldest daughter of Baptista Minola,' answered Hortensio.

'A perfect match!' exclaimed Petruchio. 'I know him slightly, though I have never met his daughter. He and my father were good friends.' So saying Petruchio prepared to rush out of the house; but Hortensio stayed him, saying:

'Wait a moment, Petruchio, and I'll go with you.' He proceeded to tell him about Bianca, and ended: 'So let me come, disguised as a musician, and you can present me to Baptista as a tutor.'

Petruchio agreed readily to this; and when Hortensio was properly disguised, they set off for Baptista's house.

They were not the only visitors: on the way they met old Gremio bringing with him Lucentio, disguised as the tutor Cambio; and at Baptista's house they found Tranio, posing as Lucentio, waiting to woo Bianca, and attended by his servant Biondello with a great pile of books.

It was not a happy morning for Baptista. For just before they arrived he had found Katharina tying up Bianca and trying to force her to tell which of her suitors she really loved. He had just managed to part them and send them to their own rooms when the three suitors and their attendants arrived.

Petruchio hardly waited to be introduced, but plunged straight into business:

'Signior Baptista, I hear that you have a daughter called Katharina, both fair and virtuous.'

'I have a daughter, sir, called Katharina,' said Baptista guardedly.

'Well, hearing of her beauty, her kindness, modesty and mild-ness of temper, I am here to woo her, with your leave. I have brought with me this man Licio, an expert in mathematics and music, to instruct her fully in both—though I am sure she is ignorant of neither.'

'You are welcome, sir,' answered Baptista, 'and Signior Licio is welcome for your sake. But I fear that my daughter Katharina may not suit you.'

'I see you do not mean to part with her,' said Petruchio. 'Or else you do not think me a suitable son-in-law.'

But here Gremio interrupted, complaining that Petruchio was talking too much and giving no one else a chance; then he introduced the tutor Cambio whom he had brought.

After this, Tranio, the pretended Lucentio, introduced himself as another suitor for Bianca, spoke of his father's enormous wealth, and presented the books that Biondello was carrying.

'Gentlemen, you are *all* very welcome!' beamed Baptista, and calling a servant, he sent the two tutors to begin their duties immediately, Biondello staggering behind them with his huge pile of books.

'Signior Baptista, I am in haste, and cannot come to woo every day,' said Petruchio when they had gone. 'You knew my father and how much he was worth: I am his sole heir. If I win your daughter's love, how much dowry shall I win with her?'

'Twenty thousand crowns on your wedding day,' answered Baptista, 'and half of my possessions on my death.'

'Excellent!' cried Petruchio. 'Let the lawyers make haste to draw up the settlements, and we'll fix the wedding day.'

'You have first to gain her love: that is the most difficult thing of all,' suggested Baptista.

'Why, that is nothing!' cried Petruchio. 'For I tell you father, she has met her match in me! I am every bit as determined as she is—and I shall woo her roughly!'

'I hope you may woo her successfully,' said Baptista anxiously. 'But you must be prepared for harsh and angry words.'

As if to give point to what he said, the door burst open at this moment, and in staggered Hortensio with the broken remains of the lute dangling round his neck.

'How now, my friend! Why are you so pale?' asked Baptista in surprise.

'From fright, I swear!' gasped Hortensio.

'Why, will my daughter not prove a good musician?'

'I think she'll prove a much better soldier!'

'Can you not break her to the lute, then?'

'No,' answered Hortensio rubbing his head ruefully, 'for she has broken the lute to me! I did no more than tell her she had struck a wrong note, when she turned on me exclaiming: "I've struck a wrong note, have I? Then I'll strike a right one!"

and hit me on the head with the lute—and here I am like a man in the pillory!'

'Upon my word, a girl after my own heart!' cried Petruchio. 'Send her to me, Signior Baptista. I long to begin my wooing!'

And when Katharina was sent alone to him Petruchio put his own peculiar plan of campaign into action.

'Good morning, Kate!' he cried as soon as she came into the room. 'That's your name I hear!'

'Then you're hard of hearing,' she snapped. 'I'm called Katharina.'

'You lie,' answered Petruchio promptly. 'You are called plain Kate, and pretty Kate, and sometimes Kate the shrew; but Kate—the prettiest Kate in Christendom, Kate of Kate-hall, my super-dainty Kate. And therefore, Kate, be consoled and listen to me. Hearing you praised for mildness and beauty, I have come to woo you.'

'Then take yourself away,' answered Katharina. 'You're no more to me than a piece of furniture, you—joint-stool!'

'A stool am I?' laughed Petruchio. 'Well then, I'm here to be sat on; so come sit on my knee, sweet Kate!'

With that, he caught hold of her suddenly and put her on his knee, where he held her by main force and kissed her. Immediately she struck him on the face.

'If you hit me again, I'll hit back!' he exclaimed.

'Then you're no gentleman!' cried Katharina. But she did not put him to the test.

'My dear, I find that you are both kind and gentle,' said Petruchio, 'and not at all cross or shrewish as some people have called you. Indeed, I do not think you can so much as frown at me, or look cross and sulky.'

'You're a fool!' snapped Katharina, frowning her hardest and looking as sulky as she knew how. 'I'll not be ordered about by you. Go away—and give orders to your own dependants.'

'That is precisely what I intend to do,' said Petruchio, still holding her firmly. 'Your father has consented to our marriage, the dowry is agreed upon, and whether you like it or not, you are going to be my wife. I am just the man for you—I'll tame you and turn you from a wild and stubborn Kate into a good, obedient, gentle, household Kate. Now Kate, be careful! Here comes your father: don't contradict me, for I am going to be your husband.'

'Well, Signior Petruchio?' said Baptista bustling in anxiously, still followed by Gremio, and Tranio disguised as Lucentio.

'Very well,' answered Petruchio promptly. 'This sweet, gentle girl loves me so much that we have agreed to be married on Sunday.'

'I'll see you hanged on Sunday!' shrieked Katharina.

'Never mind what she says,' cried Petruchio airily. 'She may pretend to be a shrew in public, but when we're alone, it's a very different matter. You should have seen how sweetly she hung about my neck and kissed me. The wedding is on Sunday, father Baptista, so invite the guests.'

'This is all very surprising,' said Baptista. 'But be it as you say. I wish you joy of your match!'

'Then I'm off!' cried Petruchio. 'Off to Venice to buy rings and things. So kiss me Kate, we'll be married on Sunday!'

With that Petruchio caught her and kissed her and was away out of the house like a whirlwind. Katharina went off like another whirlwind in the opposite direction, and Baptista mopped his brow and turned to bargain with Gremio and Tranio, dressed as Lucentio, for the hand of Bianca.

Here Tranio had much the best of it: for whatever Gremio promised, he immediately promised as much again, until Baptista said at last:

'Well, Signior Lucentio, your offer is the best. Provided that your father Vincentio comes in person to give me full assurance that what you say is true, you shall have Bianca. Next Sunday Petruchio is to marry Katharina; and the Sunday after, you will marry Bianca.'

So Tranio went off to plot with his master: they would need a false Vincentio to keep Baptista happy. Meanwhile Lucentio, disguised as the tutor Cambio, was winning Bianca for himself in secret, and soon revealed to her his true identity. It was not surprising that her other suitor, poor Hortensio, himself disguised as the musician Licio was having a very uneasy time, and becoming more and more jealous and suspicious of Cambio.

Sunday came, the feast was prepared, the guests arrived, and the bride was ready. But there was no sign of Petruchio.

After waiting for a while, Katharina burst into angry tears and went storming off to her room.

'Well, I cannot blame her,' said Baptista, who was getting rather flustered himself. 'We shall be laughing-stocks, with everyone invited to the wedding, the priest waiting, the bride ready—and no bridegroom.'

At that moment Biondello came dashing in, bubbling over with excitement at what he had to tell.

'Master, master!' he cried. 'Such news as you never heard!'

'Well, what is it?' demanded Tranio.

'Petruchio is coming!' spluttered Biondello in a torrent of words, 'in a new hat and an old jacket; a pair of old breeches all patched; a couple of boots that don't match; an old rusty sword with a broken handle and no point; riding on a saddle full of moth-holes, with stirrups of different sizes; and his horse is the oldest and sickliest you ever saw, suffering from glanders and spavins and windgalls and everything else a horse can have; and the bridle's all wrong, and mended with string. His servant's as bad as the horse, with a stocking on one leg and a gaiter on the other; with one garter red and the other blue, tied in big bows on his knees; and an old hat; and—and——'

Biondello stopped at last, being quite out of breath, and Baptista said:

'Well, I'm glad he's coming, however he's dressed.'

'But he isn't coming,' said Biondello.

'You told us that Petruchio was coming!' exclaimed Baptista angrily.

'No sir!' grinned Biondello. 'But his horse is coming—and Petruchio is on its back!'

As if to belie his words, Petruchio came striding into the house at this moment, cracking his whip and shouting for his bride.

'Good Petruchio,' said Baptista. 'We are indeed pleased to see you. But will you not change your clothes? Lucentio here will lend you something fit to be married in.'

'I'll be married as I am, or not at all!' cried Petruchio. 'She's marrying me, not my clothes!' And say what they would, Petruchio strode off to church just as he was, and was married to Katharina who seemed so scared by the mad antics of her bridegroom that she could do nothing but comply.

But after the ceremony she tried to assert herself in her usual manner. When they returned to Baptista's house, Petruchio declared that there was no time for them to join the wedding feast; they must set out at once for his country house.

'Do what you like, I will not go today!' she exclaimed furiously.

'Nor tomorrow, nor till I go to please myself. The door is open—you may go alone if you insist.'

'Come now, Kate, do not get so angry,' said Petruchio.

'I'll be angry if I want to!' she retorted. 'Be quiet, father: he shall wait until I'm ready. Now, gentlemen, forward to the bridal dinner. We'll soon see who's master here!'

'Indeed we shall!' cried Petruchio. 'Forward, gentlemen, and obey the bride. But neither she nor I are coming with you. We are leaving Padua immediately. Now, my bonny Kate, it's no use stamping and fuming, and glaring like that. I am master of what is my own, and you are my own, and you will do as I say!'

So saying, Petruchio seized Katharina, flung her over his shoulder and strode out of the house, followed by his servant, leaving all the guests open-mouthed with amazement.

Still holding Katharina, Petruchio sprang on to his horse and galloped away. Nor did he stop for several hours; but when they had almost reached his house, the horse stumbled, the girths broke, and Katharina slipped off into the mud.

Wet, weary and miserable, Katharina followed Petruchio into the house, for she was hungry as well. But she was not to get much food or rest. Petruchio continued to rave and storm like a madman, flinging the food on the floor as not fit to eat, cursing and beating the servants (who had all been instructed how to behave), and making sure that Katharina got little food and less rest. But all the time he kept assuring her that everything he did was for her good, and that every thought was for her health and comfort.

Meanwhile in Padua other plots were afoot. Tranio, disguised as Lucentio, persuaded Hortensio to give up all hopes of winning Bianca, and swore that he too would give her up as well. For he saw to it that Hortensio caught her kissing the supposed tutor Cambio. Hortensio was so disgusted that he went off immediately and proposed to a rich widow who accepted him on the spot. Baptista then announced that Bianca was to marry Lucentio next Sunday; for Tranio had bribed an old man, whom he met

in the street, to pretend to be Vincentio the rich lord of Pisa, and to promise all that Baptista hoped as a marriage portion.

The real Lucentio, however, eloped the night before the wedding with Bianca, and married her in secret.

By then, though, Hortensio had set out to visit his friend Petruchio to see how he and Katharina were getting on, and to invite them to his wedding to the widow on the same Sunday that Bianca was supposed to be marrying the pretended Lucentio.

He found Petruchio's house still in an uproar. Poor Katharina was half starved and almost worn out; but she still refused to give in to her husband or sacrifice her own will in anything.

Petruchio, who all the time professed to be doing everything in his power to make Katharina happy, welcomed his friend, and announced that they would set out next day for the double wedding in Padua.

He had already sent for the tailor and the haberdasher to make new dresses and caps for Katharina to wear. But when they arrived, he found fault with all of them, and contradicted whatever she said.

'The cap's too small!' shouted Petruchio. 'It's made for a doll!'

'It's just the right size,' said Katharina, 'and small caps like this are all the fashion with gentlewomen.'

'Then you shall have one when you are gentle,' said Petruchio severely. At this Katharina lost her temper and cursed him roundly. Petruchio pretended to believe that it was the cap and the haberdasher she was cursing, and agreed with her enthusiastically:

'What you say, dearest Kate, is perfectly true. The cap is ridiculous, stupid and all the rest. And I love you the better for not liking it.'

'Love me or love me not, I like the cap,' insisted Katharina, 'and I will have it, or none at all.'

The same thing happened over the gown, and Petruchio chased both the tailor and the haberdasher out of the house, though he privately asked Hortensio to go after them and pay them for their work.

'Well, Kate,' said Petruchio, 'since you like neither the cap nor the gown, you'll have to go in the clothes you were married in.

It's not the fine feathers that make the fine bird—we all prefer the lark to the jay—and the mind it is that makes the body rich.'

With that Katharina was forced to be content, and was ready next morning in her old clothes to start for Padua.

Petruchio, however, showed no sign of setting out until midday was passed. Then suddenly he exclaimed:

'Time to go, Kate! It's just seven o'clock, so we ought to be there by dinner-time!'

'You are mistaken, sir,' corrected Katharina more mildly than usual. 'It is almost two o'clock, so it will be supper-time before we arrive.'

'It shall be whatever time I say it is!' declared Petruchio. 'We do not start for your father's house until you stop contradicting me.'

When at last they set out, Katharina was very much subdued, but still a little rebellious and argumentative.

'Ah, how brightly the moon is shining!' exclaimed Petruchio presently.

'The moon!' cried Katharina, 'why, it is the sun! There's no moonlight in the middle of the afternoon!'

'I say it is the moon,' repeated Petruchio.

'I know it is the sun,' insisted Katharina.

'It shall be moon or sun or star or whatever I say, before we continue on our journey!' cried Petruchio. 'Turn the horses, we are going home!'

'Say what he says, or we shall never get there!' whispered Hortensio.

'Let us go on towards Padua,' said Katharina as humbly as she knew how. 'And let it be the moon or the sun, or whatever you say it is. If you call it a mere rush-candle, I vow it shall be one so far as I am concerned.'

'I say it is the moon,' declared Petruchio.

'I know it is the moon,' agreed Katharina.

'If you say that, you lie,' exclaimed Petruchio. 'It's the sun!'

'God bless us, it *is* the sun!' said Katharina promptly. 'But not when you say it isn't. Whatever you name it, that it is, and always shall be so far as I am concerned.'

The battle seemed won; but Petruchio thought it wise to try one final test. Just as they were approaching Padua they overtook an old man hurrying along the road.

'Good day to you, gentle lady!' cried Petruchio when they came up with him. 'Tell me Kate, and tell me truly, did you ever see a prettier girl? Greet her, Kate, and ask if we can see her on her way.'

Katharina had learnt her lesson, and rose nobly to the occasion:

'Young, budding maiden,' she began 'fair and fresh and sweet. Whither are you journeying? Can we not accompany you, and bring you to your parents? Or is it to the fortunate young man who is to be your husband?'

'Why, what are you talking about, Kate!' exclaimed Petruchio. 'I hope you have not taken leave of your senses? This is no maiden as you seem to think, but an old man with a white beard!'

'Pardon me, reverend sir,' said Katharina humbly, 'my eyes were dazzled by the sun. Now I see quite clearly my stupid mistake. Please forgive me!'

'Do, kind old gentleman,' cried Petruchio, 'and travel with us none the less, if your ways and ours are the same.'

'Indeed I will,' said the old man smiling in a friendly fashion. 'My name is Vincentio. I come from Pisa, and hope to find my son Lucentio in Padua.'

'Well met indeed,' said Petruchio. 'By this time your son is probably married to my wife's sister, Bianca Minola. We were hastening to the wedding, though fear that we may be a trifle late.'

So they went on together to Padua, and found there a confusion that might have ended in tragedy. For Tranio was still pretending to be Lucentio, and Baptista was still planning to marry Bianca to him that very afternoon. But the arrival of the real Vincentio proved suddenly to Baptista that neither Tranio nor his pretended father were whom they seemed to be—and that Bianca had disappeared.

However, when the real Lucentio arrived with his newly-wed wife, Vincentio readily forgave them, and persuaded Baptista to do so as well. Hortensio went off in haste to marry the rich widow; and then all three couples, with the servants forgiven and now playing their proper parts, assembled at Baptista's for a grand banquet.

All was mirth and happiness. But after dinner, when the ladies had retired, Lucentio and Hortensio thought it a good opportunity to tease Petruchio on account of his shrewish wife.

'Hortensio and I rule in our own households!' cried Lucentio; 'but we know who is master in yours, Petruchio!'

'I'm afraid, Petruchio,' nodded Baptista, 'there's no disguising the fact that you have the most disobedient wife of the three.'

'Well, I say no!' declared Petruchio. 'So let's have a bet on it. Let each of us send for his own wife to come here immediately, and see who obeys.'

'What shall we wager?' said Hortensio. 'Twenty crowns?'

'Twenty crowns!' cried Petruchio scornfully. 'Why, I'd bet as much as that on my hawk or hound, but twenty times as much on my wife.'

'A hundred, then,' said Lucentio, and this was agreed.

'Who shall begin?' asked Hortensio.

'I will,' said Lucentio. 'Biondello, go and bid your mistress come to me.'

'There's no doubt Bianca will come,' said Baptista. But scarcely were the words out of his mouth, when Biondello returned— alone.

'Sir,' said he, bowing to Lucentio, 'my mistress sends you word that she is busy and cannot come.'

'Busy, is she?' exclaimed Petruchio, 'cannot come! That's a fine answer!'

'A better one than your wife will send!' snapped Lucentio.

'Now Biondello,' said Hortensio, 'go and beg my wife to come at once!'

'Oh ho, *beg* her!' laughed Petruchio. 'Then surely she'll come!'

'I'm afraid *your* wife will not come for begging,' said Hortensio.

'Sir!' exclaimed Biondello, running in at this moment. 'Your wife says that you are having some joke at her expense. She says she will not come: if you want her, you must go to her yourself.'

'Worse and worse!' said Petruchio shaking his head. 'Now go to my wife. Say that I command her to come!'

'I know what her answer will be,' said Hortensio, when Biondello had gone with the message.

'What?' asked Petruchio.

'That she will not come,' answered Hortensio.

'Now upon my word, here *is* Katharina!' exclaimed Baptista. Katharina indeed came speeding into the room, dropped a low curtsey to Petruchio, and said:

'What do you want, sir, that you send for me?'

'Where is your sister and Hortensio's wife?' asked Petruchio.

'They are sitting and talking by the parlor fire,' answered Katharina.

'Then go and fetch them,' commanded Petruchio. 'If they refuse to come, drive them in. Quick now, and bring them!'

Off went Katharina, and everyone gasped in amazement.

'Here's a wonder indeed!' cried Lucentio.

'Certainly it is,' agreed Hortensio, 'I wonder what will come of it.'

'That I can tell you,' said Petruchio, suddenly serious. 'Peace will come of it, and love, and a quiet life; order and a house undivided. In fact, all happiness for us both.'

'Son Petruchio,' said Baptista, 'you have won the wager, and well you deserve it. Now I will add to it another twenty thousand crowns—another dowry for another daughter. For she is changed as if she were a different woman.'

'Wait a little,' said Petruchio, 'I will prove her newborn virtue and obedience still further. Here she comes, bringing your disobedient wives by womanly persuasion.'

Katharina indeed appeared at that moment, dragging Bianca and Hortensio's wife by the wrists.

'Katharina!' said Petruchio, 'that cap of yours does not suit you. Take it off and fling it away.'

Katharina obeyed without a moment's hesitation.

'How foolish to obey such a silly command!' pouted Bianca.

'I wish your duty had been as foolish!' said Lucentio severely.

'The wisdom of your duty, fair Bianca, has cost me a hundred crowns since supper-time.'

'The more fool you for making bets about my duty,' returned Bianca.

'Come Katharina,' said Petruchio, 'tell these headstrong women what their duty is to the husbands they have sworn to love, honor and obey.'

'Fie, you foolish women,' said Katharina. 'Take off those frowns and angry looks which blot your beauty and are so meaningless. An angry woman is like a muddy pool which has been stirred up: no one will come and drink from such a fountain; and no man will look upon you with love until, like the pool, you are clear and untroubled as you should be. For true happiness, *one*, in the home, must have the final word—and that is the husband, both by the will of God and by the laws of nature. Your husband goes forth into the world to labor for you by sea and land; he guards you and sees to your well-being by day and night, while you live safely and securely. Nor does he demand any tribute from you, save love, fair looks, and simple obedience —a small payment for all that he gives and does for you. To be sullen, cross and awkward is like a bad citizen breaking the laws or rebelling against the rightful authority of our rulers—who are themselves obedient to those above them, even as the greatest prince or king is to God.

'Once I was as proud, obstinate and stubborn as you are—and in open rebellion. But it brought me no joy. Only now have I learnt to be truly happy—by being truly myself, in proper relation to my husband, beneath whose foot I am ready to set my hand in token of obedience, if he so commands it.'

There was silence: Bianca, and Hortensio's wife both knew that Katharina was right, however little they liked it.

Then Petruchio said as he took her hand and their eyes met with a look of mutual love and understanding:

'Why, that's my girl! So, kiss me Kate—and away we go, to live happily for all our days!'

THE MERCHANT OF VENICE

In the beautiful city of Venice there once lived a rich
merchant called Antonio. Even in that city of wealthy merchant-
princes Antonio stood out above the rest, not only for his riches
and the success of his trading ventures, but for the directness and
honesty of his character, and his kindness and generosity as well.
There was only one thing he could not tolerate, and that was
usury—the practice of lending money to those in need, and charging a high rate of interest on it.

Antonio was always ready to help his friends. Although he had
no children, he loved Bassanio, one of his younger friends, as
much as if he were a son, and indeed treated him almost as if he
were adopted.

Bassanio was very unlike the grave, careful, sober Antonio:
he was gay and inclined to be extravagant, enjoying the company
of even wilder young men such as his friends Gratiano and
Lorenzo, spending money freely, and taking very little thought
for the future.

Antonio lent or gave Bassanio a good deal of money, and did
his best to cure him of his spendthrift ways and bring him up to
be a careful citizen of Venice. But Bassanio continued on his
reckless course, until the sudden realization that he no longer
had any money at all brought him quickly to his senses. Being at
heart a good and honest young man, he did not want to live
indefinitely on the kindness of his friend Antonio; but equally

he did not see how to make his fortune, now that all his inheritance was spent.

There was one way that at that time was very much the custom, and seemed a perfectly right and honest course, namely to marry an heiress. Many young men of good family did so, and often without any regard for who the heiress might be, provided she had enough wealth in money or lands.

Bassanio was not quite as coldly calculating as this. Some time before, he had seen and fallen in love with a beautiful girl called Portia, the only child of a rich landowner who lived at Belmont not far from Venice. At that time Bassanio was a poor scholar and soldier in the train of a wealthy Venetian marquis on a visit to Portia's father. But he had never forgotten her; and since then her father had died and left her all his fortune. Bassanio knew that Portia had many suitors, but so far none had succeeded in winning her. He loved her—perhaps she was not indifferent to him: he would risk all on the chance, and set out for Belmont to woo her.

Risk all? But he had nothing to risk, for he was penniless. A man of his rank must have rich clothes, servants, followers when he went a-wooing. Perhaps Antonio would come to his aid once more.

Bassanio sought out his friend and put the whole situation before him simply and honestly.

'I have no excuse,' he said. 'I can find no real reason why you should lend me the money on such a slender security. I can only plead that it is at least a sporting chance. When I was a boy, and had lost one of my arrows, I would shoot another in the same direction, watching carefully where it fell, and as often as not when I went to pick it up the lost arrow lay near by. I am asking you to take the same sort of chance with the three thousand ducats that I need to woo Portia in the proper style.'

'Dear Bassanio,' answered Antonio, 'you know me too well to make such excuses. I will give you everything you want, simply for the love I bear you. Most unfortunately, I have no money in hand at the moment; all that I possess is invested in my merchant ventures, and at present all my ships are on voyages to various foreign ports. But both I and my wealth are so well known in Venice that you will have no difficulty in borrowing what you need in my name, and with my word as security.'

Bassanio took advantage of his friend's generosity. But it so happened that the man whom he approached for the loan, a rich Jew called Shylock, was Antonio's deadly enemy. Shylock hated Antonio in particular because he lent money charging no interest, and, in consequence, Shylock found it more and more difficult to charge his usual excessively high rate of interest. Now he saw a chance of being revenged on Antonio—perhaps of getting rid of him altogether—and he at once devised a scheme that might allow him to murder Antonio without breaking any of the laws for which Venice was famous.

'Yes, I will lend the money,' said Shylock when Bassanio had explained what he wanted, and Antonio himself had come to ratify the bargain and sign the agreement. 'But do you not find it odd that you should be borrowing from me? You who spurn me and spit upon me for lending money as a businesslike means of increasing my own fortune!'

'I shall do as much again,' said Antonio, making no attempt to hide his contempt and loathing. 'I am borrowing from you, and breaking my rule of neither charging nor paying interest, simply to help my friend, since as you know all my own wealth is at present risked on my various trading ventures. So if you will lend, do so as to an enemy from whom you may exact the fullest penalty the law allows if he fails to pay. For between friends no such bargain for money, and payment of interest, could ever occur.'

'Good,' said Shylock. 'But Signior Antonio, in spite of all your insults, I want to be friends with you. I will charge no interest on the loan of three thousand ducats. But since this would be contrary to my usual practice, come with me to a notary and sign a bond, purely in jest, that if you do not return the money by the date agreed, you shall pay, by way of penalty, a pound of your own fair flesh, to be cut off and taken from whatever part of your body I choose.'

'Certainly,' answered Antonio shortly. 'I'll sign this bond.

And,' he added with a sneer, 'I'll say there is much kindness in the Jew!'

'You shall not sign such a bond on my account!' cried Bassanio. 'I'd rather go without the money than let you risk anything so dreadful.'

'Why, have no fear,' said Antonio. 'There's no chance of my having to pay such a forfeit. A month before the money falls due I expect three times as much from one of my ventures. Come, Shylock: I'll sign the bond at once.'

Having obtained the money, Bassanio bade farewell to Antonio and set sail for Belmont, accompanied by his friend Gratiano. His other friend Lorenzo did not go with him: he had fallen in love with Jessica, Shylock's daughter and they had eloped on the very night that Bassanio set out for Belmont. As Jessica took with her a good deal of her father's wealth, Shylock, who loved his money better than anything else, was in a terrible state. He went raving through the streets, demanding justice and crying out for his jewels and his bags of gold—wishing his daughter dead, if only he could recover his treasure.

The fact that Jessica had fled with a Christian—who was now spending the money she had taken—made Shylock even more determined to be revenged; and he greeted with delight the news that some of Antonio's ships had been wrecked on their way back to Venice.

'Let him look to his bond!' cried Shylock fiercely. 'If he does not pay me on the very day it falls due, I'll have a pound of his flesh—it will be mine by the law of Venice!'

Meanwhile Bassanio had come to Belmont, and on seeing Portia again had known that what his heart had told him was true. He had loved her since their first meeting, though he had hardly admitted the fact; and what is more, of all the suitors who had since come to woo her, none had touched her heart as Bassanio had.

All should therefore have gone well for them, and Bassanio should have returned to Venice a rich man long before Antonio's debt to Shylock was due. But to win the love of Portia was not to win her hand. For she was bound by a strange clause in her father's will which gave her no choice in the matter of a husband. True, it had so far saved her from many an unwelcome suitor; but it might equally well prevent her from marrying Bassanio; and so she put off the fatal choice from day to day.

But at last neither she nor Bassanio felt that they could wait any longer. For another suitor might appear at any moment and win Portia—a risk neither of them could bear to take. So Portia led him to a room where stood three caskets: one of gold, one of silver, and one of lead.

'In one of those caskets is my picture,' she told him. 'You must choose the correct one to win me. But before you make your choice you must swear a most solemn oath that if you fail to choose rightly, you will never tell anyone which casket you opened; further, that you will never marry but remain a bachelor all your life. My father made those conditions believing that only those who loved me truly would take such a risk—and that God would direct the choice of that man who was most suited to be my husband. Much though I love you, Lord Bassanio, I must abide by my father's will. So I beg you, do not choose yet awhile, for I cannot bear the thought of losing you altogether.'

'I must choose, and now,' said Bassanio gently. 'For to live on this rack of uncertainty is more than I can bear. Let me view the caskets.'

So saying Bassanio stepped up to the table on which they were placed and examined each in turn.

On the golden casket was written: 'Who chooseth me shall gain what many men desire'; on the silver casket were the words: 'Who chooseth me shall get as much as he deserves'; and on the leaden one: 'Who chooseth me must give and hazard all he hath.'

Meanwhile, at Portia's command, her musicians played, and one of them sang a song while Bassanio was making his choice:

> 'Tell me, where is fancy bred,
> Or in the heart, or in the head?
> How begot, how nourished?
>   Reply, reply.
> It is engender'd in the eyes,
> With gazing fed; and fancy dies
> In the cradle where it lies.
>   Let us now ring fancy's knell;
>   I'll begin it: Ding, dong bell.'

The song seemed to echo Bassanio's thoughts, and rhyme with the choice that he was already making:

'Outward shows are often the least true,' he said, 'and men's eyes are often deceived by what is mere ornament. Therefore I will not be misled by what I see. So I will not choose the gold, which is too gaudy, nor the silver, which is too like the idle coins which pass from hand to hand as a mere convenience. But as I desire nothing better than to give and hazard all I have for Portia's sake, so I choose the simple lead.'

As he spoke, Bassanio opened the leaden casket, and knew that he had chosen correctly. For there before him lay a miniature of Portia, and with it a scroll on which was written the words:

> 'You that choose not by the view,
> Chance as fair, and choose as true!
> Since the fortune falls to you,
> Be content, and seek no new.
> If you be well pleased with this,
> And hold your fortune for your bliss,
> Turn you where your lady is,
> And claim her with a loving kiss.'

'Fair lady,' said he, turning to Portia, 'I come with written authority to give and to receive!'

So saying, he took her in his arms and kissed her, and she confessed her love yet again, wishing only that she were a thousand times more fair and ten thousand times more rich, for his sake.

'Unworthy though I and all that is mine may be,' she ended, 'both mine and me are yours now and for ever. Only a few minutes ago I was the owner of this fair mansion, master of my servants—queen of myself; now house, servants, my very self are mine no longer, but are yours. I give them to you, with this ring. If you part with it, lose it or give it away, I shall know that you have ceased to love me.'

'Dear love, you have bereft me of words,' said Bassanio, holding her close to him, 'my very blood speaks to you as it courses through my veins, and I cannot find words with which to tell how much I love you. This ring shall never leave my finger while I am alive. When I part with it you will know that Bassanio is dead.'

Then Gratiano came to congratulate his friend Bassanio, leading by the hand Portia's maid Nerissa, who had agreed to marry him if Bassanio won Portia by his choice of the right casket. They also sealed their troth with a ring, which Gratiano swore should never leave his finger.

While the two pairs of lovers were making plans for their

double wedding, Lorenzo and Jessica arrived at Belmont in company with a messenger bearing a letter from Antonio.

Bassanio and Portia made them welcome, and the messenger handed the letter to Bassanio—who tore it open, and cried out with horror at what he read.

'Some dreadful news, surely!' exclaimed Portia anxiously. 'I pray you Bassanio to share your sorrow with me.'

'Sweet Portia, here are the cruellest words that ever blotted paper!' cried Bassanio wildly. 'I have told you of my friend Antonio, the great merchant of Venice, and of all his kindness to me. What I did not tell was that to supply me with money to come wooing, he borrowed from his worst enemy, and signed a bond which forfeits his very life if he does not repay his debt on the day it falls due. Now, all his ships which might have reached Venice in time have been wrecked, and he has let the day of payment go by, always hoping that one venture at least would come home.'

'If money be all,' exclaimed Portia, 'set out for Venice at once and pay his debt, with any interest that may be due. For how much was the loan?'

'For me, three thousand ducats,' answered Bassanio.

'What, no more than that?' cried Portia. 'Pay six thousand and redeem the bond. Pay twice that, and treble that again before a true friend of yours shall come to harm.'

'Alas, I fear it is too late,' said Jessica, shaking her head sadly. 'The money was borrowed from my father and I have often heard him say that he would rather have the pound of flesh which Antonio pledged than twenty times the value of the loan. I am ashamed to speak so of my own father, but I know that he hates Antonio so much for coming to the aid of those who had fallen into his clutches, that he would sooner have his revenge than recover the money.'

'Surely the Duke cannot allow such a murder to take place!' said Portia, when she realized what Antonio's forfeiture meant.

'The bond was duly and fully signed and witnessed,' said Bassanio sadly, 'and the Duke cannot alter the laws of Venice by one hair's breadth to benefit any man.'

'Nevertheless, take ten times the sum Antonio owes, and do

your best!' urged Portia. 'Let our marriages be celebrated immediately, so that what was mine may all be legally yours; set out with Gratiano at full speed, even from the very door of the church. And while you are away, Nerissa and I will live here as maids and widows until you return—bringing your dear friend Antonio with you safe and free.'

Scarcely had Bassanio and Gratiano set out for Venice, when Portia began to wonder how she could help to save Antonio. Before long she hit upon a scheme which carried with it a good chance of success, and sent a trusty messenger at full speed to Padua, to her cousin Bellario, a famous lawyer.

Then, leaving Lorenzo and Jessica in charge of Belmont, she set out with Nerissa, telling them that they were going to a monastery not far away to pray for their husbands' success and safe return.

'But really, Nerissa,' she told her maid when they were alone, 'we are going to see our husbands where they least think to see us. Of course they will not recognise us for we shall be dressed as men; I shall be a learned lawyer named Balthazar, and you shall be my clerk.'

The great day arrived when the case of *Antonio* v. *Shylock* was to be tried before the Duke and his court.

Before the actual trial began, the Duke attempted once more to persuade Shylock to forgo his cruel revenge, suggesting to him that he should show mercy and let Antonio off the actual forfeiture of a pound of flesh—particularly as he had suffered such losses from the wrecking of so many ships. But nothing would turn Shylock from his purpose.

'I have sworn a solemn oath to have my due,' he said, 'and nothing can move me. It is my wish to be rid of an enemy who, in the past, has interfered with my financial dealings.'

'This is no answer, you unfeeling man!' cried Bassanio. 'All men do not kill the people they dislike.'

'Is there any man who would not kill the thing he hated, if he got the chance?' snarled Shylock, and Antonio interrupted sadly:

'There, Bassanio, you are answered. Shylock looks at things differently from you and me. You may as well ask the wolf why he has made the ewe bleat for her lamb—you may as well stand on the beach and tell the tide not to come in—as try to change his nature.'

'Shylock, for your three thousand ducats, here are six!' urged Bassanio.

'If every ducat in six thousand ducats were in six parts and every part a ducat, it would not buy Antonio's life,' said Shylock.

'How can you hope for mercy, if you show none?' asked the Duke.

'I do no wrong, what have I to fear?' answered Shylock.

'We cannot proceed to the trial until the learned Dr. Bellario of Padua arrives,' said the Duke to Antonio. 'I have sent for him.'

At that moment a message arrived—brought by Nerissa dressed as a lawyer's clerk.

Having read the letter, the Duke turned to her and said:

'This letter from Bellario tells me that he is ill and cannot come, but that he has sent a young lawyer called Balthazar to take his place—a Doctor of Laws who has studied in Rome, and with whom he has already discussed this whole case. Is Dr. Balthazar with you?'

'He is at the door,' answered Nerissa. 'Shall I bid him enter?'

'He is very welcome,' said the Duke. When Portia entered the court he greeted her warmly without the slightest doubt that she was other than Dr. Balthazar the young Roman lawyer.

Portia seemed completely self-possessed, and fully acquainted with all the details of the case, into which she plunged immediately in the most business-like manner.

'Which is the defendant?' she asked, 'and which the plaintiff?'

'Antonio and Shylock, both stand forth,' commanded the Duke.

'Is your name Shylock?' asked Portia.

'That is my name,' he answered.

'Do you admit that you signed this bond?' asked Portia, turning to Antonio.

'I do,' he answered sadly.

'Then mercy must be shown to you,' said Portia.

'By what compulsion must I be merciful?' asked Shylock.

Portia seemed quite shocked by this: 'Mercy is not to be compelled,' she said, 'it falls like rain from Heaven, blessing those on whom it falls, and being a blessing in itself. It is the noblest token that a king can show, and it suits him better even than his crown. His sceptre shows his worldly power, but mercy, coming from God, transcends it and makes earthly power seem most like God's when mercy is mixed with justice. In the strict course of justice, none of us would be saved: we pray to God for mercy, and that very prayer should teach us all to be merciful. Perhaps this may persuade you to demand less than strict justice. For if you do demand it, this strictly honest court of Venice must give sentence against Antonio.'

'I'll answer for my own deeds,' replied Shylock. 'All I ask is that you enforce the law and give what is mine according to the bond.'

'Can the merchant not pay his debt?' asked Portia.

'Yes!' exclaimed Bassanio. 'I offer the money here and now. I will even pay ten times what is owing, if need be. But it is obvious that Shylock is swayed by his desire for revenge. I beg of you, go against the law; to do a great right, do a little wrong.'

'It must not be,' said Portia solemnly. 'There is no power in Venice to alter the law. If once it is broken by those who are here to enforce it, the law will cease to be of any worth. No, it cannot be tampered with.'

'A Daniel come to judgement!' cried Shylock. 'Oh wise young judge.'

'This bond is now overdue,' said Portia, studying the document. 'And by it you may lawfully claim a pound of Antonio's flesh to be cut off nearest his heart. But be merciful; take three times the money that is owing to you, and let me tear up the bond.'

'Only when it is paid according to the agreement,' answered Shylock. 'I swear that nothing you or anyone else can say will alter my decision.'

'I beg you to give sentence and have done,' said Antonio. 'I am prepared to die, for I know that nothing can change this man's attitude. I have confessed my sins and am at peace with the world. So I beg you to put an end to this suspense.'

'Then lay bare your breast,' said Portia solemnly, 'for a pound of flesh is forfeit: the law allows it, and the court awards it.'

'Most rightful judge,' exclaimed Shylock. He advanced upon Antonio with a great knife in his hand, and the scales ready for weighing the flesh.

'And you must cut the flesh from his breast,' continued Portia. 'It is forfeit to you according to the law.'

'Most learned judge!' cried Shylock as he approached Antonio who was being held down by four officers of the court. 'It is a sentence! Make ready to pay me what you owe!'

Shylock was already raising his arm to begin cutting into Antonio's flesh when Portia's voice cut through the horrified silence which held the court.

'Tarry a little, Shylock, there is something else. This bond does not give you a single drop of blood. The words are "A pound of flesh". Take what your bond allows you—take your pound of flesh. But if in cutting it you shed one drop of blood, your lands and goods will be confiscated by the laws of Venice.'

A great sigh seemed to go through the court, and Gratiano, being the first to see that Antonio was saved, cried tauntingly:

'Oh upright judge! Take note, Shylock! Oh learned judge!'

'Is that the law?' said Shylock slowly.

'You shall see the act, if you wish,' cried Portia. 'You have asked for justice. You shall have it.'

Shylock saw that he was trapped, and turned hastily to Bassanio. 'I'll take your offer, then!' he exclaimed. 'Pay me three times the sum owing, and Antonio shall be free.'

'Here is the money—' began Bassanio, but Portia interrupted quickly:

'Wait a little. He shall have nothing but the penalty.'

'A second Daniel!' jeered Gratiano.

'Therefore prepare to cut off the flesh,' went on Portia. 'Shed no blood, and be sure to cut no more nor less than an exact pound—or your life and all your goods are forfeit.'

'Give me my three thousand ducats and let me go!' cried Shylock.

'I have it ready—here it is!' exclaimed Bassanio. But again Portia cut in:

'He has refused it in court. He shall have nothing but justice—which gives him his forfeiture.'

'Shall I not even have my three thousand ducats?' whined Shylock.

'You shall have nothing but what is due to you—to be taken at your peril!' cried Portia triumphantly.

'Why then the devil give him good of it!' cried Shylock. 'I'll stay no longer!'

'Wait a little!' commanded Portia. 'The laws of Venice are not yet satisfied. For they lay down that if any alien seeks the life of a Venetian citizen, by direct or indirect means, half his goods are forfeit to the man against whom he has plotted, and the other half to the state. Moreover, his life is forfeit too, and only the Duke can pardon him. And I say that you, who are not a Venetian citizen, have sought the life of this merchant of Venice, both directly and indirectly: so down on your knees and beg mercy of the Duke.'

'That you shall see in what a different spirit we regard even our enemies,' said the Duke, 'I pardon you your life before you ask it. Half of your goods are forfeit to Antonio: the other half to the state—but if you show humility, the state may be content with a fine.'

'Take my life and everything!' cried Shylock. 'You take my life when you take my money—I cannot live without it!'

'What mercy can you show him, Antonio?' asked the Duke.

'I will claim not half, but only a quarter of his goods,' said Antonio, 'and I will leave it on my death to Lorenzo, who lately eloped with his daughter. But he must sign a deed here and now leaving the other quarter, and all he may then have, to Jessica and her husband on his death.'

So Shylock went off home; and when the Duke had left in state, Antonio and his friends crowded round Portia to thank her for what she had done, and ask how they could reward her.

'He is well paid that is well satisfied,' Portia declared. 'I came but to see justice done, and must now hasten back to Padua. But as a token of what I have done today, give me that ring on your finger!'

'This ring!' cried Bassanio. 'Why, it is worth nothing! Let me give you a valuable one instead.'

'I want that and that only,' answered Portia. And though Bassanio was loath to part with his wife's gift, he could not deny it to the lawyer who had saved Antonio's life.

In the same way Nerissa persuaded Gratiano to give her the ring she had given him; and then 'Dr. Balthazar' and his 'clerk' said farewell and hastened away.

Portia and Nerissa got back to Belmont first, and came upon Jessica and Lorenzo sitting happily in the moonlight telling each other stories of famous lovers in Greek and Roman legend who had met on other such nights of magic and beauty.

They too were held by the enchantment of the night and of the joy in their hearts at the success of their secret expedition to Venice.

'The light burning over there,' said Portia, as they approached Lorenzo and Jessica, 'is burning in the hall of my house. How far that little candle throws its beams! So shines a good deed in an evil world.'

'That is Portia's voice!' exclaimed Lorenzo, springing up to welcome her.

'Have our husbands returned yet?' asked Portia.

'A messenger came a few minutes ago to say they would soon arrive,' answered Lorenzo.

'Then be sure that you and Jessica say nothing yet about our absence from Belmont,' said Portia.

She was just in time with her warning, for Bassanio and Gratiano arrived almost immediately, bringing Antonio with them to celebrate. But the happiness of that night was shattered almost at once, for a violent quarrel broke out between Gratiano and Nerissa.

'Where is the ring I gave you?' cried Nerissa. 'You swore it would never leave your finger, even after your death—and now you say you've given it to a lawyer's clerk. I don't believe a word of it: you've given it to a woman!'

'I swear I gave it to a youth,' persisted Gratiano. 'A kind of boy; a little scrubby boy no bigger than yourself!'

'You were much to blame,' said Portia severely. 'I gave my husband a ring also, which he swore to wear always. I am quite certain *he* would never part with it!'

'He gave it to the lawyer, Dr. Balthazar, whose handling of the case saved Signior Antonio's life!' cried Gratiano.

'I cannot believe that he parted with my ring,' said Portia.

'Alas that I must admit it, but I did,' said Bassanio, covered with confusion.

'Then I know that you do not love me,' sobbed Portia. 'You shall not touch me until I see that ring again!'

'I gave it to the lawyer who saved Antonio's life,' pleaded Bassanio. 'He would not take the three thousand ducats I offered him, but begged only for the ring. How could I refuse him?'

'I'm sure you gave it to a woman,' cried Portia. 'You have been unfaithful to me—and I'll pay you out in your own base coin if ever that Dr. Balthazar of whom you speak comes near me!'

'I am the unhappy cause of this quarrel,' said Antonio. 'Dear Lady Portia, let me once more be surety for Bassanio. I'll wager my flesh again on his behalf, that he'll never more break an oath to you.'

'I'll take your word,' smiled Portia. 'So give Bassanio this ring, and make him swear to keep it.'

'By Heaven! The ring I gave to the lawyer!' exclaimed Bassanio.

'And this the one I gave his clerk!' echoed Gratiano as Nerissa handed a ring to him.

'Dr. Balthazar shared my bed last night and gave it to me!' said Portia.

'His little scrubby clerk shared mine!' echoed Nerissa.

Bassanio and Gratiano looked at one another with such expressions of horror and consternation that Portia and Nerissa could keep up the joke no longer, but burst into delighted laughter.

'Pardon us our jest, Bassanio,' said Portia. 'Read this letter from my cousin Bellario of Padua. There you shall find sure proof that I was Dr. Balthazar and Nerissa was my clerk! Lorenzo will bear witness that we have just returned and not yet even entered the house. Antonio, I have good news: three of your ships have come unexpectedly to harbor laden with riches. Jessica, my clerk has a deed of gift for you from Shylock—of all he dies possessed.'

'Were you the doctor of law—and I didn't recognise you?' gasped Bassanio.

'Were you the lawyer's clerk?' cried Gratiano.

'Lady, you come like a goddess,' said Antonio. 'I owe my life to you; Lorenzo and Jessica their fortune; while Gratiano and Bassanio owe you both wealth and happiness.'

'It is nearly morning,' said Portia. 'Let us go into the house.'

So the three happy couples flitted away, hand in hand in the moonlight, and behind them, as happy in their happiness as they were themselves, came Antonio.

MUCH ADO ABOUT NOTHING

Messina, that fair city of Sicily, was once governed by a Duke called Leonato whose only child was a beautiful daughter named Hero. She was not lonely, however, for her cousin Beatrice, an orphan, had been brought up with her and had always been her best friend.

These two cousins were most unlike. Hero was small, shy and retiring; but Beatrice, her elder by several years, was forthright and fearless, with a ready wit, a sarcastic tongue, and a good estimation of herself.

Neither of these young ladies was married, or had thought much about finding a husband, until chance brought a whole group of eligible young men to Messina. They came with Don Pedro, Prince of Aragon, and his half-brother, Don John, to spend a few days at Messina, while celebrating their victory in a minor war.

Beatrice already knew one of these young men, as great a talker as herself called Benedick. He was a wealthy lord of Padua —and with him came his best friend, the Florentine, Claudio.

'Signior Benedick!' exclaimed Beatrice, when the two met, 'Still talking, though no one ever listens to what you say!'

'What, my dear Lady Disdain!' cried Benedick, 'Are you still living!'

'Disdain can hardly die while there is such a man as you to treat disdainfully,' countered Beatrice.

'This is not the treatment I get from most ladies,' said Benedick. 'Yet I love none of them.'

'I am glad to hear it,' she replied, 'for if you fell in love, your lady would be bothered with a very tiresome suitor. I had rather hear my dog bark at a crow than a man swear he loved me.'

'God keep your ladyship still in that mind!' said Benedick devoutly. 'It will save at least one man from having his face scratched.'

'Scratching could not make it worse, if it were such a face as yours,' cried Beatrice. And so they went on, each determined to have the last word in the encounter.

Young Claudio, however, was of a very different temper from Benedick. While his friend was sparring with Beatrice, Claudio had no eyes nor thoughts for anyone but Hero.

As soon as he was alone with Benedick he burst out:

'Did you see Leonato's daughter?'

'I suppose I did,' said Benedick, 'but I paid no attention to her.'

'Is she not a lovely young lady?' cried Claudio.

'Well, she's too short for a high praise,' answered Benedick, 'and too dark for a fair praise, and too little for a great praise. She's handsome enough, but not at all to my fancy. Now her cousin Beatrice is much more worth looking at, and sighing after too—if only she had not such a sharp tongue!'

Benedick seemed ready to make a joke of everything; but Claudio was in earnest. Before long he sought Don Pedro's aid in his suit, with such good success that Hero, who had also fallen in love with him at their first meeting, became engaged to him.

This did not please Don Pedro's half-brother Don John, who had a spite against the world and hated to see other people happy. He had previously rebelled against his brother and, although they had made up the quarrel, he had lost his position of favor.

'Here's Claudio already being put above me, and engaged to the daughter of the Duke of Messina,' he grumbled to his two followers, Conrade and Borachio, who were always ready to agree with him, flatter him, and carry out his schemes. 'My brother has never forgiven me for rebelling. Rather than try to wheedle my way back into his favor, I'll see what I can do to upset this marriage.'

Other schemes were also afoot in the gay court of Messina: but they were of a kindlier nature than those of John the Bastard.

'Your niece Beatrice is a pleasant, spirited young woman,' said Don Pedro to his host, the Duke of Messina.

'She is certainly merry,' answered Leonato. 'Indeed I hardly think she's ever serious, except perhaps when she's asleep. She says that a star danced when she was born!'

'But she seems to hate the idea of a husband!' said Don Pedro.

'Indeed she does,' answered Leonato. 'She mocks all her wooers so heartlessly that they very soon give up.'

'She'd make an excellent wife for Benedick,' mused Don Pedro.

'Benedick!' exclaimed Leonato. 'Good heavens! If they were married a week they would have talked enough to drive each other mad!'

'Nevertheless, with your help, and with that of Claudio and Hero, I'll accomplish it—though it's a labor that might have been too much even for Hercules!' cried Don Pedro.

'My lord, I'm ready to help in any way I can,' said Claudio.

'And I also,' murmured Hero. 'For I can wish my dear cousin nothing better than a good husband.'

Leonato and his three helpers put their plans into operation that very afternoon. Benedick was sitting in the orchard reading a book of poems. He was well hidden behind a tree, and thought that he was unobserved. Don Pedro, Leonato and Claudio had seen him, however, but pretended they had not as walked up and down on the path beyond the tree, talking to one another.

'Do you really mean to say, Leonato,' remarked Don Pedro, 'that your niece Beatrice is in love with Benedick?'

'I never thought that she would love anybody!' exclaimed Claudio.

'Nor I either,' agreed Leonato, 'but it's true none the less that she absolutely dotes on Benedick, in spite of the way she has always seemed to flout and scorn him.'

Benedick was listening now, his mouth open with surprise, and Leonato went on:

'It is most extraordinary: it seems that she is truly and deeply in love with him.'

'Has she told Benedick of this, or let him know in any way?' asked Don Pedro.

'No,' answered Leonato, 'and she swears she never will.'

'This is certainly true,' said Claudio. 'Your daughter Hero has told me. For Beatrice says that he would only make fun of her if he knew.'

'It's all very sad,' sighed Leonato, 'and my daughter is afraid that Beatrice may do herself some injury in her despair. She is in a terrible state, though she hides it well; and I am most anxious about her.'

'Surely we ought to tell Benedick,' suggested Don Pedro.

'Hero thinks that it will be the end of Beatrice,' said Claudio. 'For she says she will die if Benedick does not love her, and she would die rather than tell him; and if he finds out and woos her she would die rather than show her love or abate one scrap of her usual crossness to him.'

'I suppose she's right,' said Don Pedro, 'for Benedick would only laugh at her and scorn her. He's a good soldier and has a pretty wit, but I cannot see him as a lover! I feel so sorry for your niece, Leonato, that I think we should tell Benedick privately how she feels.'

'Never, my lord,' said Claudio. 'It would do no good. Poor Beatrice must learn to forget her love.'

'That's impossible,' said Leonato. 'She would wear her heart out sooner.'

'Well, we must see what Hero says,' concluded Don Pedro as they began to move away. 'I love Benedick well; I wish he could come to realize how ill he is behaving to Beatrice; she is so good and sweet a lady.'

When they had gone into the house, Benedick, who had

overheard the whole conversation, began pacing anxiously up and down, pondering on their words.

'This can be no trick,' he told himself. 'They were in earnest. They have learnt the truth from Hero. Beatrice loves me. . . . Why, I must requite her love. . . . She is a fair lady, and a clever one. I said I would die a bachelor—but I meant that I did not expect to live until I was married!'

So Benedick thought, pacing up and down in the orchard, and had more than half persuaded himself that he had been in love with Beatrice all the time—when suddenly he saw her coming from the house.

'Ah,' he thought, 'she is fair indeed! Yes, I already see signs of love in her!'

Whatever Benedick thought he saw in Beatrice was not due to any conscious change in her attitude.

Up she came, much as usual, dropped him a mocking curtsey and said off-handedly:

'Against my will, I am sent to fetch you in to dinner.'

'Fair Beatrice, I thank you for your trouble,' answered Benedick awkwardly.

'I took no more trouble for those thanks than it gives you trouble to thank me,' said Beatrice. 'If it had been troublesome, I would not have come.'

'You take pleasure, then, in bringing the message?' hesitated Benedick.

'Indeed I did—so small a crumb that it is invisible!' said Beatrice sarcastically. 'But I see you are not hungry, so farewell!'

Off she ran, back to the house, and Benedick followed slowly after her, saying to himself:

'There's a double meaning in all her words: "no more trouble for those thanks than it gives you trouble to thank me"— that means that any trouble she takes for me is as easy as thanks. . . . It's quite obvious that she loves me, and if I do not take pity on her and love her in return, I am a villain!'

Later that same day Hero saw to it that Beatrice received a dose of the same medicine that had already wrought such a marvellous change in Benedick.

'Margaret,' she said to her waiting woman, 'go to Beatrice who is in the parlor, and tell her that Ursula and I are sitting in the orchard talking about her, and that she'll be able to overhear everything we say if she steals up behind the tree. Her curiosity will surely drive her to come. Give us time to get to our place, and then see what you can do.'

So Hero and her other waiting women settled themselves in the orchard where Benedick had sat reading earlier in the day;

and presently, sure enough, they saw Beatrice flitting along behind the tree like a bird.

'No, truly, Ursula, she is too disdainful,' Hero was saying when Beatrice came into earshot, 'and she's as wild and un-restrained as a bird.'

'But are you sure that Benedick loves Beatrice so deeply?' asked Ursula.

'Both Don Pedro and Claudio say he does,' answered Hero.

'And they asked you to tell her?'

'They did,' replied Hero, 'but I said it would be much better for them to tell Benedick that his suit was hopeless and he must try to forget her. For he deserves a kinder fate than to pine for

Beatrice who is so proud and scornful that she will only break his heart, and then laugh in triumph at him.'

Then Hero and Ursula went on to discuss Beatrice in far from complimentary terms, before turning back to Benedick whom they decided was one of the handsomest and finest young men in Italy. They went off, regretting that so fine a man should pine for a lady who was too proud to recognize true love when she saw it.

Beatrice, who had overheard all this, was dazed, both at hearing what other people thought of her proud and scornful ways, and at knowing of Benedick's love for her. For already love was leaping up in her heart; and presently she went slowly after her cousin and Ursula, determined both to mend her ways and to requite Benedick's affection.

The change in both Beatrice and Benedick was immediate; it was noted with great amusement by the plotters. Benedick had his beard shaved off, took to wearing finer and finer clothes, and went about sighing and dejected as a lover should. Beatrice grew melancholy and had hardly a word of jest to throw at anyone; she complained of being ill, and began really to pine for Benedick.

Don Pedro, Leonato, Hero and Claudio viewed this change with great pleasure and satisfaction; but before they could drive their jest further, tragedy came suddenly to the happy court of Messina: Don John brought a strange and disquieting story to Don Pedro and Claudio.

'It grieves me very much,' said he, 'but I have it on the best authority: Hero, Leonato's daughter, is false to Claudio. And I can prove it. She has another lover—who visits her secretly. This very night, the eve of her wedding to Claudio, you shall come with me and see the villain bidding her farewell and climbing down from her bedroom window.'

'If this be true,' said Claudio wildly, 'I'll shame her in public; I'll do it tomorrow in the church, on the very steps of the altar when we meet there to be married.'

The day of Hero's wedding dawned without Leonato having any suspicion of what was about to happen; yet he had a warning which went unrecognized.

Just before it was time to lead his daughter to church, Dogberry the head constable of Messina came to see him on urgent business accompanied by his assistant constable, Verges. Neither of these worthies was particularly bright, and Dogberry himself was fat, foolish and immensely self-important, with a bad habit of using long words in the wrong places, and a worse one of telling any story in such a way that no one could make head nor tail of it.

'Sir,' said Dogberry when he was brought before Leonato, 'I have come to hold a confidence with you about something that discerns you particularly.'

'You wish to confer about something that concerns me?' interpreted Leonato smiling. 'Well be quick, good Dogberry, for you see what haste I am in.'

'Then sir, this is it!' began Dogberry.

'Now you shall hear the truth, sir!' piped old Verges.

'Never listen to him, sir!' exclaimed Dogberry. 'He is an old man, and his wits are not so blunt as those of us younger men. Yet he is an honest man.'

'Yes, thank God,' added Verges, 'I am as honest a man as any living old man that is no honester than I!'

'Comparisons are odorous,' declared Dogberry grandly, 'so enough, good neighbour Verges!'

'Friends, you are tedious!' exclaimed Leonato, anxious to get rid of them quickly.

'Tedious!' exclaimed Dogberry, thinking this was a compliment. 'I thank your worship for saying so. Truly, if I were as tedious as a king, I would give it all to your worship!'

'All your tediousness to me?' sighed Leonato. 'But tell me what you have to say.'

'Well sir, our watch last night arrested two villains, as wicked as any in Messina——' began Verges.

But Dogberry interrupted again, wasting more time, and ending up: 'We have indeed comprehended two auspicious persons, and wish to bring them before your worship to be questioned.'

'I have no time left!' exclaimed Leonato. 'But question these two suspicious characters you have apprehended, and bring the report to me.'

So off went Dogberry and Verges, full of importance, and Leonato set out for the church with Hero and her cousin Beatrice.

There Claudio was waiting, accompanied by Don John, Don Pedro and Benedick; and the priest Friar Francis, began the ceremony at once by asking if either Claudio or Hero knew of any cause why they should not be joined together in holy matrimony.

'Do you know of any cause, Hero?' asked Claudio.

'None, my lord,' answered Hero.

'But I do!' cried Claudio. And he accused Hero in bitter, biting terms of being false, impure, unchaste and a liar.

'What does this mean?' gasped Leonato, turning to Don Pedro.

'All that he says is true, though I grieve to tell you,' was the answer.

'True? Oh God!' sobbed Hero.

'Leonato, bid her answer truly,' said Claudio. 'Hero, what man was it you talked with at your window last night between twelve and one? If you are true, answer this truly.'

'I talked with no man at that hour, my lord!' cried Hero indignantly.

'Then indeed what Claudio says is true,' said Don Pedro sadly. 'Leonato, last night Claudio and my brother and I saw your daughter at her bedroom window talking with a ruffian who has confessed that he has long been her lover.'

'I could tell you all that he told me,' added Don John soberly. 'But it is too shameful. Enough has been said.'

'Oh Hero, if only you had proved as pure of heart as you are lovely to look at!' cried Claudio. 'But farewell, pure impiety—impious purity. Never again can I trust a woman, nor judge her by her face.'

All this was too much for Hero, who sank to the ground in a dead faint.

'Let us go,' said Don John. 'She is overcome at the sudden exposure of her wickedness.'

So saying, he strode out of the church, followed by Claudio and Don Pedro.

But Beatrice bent over her cousin, assisted by Friar Francis, while Leonato and Benedick stood by, hardly knowing what to do.

'You may call me a fool,' said Friar Francis, 'but I am sure Hero is innocent and that some strange mistake has been made.'

'I cannot believe that either Claudio or Don Pedro would act but in good faith,' said Benedick. 'If they have been deceived in this, the fault must lie with Don John, who is capable of any villainy.'

When she recovered consciousness, Hero continued to insist that she was innocent.

'Now my advice is for a small deception,' said Friar Francis. 'Give out that Hero died of a broken heart, the result of this false accusation. Keep her well hidden. The true explanation will surely come to light—and may do so more quickly at the shock of her supposed death.'

'Do as the Friar suggests, Signior Leonato,' urged Benedick. 'Though Claudio and Don Pedro are my close friends, I will keep your secret—and do all I can to unravel this mystery.'

So Leonato and Friar Francis led Hero away, but Benedick turned to Beatrice who was now alone with him in the church, and said:

'Lady Beatrice, have you been weeping all this while?'

'Yes,' she sobbed, 'and will continue to do so.'

'I am sure your cousin is wrongly accused,' he said.

'Ah, what I would not give to the man who would vindicate her,' she cried.

'Is there any way it can be done?' he asked.

'Yes, there is,' she said, 'but no one to do it.'

'May a man do it?' he asked.

'It must be done by a man,' she answered, 'but not by you.'

'Yet I love nothing in the world so much as you,' said Benedick. 'Is that not strange?'

'No stranger than that I love you in just such measure,' she said.

'Then command me to do anything for you,' cried Benedick.

'Kill Claudio!' cried Beatrice, her eyes flashing.

'Not for all the world!' said Benedick.

'Then you do not love me,' she replied. 'Farewell.'

'Sweet Beatrice,' begged Benedick. 'Do you believe truly and in your very soul that Claudio has wronged Hero?'

'Yes, as surely as I have a belief or a soul,' she answered.

'Then I will challenge him,' said Benedick. 'Let me kiss your hand, and I will set out in search of him. And you go to comfort your cousin.'

Benedick found Claudio later that day, in company with Don Pedro, waiting in the hall of Leonato's house. He called Claudio a villain, and arranged to meet him and fight early the following morning. Then he strode off to tell Beatrice that he had taken the first step towards obeying her command.

Had he waited a few moments longer he would have had far better news to tell her, for scarcely had he gone when Dogberry arrived to see Leonato, bringing with him Don John's two men Conrade and Borachio, securely bound and led by several watchmen.

'What does this mean?' cried Don Pedro. 'Two of my brother's men prisoners of the watch! Officers, what have these men done?'

'So please you, sir,' said Dogberry, rather flustered to be questioned by the Prince himself, 'they have committed a false report; moreover, they have spoken untruths; secondarily, they are slanders; sixth and lastly, they have told lies about a lady; thirdly they have proved false facts, and finally, they are lying knaves.'

'First, I ask you what they have done,' said Don Pedro gravely, imitating Dogberry's high-flown style. 'Thirdly, I ask you what their offence is; sixth and lastly, why have you arrested them; and finally what crime do you charge them with.'

Dogberry was so dumbfounded that he did not know what to say. But Borachio flung himself on his knees before Don Pedro and confessed his crime:

'Good prince,' he cried, 'I have deceived you all; and what you in your wisdom could not discover, these fools of constables have brought to light. Last night, when I was drunk, they heard me confessing to Conrade that Don John bribed and persuaded me to slander the Lady Hero; and that he brought you secretly to the orchard where you saw me at the window with Margaret, disguised in Hero's garments. She thought it only a jest, but I knew of the trap. And now by my fault Hero is dead, and my master has fled from Messina. . . .'

'Oh, he is composed and framed of all that is evil!' cried Don Pedro, while Claudio buried his face in his hands and sobbed.

'Come now, men, drag the plaintiffs off to prison!' cried Dogberry. 'By this time neighbour Verges has reformed Signior Leonato of the matter.'

When Leonato appeared, Claudio flung himself at his feet and begged forgiveness.

'Give me any penance,' he cried. 'Decree any punishment. Even though I sinned in innocence, I will endure it.'

'I cannot bid you bring my daughter back to life,' said Leonato. 'But you can proclaim her innocent this very night to all Messina. Then tomorrow come to me here and I will give you in marriage a niece of mine whom you have never seen, the living image of my dead Hero. Will you do this?'

'Noble sir,' cried Claudio, 'your kindness draws more tears from my eyes. I will do all that you command.'

'Moreover!' interrupted Dogberry, who felt that he was being neglected, 'let me inform you sirs, though it is not down in white and black, that this villain the plaintiff here, the defender, did call me an ass. When you come to punish him, sir, do not forget that I am an ass!'

Now there was no need for Benedick to fight Claudio, so next morning both Benedick and Beatrice went to meet Claudio and Don Pedro at Leonato's house to see the end of the matter.

There Leonato brought to them a veiled woman and set her hand in Claudio's, saying:

'Take her before good Friar Francis, and swear to marry her.'

'Give me your hand before this holy man,' said Claudio. 'I am your husband, if you will have me.'

'And when I lived I was your other wife,' said Hero, flinging back her veil, 'and when you loved, you were my other husband.'

'Another Hero!' gasped Claudio.

'One Hero died, defiled by your words,' she answered, 'but now I live, true and pure.'

'Hero herself!' gasped Don Pedro. 'Hero that is dead!'

'She died only while her false accusation lived,' said Leonato; and Friar Francis told how and why he had suggested the deception.

Now that Hero and Claudio were about to be married, Benedick thought the time had come for him and Beatrice to be married also.

'Come Beatrice,' he said, 'let us to church. You love me, do you not?'

'Why no,' she answered, 'not more than is reasonable.'

'Then your uncle, and the prince, and Claudio were all deceived,' he exclaimed, 'for they swore you loved me.'

'Do you love me?' she asked.

'Why no, not more than is reasonable,' answered Benedick.

'Then my cousin, and Margaret, and Ursula were all deceived,' said Beatrice, 'for they swore that you loved me.'

'They swore that you were ill because of me,' said Benedick.

'They swore that you were nearly dead because of me,' said Beatrice.

'Come, I will have you,' said Benedick. 'But I swear I only take you out of pity!'

'I will marry you,' mimicked Beatrice. 'But I swear I yield only on great persuasion—and partly to save your life, for I was told you were dying of a consumption, having gone into a decline for love of me.'

'Peace, I will stop your mouth!' laughed Benedick, kissing her.

'How do you feel, Benedick, the married man?' teased Don Pedro.

'Ah, you poor fellow,' sighed Benedick. 'Truly I pity you, and any man who has not got a wife. Get one quickly, prince—for there is nothing like it!'

And so, laughing merrily, they all set off to church where Friar Francis celebrated their double wedding.

THE MERRY WIVES OF WINDSOR

EARLY IN THE reign of King Henry V there lived at Windsor two wealthy, middle-aged gentlemen named Ford and Page, both happily married, though only the Pages had children—a little son called William, and a grown up daughter, Anne.

As Anne was a pretty young thing, and likely to be an heiress, she had several suitors. There was a well-to-do Frenchman, Doctor Caius, whom Mistress Page thought would be the best husband for her daughter; and there was a foolish young country gentleman called Slender with plenty of money, and he was the suitor chosen by Anne's father. Anne herself, however, cared for neither of these two: her own choice was for a young gentleman called Fenton who had been favored by her parents before either of the more wealthy wooers appeared on the scene; but he had been sent about his business when the rich men appeared—he had far less money than either of them.

Slender was put forward as a suitor by his cousin Justice Shallow. He arrived at Windsor determined to have the law on a certain Sir John Falstaff, recently come to stay at the Garter Inn with three disreputable followers, Pistol, Bardolph and Nym. Falstaff had been a close companion of King Henry when Prince of Wales; for Henry had been a wild youth who liked to escape from the court and drink and join in mad escapades with the fat old knight and his friends. But when he came to the throne, Henry reformed his ways completely, cut himself off

from his old life and his low acquaintances, and banished Falstaff
from the court. In consequence, Falstaff and his followers found
themselves practically penniless. They had lived for so long with
the aid of the Prince; now they had only their wits to depend on,
and these soon got them into trouble.

As soon as Justice Shallow arrived in Windsor, he went straight
to Master Page's house, accompanied by his cousin Slender, and
before long Falstaff and his followers arrived there to answer his
accusations.

'I will take this case to London!' cried Shallow. 'Yes, it shall
come up before the Court of Star Chamber! Sir John Falstaff,
you have stolen my deer and beaten my keepers when they tried
to do their duty and drive you out of my park!'

'And what if I have helped myself to some venison?' said fat
Sir John, beaming superciliously at the angry old man. 'There's
no harm done! And if you take such a case to London, you'll
only make a laughingstock of yourself.'

'Moreover,' went on Shallow severely, 'you or your followers
are pickpockets, and have robbed my good young cousin
Slender.'

'Robbed!' cried Sir Hugh Evans, the Welsh parson, who was
acting as clerk at this unofficial trial. 'I must make a note of that!'

'Pistol!' cried Falstaff.

'He hears with ears!' answered that worthy, striking an
attitude, and glaring round at everybody; for he was a great
bully, and pretended to be wild and fierce, though really he was a
coward.

'Did you pick Master Slender's purse?' asked Falstaff.

'Froth and scum, thou liest!' roared Pistol, whipping out his
sword and waving it at Slender.

'Then—then it was this man!' hesitated Slender, who was at
least as great a coward as Pistol, turning to Nym.

'Be careful, sir,' growled Nym. 'Don't try to trap me; you
might get caught yourself—that's my line!'

'I swear it was one of you!' cried Slender. 'One of you took
my money when you had made me drunk! It must have been this
red-faced fellow!'

'Well, Bardolph?' asked Falstaff.

'Why sir, the gentleman had drunk himself out of his five sentences——' began red-nosed Bardolph stolidly.

'Sentences?' cried Sir Hugh, 'Senses, you mean! Fie, what ignorance!'

'And being tipsy, lost all his money,' concluded Bardolph, paying no attention to the interruption. 'What else can he expect, if he gets dead drunk?'

'I-I'll never get drunk again so long as I live!' cried Slender. 'And when I do, it shall be with honest men, and not with drunken villains.'

At this moment Mistress Page came out of the house to the porch where they were, carrying wine, and with her came Anne Page and Mistress Page's closest friend, Mistress Ford. Very wisely, Justice Shallow dropped the whole matter of the poached venison and Slender's empty purse, and made haste to press his cousin's suit instead.

Master Page was a merry, friendly man so, to heal any quarrel that might still remain, he invited the whole party in to dinner. This gave Anne Page full opportunity to sum up her new suitor, Slender, as a brainless young fool with whom she would have nothing to do. But it also gave Falstaff the chance of meeting and flirting with both Mistress Page and Mistress Ford; and this gave the conceited old knight an idea for a new way of making some of the money he needed so badly. It was both shameful and dishonest, but he was far past caring about such things; and when he got back to the Garter Inn he at once laid his scheme before his three followers.

'I have no money,' he said, 'and I can no longer keep you. I have arranged for Bardolph to work as a waiter here at the inn. But you, Pistol and Nym, must help me in my scheme, or starve. You know a certain Ford, of this town?'

'Yea, I know the fellow, he is finely rich!' cried Pistol, in his usual swaggering way.

'Then, my honest lads, I'll tell you what I'm about.'

'Two yards about, at least!' cried Pistol.

'This is no joking matter,' said Falstaff severely. 'I may be two yards round the waist—but there will be no waste in my plan. I shall make love to Ford's wife. She must be tired of her cross old husband, and ready to smile on someone of my importance. . . . Moreover, I've found out that Ford is very rich, and his wife has as much money as she wants. So I've written her a letter; and one to Page's wife as well, just to have two strings to my bow; after all, she flirted with me as readily as Mistress Ford—and she too has plenty to spend. You two must take the letters.'

'Shall I, who wear steel at my side, descend to such base employment?' cried Pistol, who saw no chance of getting anything out of this scheme except a beating or a broken head from one of the angry husbands. 'The devil take me if I stoop to such a thing!'

'I'll touch no such letter,' agreed Nym, 'it's not at all in my line.'

'Then pack off, you rogues!' shouted Falstaff. 'Fend for yourselves! I'm only doing what everyone does nowadays. My page Robin shall deliver the letters—and make his fortune instead of you!'

Off stamped Falstaff. Pistol swore after him loudly: 'Base Turk!' he cried finally. 'You'll be starving when my pocket's full of money!'

'I'll be revenged, that's my line,' growled Nym. 'I'll go straight to Page and tell him.'

'I'm with you!' agreed Pistol. 'Let us away! I'm off to tell Ford what this vile varlet Falstaff has in mind!'

Meanwhile other plots were brewing over the winning of sweet Anne Page. Although Doctor Caius was one of her wooers, his housekeeper Mistress Quickly was quite ready to help his rival Slender, whose man, Peter Simple, had come to beg her aid and bring her a good big bribe from his master.

Unfortunately for them both, fiery little Doctor Caius surprised them, and in her flurry Mistress Quickly said that it was Sir Hugh, the Welsh Parson, who had sent Simple to plead for his friend.

The angry Frenchman immediately sat down and scribbled a note.

'There!' he cried, handing it to Simple. 'Give-a dis letter to Sir Hugh; by gar, it is a shallenge to fight-a se duel! I vill cut his troat in de Park! I vil teach dis scurvy priest to meddle vit me!'

Off went Simple one way, and Doctor Caius another—and just in time, for Fenton, the suitor whom Anne really loved, arrived with an even bigger bribe for Mistress Quickly—who took it without any hesitation, and promised to help him in his suit, just as she had promised both Slender and Doctor Caius.

Pistol and Nym went straight to Ford and Page, and told them what Falstaff was up to. Page laughed heartily, and treated it all as a huge joke; but Ford was a jealous, suspicious man, and set out at once to spy on Falstaff. This he did by bribing the innkeeper of the Garter to introduce him to Sir John as a stranger called Brook.

Falstaff had scarcely seen Ford, and suspected nothing when Mr. Brook bought him a drink and offered him money if he would help him to woo Mistress Ford.

'You have come to the right man, Master Brook!' said Falstaff, draining his mug of sack, the light Spanish wine that was his favorite drink, and clattering it down on the table as a gentle hint that he wanted more. 'Why, just before you came I had a message from Mistress Ford in answer to a letter of mine. She invited me to go to her house between ten and eleven this morning, when her jealous, rascally knave of a husband will be out. I'll get my hands into his moneybags, depend upon it— and you shall have his wife as your mistress!'

Off went Falstaff to his assignation, and Ford, full of rage and jealousy, set out to find some friends to help him outwit the fat knight. He met a whole crowd coming back into Windsor from that part of the Great Park down by the river Thames. For there it was that Doctor Caius had bidden Sir Hugh the parson to meet him and fight a duel for the sake of sweet Anne Page. The kindly host of the Garter Inn had, however, learnt of what was going on, and with the aid of Shallow, Slender and Page had prevented the combatants from meeting until they had been dissuaded from any idea of fighting—much to the relief of Parson Hugh, who was as great a coward as Slender himself. They were all delighted when Ford met them and invited them to dinner with him. Shallow and Slender excused themselves, Slender being determined to go off and woo Anne Page; but the rest of them set out towards Ford's house, having been promised not only a dinner, but the sight of 'a monster' as well.

When Mistress Ford and Mistress Page had received their letters from Falstaff, each was filled with fury and disgust at the wicked old knight's impudence, and both were determined to be revenged on him and to ask the other's help; and when they discovered that they had received identical letters, they decided to work together to punish the fat knight and put him to open shame.

So Mistress Ford sent a message asking him to visit her, and she and Mistress Page arranged a plot; it centered on a large hamper of dirty clothes that was set ready in the room, and two strong serving men were given certain instructions.

When Falstaff arrived by the back door, Mistress Page slipped out by the front, and waited there to come and interrupt the meeting with a false warning that Master Ford was coming. No falsehood was needed, however, for within a few minutes she saw Ford himself hastening towards the house with Master Page, Sir Hugh Evans and Dr. Caius.

Falstaff had scarcely time to sink (with some difficulty) to his knees and begin his wooing, when there was a knock at the door and they heard Mistress Page calling to be let in.

'She must not see me!' exclaimed Falstaff, struggling to his feet. 'I will hide here, behind the curtain!'

'Yes, do!' said Mistress Ford. 'She's a terrible gossip, and no one must know, dear Sir John, that you were visiting me.'

No sooner was he hidden than Mistress Page burst into the room, crying:

'Oh, Mistress Ford, what have you done? Your husband's coming up the street with all the constables and officers in Windsor, to search for a gentleman he says is in the house with you. If he's here now, get him out quickly, for your husband will certainly harm him if he catches him.'

'Alas!' cried Mistress Ford, 'there *is* such a gentleman—an old family friend. But my husband is so jealous! What shall we do?'

'You cannot hide him here!' exclaimed Mistress Page, 'and the back door is already guarded. . . . Ah, I know! Look, here is a hamper of dirty clothes; if your friend is not too big a man, he could hide in it and we could cover him with the washing.'

'Alas, he is too big to fit in there!' cried Mistress Ford. 'Oh, what shall I do?'

This was more than Falstaff could bear, and he came rushing out from behind the curtain, shouting:

'Let me see it! Let me try to get into it! I'll get in somehow! Do what your friend suggests, only save me!'

With great difficulty the two women managed to force Falstaff into the hamper and to hide him under a tight packing of the filthiest old sheets they could find. They found it even more difficult to prevent themselves from screaming with laughter at his terror; but they managed to keep straight faces until the two serving-men had slung the hamper on a pole which they raised with some difficulty to their shoulders.

Just as the men were staggering to the door, it burst open and in rushed Ford, waving a stick, and shouting to his friends to search the house.

'What's this?' he cried, seeing the hamper.

'Dirty linen,' answered Mistress Ford. 'They are carrying it to the laundress at Datchet.'

'Then away with it!' shouted Ford, and as soon as it was out of the house, he locked the door, and began his search.

But there was no one there; and Mistress Ford began to weep, and pretend to be terribly upset by her husband's suspicions.

'I cannot find him!' panted Ford at last. 'Perhaps the villain boasted of more than he could accomplish!'

Mistress Ford pricked up her ears at this; and when Ford had apologised to her and begged forgiveness and taken his friends off for a drink, she said to Mistress Page:

'My husband is always jealous; but this time I think he had some

special reason for thinking that Falstaff was here. Someone is telling tales—Mistress Quickly, perhaps. . . . Anyhow, I'll send the fat knight a very humble, loving message by her, arranging another meeting. He's sure to rise to the bait. Then we'll see whether my husband arrives again to take him.'

So, when Mistress Quickly called on Mistress Page again, bringing love-messages for Anne from Dr. Caius (but also, in secret, from Fenton), she was given a fresh message to Falstaff, and set off willingly for the Garter Inn.

Here she found the fat knight with his feet in a mustard bath, drinking hot sack, and sneezing like a volcano, while Bardolph tended him as best he could.

'To think!' sneezed Falstaff, 'that I, at my age, should be tipped into the Thames like a barrow of rubbish! And I sink easily, as you might guess from my size!'

'I come from Mistress Ford,' began Mistress Quickly.

'Ford!' choked Falstaff. 'I have had ford enough! I was thrown into the ford! My belly is full of ford!'

'Alas, poor woman!' cried Mistress Quickly. 'You should see how she weeps! And how she curses the men for misunderstanding their orders. She yearns to see you again, and to tell you how sorry she is for your misfortune. . . . Her husband is going shooting this morning between eight and nine, and I must hurry and tell her if you are coming. She'll more than make up to you for what happened yesterday, that I promise!'

'Well, I will come!' said Falstaff. 'Between eight and nine— that's very shortly. Good, bid her expect me!'

Off went Mistress Quickly on her errand; and before Falstaff was ready to set out, Ford arrived, disguised as Master Brook, to ask how he had fared the day before.

'Certainly I was at her house at the hour we agreed on,' boasted Falstaff, 'and I was doing very well indeed—your suit was half won—when we had word that her jealous rascal of a husband was coming with a whole gang of ruffians to search the house for her lover.'

'While you were there?' asked Ford.

'While I was there!' beamed Falstaff.

'And they could not find you?' exclaimed Ford looking incredulously at Falstaff's enormous size.

'By good luck, there was a hamper of dirty linen standing in the room,' said Sir John. 'In this I hid, among stinking shirts and smocks and stockings and greasy napkins, and was carried out under Master Ford's nose. But mark what I suffered on your account, Master Brook! Not only was I bent double and nearly suffocated in dirty clothes—nearly melted in grease—but I was tipped into the Thames when glowing hot, to be cooled like a horseshoe!'

Falstaff paused to sneeze loudly, and Ford said:

'I am sorry, sir, that you have suffered this for my sake. I presume that my suit is now desperate, and you will not risk pressing it again?'

'Master Brook,' answered Falstaff grandly, 'I will be thrown into Etna before I give up what I have promised to perform. Her husband has gone out shooting this morning, and she has already arranged another meeting—between eight and nine.'

'It's past eight already!' exclaimed Ford.

'Then I must hurry. Meet me here later, Master Brook, to hear of the success of my venture!'

Off bustled Falstaff, and as soon as he was gone, Ford, even madder with rage and jealousy than before, tore off his disguise and went to collect his friends to go again and surprise the fat knight at his wife's house.

There Falstaff had not been many minutes with Mistress Ford before Mistress Page arrived to warn them that Ford was coming. As before, Falstaff hid when Mistress Page came, and the two merry wives were left to devise a scheme for his escape.

'Oh, Mistress Ford!' cried Mistress Page. 'Your husband is even madder than he was yesterday! He has the same party of friends with him, and he is going to search the house—he is in the street already. I am glad Sir John Falstaff is not with you this time!'

'Why?' cried Mistress Ford, making sure that Falstaff should hear every word in his place of hiding behind the curtain. 'Does my husband suspect him?'

'He talks of nothing but the fat knight,' answered Mistress

Page. 'He swears they carried him out in a hamper; and he declares that Falstaff is here now; a great rabble have come to take him and punish him. I'm so glad you are alone—for now your husband will truly discover how foolish he is to be so jealous.'

'Woe is me, Sir John *is* here!' cried Mistress Ford. 'What shall I do?'

'Then you will be put to shame, and he will be murdered!' exclaimed Mistress Page. 'Better shame than murder—you *must* get him out of the house.'

'How can I?' asked Mistress Ford. 'Unless we put him in the hamper again!'

'No! No!' cried Falstaff rushing out from behind the curtain. 'I'll not go in the hamper again! Can't I get out by the door before anyone comes?'

'Impossible,' exclaimed Mistress Page. 'They are waiting outside with pistols!'

'What shall I do?' gasped Falstaff. 'I'll hide in the chimney!'

'No good,' said Mistress Ford. 'My husband always discharges his gun up it when he comes in from shooting. And it's no good hiding in the baking oven, or the wine-cellar, or down the well, or under the bed, or in any cupboard or chest; my husband will look in all of them. No, there's nowhere to hide you in the house.'

'Then I'll go out,' said Falstaff.

'If you go out, you will be shot,' said Mistress Page. 'Unless you go in disguise. . . .'

'I have it!' cried Mistress Ford. 'My maid's aunt is the fat woman of Brentford. She has one of her dresses upstairs—it will fit Sir John, she's as big as he is. And we'll find a hat with a wide brim, and a muffler and wimple to hide his face. Run up, Sir John! We'll come and dress you in a moment.'

'I hope my husband will meet him in this disguise,' said Mistress Ford as soon as Falstaff was out of the room. 'He cannot bear old Mother Pratt of Brentford, but swears that she is a witch, and has threatened to beat her if ever she comes into this house again.'

'Well, Heaven guide your husband's stick to Falstaff's shoulders!' exclaimed Mistress Page fervently. 'For he deserves a beating if anyone does!'

'But is my husband really coming?' asked Mistress Ford.

'Indeed he is,' answered Mistress Page, 'waving his stick and talking about the villain who was carried out in the basket yesterday; he has learnt about Falstaff somehow.'

'The hamper! Well remembered! I'll instruct the servants, and then join you upstairs!' said Mistress Ford, hastening towards the kitchen, while Mistress Page set off to help Falstaff put on his disguise.

'Take up the hamper again,' she instructed the two serving men, 'and carry it out. Your master is at the door; if he tells you to put it down, obey him at once.'

'I hope the hamper isn't full of knights again!' grumbled one of them.

'I hope not, indeed,' agreed the other. 'If it had been full of lead, it could not have been heavier!'

Scarcely had they taken up the hamper and slung it on the pole between them, when in rushed Master Ford, followed by Page, Shallow, Dr. Caius and Sir Hugh Evans. He was shouting wildly, while his friends tried to calm him; and the moment he saw the hamper, he burst out again:

'Set it down, you villains! Now shall the devil be shamed. Call my wife, somebody! She shall see what honest clothes she sends to the laundry!'

'Whatever is wrong, Master Ford?' exclaimed Mistress Page rushing in. 'Save us! The man's mad!'

'He is lunatic!' agreed Sir Hugh. 'Mad as a mad dog!'

'Come here, wife!' yelled Ford, paying no attention to them. And when Mistress Ford came trembling into the room, he continued. 'Now, you modest, virtuous woman, who has a jealous, foolish husband? I suspect without cause, do I? Wait till we turn the villain out of this hamper!'

With that, Ford began throwing the clothes about the room, shouting: 'There was a man carried out in this hamper yesterday, I tell you! Why may he not be there again? He's in my house I know.'

'Master Ford, you must pray for guidance, and not follow the wicked, jealous imaginings of your heart,' said Sir Hugh gravely.

'I tell you, he's in the house!' repeated Ford. 'And I'll search it till I find him.'

'Mistress Page!' called Mistress Ford up the stairs. 'Come down, and bring the old woman with you—my husband is coming up to search all the rooms.'

'Old woman? What old woman?' asked Ford.

'Why, only old Mother Pratt, my maid's aunt,' answered his wife.

'She's a witch and a thief,' cried Ford. 'I forbade her to enter my house again. She uses charms and spells, and I will have none of such wizardry here. Come down you witch! Come down, I say!'

'Dear, kind husband, do not harm the old woman!' begged Mistress Ford.

But when Falstaff came in, all dressed up as the fat woman of Brentford, with a great skirt and his face muffled under a wide-brimmed hat, Ford went for him and gave him a good thrashing as he drove him out of the house. Then Ford locked the door and rushed upstairs, followed by his friends.

The moment they were alone, Mistress Page said: 'Well, Sir John has had the beating he so richly deserved. I'm sure he won't come near you again! We've proved to him he only gets into trouble if he tries his wicked tricks on Windsor wives.'

'Wives can be merry, and yet remain honest!' agreed Mistress Ford. 'But I think the time has come to tell my husband everything, and show him the two letters which Falstaff sent to us!'

When Ford saw the letters and heard how his wife and Mistress Page had set out to punish Falstaff, he was truly sorry for his behavior.

'Forgive me, my dearest Alice,' he said. 'Henceforth, do what you like—I'll never suspect you, or be jealous again.'

'But let us try one further plot,' suggested Page. 'Let our wives arrange one more meeting with this silly old fat man at which we can all hold him up to ridicule and scorn.'

'Let's send Mistress Quickly to him again,' said Mistress Page. 'She can bear him a message telling him to meet us in Windsor Park at midnight.'

'He'll never come,' said Page.

'He's been thrown in the river, and beaten,' agreed Sir Hugh. 'He'll not risk any further punishment.'

'You plan what to do to him when he comes,' said Mistress Ford. 'We'll think of a way of bringing him!'

'I know what we can do!' exclaimed Mistress Page. 'You know the legend about Herne the Hunter, who was once a keeper in Windsor Forest, and how he must walk forever round and round an old oak tree at midnight, with deer-horns on his head and a gallows chain hanging from his arm?'

'There are many who would be afraid, even now, to go near Herne's Oak at midnight,' agreed Page. 'But how can this ghost help us?'

'Why, we shall suggest to Falstaff that he should meet us at the Oak, dressed as Herne the Hunter,' she answered. 'It will seem an excellent scheme to him; in this disguise he will frighten away anybody who sees him, and so he'll be certain that this time no one will interrupt us.'

'Excellent,' said Page. 'And what then?'

'I've been thinking of that,' said Mistress Page. 'Our daughter Anne shall be hidden in the saw-pit which is near the Oak, dressed all in white as the Queen of the Fairies. And with her shall be a whole troop, headed by our little William, pretending to be fairies and goblins and elves. When Mistress Ford and I have been with Falstaff a few minutes, these must all rush out, waving tapers and singing some suitable song. Then we'll pretend to be frightened and run away. But the fairies shall pinch Falstaff, and burn him with their tapers, and ask him what he is doing beneath the tree where they meet to dance at midnight. He will think they are real fairies, and tell the truth. Then we can all present ourselves and mock him home to Windsor.'

'A good device,' said Sir Hugh. 'The children will need to be taught their parts and rehearsed carefully. I will undertake that.'

So everyone went off to get ready for the final exposure of Falstaff—but Page prepared a little plot of his own. He was tired of constant arguments with his wife as to who should marry their daughter Anne, so he decided to instruct Slender to steal her away when she had finished her duties as Fairy Queen, take her to Eton near by, and there marry her.

It happened, however, that Mistress Page thought of the very same idea, and went off to instruct Doctor Caius how *he* might steal Anne away that night and marry her in Windsor at the deanery.

'She shall be dressed in green,' she said, 'so that you may know her among the rest of the fairies, and slip off without saying a word.'

Now both Page and his wife issued their commands to Anne, but she decided that, as her father wanted her to run away with one man, and her mother was plotting to marry her to another, she was quite at liberty to choose for herself. So she too made plans; and presently Fenton was arranging with the host of the Garter Inn to have a priest waiting at Windsor Church, with himself and Bardolph for witnesses, between twelve and one that night.

Mistress Quickly found little difficulty in persuading Falstaff to make one more attempt.

'It's the third time,' he said, 'and there's luck in odd numbers. If you can find me the horns, I'll be Herne the Hunter!'

She had scarcely gone when Ford arrived in his disguise as Master Brook, and Falstaff told him the whole scheme, bidding him come to Herne's Oak shortly after midnight, and not to be frightened if he saw Herne the Hunter in person waiting under it.

'Did you visit Mistress Ford yesterday, as you said you were going to do?' asked Master Brook.

'Indeed I did,' replied Falstaff, 'and though I went in as a man, I came out as a woman! So as to cause no trouble, and deceive that jealous knave her husband, I disguised myself as the old witch of Brentford—yes, and let that wretch Master Ford beat me, too. Had I not been in disguise, I'd have beaten him instead—for I fear no one and nothing!'

Midnight was striking on the great bell in the Curfew Tower of Windsor Castle when Falstaff reached Herne's Oak. He was dressed in a huge, black, ragged cloak, and had a stag's horns on his head and a rusty chain dangling from his arm.

Scarcely was he there when Mistress Ford and Mistress Page came stealing out of the wood. Falstaff took one of them on each knee and had just begun a rather complicated attempt at making love to two ladies at once, when a weird, strange sound of music caused them both to spring to their feet in pretended terror.

'Oh, what is that?' shrieked Mistress Page.

'Heaven forgive our sins!' shrieked Mistress Ford.

Upon which they fled screaming, while out of the wood came troops of fairies and goblins, with lighted tapers, who began to circle round Herne's Oak.

'Fairies, black, grey, green and white!' chanted the Fairy Queen. 'You moonshine revelers and shades of night!'

'They are fairies!' gasped Falstaff, flinging himself on his face and hiding his eyes. 'Whoever speaks to them will die. I'll shut my eyes and lie still on the ground. Perhaps they will not harm me if I don't look at them.'

The fairies gathered closer round the tree, and their Queen gave them their commands:

'About! About!' she cried. 'Search Windsor Castle, elves, within, without!' And she went on to instruct them how they were to punish the lazy maids who had left the hearths unswept and the dishes unwashed by pinching them black and blue, and by giving them nightmares. But to those who had cleaned the house and said their prayers, they were to give sound, sweet sleep and happy dreams. 'But first of all,' she concluded, 'let us dance round Herne's Oak as is our custom, until the Curfew Bell strikes one.'

'But stay!' cried a fairy with a Welsh accent, who was dressed as a hobgoblin, 'I smell a man of middle-earth!'

'See where he lies!' cried another. 'Vile worm, cursed from birth by the evil eye!'

'First touch his fingerends with trial-fire,' directed the Fairy Queen. 'If he be pure of heart, the fire will turn away without hurting him. But if he feels the pain, it is a sure proof that he is a man with a heart full of evil and corruption.'

Falstaff felt the pain of the lighted tapers all right, and cried out for mercy, still hiding his eyes in the grass.

'Corrupt and tainted with evil desires!' cried the Queen. 'Pinch him, Fairies, pinch him black and blue—

> Pinch him, and burn him, and turn him about,
> Till candles and starlight and moonshine be out!'

So Falstaff got what he deserved, and lay rolling and roaring on the ground until, at a sudden sound of horns, the fairies fled away in all directions.

Falstaff sat up cautiously, to see the Fords and the Pages coming towards him arm in arm.

'No, do not try to run away,' said Ford. 'You are a Herne the Hunter who will hardly frighten *us*!'

'Now, Sir John,' said Mistress Page. 'What do you think of us two merry wives of Windsor?'

'Well, Sir John,' said Ford, 'how have you fared in the winning of my wife for Master Brook?'

'You could not be my love, Sir John,' said Mistress Ford. 'But if you wear those horns you shall always be my deer!'

'It seems to me that I have been proved an ass,' said Falstaff slowly. 'Nor do I even believe now that these were fairies. Once or twice I had my doubts. One of them had a Welsh accent, and another spoke uncommonly like that knave Pistol.'

'You have not yet offered to pay back to Mr. Brook all the money he gave you to win Mistress Ford for him!' said Ford severely.

'Forgive him the debt,' said Mistress Ford laughing. 'Then we can all be friends and think no more of what has passed.'

'Well, here's my hand!' cried Ford. 'Let all be forgiven.'

'Cheer up, Sir John!' exclaimed Page. 'Come back with us to my house for a goodnight drink. And if my wife laughs at you, you may laugh at her and tell her that by now her daughter Anne is married to Master Slender!'

Scarcely had he spoken when Slender himself appeared looking very miserable and cross.

'What has happened, son?' cried Page. 'Are you not married to Anne?'

'I took her all the way to Eton,' complained Slender, 'and when I lifted her veil as we stood before the altar, it was not Mistress Anne at all, but a great hulking boy all dressed up. I'd have thrashed him there and then, had we not been in church.'

'Then, like a fool, you took the wrong fairy!' exclaimed Page 'I told you how to recognise Anne; she was the only one in white!'

'Do not be angry,' said Mistress Page laying her hand on her husband's arm. 'I knew about your plan, and I dressed my daughter in green instead of white—so that Dr. Caius should know which she was. . . . *He* has married her by now!'

But Dr. Caius did not have her either, and arrived shortly afterwards, ready to fight anybody:

'By gar!' he cried. 'I take-a ze fairy in green—and she is *un garçon*, a boy an' not Anne Page! By gar, I kill everybody in Windsor!'

'Then who has married Anne?' cried Ford.

'I can guess,' said Page. 'Yes, here they come.'

Sure enough Fenton and Anne came hand in hand to kneel at

the feet of Page and his wife, tell them they were married, and beg their forgiveness.

'Well, I'm glad you've not had it all your own way!' chuckled Falstaff.

'Fenton, I give you joy of her!' cried Page, clapping him on the back. 'What cannot be mended must be endured. I know you love each other, and I'm sure you'll make her a good husband.'

'Heaven give you many merry, happy days,' said Mistress Page, kissing him. 'Now let's all hasten back to Windsor and laugh over what has happened, as good friends should.'

'Let it be so,' said Ford. 'Come on, Sir John, let Herne the Hunter lead the way!'

AS YOU LIKE IT

NOT FAR FROM the Forest of Arden there once lived a Duke who was loved by his people for his gentle ways and his happy contented nature. He had, however, a brother called Frederick who was so jealous of him, and so full of energy and ambition, that one day he raised a rebellion against his kinsman, drove him out, and seized the dukedom for himself.

The banished Duke was accompanied into exile by many of his friends, and they settled themselves in the Forest of Arden where they lived a pleasant, easy life just as Robin Hood had done in Sherwood Forest. The Duke did not want to make war against his brother, and was quite content to wait until Frederick made himself so unpopular that another revolution would bring him back to power. He was an easy-going man; he preferred a simple, open-air life to the formality and intrigue of a court, and there was plenty of food to be found by hunting the deer.

The Duke did not even worry overmuch about his only child, Rosalind, who had been left behind at court. For he felt sure that Frederick would look after her, especially since she was the close friend and companion of his daughter Celia.

Now, Frederick's behavior had been a bad example to at least one of his followers, a young man named Oliver de Boys whose dead father had been a close friend of the banished Duke. Oliver had two younger brothers; the next in age to himself was away at the university, but the youngest of the three, Orlando, remained at home. He was an honest, straightforward youth whom everyone loved—and Oliver was intensely jealous of him. He gave him no education, treated him as a servant, and refused to let him go and seek his fortune or to give him any of the money which old Sir Rowland de Boys had left to him.

'I will not endure it,' said Orlando one day to his only friend, old Adam who had been his father's faithful servant. 'If I knew how to get my rights, I would!'

At this moment Oliver came striding out of the house. When he saw Orlando talking to Adam, he ordered him to get to work, and struck at him with his whip.

This angered Orlando so much that he seized hold of his brother and flung him to the ground, hardly realizing his own strength.

'Are you going to murder me, you villain?' gasped Oliver.

'I am no villain,' said Orlando, still standing over him. 'I am the youngest son of Sir Rowland de Boys, and whoever says that he was the father of villains is a liar. If you were not my brother, I would tear out your tongue for saying so.'

'Dear masters, do not quarrel!' begged old Adam anxiously.

'Let me up, I say!' cried Oliver.

'I will not until I please,' answered Orlando. 'My father left instructions in his will that I should have a good education: but you have brought me up as if I were a peasant, and I will no longer endure it. Give me the portion which my father left me, and I will trouble you no longer.'

'Certainly I shall not be troubled with you much longer,' said Oliver. 'You shall have part at least of what you want. Now let me up, and go into the house. I'll speak with you again presently.'

'I don't want to hurt you more than I need,' said Orlando releasing Oliver. 'But I must have my rights.'

When Orlando and Adam had left him, Oliver decided to get rid of his brother altogether: he set out for Duke Frederick's court where he knew that a great wrestling match was to be held next day. The wrestling champion, Charles, was a friend of his, and now he went to him and said:

'I understand you are to show your skill before Duke Frederick and his court. Well, my brother Orlando, who is ridiculously proud of himself, is coming to contend against you.'

'I had heard that he was,' answered Charles, 'and I was coming to tell you, and beg you to prevent him from challenging me. Tomorrow I wrestle for my reputation—and if your brother comes against me, he is certain to get hurt.'

'Charles,' said Oliver, 'you are my friend, and I can speak the truth to you. My brother is a villain who seeks my life—he has several times tried to poison me, and once to burn down the house in which I was sleeping. So I do not mind if you break his neck, and not just a rib or two. Indeed it would be dangerous for you merely to injure him; he would have his revenge if he recovered, and your life would not be safe. . . .'

Next day, during the great wrestling match, Charles did terrible feats of strength, and had fatally injured three opponents before Orlando came to challenge him.

'Try to persuade this young man not to contend with Charles,' said Duke Frederick to his daughter Celia and her cousin Rosalind. 'It would be a pity if so fine a youth suffered any serious injury.'

Both Rosalind and Celia did their best, but Orlando was not to be turned from his purpose. However, he proved right in thinking it was a fair match, for he was stronger than he knew, and in the first bout threw Charles to the ground where he lay unable to move hand or foot.

Duke Frederick congratulated Orlando warmly on his triumph, and it seemed that his fortune was made. But when he learnt that Orlando was the son of Sir Rowland de Boys, his brother's best friend, his manner changed suddenly:

'You would have pleased me better if you had belonged to some other family,' he said coldly. 'I wish you could have told me of a different father.'

When Frederick had gone, Orlando exclaimed angrily: 'I am prouder to be even the youngest son of Sir Rowland than I would be if Frederick made me his heir.'

'If I had known who you were,' said Rosalind, 'I would have added tears to my entreaties when I asked you not to wrestle. Now

I beg you, wear this chain in memory of me. If I had more to give I would give more.'

Orlando seemed quite tongue-tied, and Rosalind and Celia left him standing gazing after them with never a word to say. The moment he had seen her, Orlando had fallen in love with Rosalind; and when she had drawn near and hung her chain round his neck, the sudden knowledge of his love had left him dumb with awe and wonder.

He was not left standing as if thunderstruck for long, however. One of Duke Frederick's lords came to warn him that the usurper was plotting against him because he was Sir Rowland's son.

Orlando was certainly out of fortune. For as soon as he reached home, old Adam met him with another warning:

'You must fly, good master,' he said. 'This very night your wicked brother plans to murder you. Do not enter the house, for you will never leave it alive.'

'But where can I go?' asked Orlando. 'I have no money.'

'Here is the sum of five hundred crowns, all my savings,' said Adam, giving it to him. 'Take it, dear master, and take me with you to be your servant still. I know that God will not let me starve in my old age.'

Orlando was deeply touched by Adam's devotion; and presently they set out together to seek their fortune.

They were not the only exiles to leave the court that day. Frederick seemed determined to get rid of everyone connected with his brother the rightful Duke, and not long after the wrestling match he strode suddenly into his daughter's room, and said to Rosalind:

'Niece, you must leave the court at once. If you are found within twenty miles of this spot ten days from now, you die.'

'Dear father, let her stay!' begged Celia. 'I cannot live out of her company. We have always been together in all things. What has she done to deserve this?'

'She is too subtle a traitor for you to understand,' said Frederick. 'Her silence and her patience make the people pity her and take her part. You are a fool; she is robbing you of your place. No, not another word. Nothing will make me change my mind; she is banished.'

Duke Frederick swept out of the room, and Celia strove to comfort her cousin.

'Dearest Rosalind,' she said. 'Do not weep. Surely you realise that the Duke has banished me his daughter as well as you?'

'That he has not!' exclaimed Rosalind.

'Has not?' cried Celia. 'Then, Rosalind, you lack the love which teaches me that you and I are one. Shall we be parted? Never! Let my father seek another heir. So let us now plan how we can slip away together unseen and go to find your father in the Forest of Arden.'

'What terrible dangers we shall run into,' hesitated Rosalind. 'Two girls, wandering alone. . . .'

'I'll put myself in poor clothes,' said Celia, 'and stain my face with umber. If you do the same, anyone we meet will think we are simple country girls, or shepherdesses.'

'Why should I not dress as a man!' exclaimed Rosalind eagerly. 'I am taller than most girls of my age, and good at acting a part. I'll stride along in my doublet and hose, with a woodman's axe at my belt and a boar-spear in my hand, and look as brave as any man. I'll be called Ganymede; you can be my sister.'

'I'll call myself Aliena,' said Celia.

'I've another idea!' exclaimed Rosalind, her eyes sparkling now with excitement. 'Why not ask Touchstone the jester to go with us? He'll be a protection, and a comfort on our wanderings.'

'He'll go along with me the wide world over!' said Celia. 'I'll ask him. Then we can slip away as soon as it's dark. Cheer up, dear cousin; it is liberty we are going to enjoy, and not banishment!'

They were not feeling so cheerful by the time they reached the Forest of Arden. They sat down to rest under the shade of the trees.

'I am weary and can go no further,' sighed Rosalind. 'I could almost disgrace these men's clothes and cry like a woman. But I must remember to encourage the weaker vessel. Courage, good Aliena! . . . Oh, how weary are my spirits!'

'I don't mind about my spirits,' said Touchstone. 'If only my legs were not so tired!'

'Well, here we are in the Forest of Arden,' said Celia.

'Yes,' agreed Touchstone. 'Now I am in Arden. . . . More fool I! I was in a better place when I was at home, but travellers must be content with what they can find.'

As they sat resting under the tree, there came an old shepherd leaning on his crook, and a young man with him.

'Oh Corin, if only you knew how much I love her!' the young man was saying.

'I can guess, Silvius,' grinned old Corin. 'I've been in love too, in my time!'

'No, Corin, you are so old you cannot possibly understand!' cried the lovelorn Silvius. 'Even if you were as true a lover as ever sighed wakefully all night through, you cannot have loved as much as I do now. How many mad actions did your love lead you into?'

'Into a thousand that I have long forgotten!' chuckled Corin.

'Then you never loved as I do!' cried Silvius. 'If you cannot recall even the slightest folly that love led you into—then you have not loved! Or if you have not sat, as I am doing now, boring everyone who heard you with your beloved's praises—you have not loved! Or if you have not felt suddenly that you must be alone, as I feel now—you have not loved! Oh Phoebe, Phoebe, Phoebe!'

So saying, Silvius sprang to his feet, and with a tragic gesture fled away into the forest, while old Corin sat back and laughed until the tears ran down his face.

'Alas, poor shepherd,' said Rosalind, tears springing to her eyes for quite another reason. 'Talking of your own wounded heart, has reminded me of mine!' For it was not only Orlando who had fallen in love at first sight at Duke Frederick's wrestling match.

'And mine too!' said Touchstone, winking at Celia. 'I remember when I was in love how I broke my sword on a stone, and bade it take that for coming by night to visit Jane Smile. Oh, we that are true lovers behave so absurdly.'

'You speak more sense than you intend,' said Rosalind. 'But

go now and ask this old shepherd if he will sell us something to eat. I am ready to faint with hunger.'

Touchstone went and talked with Corin, who proved very friendly and hospitable. Before long he told them that the farmer for whom he worked was about to sell his cottage, flock and pastures, and that Silvius had made an offer for it, but had forgotten all about such things when he fell in love with the scornful Phoebe.

Rosalind had brought both money and jewels with her; now she instructed Corin to buy the farm on her behalf and manage it for her. Corin accepted gladly; and so very soon 'Ganymede' and his sister 'Aliena' were settled on the edge of the Forest of Arden in a pleasant cottage of their own.

They had so far seen nothing of the banished Duke, and, for a while, made no attempt to find him. On one occasion Touchstone met a friend of the Duke's called Jacques who was a melancholy philosopher always ready to argue and say clever or cutting things; and these two got on well together, though Touchstone was careful not to say anything about Rosalind.

Meanwhile Orlando and Adam had also come to the Forest of Arden, though they reached it at a point quite distant from where Rosalind and Celia were living. They wandered in it for a long time without meeting anybody or finding any food, and at last Adam grew too tired to walk any more. For a time Orlando supported him; but at length Adam could go no further, and Orlando laid him carefully on a soft, grassy bank and went on alone in search of food and shelter.

He came before long to where a fire was burning over which a deer hung roasting. About the fire sat a large group of men dressed as foresters, laughing and talking as they drank from large horns, and eating bread and fruit while waiting for their venison.

Thinking that they must be robbers who would yield nothing to polite words, but only be impressed by force, Orlando drew his sword and rushed forward, crying:

'Stop, and eat no more!'

'Are you made so fierce and rude by distress?' said the man who was obviously the leader of the band. 'Or are you a mere despiser of good manners? What is it you want? You are likely to gain more by gentleness than force.'

'I am dying of hunger,' said Orlando. 'Let me have food!'

'Sit down and feed, and be welcome to our table,' was the answer.

'Forgive me, I beg,' said Orlando. 'In this savage place I expected to find only savages. But if you are men who have looked on better days, who have lived where bells have called you to church, have sat at table with law-abiding men, and know what it is to pity and to be pitied—let gentleness give me what I ask. And in that hope I blush for my rudeness, and sheath my sword.'

'It is true that we have seen better days,' answered the leader, who was none other than the banished Duke, Rosalind's father, 'and we have been called to church by holy bells, and indeed know what it is to pity. So tell us what we can do for you, and whatever you ask shall be yours.'

'Then wait a while before you begin your meal,' said Orlando. 'There is a poor old man who, for love, has followed me many miles. Until he has had food and wine, I will not eat. He lies only a little way from here.'

'Go quickly and bring him,' said the Duke. 'We shall await your return.'

As soon as Orlando had gone, the Duke remarked:

'You see that we are not alone in misfortune. This wide and universal theater, the world, presents plays far more sad and tragic than that in which we take part.'

'All the world's a stage,' amplified Jacques, seizing his chance, 'and all the men and women merely players. They have their exits and their entrances, and one man in his time plays many parts . . .'

So he went on, pointing out that a man's life might be divided into seven ages, and describing each—the baby, the schoolboy, the lover, the soldier, the councilor, the pensioner, and finally the old man in his 'second childhood'—until Orlando returned carrying Adam.

'Set him down—and eat, both of you,' said the Duke kindly. 'We will wait to ask who you are or how you come to be here; and now my cousin Amiens shall sing for us.'

So Amiens sang,

> 'Blow, blow, thou winter wind,
> Thou art not so unkind
>   As man's ingratitude;
> Thy tooth is not so keen,
> Because thou art not seen,
>   Although thy breath be rude.'

And when he had eaten all he needed, Orlando told the Duke who he was, and was welcomed even more warmly. And after this Orlando lived with the Duke and the other exiles in Arden, and helped them to hunt the deer for food.

But he was not a very good huntsman, for the same reason that Silvius was no longer a very good shepherd: he was in love.

Now that there was no danger from his brother Oliver, nor any need to care for Adam as he had done on their wanderings, Orlando had plenty of time to think about Rosalind. And he fell more and more deeply in love, until he could do little but carve her name on the forest trees, and write sentimental poems in her praise. These he attached to the bushes under which he sat lamenting his hard fate for their cruel separation.

One day Rosalind found one of these poems and read it to Touchstone, who was most contemptuous:

'All the pictures fairest lined
Are but black to Rosalind.
Let no face be kept in mind
But the fair of Rosalind,'

she read, and Touchstone remarked scornfully:
'I can rhyme for you like that for years on end! For a taste:

If the cat will after kind,
So be sure will Rosalind.
Winter garments must be lined,
So must slender Rosalind!

'But why do you make such verses?'
'Peace, you dull Fool,' answered Rosalind. 'I found them on a tree!'
'Then the tree yields very bad fruit!' commented Touchstone.

Before Rosalind could think of any suitable retort, Celia appeared reading yet another set of badly constructed verses addressed this time to 'Heavenly Rosalind'.

When the two girls were alone together, Celia asked:
'Are you not surprised to find verses in your honor hung from the trees, and your name carved in their bark? Do you know who has done this?'

'Is it a man?' asked Rosalind.

'And a chain that you once wore is about his neck,' said Celia. 'Ah-ha! You blush!'

'Tell me who it is!' begged Rosalind.

And when she had teased her cousin a bit longer, Celia said: 'It is young Orlando, who tripped up the wrestler's heels and your heart all in a moment!'

'Orlando!' gasped Rosalind, 'Oh, what was he doing when you saw him? What did he say? How did he look? Where was he going? What is he doing here? Did he ask for me? Where is he now? Answer—answer!'

'I would need a giant's mouth to answer so many questions at once!' laughed Celia. 'You must let me tell my tale without interruptions.'

'Because I am dressed like a man, do you think I have a doublet and hose in my disposition?' cried Rosalind. 'Do you not know that I am a woman? When I think, I must speak!'

'Then I'll tell you—' began Celia. 'But sssh! Here he comes in person!'

'Yes! It's Orlando!' breathed Rosalind. 'Let's hide and see what he does!'

Orlando was walking slowly through the forest, trying to get rid of Jacques, who was being more of a pest than usual:

'I thank you for your company,' he said at last. 'But to tell you the truth, I prefer to be alone.'

'And so do I,' answered Orlando. 'But for the sake of good manners, I thank you for your society.'

'Goodbye. Let's meet as seldom as we can,' said Jacques.

'I hope we may become better strangers,' replied Orlando.

'I beg you to ruin no more trees by carving love-songs on them,' said Jacques, determined to have the last word.

'I beg you to ruin no more of my poems by reading them badly,' retorted Orlando.

'Rosalind is your love's name?' queried Jacques. 'I do not like it.'

'There was no thought of pleasing you when she was christened,' Orlando parried.

'How tall is she?' Jacques tried again.

'Just as high as my heart!' cried Orlando devoutly.

'You are full of pretty answers,' snapped Jacques. 'All lovers are fools. And indeed I was looking for a Fool when I found you.'

'He is drowned in the brook,' said Orlando seriously. 'You have only to look in, and you will see him.'

'There I shall see my own reflection,' said Jacques, taken off his guard.

'Which I presume is that of a fool!' cried Orlando.

'I'll stay no longer!' growled Jacques, seeing that he could not get the better of the argument. 'Farewell, good Signior Love!'

'Goodbye, good Cavaliero Crosspatch!' cried Orlando; and he settled himself down under a tree to write another poem to Rosalind, well satisfied that he had won his duel of words with Jacques. But he had another duel before him which he little expected—and the nature of which he did not then understand at all.

For now Rosalind, in her disguise as Ganymede, came forward and slapped him on the back, beginning a conversation by asking him what time it was.

'There are no clocks in the forest,' said Orlando.

'Then there is no true lover in the forest!' cried Ganymede. 'For if there were he could tell the time as well as any clock— sighing every minute and groaning every hour!'

So they began a brilliant battle of wits, and Orlando almost forgot to pine for his Rosalind, until the young shepherd who talked so well of love said:

'There is a man in this forest who is really in love. Not you, obviously. He hangs poems on bushes and carves verses on trees, which all declare his love for some girl called Rosalind.'

'I am that lover,' said Orlando. 'What makes you think I could not be he?'

'There are no signs of a true lover about you!' was the answer.

'I wish I could make you believe how truly I love,' said Orlando.

'Me believe!' cried Ganymede gaily. 'You will as soon convince the lady whom you say you love! Though I'll wager she is readier to believe you than to confess she does! But are you really as much in love with Rosalind as your rhymes suggest?'

'Neither rhyme nor reason can express how much!' cried Orlando.

'Love is merely a madness,' said Ganymede wisely, 'and I will guarantee to cure it, if you will pretend that I am your Rosalind, and woo me day by day. For I will make you all the answers girls in love give to the young men who love them, and—and this will cure you in time!'

'I do not wish to be cured,' said Orlando.

'But—but I would like to cure you,' said Ganymede.

'Now, by the truth of my love, I will let you try!' laughed Orlando. 'Show me the way to your cottage, and I'll come there to woo you, good Ganymede.'

'You must call me Rosalind. . . . Come, sister Aliena, we'll show this young forester where we live. . . .'

There were other love affairs in the Forest of Arden: the jester Touchstone, in spite of teasing Rosalind about her love, decided to find himself a wife. He chose a rather simple country girl called Audrey who was loved already by an even simpler clod-hopper called William. Touchstone, however, was such a good talker that he argued the rather stupid William into giving up all claims to Audrey, and carried her off in triumph.

Then there was also the affair between the lovelorn shepherd Silvius and the disdainful Phoebe. Corin brought Rosalind and Celia to see them not long after Rosalind had first met Orlando in the forest; and after they heard Silvius wooing in the most poetic terms, and Phoebe making fun of him, Rosalind decided that she must take a hand in the game. So she in turn made fun of Phoebe, scorning her and jeering at her:

'Who are you to exult over the wretched, and scorn a poor lover?' she cried contemptuously. 'You have no beauty yourself, and are hardly likely to get other offers of marriage! You should be on your knees, thanking God for having sent you a good man to love you as truly as Silvius does—you'll not get another chance!'

Off went Rosalind, pretending to be full of scorn and contempt. But Phoebe, thinking her to be indeed the young shepherd Ganymede, had fallen in love with her on sight, and asked the wretched Silvius for help.

'So perfect is my love,' said poor Silvius, 'that your very word is law, and I will do anything you ask for the chance of a smile and a kind word now and then.'

'Do not think that I love this fellow Ganymede,' Phoebe hastened to assure him—and herself. 'He's a rude boy, who made unkind remarks about me. I should like to write him a very taunting letter, telling him just what I think of him. You'll carry it to him for me, won't you Silvius?'

'With all my heart,' answered Silvius, and off went Phoebe to write her letter.

Meanwhile Orlando and Rosalind were meeting again to continue their wooing, which Orlando, in spite of thinking she was the boy Ganymede, found strangely attractive.

'I must leave you now for two hours,' said Orlando at last.

'Alas, dear love, I cannot be without you for two whole hours!' cried Ganymede-Rosalind.

'I must attend the Duke at dinner,' explained Orlando. 'But I'll be with you again by two o'clock.'

'Be sure you are punctual,' said Rosalind severely. 'If you are so much as a second late, I shall know that you do not really love your Rosalind.'

Off went Orlando, and Rosalind flung herself down by her cousin, exclaiming rapturously:

'Oh Celia, Celia! If only you knew how many fathoms deep I am in love! I tell you, I cannot bear to be out of sight of Orlando. I can do nothing but sit and sigh until he comes back!'

'You sigh if you like,' said Celia, 'but I'm going to sleep! Two hours will soon be up.'

But more than two hours passed, and there was no sign of Orlando.

'It's long after two!' pouted Rosalind. 'And where is Orlando!'

'I expect that, full of love, he has taken his bow and arrows and gone out—to sleep!' suggested Celia reproachfully at being awakened. 'But look who is here?'

It was Silvius, the lovelorn shepherd, with the letter from Phoebe. Rosalind read it aloud—an ardent love letter to Ganymede

—making fun of it and pretending that everything it said was a gibe. At last she said:

'Poor shepherd, will you still love such a woman? Well, go back to her, for I see that love has made you a tame snake, say to her that if she loves me, I command her to love you. Now off you go, and deliver my message!'

Hardly had Silvius gone on his forlorn errand, when a stranger appeared walking fast through the trees. On seeing Rosalind and Celia he hastened towards them and asked the way to a cottage which, by his description, they recognised as their own.

'But,' said the stranger, 'I think that I need go no further. Are you not the two who live in this cottage? Young Ganymede, and his sister Aliena?'

'You are right,' said Celia. 'Why do you seek us?'

'Orlando has sent me as his messenger,' was the answer, 'and he bade me give this blood-stained handkerchief to you, young sir—the boy he calls his Rosalind.'

'What is the meaning of this token?' asked Rosalind, turning pale.

'Let me tell you the story,' answered the stranger, 'though to do so is to reveal my shame. When Orlando left you, he intended to return in two hours' time. But as he walked through the forest, his mind on other things, he came upon a wretched, ragged man lying asleep under a tree. Crouched beside him was a hungry-looking lioness waiting for him to wake: for, as you know, lions will never prey on anything which seems to be dead. Advancing cautiously, Orlando saw to his surprise that the man lying there was his brother Oliver.'

'I have heard him speak of that brother!' exclaimed Celia. 'He said that he was the unkindest brother that ever lived.'

'He spoke only the truth about him,' said the stranger 'as I have good reason to know.'

'But what happened?' exclaimed Rosalind impatiently. 'Did Orlando leave his wicked brother as food for the lioness?'

'Twice he turned away, meaning to do so,' answered the stranger, 'but forgiveness and his natural instinct to save a life, prevailed. He turned and attacked the lioness, quickly overcame her, and killed her with his spear—and I woke to find the battle ended.'

'Are you the brother who tried so often to kill him!' exclaimed Celia.

'Was it you he rescued?' asked Rosalind.

'It was I,' answered Oliver. 'But not the "I" I was. I am not ashamed to tell you what I used to be, since my conversion has made me so happy.'

'But the stained handkerchief——' interrupted Rosalind anxiously.

'When I had begged his forgiveness,' continued Oliver, 'Orlando led me to the banished Duke, who welcomed me when he heard how wicked Frederick had turned me out of house and home, and how Orlando and I were now reconciled. He gave me fresh clothes, and fed me, and then I returned with Orlando to the cave where he lives. There he stripped off his shirt, to discover that the lioness had cruelly torn the flesh of his arm. It had been bleeding all the time. The pain caused Orlando to faint; and when I had bound up his wound, he sent me to seek you and explain why he had broken his promise.'

At this Rosalind fainted also, and Celia and Oliver bent hastily over her.

'Many will faint at the sight of blood,' said Oliver.

'There is more than that in it,' exclaimed Celia, forgetting the secret for the moment. Perhaps Oliver guessed something of the truth, for when Rosalind sat up, he said:

'Buck up, young fellow! You a man? You lack a man's heart!'

'I do indeed,' sighed Rosalind, and then she added hastily: 'Ah sir, didn't I pretend to faint well? Please tell your brother how well I acted!'

'This was no pretense,' said Oliver. 'This was a real faint.'

'All pretense, I assure you!' insisted Rosalind.

'Well then, cheer up, and pretend to be a man!' said Oliver.

'He looks paler and paler!' interrupted Celia hastily. 'Help me to lead my brother to the cottage. . . .'

Later in that eventful day, Oliver returned to where Orlando was waiting, and told him how his message had been received. He also told him of his own wonderful fortune. How he and Celia had fallen in love at first sight, told one another of their passion, and agreed to get married the very next day.

'Do not think we are foolish,' ended Oliver. 'I love Aliena with all my heart, and she loves me. You shall have Sir Rowland's lands and goods, and I will live and die a shepherd here in Arden.'

'Then let your wedding indeed be tomorrow,' said Orlando, 'and I will invite the Duke and all his followers to it. Go and tell Aliena. . . . But look, here comes my Rosalind!'

'Greetings, good brother!' exclaimed Rosalind as she passed Oliver.

'The same to you, fair *sister*,' cried Oliver as he ran off to find Celia.

'Ah, my dear Orlando!' said Rosalind hastily. 'I hope your brother told you how well I pretended to faint?'

'Yes,' answered Orlando slowly, 'and greater wonders than that!'

'Oh, you mean their sudden falling in love!' cried Rosalind hastily.

'They are to be married tomorrow,' said Orlando. And he added with a deep sigh: 'How bitter it is to look into happiness through another man's eyes.'

'Then I cannot serve your turn as Rosalind tomorrow?' she asked.

'I can no longer live on pretense,' answered Orlando.

'Then I will plague you no longer by pretending,' said Rosalind. 'Learn that I am a magician; the magic was taught me by my old uncle and is white magic—all quite lawful. By its power, I will produce Rosalind for you, and you shall marry her tomorrow. So prepare for your wedding! . . . Look, here comes a lover of mine and a lover of hers!'

'Dear Ganymede!' cried Phoebe, for it was she, followed by Silvius. 'You have been most unkind! Why did you show Silvius my letter to you?'

'I intend to be unkind to you,' said Rosalind, 'You are followed there by a faithful shepherd who loves you truly. Look at him, not me—and love *him*.'

'Good shepherd, tell this youth what it is to love truly,' said Phoebe, and Silvius replied:

'It is to be all made of sighs and tears, of faith and service, of adoration, duty and obedience, of humbleness, patience and impatience. . . . And so am I for Phoebe.'

'And so am I for Ganymede!' cried Phoebe.

'And so am I for Rosalind!' cried Orlando.

'And so am I for—no woman!' cried Rosalind. 'But enough of this. Let us all meet tomorrow. I will marry you, Phoebe, if ever I marry a woman, and I'll be married tomorrow. I will satisfy you, Orlando, if ever I satisfy a man, and you shall be married tomorrow. I will make you happy, Silvius, if what you most wish for will make you happy, and you shall be married tomorrow. Do not fail me—tomorrow we meet!'

Next day the Duke and his followers assembled for the complicated marriage ceremony to which Orlando had invited them.

Rosalind met them, still disguised as Ganymede and exacted promises from them all:

'You will let Orlando marry Rosalind if I produce her for you?' she said to the Duke.

'Indeed I will,' he answered, 'and would, if I had kingdoms to give with her.'

'And you will marry her, Orlando?'

'If I were king of all the world, she should be my queen,' he answered.

'You will marry me,' she said to Phoebe, 'if you still wish to do so half an hour hence? And if you change your mind, you will marry Silvius?'

'I promise,' said Phoebe.

'Then in half an hour your wishes shall all be granted,' cried Rosalind. 'Orlando shall marry Rosalind; Oliver shall marry Celia; and Phoebe shall marry me, or if she refuses me, Silvius. Wait here while I go and prepare my spell!'

'I think there must be another Flood on the way?' exclaimed Jacques presently. 'There are so many couples coming to the Ark! Here is a very strange pair of beasts, called fools!'

It was Touchstone and Audrey who had decided not to be left out of the general marrying; and when Jacques introduced them to the Duke, Touchstone entertained him with so many amusing remarks that the time sped by until suddenly Rosalind re-appeared as her own proper self, hand in hand with Celia.

'To you I give myself, for I am yours,' she said, kneeling to the Duke her father. Then rising, she went over to Orlando and curtsied to him, saying: 'To *you* I give myself, for I am yours!'

'If there is truth in sight, you are my daughter!' exclaimed the Duke.

'If there is truth in sight, you are my Rosalind!' gasped Orlando, raising her and taking her in his arms.

'If sight and shape be true, farewell to my love!' cried Phoebe, realizing that Rosalind and Ganymede were one and the same. Then she turned and took Silvius timidly by the hand. . . .

So the quadruple wedding was performed in the happy Forest of Arden, and not long afterwards the wicked Frederick gave up the dukedom to his brother. Oliver and Celia were given all the lands which had belonged to Sir Rowland de Boys; for Orlando, by marrying Rosalind, became heir to the Duke, who had no son. And so they all lived happily ever after.

TWELFTH NIGHT

SEBASTIAN AND VIOLA were twins, a boy and a girl so like that they could hardly be told apart. They were the children of a rich Italian merchant, and once when they were traveling together in one of their father's ships, a great storm arose suddenly and wrecked it on the coast of Illyria. Sebastian escaped by clinging to the mast which was washed out to sea where he was picked up by a passing ship. But Viola came safely to shore with the captain and most of the sailors.

Thinking that Sebastian was dead, Viola had no heart to return home. Instead, she dressed herself as a boy, took the name of Cesario, and became the trusted servant of Orsino, the Duke of Illyria.

Now Orsino was in love with a young lady called Olivia, the daughter of a rich count who had died a year or so before and left her his mansion and a considerable fortune. This she had shared with her only brother, until his sudden and unexpected death cast her into such melancholy and gloom that Orsino despaired of winning her. She shut herself up in the house, refused even to receive messages from Orsino, and swore that she would remain in this solitary condition for seven years, mourning for her brother.

Orsino was not Olivia's only suitor. Her uncle, Sir Toby Belch who had come to stay with her to try and comfort her after her double loss, had introduced a wealthy, but extremely brainless young knight, Sir Andrew Aguecheek, to woo her. Olivia would have none of him, and she did not at all approve of her uncle who was inclined to be boisterous and drunken—particularly when he had a friend to drink and revel with. But Sir Toby's real enemy was Olivia's chamberlain, Malvolio, a conceited, sour-tempered man with no sense of humor but a very high opinion of himself. He disapproved strongly of Sir Toby's goings on, and was always scolding Olivia's maid, Maria, for encouraging the old man; and he heartily disliked the jester, Feste, who made fun of him and cracked jokes which he did not understand. Needless to say, Malvolio was equally unpopular with Feste, Sir Andrew, Sir Toby and Maria, as well as with the other servants under his authority.

It was into this strangely mixed household that Viola found herself thrust not long after she had become Orsino's page. The Duke had taken an instant liking to her, and after only three days was already telling 'Cesario' all the secrets of his heart, and begging 'him' to visit Olivia and plead for him.

'Do not take no for an answer,' urged Orsino. 'If they refuse to let you in, swear you will stand at the gate until you take root there. And when you win your way to Olivia's presence, woo her for me with the sweetest words you know.'

'I'll do my best,' said Viola, bowing to the Duke before setting out. But as she went she said to herself with a sigh: 'Yet I pray that my wooing of Olivia for Orsino may not succeed; for I myself love him, and would like to be his wife.'

When Viola reached Olivia's mansion, she was kept at the gate by Sir Toby, who was very drunk, in spite of it being early morning. But Maria went to tell her mistress. She found Olivia in black mourning clothes, delivering her orders for the day to Malvolio. Feste, who had been away, had just returned and had come to pay his respects to his mistress. Olivia did not seem pleased to see him:

'Take the fool away,' she said to Malvolio.

'Do you not hear, fellow?' exclaimed Feste. 'Take away the Lady!'

'How do you prove that I am a fool?' asked Olivia, wondering what Feste had in mind.

'You must answer my questions, then,' he said.

'Well, for want of anything better to do, I'll humor you.'

'Madam, why do you mourn?' began Feste.

'Fool, I mourn for my brother's death.'

'I think his soul is in Hell, madam.'

'I know his soul is in Heaven, fool.'

'The more fool you, madam!' cried Feste triumphantly. 'To mourn because your brother's soul is in Heaven! Fellow, take away the Lady!'

'What do you think of this fool, Malvolio?' asked Olivia. 'Is he not better at his job than before he went away?'

'Yes,' sneered Malvolio, 'he grows better the older he becomes; he'll be the biggest fool possible when he's senile.'

'Madam,' Maria interrupted at this moment, 'there is a young gentleman at the gate who wishes to speak to you.'

'Is he from Duke Orsino?' asked Maria.

'I do not know,' answered Maria. 'Your uncle, Sir Toby, is talking to him.'

'Go and fetch Sir Toby!' exclaimed Olivia. 'Quickly! He'll be saying something foolish.' And when Maria had gone she turned to Malvolio and said:

'And you go, Malvolio, and see what the youth wants. If he is from the Duke, say I am ill, or not at home, or what you will—but dismiss him.'

Off went Malvolio, full of importance. But he returned in a few minutes looking rather nonplussed.

'Madam,' he began in his usual pompous manner, 'yonder young fellow swears he will speak with you. I told him you were ill; he replied that he knew you were, and has come to see you for that very reason. I told him you were asleep, and he said he guessed as much, but knew you would wake soon, and so had come at this moment. What can I say to him, lady? He seems to have an answer ready for everything.'

'Well, let him come in,' sighed Olivia. 'We'll hear once more what Orsino has to say. Maria, my veil.'

Viola made a very handsome young man as Cesario, and affected a rather pert, off-hand style which caught Olivia's attention at once.

'Which is the lady of the house?' she asked.

'You may speak to me. I will answer for her,' replied the veiled Olivia.

'Most radiant, unmatched and exquisite beauty,' began Viola dramatically, and then added in her ordinary voice: 'Please tell me if you really are the Lady Olivia. I should hate to waste all the speech, which I've learned with such care.'

'I am,' she answered with a smile. 'But just tell me the important things—leave out all the compliments.'

'Oh dear,' sighed Viola in comical distress. 'I worked so hard learning it, and I promise you it's very poetical.'

'Then it's more likely to be false,' said Olivia. 'So be brief and give me your message. I hear you were impertinent to my chamberlain, and I sent for you more to see who it was who behaved like this than to hear what you had to say.'

'And now, young man, you may leave,' added Malvolio. 'Here is the door.'

'No, my good commissionaire, you cannot see me off the premises just yet,' retorted Viola, determined to outdo Malvolio in insolence. 'I have secrets to disclose to this lady too sacred for profane ears.'

Olivia dismissed all her attendants, and Viola proceeded to plead Orsino's suit in her own words, which were much sincerer than the Duke's carefully polished phrases and protestations of undying love.

Olivia, however, was not interested in Orsino or his suit. Already she was fascinated by his youthful messenger, Cesario, who had such a gift of words and was so young and handsome himself.

Finally Viola described how she would woo if she were Orsino, and Olivia said:

'You might well prove more successful; but tell me who you really are. Who were your parents?'

'I come of a higher rank than my present position might suggest,' answered Viola. 'Chance has turned me into a servant, but I was born a gentleman.'

'Well, return to your master,' said Olivia, 'and tell him that I can never love him, valiant, learned and handsome though I admit he is. Let him send me no more messengers of love—unless you come to tell me how he received my message.'

'Farewell, fair cruelty,' said Viola, bowing low. 'As you have disdained my master, I hope the man you love may disdain you, and may he hold your love in as much contempt as you hold Orsino's.'

As soon as Viola had gone, Olivia began to wonder who he was, and to wish him back again.

'Malvolio!' she called, and when her chamberlain came in she bade him hasten after the Duke's messenger with a ring he had left behind.

'It was a present from his master,' she said. 'But I will not have it. So hurry, good Malvolio, and give it to Cesario.'

But the ring was one of her own, and when Malvolio overtook Viola and insisted on her taking it, she began to realise that Olivia had fallen in love with her.

Malvolio was even ruder to Viola when he gave her the ring than he had been before; but she was too much concerned with her own love for Orsino and Olivia's love for her to bother about him.

Sir Toby and Maria, however, were not so forgiving. And that very evening Malvolio behaved with such insolence towards them that they set about devising a suitable revenge.

Sir Toby and Sir Andrew were sitting up talking and drinking late, for Sir Toby declared that 'not to be in bed by midnight was the same thing as being up early in the morning', and that therefore late hours were really a sign of virtue. When Feste the jester joined them, they added singing to drinking, for he had a sweet voice and began with a love-song:

'Oh mistress mine, where are you roaming?
Oh stay and hear; your true love's coming,
   That can sing both high and low:
Trip no further, pretty sweeting;
Journeys end in lover's meeting,
   Every wise man's son doth know.'

Sir Andrew Aguecheek declared that Feste's voice was 'sweet
and contagious', and to prove his point started to sing himself—
anything but sweetly.

'Ha!' cried Sir Toby, 'shall we make the rafters ring? Shall we
rouse the night-owl with a catch?'

And with that he added his own bellow to Sir Andrew's more
warbling strain, until Maria came rushing in, exclaiming:

'What caterwauling is this! If you make such a noise, my lady
will send for Malvolio and bid him turn you out of the house.'

'He'll do no such thing!' hiccupped Sir Toby. 'Am I not
Olivia's uncle? Have I not rights.' And he began to sing again
at the top of his voice.

Sure enough before long Malvolio came hurrying into the
room in his nightgown and cap, carrying a candle:

'Are you mad?' he cried. 'Or are you only stupid? Or just bad
mannered? How dare you treat my lady's house as if it were an
inn, and disturb everyone with your low songs? Have you no
idea of place or time?'

'We kept time in our catches very well!' exclaimed Sir
Andrew indignantly.

'Sir Toby, I'll be blunt with you,' said Malvolio. 'My lady is
pleased to have you in the house if you behave properly. But if
you cannot do so, she is very ready to bid you farewell.'

'Farewell, dear heart, since I must needs be gone!' sang Sir Toby.

'His eyes do show his days are almost done!' Feste joined in.
And so they went on, singing suitable lines from songs and dancing
drunkenly round Malvolio, until he strode angrily from the
room, threatening to tell Olivia.

'He deserves challenging to a duel, and then being laughed
off the field of battle!' cried Sir Andrew indignantly.

'You write a challenge, and I'll see that he gets it!' roared Sir Toby.

'Sweet Sir Toby, be quiet!' begged Maria. 'My lady is much disturbed ever since she spoke with young Cesario, the Duke's new messenger. She cannot sleep, and so she is inclined to be bad tempered. As for Malvolio, let us make a plot to show him up for the ass we all know him to be. I have an idea how we may make a fool of him.'

'Tell us, tell us!' cried Sir Toby.

'You know how conceited he is,' said Maria. 'He thinks every one admires him, and that no woman can look at him without falling in love. I will use his conceit to help my revenge.'

'But how?' asked Sir Toby.

'I will write a letter that he will think is from my lady,' answered Maria. 'I'll imitate her hand and write such things that he'll think she is dying of love for him. And I'll bid him show that he has found the letter by wearing yellow stockings with cross-garters (both of which she detests), and by smiling all the time, and being even more commanding than usual to you and the servants. We'll drop this letter where he'll find it when he is walking in the garden; then we can hide behind a hedge and watch him reading it. When he starts behaving as the letter tells him to, my lady will think he is mad!'

'Oh, it will be admirable!' cried Sir Toby.

'To bed now, then,' said Maria. 'Do not offend my lady any more. I'll go and write the letter.'

'That's a clever girl,' said Sir Andrew when Maria had gone.

'She's a fine lass—and she adores me!' agreed Sir Toby.

'I was adored once, too,' said Sir Andrew sadly.

'Come,' said Sir Toby. 'It's too late to go to bed now; let's go to my room and mull some sack.'

When Viola returned to Orsino with Olivia's message, it made him even more melancholy and depressed than he was already—though indeed his passion for Olivia was fast becoming an obsession that could scarcely be called love.

In keeping with his mood, he sent for Feste who was famous in Illyria for his sweet voice, and bade him sing a sad song:

> 'Come away, come away, death,
>   And in sad cypress let me be laid;
> Fly away, fly away, breath;
>   I am slain by a fair cruel maid.
> My shroud of white, stuck all with yew,
>   Oh, prepare it!
> My part of death, no one so true
>   Did share it.'

When the music had put him into the very depths of love-lorn melancholy, Orsino spoke again to Cesario of his passion for Olivia.

'You must go to the Countess again,' he said, 'and plead with her. Tell her once more that it is for herself alone and not for her lands and riches that I love her—I would love her as much were she a beggar-maid.'

'But if she cannot love you?' said Viola.

'I will not accept such an answer,' replied the Duke.

'But perhaps you must,' said Viola. 'Suppose some lady were as deeply in love with you as you are with Olivia; you cannot love her, and you tell her so. Must she not accept such an answer?'

'No woman is capable of loving as I do!' cried Orsino. 'You cannot compare the love with which a woman might love me, and that with which I love Olivia.'

'Yet I know only too well how deeply a woman can love a man,' said Viola, thinking of her own feelings for Orsino. 'They can be as true to love as we are. My father had a daughter—she loved a man as truly as, were I a woman, I might love you.'

'And what was her history?' asked Orsino, interested in spite of his own selfish passion.

'A blank, my lord—she never told her love,' said Viola. 'She pined in secret, hiding her passion until her beauty wasted away, and her cheeks that had been as smooth as damask became all lined with care. She sat like patience on a monument—

smiling at grief. Surely this was love? We men say more, swear more oaths of constancy—but often we prove less faithful than women.'

'But did your sister die of her love, boy?' asked Orsino.

'I am all the daughters of my father—and all the sons too, I fear,' said Viola, sighing as she thought of Sebastian. Then anxious to change a dangerous subject, she said quickly: 'Shall I go to the Lady Olivia, none the less?'

'With all the speed you can,' answered Orsino. 'Take her this jewel, and tell her my love can bear no denial.'

While Viola was speeding towards Olivia's house, Maria was carrying out her plot against Malvolio, who was walking in the garden—practising courtly gestures, and watching his own shadow to see how they looked.

When she had dropped the letter where Malvolio was sure to see it, Maria hastened to hide with Sir Toby and Sir Andrew behind a convenient hedge, there to await developments.

Sure enough, Malvolio came mincing along the path, as proud as a peacock, talking to himself to practise his diction and see how like a great lord he could speak:

'To be Count Malvolio!' he said, while Maria and Sir Andrew had great difficulty in keeping Sir Toby quiet. 'Yes, having been three months married to Olivia, sitting in state, in my velvet gown, I shall send for my kinsman Toby . . . Toby approaches, he bows low to me——'

'And knocks you down with a blow in the mouth!' muttered Sir Toby behind the hedge.

'I extend my hand to him,' went on Malvolio grandly, 'and say: "Cousin Toby, as Heaven has made me your niece's husband, I have the right to speak to you as one of the family. So let me warn you to regulate your drunkenness—to cure it altogether. Moreover you waste your time with a foolish knight—" '

'That's me, I suppose!' whispered Sir Andrew.

' "Called Aguecheek" '—went on Malvolio.

'I knew he meant me,' sighed Sir Andrew. 'For many people call me a fool.'

But here Malvolio broke off his daydream, for he had just seen the letter lying on the path. Stooping with an elegant gesture he picked it up and looked at it carefully.

'This is in my lady's writing!' he exclaimed: ' "To the Unknown Beloved. I may command where I adore..." Mmm ... "M.O.A.I. doth sway my life . . ." Surely she means me! It is a kind of hidden message.... What else? Ah: "Some are born great, some achieve greatness, and some have greatness thrust upon them. . . . Do not be afraid of greatness. . . . Be short with the family, and order the servants about..." What else?' Malvolio went on spelling out the letter, sometimes to himself, sometimes out loud.

'This is as clear as daylight!' he cried when he had finished. 'My lady loves me, and tells me how to show that I have seen this letter, and will accept the great fortune she offers me. Yes, I will do all she tells me—be short with Toby, show my superiority to the servants, wear yellow stockings with cross-garters, and smile whenever I am in her presence! Oh, I will do everything she commands!'

So saying Malvolio strode away to change into yellow stockings, and the plotters behind the hedge were able to give way to their laughter and delight. But they had further business at hand, for Sir Toby feared that Cesario, the Duke's 'gentleman' was robbing his own friend Sir Andrew of Olivia's affection, and should be challenged to a duel.

Sir Andrew was a great coward, but Sir Toby persuaded him that Cesario would be easy to beat—until the challenge had been written and delivered. Then he and his friends began to tell Sir Andrew how fierce Cesario was, and the poor knight quaked with terror.

Meanwhile, Viola continued to visit Olivia with messages from Orsino; and Olivia became more and more deeply in love with 'him', in spite of Cesario's scorn, and of his declaration that he could never love her.

'I swear,' said the supposed Cesario to Olivia after she had declared her love and offered him herself and all her possessions, 'I swear that I have but one heart, and that is given completely and forever to no woman living—nor shall any ever sway it save myself alone.'

Cesario then vowed never to come near Olivia again. But the Countess sent such pathetic messages to him that at last he relented, and wrote to say that he would come to dine with her.

'How shall I entertain him?' Olivia asked Maria. 'Send for Malvolio. He is so sober and serious, he will show by his glum looks and his black suit how sunk in sorrow this household is.'

'He is coming, madam,' answered Maria, 'but he is so strange today that I'm sure he must have taken leave of his senses.'

'What is the matter with him?' asked Olivia. 'Is he raving?'

'No, madam, he does nothing but smile,' answered Maria. 'You had better have someone near to protect you, for I am sure he's not right in the head. Look, here he comes!'

Sure enough, Malvolio came sweeping into the room in yellow stockings with cross garters, grinning like a hyena.

'How are you, Malvolio?' asked Olivia anxiously.

'Sweet lady, ho, ho!' replied Malvolio, smiling more than ever.

'You smile?' queried Olivia. 'I sent for you for sad reasons.'

'Sad?' grinned Malvolio. 'I would be sad, for these garters are infernally uncomfortable. But I will do anything to please you.'

'To please me?' asked Olivia. 'Why do you smile so, and kiss your hand to me all the time?'

'By your command,' leered Malvolio. '"Be not afraid of greatness," and so forth. "Remember who longs to see you in yellow stockings and cross-garters". I know well the sweet Roman hand!'

'Why, this is midsummer madness!' exclaimed Olivia.

At this moment a servant came to tell her of Viola's arrival, and she sent hastily for Sir Toby Belch to look after Malvolio. And, with the aid of Sir Andrew and Feste, Sir Toby very soon had the poor man locked up in a dark room.

Olivia was as unsuccessful as usual in winning any token of love from Cesario.

'Ask of me anything you wish,' she cried at length, 'and I will give it to you.'

'Your love for my master Orsino,' answered Viola.

But this was the one thing Olivia could not give, though she persuaded Viola to come again next day in case it might grow more possible in time.

Viola was just leaving the house when Sir Toby overtook her and gave her the challenge from Sir Andrew.

'I do not know what injury you have done him,' said Sir Toby, looking as grim as he knew how, 'but I know that he is breathing fire and waiting to cut you to pieces at the end of the orchard.'

'You—you have made a mistake, sir,' stammered Viola, 'I have offended nobody, and he cannot mean to challenge me.'

'*You* are mistaken,' Sir Toby assured her. 'Therefore get ready to sell your life dearly. Sir Andrew is a terrible, grim fighter; he has already killed three men in duels.'

Viola, who was almost afraid even to look at her own sword, would have run away while Sir Toby was fetching Sir Andrew, but the knight left his friend Fabian to keep an eye on her. And Fabian improved the occasion by describing how fierce a duellist Sir Andrew was—until Viola was almost ready to reveal that she was a woman, rather than fight.

Meanwhile Sir Toby was telling Sir Andrew how terrible a fighter Cesario was, until he too was ready to run a mile rather than fight. In the end, almost by pushing them, Sir Toby and Fabian brought the two combatants together, and even got them to draw their swords and advance towards one another as if the fight were really about to take place.

The blades had scarcely clashed together, however, when a tall sea-captain in a foreign dress, dashed suddenly up and shouted to Sir Andrew:

'If this young gentleman has offended you in any way, I take the fault on me and will fight you on his behalf.'

At this Sir Toby whipped out his own sword and turned angrily on the stranger, who at once drew to defend himself. Almost immediately the Duke's officers appeared and the leader addressed the stranger:

'Antonio, I arrest you by order of Count Orsino.'

'I must obey,' said Antonio, sheathing his sword. 'This comes of seeking you in a city where my life is in danger,' he added to Viola. 'Now, before they take me, please give me some of that money.'

'What money, sir?' asked Viola, completely surprised, for she had never seen Antonio before. 'For the kindness you have shown me, I'll give you half what I have, though I fear it's little enough.'

'Do you deny me now?' cried Antonio. 'Remember all the kindnesses I have done you.'

'I know of none,' said Viola, 'nor do I know you by your voice or feature. I hate ingratitude worse than any vice—but you are a complete stranger to me.'

'Oh Heavens?' cried Antonio as he was dragged away. 'I rescued this youth from death, and thought from his face that he was an honorable man! Sebastian, you have brought shame on what seemed an honest countenance, and perhaps death on me who saved your worthless life!'

While Antonio was being dragged off in one direction, Viola took the opportunity of slipping off in another before Sir Andrew could propose continuing the duel. But as she went she thought to herself: 'He called me Sebastian! Does that mean my brother is alive and here in Illyria?'

Viola had scarcely gone, when Sir Toby began to tell Sir Andrew what a coward Cesario was.

'I'll go after him!' cried Sir Andrew valiantly. 'I'll not draw my sword on him, but I'll give him a good beating, which is what he deserves for running away!'

He came up with Cesario just outside Olivia's house, and struck him, crying: 'Now, sir, I have you! I'll give you what you deserve!'

'Why then, I'll give you the same!' was the answer; and the supposed coward turned and began to beat Sir Andrew, who yelled for help.

Up rushed Sir Toby and drew his sword—only to find himself matched with a better swordsman than himself.

But before things went very far, the door opened and out came Olivia:

'Stop, Toby!' she cried. 'Out of my sight, you barbarian! Cesario,' she said, when Sir Toby and Sir Andrew had gone, 'I am sorry these troublesome wretches have behaved like this to you. Come into the house with me, and I will tell you of all the trouble they have been making.'

'Madam, I will,' said the young man, taking the hand which Olivia held out to him; and together they passed into the house.

Later that same day Orsino came in person to conduct his wooing of Olivia, and when he and Viola were just outside Olivia's house, the officers met them leading Antonio.

'I remember this man!' exclaimed Orsino. 'Though last time I saw him it was in the heat of battle when he fought so valiantly against us that we could not help but praise him. What is he doing here?'

'Lord Duke, it is indeed that same Antonio,' said the officer in command. 'He who took the *Phoenix* at Candia, boarded the *Tiger*, and wounded your nephew.'

'He did me a kindness, sir,' said Viola. 'He drew his sword to defend me when I was attacked; though afterwards he spoke very strangely.'

'A notable pirate indeed,' said Orsino. 'Antonio, what foolish boldness has brought you to Illyria?'

'Noble Orsino,' answered Antonio, 'I am no pirate, though I admit that I have fought against you. As for what drew me to Illyria, it was surely witchcraft. That boy beside you, I rescued from the sea—he would have died otherwise. I gave him his life, I gave him my love—for his sake I dared to land here in Illyria— and today he has denied knowing me.'

'When did you come to this town?' asked Orsino.

'Today, my lord,' replied Antonio. 'But day and night for the last three months, this young man and I have never been apart.'

'Here comes Olivia—and Heaven walks on earth!' exclaimed Orsino as the door of the house opened. 'As for you, Antonio, what you say is madness. This youth has been my attendant, here, for the past three months. But stand aside now. I'll question you further later on.'

'What do you seek, my lord?' asked Olivia, curtseying to Orsino. 'Surely not that which you know you can never have? If it is, you may spare your words, for they are loathsome to me.'

'I know what it is that has turned you against me!' cried Orsino. 'It is this boy Cesario. Be sure I shall see to it that you never set eyes on him again!'

'Most willingly would I die, my lord, if it would do you any service,' said Viola.

'Where are you going, Cesario?' cried Olivia.

'After him I love,' answered Viola. 'Him I love more than life!'

'Have you forgotten already?' exclaimed Olivia. 'Call for the priest!'

'Come, Cesario,' said Orsino, turning away.

'Stay, stay!' cried Olivia. 'Stay Cesario—husband!'

'Husband!' exclaimed Orsino.

'Yes, my husband! He cannot deny it!' said Olivia.

'Are you her husband, Cesario?' asked Orsino.

'No, my lord, I am not!' exclaimed Viola indignantly.

But scarcely had he spoken when a priest came out of Olivia's house and swore solemnly that he had just married Cesario to the Countess.

'Oh, you dissembling cub!' cried Orsino. 'Take her and go. But never let me set eyes on you again!'

Before Viola had a chance to say anything else, Sir Andrew came rushing out of the house with a broken head crying for a surgeon, and after him reeled Sir Toby in the same condition.

'Who has done this?' asked Olivia indignantly.

'The Duke's gentleman, Cesario!' sobbed Sir Andrew. 'We took him for a coward, but he's the very devil incardinate!'

'Why do you accuse me?' asked Viola. 'You wanted to fight me for no cause, but I spoke fairly to you, and certainly did not hurt you.'

At this moment a young man came out of the house and took Olivia by the hand, saying:

'Forgive me, sweet love, that I have hurt these two guests of yours. But as they attacked and insulted me, I could do no less than punish them as they deserved.'

'One face, one voice—and two persons!' gasped Orsino, looking from the young man to Viola and back again.

'Antonio! Oh my dear Antonio!' cried the young man springing forward suddenly. 'Oh, what has happened to you since we parted on landing?'

'Sebastian? Are you really Sebastian!' exclaimed Antonio, bewildered.

'Who else can I be?' was the answer.

'Then you have divided yourself into two parts,' said Antonio pointing to Viola.

'Is it I who stand there?' gasped Sebastian. 'I never had a brother. I had a sister, but she was lost at sea. Who are you? What is your name? Who were your parents?'

'I come from Messaline,' answered Viola. 'My father's name was Sebastian. And I had a brother called Sebastian who was also lost at sea—and he was even such a man as you, and dressed always in such garments as you are wearing. . . . And if it is only garments that stand in the way of our happiness, and my masculine attire which misleads you, let me admit that I am your sister Viola. To prove which, I can refer you to a sea-captain in this town by whose help I was able to disguise myself as Cesario and become the servant of this noble Duke.'

'Then, lady, you mistook me for my sister!' said Sebastian to Olivia. 'Yet nature guided the mistake, for though you loved a girl, you have married a man!'

'Cesario,' said the Duke to Viola. 'You have often said that you would never love a woman as you love me.'

'All that I said, I will swear to,' answered Viola, 'and all that I swear, I will keep as true as steel.'

'Then give me your hand,' said Orsino. 'And let me see you in your woman's clothes.'

'The captain who rescued me has my clothes,' said Viola. 'But he is in prison, on account of some suit brought against him by Malvolio, the Countess Olivia's gentleman.'

'We shall set him at liberty!' exclaimed Olivia. 'Fetch Malvolio. . . . Yet, I remember now, the poor man is out of his wits. . . . But bring him.'

When Malvolio appeared and showed Olivia the letter he had found in the garden, all was turned to mirth. For Olivia recognised the writing as Maria's, and Feste the jester told her the whole story.

So all was forgiven, and all injuries forgotten, and Sebastian and his wife Olivia led Viola into their house to be married to the Duke Orsino.

Part II

THE TRAGEDIES

ROMEO AND JULIET

THERE WERE ONCE two rich and powerful Italian families,
living in the city of Verona, who were at war with one another.
When a young Capulet and a young Montague met, there was
sure to be a fight, and often one or other was killed or severely
wounded. Their friends and servants joined in the quarrel; so
Verona was almost in a state of civil war.

One day a brawl in the streets between a few servants of the
two families grew and grew until there was a real battle. Benvolio,
one of the Montagues, tried his best to break up the fight, but
young Tybalt, a fiery Capulet, called him a coward and attacked
him.

Then, as the noise of battle swelled, the citizens of Verona
joined one side or the other, and the two heads of the families,
both elderly men, came hastening out to cheer on their several
followers.

But Escalus, the Prince of Verona, was determined to put an
end to all these riots and duels between the Capulets and the
Montagues. He and his guard arrived before the battle had gone
very far; and when the tumult was quelled and all stood in
respectful silence, he issued a decree:

'If ever you disturb our streets again, the penalty shall be death
or banishment for those who are guilty. This time I will enquire
no further as to who began the battle: but in the future, if the
peace is broken, I shall punish without mercy.'

Capulets and Montagues dispersed to their homes, and Benvolio went to seek his friend and cousin Romeo, Montague's son, who had not taken part in the battle, and tell him what had occurred.

When he found him he soon discovered that Romeo was interested in other matters than the family quarrel.

'You are so sad and serious these days,' said Benvolio teasingly to his friend. 'I think you must be in love!'

'Out!' sighed Romeo.

'Out of love?' smiled Benvolio.

'No. In love, but out of love's favor!' declared Romeo with another great sigh, and went on to tell of his passion for the beautiful, disdainful Rosaline, in such flowery and extravagant terms that Benvolio felt sure there was no danger of any real heartbreak.

'If she will have none of you,' he exclaimed, 'stop making yourself miserable over her. There are other pretty girls in Verona; look about you, you'll find fairer ladies than Rosaline, and kinder too.'

'To look on others is but to prove how far, far fairer is she than all the rest,' insisted Romeo. 'And I am wounded to the heart. I can never be cured.'

'Nonsense, my dear fellow,' said Benvolio. 'One fire burns out another's burning. Fall in love with someone else and you'll forget all about Rosaline in a moment.'

At this Romeo took offence, and was just about to stalk off in a huff when he bumped into one of Capulet's servants, a man called Peter, who was standing stock still in the middle of the street looking hard at a list of names. First he looked at the list rightside up; then he turned it upside down; and just to make sure he examined it sideways.

'Good day, sir!' he said with great relief when Romeo ran into him. 'Can you read?'

'Only too well!' sighed Romeo—'All my sad future in the misery of the moment!'

'Well, you may have learnt that without going to school,' said Peter. 'But can you read written things—things you've never seen before?'

'Indeed I can!' smiled Romeo; and taking the paper from the man's hand he read out the list of names, dwelling lovingly over one of them, 'my fair niece Rosaline.'

'This is a fine company,' he said when he had finished. 'Where are they to come?'

'Up,' answered Peter.

'But where?'

'To supper at our house.'

'Whose house?'

'My master's.'

'I suppose I should have begun by asking that,' said Romeo.

'Well, I'll tell you without asking,' said Peter. 'My master is the great rich Capulet, and if you are not one of the Montagues, I invite you in his name to come and join the feast tonight. Rest you merry!'

With that Peter hastened away on his errand, and Benvolio said:

'Let us go to this party. Most of the guests at these gatherings wear masks so no one will recognize us as Montagues. The beautiful Rosaline whom you love will be there, and you can compare her with all the fairest ladies of Verona.'

'I'll come,' declared Romeo, 'just to prove how impossible it is to find one fairer than my love!'

So the two went off to seek their friend Mercutio and persuade him and several others to go with them in disguise to the Capulet's masked ball that night.

Meanwhile the great house of the Capulets was all in a bustle of preparation, with old Capulet ordering the servants about in every direction until they fell over one another in their haste and anxiety.

Capulet's young wife at last left her excitable, quick-tempered husband to direct the preparations himself, and sought refuge with their fourteen-year-old daughter Juliet and her old nurse. She had something of great importance to tell Juliet before that evening, and this seemed a good opportunity for a quiet chat.

'Nurse,' said Lady Capulet, wondering how she would lead up

to what she had to tell, 'my daughter is growing up quickly. She's almost a young woman, is she not?'

'Faith, I can give you her age to a day!' cried the nurse who was extremely fond of hearing her own voice. 'If my daughter Susan had lived—God rest all Christian souls!—She was too good for me—they would have been the same age—but God called Susan out of this wicked world, and Susan would have been fourteen on—let me see! How long is it since the earthquake? It must be eleven years—How well I remember that day! I was sitting in the sun over by the wall of the dovecote. . . . Where was I? Yes, it must be eleven years since then, and Juliet was three, and could run and waddle all about—Why, only the day before she fell and cut her forehead, and my husband—he was still alive then —God rest his soul!—He was a merry man—he picked her up when she fell, and to stop her crying, he said——'

'And do you stop too, good Nurse!' Lady Capulet managed at last to get a word in.

'I have done!' puffed the nurse. 'God bless you, my Julie! You were the prettiest baby I ever nursed; and now my wish is to live long enough to see you happily married.'

'That is just what I came to talk about,' exclaimed Lady Capulet, thankful for so good a chance. 'Juliet, my dear, would you like to be married soon?'

'It is an honour I have scarcely thought about,' hesitated Juliet.

'Well, think about it now,' said her mother. 'Many ladies of Verona, quite as young as you, are already wives and even mothers. Why, you yourself were born when I was not much older than you now. Anyway, Count Paris, a young man both handsome and rich, has asked for your hand in marriage. You will see him tonight at our feast, and may tell whether you can love him. What do you think?'

'I'll try to love him, if to look and like is to love,' murmured Juliet confusedly.

Lady Capulet had more to say, but at that moment a servant dashed in to tell her that the earliest of the guests had arrived, that everything was in a muddle, and that she must come at once. Nor did she get another chance to speak with Juliet during the rest

of that day. Guests from a distance kept arriving, and old Capulet's attempts to greet them and superintend all the preparations at
the same time kept her fully occupied trying to restore order out
of the chaos which he created in his enthusiasm.

He was still busying himself later that evening when guests
were pouring in thickly, both friends and comparative strangers,
now mostly in cloaks and masks. Among them came Romeo,
with his friends Mercutio and Benvolio. They were welcomed
with the rest by Capulet who, at first, had no suspicion that they
were Montagues, and therefore his enemies.

Benvolio and Mercutio were soon joining in the dances and
feasting merrily with the other guests. But Romeo moved
moodily from group to group, looking for his lady-love the dark,
disdainful Rosaline, determined to appear lonely and miserable
to reproach her for her scorn.

Suddenly, however, he saw Juliet—and the dream-world in
which he had been playing with love fell away from him and
was forgotten as he realized what real love meant. He had fallen
truly and deeply in love at first sight.

When he had recovered a little from the shock of this new and
wonderful experience, he stopped one of the servants to ask:

'Who is that lady whose hand young Tybalt is holding in the
dance?'

'I do not know, sir,' answered the man, who chanced to be one
whom Capulet had hired for that night only.

'Even in this rich gathering she seems to shine so brightly that
the candles themselves might learn from her how to give light!'
murmured Romeo. 'She is like a single white dove in a whole
flock of crows. Could I but touch her hand, my own would be
blessed for ever more. Did I know love till now? It was some
shadow; for until this night I have never known what real beauty
is.'

Unfortunately, Juliet's wild and bloodthirsty young cousin
Tybalt heard Romeo's voice, if not his words, and exclaimed:

'By his voice, this must be a Montague! Boy, fetch me my
rapier! What, does this slave come in disguise to mock us? By

my honor, it would be no sin to strike him dead here and now!'

'How's this, nephew?' asked Capulet, 'Why are you storming and raging so?'

'Uncle!' spluttered Tybalt. 'That man over there is a Montague, one of our enemies. He has come here in disguise to mock and jeer at us.'

'It must be young Romeo,' began Capulet.

'Yes!' raged Tybalt. 'It's that villain Romeo!'

'Be quiet, nephew,' said Capulet. 'I have always heard of him as a noble and well behaved young man, and I will have no insult offered to him or to anyone who is a guest in my house.'

'I'll not endure him!' cried Tybalt.

'He shall be endured if I say!' exclaimed Capulet, beginning to lose his temper. 'Am I master here, or are you? Do as I tell you, and keep quiet—or I'll make you quiet.'

'Since I cannot punish him now, I'll go. But I shall pay him back for this insult.'

So saying, Tybalt raged out of the house, which was the most foolish thing he could have done. For now Romeo found his chance to take Juliet by the hand and lead her away in a dance.

Presently they paused together in an alcove, and Romeo said:

'Forgive me, fair saint, for profaning your hand with my own, so unworthy. My lips, like two blushing pilgrims, stand ready to smooth away my rough touch with a tender kiss.'

'Good pilgrim, you blame your hand too much,' murmured Juliet. 'Even a saint's hand may be touched by a true pilgrim—so I cannot blame you for taking mine.'

'Have not saints lips as well as hands—and pilgrims also?' asked Romeo.

'Yes, pilgrim. But lips to be used only for prayers.'

'Then, dear saint, grant what my lips pray for, lest faith turn to despair,' urged Romeo.

'But saints do not move, even when they grant prayers,' answered Juliet, not knowing what else to say.

'Then do you not move, sweet saint, until my prayer is answered,' said Romeo, kissing her. 'There! Now your lips have purged away the sin from mine.'

'But does not your sin now remain on my lips?' asked Juliet, longing now to be kissed again.

'Sin from my lips? Then give me back my sin!' whispered Romeo, drawing her to him and kissing her once more.

But meanwhile the old nurse had been keeping an eye on Juliet, and though she did not know who Romeo was, she felt that things had gone quite far enough. So now she bustled up, exclaiming:

'Madam, your mother wishes to speak with you.'

Full of confusion, Juliet hastened away, and Romeo asked the nurse:

'Who is her mother?'

'Why indeed, young sir, she is the lady of the house,' answered the nurse severely. 'And a good lady, and a wise one, and virtuous too. I nursed her daughter whom you were talking with. . . .'

But Romeo was not listening. 'She is a Capulet!' he thought. 'Then my very life belongs to one of my enemies!'

As Romeo stood like one dazed, Benvolio caught him by the arm and led him away, fearing that Tybalt would return and a fresh brawl break out.

It was some time after this that Juliet found the nurse again as many of the guests were leaving. She began hastily to ask who this and that one was, and as Romeo left asked his name too. The nurse who had just learnt it replied:

'His name is Romeo. He is the only son of your great enemy Montague.'

'Alas, alas! My only love given to the only man that I should hate!' cried Juliet, and fled weeping to her own room.

In the press of departing guests, Romeo broke away from Benvolio and Mercutio and dodged out of sight through the narrow streets of Verona.

'Romeo! Romeo!' shouted Mercutio drunkenly, trying in vain to overtake his friend. 'Come out from wherever you are hiding! I conjure you, by Rosaline's bright eyes and sweet red lips, to show yourself! Come out, mad lover, even if you come disguised as a sigh!'

But Romeo was not to be moved by the old magic, and

presently Mercutio and Benvolio gave up the search and reeled off to bed.

As if by instinct, Romeo had made his way round to the wall of Capulet's orchard, scrambled over, and hidden in the darkness beyond. When his two friends were far enough away, he crept out of hiding—only to linger in the shadows below the balcony of a lighted window.

There, very soon, Juliet appeared alone, seeming to him as bright as the very sun which kills the pale, cold moonbeams when it rises.

'It is my lady, oh it is my love!' Romeo's heart turned over, and he caught his breath in a sob of wonder and longing: 'Oh that she knew she were!'

Juliet's own love and longing were as intense as Romeo's, and now when she thought herself alone her feelings overflowed in words.

'Oh Romeo, Romeo!' she murmured, dwelling wistfully on the name. 'Oh why are you called Romeo? It is only your name that is my enemy. For, after all, what's in a name? A rose by any other name would smell as sweet. Then throw your name away, it is no part of you—and in exchange take me and all my love!'

'I take you at your word!' cried Romeo coming forward into the light from the window. 'Do but call me your love, and I'll be newly christened, and never more be Romeo!'

'My ears have not yet drunk in a hundred words uttered by that tongue—yet I know its sound!' gasped Juliet. 'You are Romeo—and a Montague.'

'No longer one nor the other, if you dislike either!' cried Romeo.

'Why have you dared to come here?' asked Juliet, looking anxiously behind her. 'This place is death for a Montague. If any of my relations see you, they will murder you.'

'It is a surer death to be away from you,' protested Romeo. 'Love drew me here and will not let me go.'

'I would not have told you that I loved you before you had asked me,' said Juliet softly. 'But since you have already heard me confess it, I'll not take back my words. But you must not think that so quick and readily confessed a love is of small worth. In truth, I shall prove more constant than those who are coy and take most wooing.'

So the two lovers continued telling each other the depth and constancy of their love, until Juliet heard the nurse calling her from inside the house.

'Just three words more, dear Romeo, and then goodnight,' she said. 'If you love me truly and honorably, and wish me to be your wife, send word tomorrow where and at what time we can meet to be secretly married. I'll find you a messenger whom I can trust.'

Again the nurse called, and Juliet sped in—only to return a few moments later.

'For the last time, my love. Goodnight! Goodnight! Parting is such sweet sorrow, I could say "goodnight" till morning!'

When he was sure that Juliet would come no more to the window, Romeo climbed back over the orchard wall, and set out for the cell where Friar Laurence, his Father Confessor, lived, for he now greatly needed help.

The good old priest was already up, though day was scarcely dawning, gathering herbs to make ointment and medicines for his poorer parishioners. He listened to Romeo's confession with an amused smile, and asked if he had so soon forgotten Rosaline.

'You often blamed me for loving Rosaline!' exclaimed Romeo.

'For doting foolishly, not for loving!'

'And you told me to bury this love.'

'Certainly. But not to put it in the grave and take out another instead!'

'Ah, but she whom I love now is different!' cried Romeo. 'She is as eager as I, and returns me love for love.'

'Rosaline knew well that you were in love with love and not with her,' said Friar Laurence gently. 'But this time I believe you, and will do all I can to help you and Juliet. For this marriage may prove a happy union to more than yourselves; it may end forever the quarrel between the houses of Montague and Capulet.'

Having made his arrangements with Friar Laurence, and spent

a little time with him in prayer, Romeo set out to find his friends
Benvolio and Mercutio, and waited for the messenger from
Juliet to find him.

Scarcely had he discovered them, when the old nurse arrived,
and Romeo told her what he had planned with Friar Laurence,
and sent her back to tell Juliet to come to the cell that afternoon
to be shriven—and also to be married.

Juliet was waiting impatiently when the old woman returned,
and the nurse could not forebear teasing her and keeping her
waiting for the news, until Juliet was nearly frantic.

'Sweet Nurse,' she sobbed, 'tell me what Romeo says!'

'Have you got leave to go for shrift today?'

'I have,' answered Juliet, wondering if the nurse was going to
change the subject yet again.

'Well then, off you go to Friar Laurence's cell. There waits a
husband to make you a wife! Ah-ha!' chuckled the nurse kindly,

'now your cheeks are pale no longer! Well, off to church you go, while I meet Romeo's man who is to give me a rope-ladder which Romeo may climb tonight!'

So the two lovers were married, and kind old Friar Laurence called down blessings on their union, and bade Juliet hasten home so that nothing might be suspected from too long an absence.

Shortly after she had gone, Romeo left the cell also, and was walking quietly through the streets of Verona when suddenly he came upon Tybalt, Juliet's fiery cousin, with several of the Capulets, exchanging high words with Benvolio and Mercutio.

'Ah-ha!' cried Tybalt as soon as he saw Romeo. 'Here's the villain I want!'

'Tybalt, I am no villain,' answered Romeo. 'I hope that you may learn to know me better, and find that I do not deserve such a greeting.'

'Boy,' snapped Tybalt insolently, 'this shall not excuse the injuries you have done me. So draw your sword and defend yourself.'

The last thing in the world Romeo wanted to do was to fight with a Capulet, and his wife's cousin at that. So he replied as mildly as possible:

'Tybalt, I never injured you. Indeed I love you better than you can realize, till you know the reason for my love. And so, good Capulet—a name I hold as dear as my own—be satisfied.'

But this gentleness on Romeo's part seemed to Mercutio mere cowardice. 'Tybalt!' he shouted, drawing his sword, 'come with me!'

'What do you want with me?' asked Tybalt.

'Good king of cats, nothing but one of your nine lives!' jeered Mercutio. 'So out with your sword before I thrash you with the flat of mine.'

'I'm ready for you!' cried Tybalt, drawing his rapier and standing on guard.

'Gentle Mercutio, sheath your sword!' begged Romeo.

But Mercutio would pay no attention, and engaged with Tybalt.

'Draw, Benvolio!' cried Romeo. 'Draw, and help me beat down their weapons! Gentlemen, for shame! Tybalt! Mercutio! Remember the Prince's decree against any further warfare between our houses! Hold Tybalt! Good Mercutio!'

Romeo caught his friend's arm in a vain attempt to stop the fight, and Tybalt took advantage of this to run Mercutio through with impunity, and then turn and fly.

'I am hurt!' gasped Mercutio, sinking to the ground. 'I am killed! A plague on both your houses! Why the devil did you come between us? I was hurt under your arm.'

'I thought all for the best,' said Romeo, kneeling by his friend's side.

'Help me away, Benvolio!' gasped Mercutio, 'I do not want to die in the very streets! Oh, a plague on your houses!'

Romeo had scarcely time to collect his thoughts, before Benvolio came back to tell him that Mercutio was dead; and at that very moment Tybalt came stalking proudly past again.

This was more than Romeo could bear:

'Alive, in triumph, and Mercutio slain!' he exclaimed. 'Now Tybalt, take back the name of villain, or stand and fight! Mercutio's soul waits for one or both of us to accompany him!'

Tybalt asked for nothing better, and a moment later their swords clashed together. But he had met his match this time; and it was not long before he lay dead, with Romeo standing above him, stunned and horrified at what he had done.

'Romeo! Away quickly!' cried Benvolio. 'If you are caught, the Prince will condemn you to death!'

'Oh, I am fortune's fool!' exclaimed Romeo, and turning, he ran to seek shelter in Friar Laurence's cell.

He was only just in time, for when Prince Escalus arrived on the scene a few minutes later, both Capulet and Montague were there, crying for vengeance on the slayers of Tybalt and Mercutio.

Having heard all that had happened, Escalus pronounced solemn sentence:

'Tybalt began the quarrel and killed Mercutio, therefore I will not condemn Romeo to death. But as he killed Tybalt, I will banish him from Verona. If he is found anywhere in Verona after sunrise tomorrow, he dies.'

Juliet was waiting eagerly for the coming of night which should bring Romeo to her, when the old nurse arrived with the news. 'Ah, well-a-day! He's dead!' she cried. 'He's dead! He's dead! We are undone! He's gone, he's killed, he's dead! Oh Romeo, Romeo, who ever would have thought it!—Romeo!'

For a long time Juliet thought that it was Romeo who was dead, for the old woman wandered on in her usual muddled fashion without explaining what had happened.

When at last she learned the truth, Juliet's grief knew no bounds. At first she blamed Romeo, calling him a beautiful tyrant, an angelic fiend, a wolfish lamb and a dove-feathered raven. But very soon she was lamenting the banishment of her husband, finding a hundred excuses for Romeo, and realizing that the one word 'banished' brought her greater grief than the death of ten thousand Tybalts. Indeed, she seemed almost ready to die of grief, until the kind old nurse brought her true comfort:

'Go to your room,' she said. 'I know where Romeo is hiding. He's in Friar Laurence's cell. Take the cords up which he may climb to your balcony. I'll send him to comfort you.'

Romeo himself was in just such grief, and it took Friar Laurence a long time to make him see reason, even after the nurse arrived with her message from Juliet.

'Go now to your wife,' said the Friar, when at last Romeo grew calm. 'But be sure you are away from Verona by sunrise. Go straight to Mantua and stay there. Leave your servant Balthasar here, and I will send messages to you by him. I must find some way of reconciling your parents by means of the marriage, and of winning your pardon from the Prince.'

So Romeo spent this one night with Juliet; and early in the morning when the first lark sang—which Juliet in vain wished was the nightingale—he stole out of Verona and rode away to Mantua.

But there was more trouble waiting for this poor pair of star-crossed lovers. Seeing that Juliet was pining, as they thought, for

Tybalt's death, her parents quickly prepared for her wedding with young Count Paris, telling her nothing about it until two days before.

Poor Juliet refused to marry Paris. But her parents insisted, and since in those days parents had absolute control over their children, there was nothing she could do. Even the nurse could not help—she could only advise Juliet to forget about Romeo and marry Paris.

In absolute despair, and thinking of killing herself if all else failed, Juliet went to consult Friar Laurence. She was not allowed out of her parents' house without an armed guard; but the men remained outside the Friar's cell, so she was able to tell him all her troubles in complete secrecy.

When he realized that Juliet was actually ready to stab herself rather than marry Paris, the Friar proposed a bold and desperate scheme.

'Tomorrow is Wednesday,' he said, 'and your wedding to the Count is fixed for Thursday morning. Go home now, and tell your parents you are sorry, and will obey them. But tomorrow night take this drug and hide the bottle. You will fall asleep so deeply that to all who see or touch you it will seem that you are dead; for you will be cold and stiff just like a corpse, and will remain in that state for forty-two hours. Your parents will bury you in the vault under the Capulet monument in the churchyard, replace the stone slabs over the top, and leave you there. I will send a message to Romeo to return by night, and he and I will be ready to rescue you from the crypt when you wake. Can you dare to do this?'

Juliet readily agreed, took the phial which the Friar gave her, and on the following night drank the potion as he had instructed —though not without many fears of waking too soon in the tomb, or of being left there to die among the bones of her ancestors if anything happened to Friar Laurence.

Next day, when Count Paris came to lead her to church, he found himself following instead, as a mourner at her funeral. Another mourner was Balthasar, Romeo's servant; and when he had seen Juliet laid in her grave, he took horse and galloped to

Mantua without even stopping to see if there was any message from Friar Laurence.

There he found Romeo, and told him that his lady was dead and buried.

Life was now not worth living, and Romeo, having bought a deadly poison, set out that night for Verona intending to die beside Juliet in the tomb.

There he arrived just too soon. For Friar Laurence's messenger had been stopped on the way, and had never reached Mantua. He had hastened back to the Friar who at once set out for the tomb to be there when Juliet woke from her drugged sleep.

But Romeo arrived first. As he was breaking open the tomb, Count Paris came to strew flowers on Juliet's grave, and would not listen to explanations. He attacked Romeo who was forced to kill him in self-defence.

Then Romeo raised the slabs of stone in the floor of the Capulet monument, and climbed down into the vault where Juliet lay cold and still, but as beautiful as ever.

Kneeling beside her, Romeo bade her farewell:

'Eyes, look your last,' he murmured. 'Arms, take your last embrace; and be this my final kiss the seal of faith testifying that my love is true to all eternity.'

Then he drank the poison, and sinking down beside Juliet, was dead in a few moments.

Scarcely had he ceased to breathe when Friar Laurence arrived at the monument, stumbling over the graves in his haste. But he was too late. As he bent over Romeo, Juliet woke suddenly from her trance and sat up, exclaiming:

'Dear, faithful Friar! Where is my husband? I remember where I should be, and there I am. But where is Romeo?'

'Lady,' said Friar Laurence solemnly. 'We may plan, but God directs what shall happen, and He has decreed otherwise than we intended. Your husband lies dead beside you, and Paris is dead too. Come away with me, and I will hide you among a sisterhood of holy nuns. Come quickly, for the watch is on its way and will arrest us. Follow me! I can wait no longer!'

Friar Laurence scrambled out of the vault and fled across the churchyard, where the watchmen were already looking for Romeo, having been called by Paris's servant.

But Juliet did not follow him. She realized at a glance what had happened, and decided to stay with Romeo. She took the cup from his hand and saw that he had taken poison.

'Ah, how mean of you to drink it all,' she whispered, 'and not to leave one friendly drop to help me on my way to join you!'

Now she heard the watchmen drawing near above her and shouting to one another. Swiftly she took Romeo's dagger and sheathed it in her heart, kissing in death his lips that were still warm.

Then the watch arrived at the tomb, having caught Friar Laurence, and also Balthasar who had hidden in the churchyard to see what would happen. Soon both Capulet and Montague followed, and with them Prince Escalus. Friar Laurence told the whole tragic story, and Balthasar added all he knew and gave the Prince a letter which Romeo had left with him to give Montague.

'See, Capulet and Montague, the terrible result of your quarrel,' said the Prince solemnly. 'Even the love which God sent to join these two has been turned into a punishment on you both.'

'Brother Montague,' said Capulet, 'Forgive me. Here is my hand. This is my daughter's marriage portion, I can give no more, nor ask more of you.'

'But I can offer more,' said Montague, taking his old enemy's hand. 'For I will have a statue of Juliet made in pure gold, which shall be among the chief treasures of Verona so long as our city endures.'

'As rich shall Romeo lie in gold beside his Juliet,' said Capulet. 'Poor sacrifices to our foolish quarrel.'

And so in this sad way peace was made between the Capulets and Montagues, and the statues of the two lovers remained as a warning of what such quarrels might lead to.

> 'For never was a story of more woe
> Than this of Juliet and her Romeo.'

HAMLET

HAMLET, KING OF DENMARK, died suddenly one afternoon while sleeping in his orchard. It was given out that a strange serpent had bitten him, and certainly when he lay in state everyone could see that his skin was covered with spots and blotches as if a sudden leprosy had seized him and killed him in an instant.

At that time kings in Denmark were elected; and though many people expected the late king's son, Hamlet, to succeed him, his brother Claudius was chosen instead. No one dared to question his doings even when, to make his throne more secure, he married his brother's widow, Queen Gertrude, contrary to the rules of the Church.

Claudius was both crowned and married by the time young Hamlet returned to his home in Denmark from Wittenberg where he had been studying at the University. And young Hamlet found himself in both a difficult and dangerous position. He and his friends felt that Claudius had rushed the election in order to become king before Hamlet could challenge his succession; and it was whispered that Claudius, who was known to be unscrupulous, knew more than he should of the late king's death—and had had an understanding with the Queen during her first husband's life.

But Hamlet could do nothing. He had but the barest of suspicions—any suggestion of which would merely be taken as an attempt to stir up trouble because he had not been elected to

succeed his father. Claudius was a hard liver, a hard drinker—and
a hard hater; and Hamlet knew that his life would be in danger if
he made any attempt to accuse him or suggest that something was
rotten in the state of Denmark. Claudius in fact would leap at any
chance of removing so dangerous a rival.

The state was certainly in a far from healthy condition. Fortinbras, the brave and gallant young Prince of Norway was gathering his army to invade Denmark, demanding the return of lands
which the late King Hamlet had taken from his father in an earlier
war; and Claudius felt that there might be many, even in Denmark, who would side with Fortinbras who, besides Hamlet,
should also have been a candidate for the Danish throne on the old
king's death.

To make matters worse, there were ugly rumors among the
soldiers on guard in the royal castle of Elsinore. Not one of them
would keep watch alone on the high stone platform overlooking
the sea during the hours of darkness. As midnight drew near,
the sentry became more and more anxious and afraid lest his
relief and an officer should fail to arrive before the clock struck
twelve. . . .

One night, not two months after the king's death, Francisco
was pacing anxiously up and down with his pike at the ready,
waiting to be relieved. The castle clock struck twelve, the
deep strokes echoing on the frosty air. . . . There was a slight
sound:

'Who's there?' shouted Francisco, whipping round, the end of
his pike waving wildly.

'You answer first! Who are you?' cried another voice, almost
as scared as his. It was Bernardo, his relief. 'Have you had quiet
guard?' he asked anxiously.

'Not a mouse stirring,' said Francisco thankfully.

'Well, goodnight,' said Bernardo, taking up his position on the
platform. 'If you see Marcellus and Horatio, who should also be
on watch, tell them to hurry!'

'I think I hear them,' answered Francisco; and he strode
away saluting the two officers as he passed.

'Has the thing appeared again tonight?' asked Marcellus as soon as he and Horatio had joined Bernardo.

'I have seen nothing,' answered Bernardo.

'Horatio says it is only our imagination,' said Marcellus, 'and he does not believe that we have twice seen this terrible sight. But I have begged him to come and watch with us, so that if it appears again we may prove that we spoke the truth—and he may speak to it if he dares.'

The three of them sat down by the fire while Bernardo began to tell Horatio what he and Marcellus had seen only the previous night as the clock was striking one.

'Sssh! Stop talking!' interrupted Marcellus suddenly in a tense whisper. 'Look! Here it comes again!'

'The very same!' gasped Bernardo. 'The very image of the dead king. Look, Horatio! Is he not like the king? . . . Speak to it, Horatio!'

'What are you?' asked Horatio taking a step towards the ghostly figure which had appeared out of the darkness. 'Why do you wear the likeness of King Hamlet, who is dead and buried? By Heaven, I bid you speak!'

But the ghost only faded away; and the three men returned to their seats by the brazier, casting apprehensive glances around them, to discuss their extraordinary experience.

'I would not believe this if I had not seen it with my own eyes,' said Horatio who, being young Hamlet's close friend and fellow scholar at Wittenberg, was not inclined to be as superstitious as the two regular soldiers.

'Is it not like the king?' queried Marcellus.

'As like as you are to yourself,' answered Horatio with conviction. 'I saw him just as he is now, in full armor, on the day he won his victory over the Poles in the great battle on the ice. . . . In my opinion this means that something is wrong in Denmark, and we may expect a terrible crisis.'

At this Marcellus and Bernardo fell to discussing the current news, and Horatio told them all he knew of the preparations for war with Norway. Then they went on to compare this with other cases of ghostly appearances foreshadowing dreadful events, and

Horatio was just telling them of the signs and portents seen in Rome before the murder of Julius Caesar, when suddenly the ghost came gliding towards them again.

'I'll cross it, though it should blast me!' exclaimed Horatio, springing to his feet and advancing towards the apparition, making the holy sign of the Cross as he did so. 'Stay and speak!' he cried to the ghost. 'Tell us, if there is anything we can do which can set your soul at rest so that you may lie quietly in your grave. Speak, if you know of any danger threatening your country. . . . Stay and speak! Stop it, Marcellus!'

'Shall I strike at it with my pike?' cried Marcellus.

'Do, if it will not stand!' commanded Horatio.

The three men tried to surround the ghost, but it faded from sight, leaving them standing round an empty space.

'It was about to speak, when the cock crowed,' said Bernardo.

'Then it started, as if summoned away,' agreed Horatio. 'Now I suggest that as soon as it is morning we go and tell young Hamlet all that we have seen. I am certain the ghost will speak to him. . . .'

Hamlet was in a mood of deep depression when Horatio found him. He was utterly disgusted with the way his uncle, King Claudius, behaved—and even more so at his mother's hasty remarriage to such a vile man after being the wife of so noble a husband as the late king. 'My own flesh is stained and sullied through what she has done,' he thought; 'if only it could melt into a fog and drift away! If only suicide were not contrary to God's law. . . . Everything is wrong, wretched and evil. But I may not breathe a word of what I feel. My heart must break in silence.'

Horatio wasted no time in telling Hamlet of what he and Marcellus and Bernardo had seen, nor did Hamlet find it hard to believe:

'My father's spirit—and fully armed!' he thought. 'I suspect there *has* been foul play. Such deeds cannot be hidden, though buried under the very earth.'

'I will watch with you tonight,' he said to Horatio and the two soldiers. 'If it assumes my father's form, I'll speak to this ghost, though Hell itself should open to prevent me. I beg you all to keep silent about what you have seen—and still more, about what we may see tonight. . . .'

It was colder than ever on the battlements when Hamlet joined Horatio and Marcellus who were waiting there for him as midnight was striking. Below them in the castle King Claudius and his drunken followers were still feasting and—according to an old custom which he had revived—whenever he drained his goblet, there was a flourish of trumpets, and a cannon boomed out over the frosty air.

'No wonder other countries call us drunkards,' remarked Hamlet bitterly. 'My uncle's way of life is already infecting the court; and this old custom, which to my mind is more honoured in the breach than in the observance, sets an example to the whole nation. So one canker spreads——'

'Look, my lord!' interrupted Horatio suddenly. 'Here it comes!'

'Angels and ministers of grace defend us!' gasped Hamlet, crossing himself as the shadowy figure drew near. 'Stay and speak, whether you are a fiend from Hell come to tempt me, or a Heavenly soul returned to earth for some divine reason. Answer me! Let me not burst in ignorance! Hamlet! Father! King! Royal Dane! Say why you have broken out of the tomb and, clad in armour, revisit these glimpses of the moon, making night terrible by your ghostly presence?'

'It beckons to you,' cried Horatio.

'Do not go with it!' cried Marcellus.

'By no means,' agreed Horatio. 'Suppose it should lead you to the edge of the cliff and tempt you to fling yourself over into the sea far below?'

'Nevertheless, I'll follow it!' cried Hamlet. 'I set no value on my life—and it cannot harm my soul. Go on, I'll follow!'

The ghost moved away into the darkness, and Hamlet went where it led until they were beyond sight and hearing of Horatio and Marcellus.

'Listen,' said the ghost suddenly. 'I have only a little time, for very soon I must return to Purgatory where the sins of my lifetime are being burnt away.'

'Alas, poor ghost,' gasped Hamlet.

'Do not pity me, but listen carefully,' the ghost continued. 'I am your father's spirit, doomed for a certain time to walk by night, and by day to fast in fires. If ever you loved me, your father, revenge my foul and most unnatural murder.'

'Murder!' cried Hamlet.

'Murder most foul,' went on the ghost solemnly. 'It is said that while I slept in my orchard as usual, a serpent stung me. But this is a lie by which all Denmark is deceived. The serpent that caused my death now wears my crown!'

'Oh my prophetic soul—my uncle!' gasped Hamlet.

'Yes, that vile and impure man,' said the ghost. 'Not content with leading your mother astray and persuading her to help in all his wicked schemes, he stole upon me as I slept and poured poison into my ear. . . . Hamlet, revenge this most horrible murder. But whatever you do, take no vengeance on your mother. Leave her punishment to Heaven. I must go. Farewell. Remember me!'

'Remember you? Always—forever!' sobbed Hamlet as the ghost faded from sight. The shock of his experience was almost more than he could bear; but he managed, when Horatio and Marcellus found him, to swear them to even greater secrecy.

'Swear never to tell what you have seen tonight,' he insisted holding the cross-hilt of his sword for them to lay their hands on. 'Swear to stand by me in whatever I decide to do. If I pretend to be mad, which I may do, swear not to show that you know I am only pretending—or that you know any reason for it. Swear on my sword!'

And the ghost echoed his word with a solemn 'Swear!' as he held the sword for them.

'Oh day and night, but this is indeed strange,' said Horatio, quite overcome.

'There are more things in Heaven and Earth, Horatio, than philosophy dreams of,' said Hamlet solemnly, taking his friend's arm. 'The time is out of joint, but that I was born to put it right is almost more than I can endure.'

Hamlet, indeed, was so upset by his interview with the ghost that it was not difficult for him to pretend to be mad. For he was suffering from terrible doubts. He had no way of knowing whether the ghost had indeed been his father's spirit, sent by God with a true message; or whether it was a fiend from Hell come to tempt him to damnation. And he brooded on this problem until he became pale and ill, and could think of little else.

Queen Gertrude was much troubled by her son's mental sickness; and although he may secretly have been pleased, King Claudius did his best to find out what was troubling Hamlet. His most faithful councillor was a pompous, long-winded old man called Polonius. Now Polonius had a daughter, Ophelia, with whom it seemed that Hamlet was in love. When she confessed Hamlet's attentions to her, Polonius, who delighted to meddle in other people's affairs, warned her solemnly that Hamlet was only flirting. He commanded her to give back all Hamlet's presents, and advised her to treat him coldly.

One day, not long after Hamlet's meeting with the ghost, Ophelia came to her father in tears, telling him that she was sure Hamlet had gone mad through unrequited love, and that she was the cause.

Polonius was delighted at having discovered the reason for the prince's madness, and hastened to tell the King and Queen. The King was doubtful; but the easy-going Queen felt quite confident that his disappointment in love, added to the shock of his father's death, was quite enough to account for Hamlet's condition. However, she readily agreed with the King's suggestion that two friends of Hamlet's, Rosencrantz and Guildenstern, should be paid to spy on him and try to discover from him what the trouble was.

This method, however, proved unsuccessful, for neither of these dishonest young men was clever enough to conceal from Hamlet that they had been sent by the King to keep him company.

Following up Polonius's suggestion, the King then set himself to spy on Hamlet when he was alone with Ophelia.

Now, part of Hamlet's reason for pretending to be mad had been to give Ophelia an excuse to refuse his love, for he loved her deeply enough not to want her involved in any plot against King Claudius. The interview on which the King and Polonius were spying had not gone very far, however, before Hamlet began to suspect what was happening. Realizing that Ophelia must be in the plot as well, he became harsher and harsher, and more abusive in what he said, ending:

'I say we will have no more marriages. Those that are married already, all but one, shall live; the rest shall keep as they are. To a nunnery, go!'

Hamlet dashed away in a frenzy, leaving Ophelia in tears, and the King and Polonius came out from hiding.

'This madness of Hamlet's has nothing to do with love,' said the King. 'Indeed, though he spoke oddly, it was not like madness. He has something on his mind, and I greatly fear that he may become dangerous. I will send him to England on a mission, which will give him something else to think of, and may perhaps cure him.'

'I still think his madness springs from unrequited love,' insisted Polonius. 'To send him to England is a good idea; but make one more attempt to find out what is troubling him. Let his mother entreat him, all alone, to tell her what is upsetting him so. I will hide behind the curtain in her room and listen to all he says. That must be later this evening. Before then we shall attend the players who have come to Elsinore and are giving a performance at Lord Hamlet's special request.'

'It is well to humor him,' agreed the King. 'I will tell the Queen to send for him after the play. Be sure you are there in hiding. Madness in great ones must not go unwatched.'

Hamlet was indeed on the edge of madness. He could not make up his mind what to do; and once again his unhappiness and uncertainty were turning his thoughts towards suicide. He was debating endlessly, endlessly with himself whether it was better to be alive or dead, braver to endure whatever might happen or to plunge a dagger into his own heart.

'To sleep,' he moaned. 'To die and so find rest—so end all the heartaches and mischances that are the lot of mankind. To die . . . To sleep. . . . But perhaps to dream. . . . That's where the trouble lies. What dreams are there in death? What makes us fear to end our life with the help of a naked dagger? The dread of something after death, the undiscovered country from whose border no traveller returns, makes us rather endure the misery we know of than fly to sufferings of which we know nothing.'

Such was his mood when he learnt that the players had come to Elsinore. On former visits no one had delighted more in their performances than he had; and now he was able to forget his troubles for a few minutes as his old friends acted fragments of plays for him. Yet when one of them gave a speech about the death of King Priam of Troy and was moved to tears by his own narrative, Hamlet felt it as a reproach to him that he had still done nothing to avenge his father's murder. Now suddenly he saw a chance of proving that the ghost had brought a true message—and that to kill Claudius would be no more than an act of justice.

'I have heard,' he thought, 'that guilty people sitting at a play have by the very cunning of the scene been moved immediately to confess their wicked deeds. . . . Though it has no tongue, murder will speak out most wonderfully. . . . I'll get these players so to act a scene, like the murder of my father—in front of my uncle. . . . I'll watch his every look, his every move. If he shows any sign of guilt, I'll know that the ghost was indeed my father's spirit, and spoke only the truth. Yes! The play's the thing wherein I'll catch the conscience of the King!'

When Hamlet had instructed the players, and made sure that the King and the rest of the court were coming to the play, he drew Horatio aside and said:

'Horatio, you are my dearest—my only true friend. Help me now. One scene of the play tonight is very near the circumstances of my father's death, about which I told you. Watch the King—watch his every expression. If what he sees tonight does not reveal his guilt, the ghost comes from Hell—and my imagination is more vile than words can describe. Sssh! They are coming. Choose a good place from which you may watch.'

When all the audience was assembled, the play began. At first Claudius treated it with a bored condescension, but soon he began to get interested. . . . The Player King and the Player

Queen vowed their eternal love and faith to one another. The
Player King hinted that he might soon die, and his wife find
another husband to comfort her—but she would have none of
such a suggestion:

> 'In second husband let me be accurst!
> None wed the second but who killed the first,'

she declared, and continued to profess her love and constancy at
great length. At last the Player King bade her leave him to sleep
on the flowery bank in the garden, and having blessed him, she
stole softly away.

'How do you like the play?' Hamlet asked his mother.

'I think the lady protests too much,' she answered.

'Oh, but she'll keep her word!' cried Hamlet.

'Do you know what happens in the play?' asked the King. 'I
hope there is nothing offensive in it?'

'Oh no,' answered Hamlet. 'They only jest—*poison* in jest!
Nothing offensive. . . . Why, it is based on a murder that happened in Vienna. . . . Sssh! This is one Lucianus, the King's
nephew.'

A dark-cloaked, villainous figure slunk onto the stage, and
went through such antics of wickedness that Hamlet lost patience:

'Begin, murderer!' he shouted. 'Stop making those damnable
faces, and begin!'

After making a suitable speech, Lucianus held up his vial of
poison and poured it into the Player King's ear. . . .

'He poisons him in the garden for his kingdom!' cried Hamlet,
unable to wait for the play to speak for itself. 'You may find the
story in Italian. Presently you shall see how the murderer gets the
love of the Queen!'

This was more than Claudius could stand. With a cry, he leapt
to his feet and rushed from the room, the whole court following
him until only Hamlet and Horatio remained.

'I'll take the ghost's word now!' cried Hamlet. 'Did you see?'

'Very clearly, my lord,' answered Horatio.

'When poisoning was mentioned', went on Hamlet—but

broke off suddenly as Rosencrantz and Guildenstern came hastening back to tell him that the King was much annoyed by his
behaviour, and that the Queen wished him to go and see her later
on. Meanwhile they continued their clumsy attempts at spying,
until Hamlet lost patience with them, and told them off for their
impertinence.

They had no answer to make, and were looking thoroughly
tongue-tied and sheepish, when Polonius came bustling in to say
that the Queen was waiting for Hamlet.

'Go and tell her I am coming,' said Hamlet shortly, and off
went Polonius.

'Now, leave me, friends,' said Hamlet, and Horatio also went,
while Rosencrantz and Guildenstern hastened away to consult
with the King—who told them that they must be ready to accompany Hamlet to England as soon as possible.

Left alone, Claudius broke down for a moment. 'My crime is
like a hideous stink rising up to God for vengeance,' he thought.
'It has the same curse on it as that of the first murder, when Cain

slew his brother Abel. . . . Yet there is forgiveness even for such a sin as mine—even though my hand were thicker than itself with brother's blood. . . . But how can I pray for mercy? It cannot be true repentance to keep those things for which I did the murder—the throne and my queen. . . . Can I be pardoned, and still keep the proceeds of crime? Yet what else can I do? Help, angels—let me repent truly and pray sincerely. All may yet be well with my soul.'

Thinking such thoughts, Claudius sank to his knees in the little oratory curtained off from the throne-room, buried his face in his hands, and strove to pray with more than mere words.

He was kneeling thus when Hamlet passed through the room on his way to visit the Queen, and he did not see or hear him. But Hamlet caught a glimpse of his uncle through the curtains of the oratory, and paused, his hand on his sword.

'Now I could kill him easily,' he thought. 'Yes, I'll kill him while he kneels there. But if I kill him praying, his soul goes to Heaven; yet he murdered my father who was asleep and unprepared, who had not made confession nor received absolution. . . . This is merely to be an executioner, not to be the minister of vengeance. No, live a little longer, villain though you are, until I can cut you off in the middle of some sin—and send you straight to Hell.'

So thinking, Hamlet pushed back the half-drawn sword into its sheath, and went quietly on his way still making excuses to himself for not coming to the point and killing his father's murderer. Claudius rose from his knees a few minutes later groaning, 'I can only utter empty words, my thoughts cling to the fruits of my crime. Words without thoughts of true repentance cannot win to Heaven.'

Hamlet came to his mother's room with his mind already inflamed with anger at his own failure to kill Claudius, and she made matters worse in her usual thoughtless way by beginning immediately:

'Hamlet, you have offended your father deeply——' meaning his stepfather the King.

'Mother, you have offended *my* father deeply,' he replied, trembling with rage and disgust.

'Have you forgotten who I am?' cried the Queen, annoyed by Hamlet's tone.

'No, I have not,' he answered coldly. 'You are the Queen— your husband's brother's wife, and—I wish it were not so—you are my mother.'

'If that is your way of speaking to me, I'll leave you to those who can answer you as you deserve,' she exclaimed, springing to her feet.

Hamlet caught her by the wrists and forced her back into her seat, hissing, 'Stay where you are; you shall not move until I have set before you a glass in which you may see to the very depths of your wicked soul.'

'What are you doing?' screamed the Queen. 'You are not going to murder me, are you?'

At this Polonius, who was hidden behind a curtain, lost his head and shouted for help. Hearing him, Hamlet thought it was the king and drawing his sword lunged at the curtain, crying: 'A rat! A rat!'

'What have you done?' gasped the Queen, as there came a cry and a groan, and then silence. 'What rash and bloody deed is this?'

'Almost as bad, mother,' said Hamlet grimly, 'as to kill a king and then marry his brother.'

'Kill a king!' gasped the Queen.

'That was what I said,' answered Hamlet as he drew back the curtain, hoping to find Claudius lying there dead. He was sorry to find Polonius, but felt that the old man had brought his death on himself. He had played the spy once too often. Moreover, to kill Polonius under whatever circumstances was not so serious a matter in those days as to kill a king who reigned by divine right and, however badly he might fill the position, was none the less God's viceroy on earth.

Nevertheless Hamlet was upset by what had occurred, and he proceeded to become more and more hysterical as he scolded his mother and reproached her for deserting his father for such a man as Claudius.

Suddenly, like a cold breath across his hot torrent of

words, the ghost of King Hamlet appeared to him once more, and spoke to him—though the Queen could see and hear nothing.

'Do not forget,' said the ghost solemnly. 'This visitation is to remind you of the duty which you seem almost to have forgotten. Now speak to your mother—and be pitiful to her.'

Then he faded away, nor could Hamlet understand how his mother had been unable to hear or see what he had heard and seen. And indeed when Hamlet told her, it merely confirmed her belief that he was mad.

The death of Polonius gave Claudius an excellent excuse for sending Hamlet off to England immediately. But the King realized only too well that it might have been himself rather than Polonius who had fallen before Hamlet's sword, and decided to be rid of him once and for all. So he gave to Rosencrantz and Guildenstern a secret letter for the King of England, who at that time accepted the ruler of Denmark as his overlord, commanding him to put Hamlet to death immediately.

Hamlet, however, suspected Claudius and knew that his two companions carried a letter of importance. So one night during the voyage he crept to their cabin and stole the letter. When he had read it, he wrote another in the same style, but bidding the King of England have the two messengers who gave him the letter executed immediately. He folded this so as to look exactly like the original letter, sealed it with the royal Danish seal which he had on his father's ring, and returned it without Rosencrantz and Guildenstern suspecting anything.

The very next day the ship was attacked by pirates. They were beaten off, and the ship continued on its way to England. But Hamlet was captured by the pirates during the battle, and was set safely ashore in Denmark, leaving Rosencrantz and Guildenstern to go on to meet their fate.

Hamlet returned to find Denmark in an even more troubled state than when he had left it. For Polonius had a son called Laertes who had been away at the time of his father's death, but came hastening home eager to avenge it. He was even more anxious to do so when he found that his unfortunate sister Ophelia had been driven mad by the shock, coming so soon after the sad ending of her love-affair with Hamlet.

Laertes gathered a great band of followers and marched to Elsinore, meaning to kill Claudius whom he thought was responsible for Polonius's death. But the cunning King soon persuaded him that Hamlet was entirely to blame, and would have been punished at once had it not been that the ordinary people of Denmark loved him for his father's sake and might have caused a revolution.

When news came that Hamlet had returned alone, Claudius at once began to plot his death. Laertes seemed the best tool he could use, particularly since Ophelia fell into a stream in her madness and was drowned. Claudius played so cleverly upon Laertes's grief and anger that the young man was ready to take his revenge on Hamlet by any means in his power:

'I'd cut his throat in church!' he raved.

'Then do as I suggest,' said Claudius. 'Keep to your room so as not to meet him when he returns. I hear that you have become an expert swordsman while you have been away: Hamlet is well skilled with rapier and dagger, and by praising you we'll bring about a friendly fencing match with foils, on which we can lay bets. Hamlet will suspect nothing: but one of the foils will have no button and so really be a sharp sword. You must make sure to get the sharp weapon; then you may take your revenge, killing him as if by accident.'

'I'll do it!' cried Laertes. 'And to be doubly sure, I'll anoint the end of the sword with a deadly poison.'

'Good,' agreed Claudius, realizing that Laertes would now stick at nothing, however treacherous and wicked. 'And to make even more certain, I'll have a poisoned cup of wine ready. Hamlet is out of practice, and will get hot from fencing. Make your bouts as violent as possible then he'll call for drink—and I'll see to it that he gets the right cup.'

Hamlet arrived at Elsinore just in time for the funeral of Ophelia, about whose madness and death he knew nothing. He and Horatio passed the burial ground as the grave-digger was finishing his work.

'Whose grave is that?' asked Hamlet idly.

'Mine, sir!' answered the grave-digger with a grin.

'I think it must indeed be yours,' agreed Hamlet, 'for you lie in it! Graves are for the dead, not for the quick!'

'Then it's a quick lie,' retorted the grave-digger.

'How long have you been a grave maker?' asked Hamlet.

'I began on the very day the old King conquered Norway,' was the answer. 'The day young Hamlet was born—he that is mad, and is sent to England.'

'Why was he sent to England?' asked Hamlet.

'Because he was mad,' answered the grave-digger. 'No one will notice anything wrong with him there.'

'Why not?' asked Hamlet.

'Because there the men are as mad as he!' the grave-digger replied.

While they were still talking, Ophelia's funeral procession arrived, and Hamlet was horrified to discover who was to be buried in the grave he had been jesting over.

When Laertes saw Hamlet, who protested how much he had loved the dead Ophelia, he attacked him. The King and Queen who were there too, managed to part them; and when Hamlet had gone, the King suggested that his behaviour was due to madness, and reminded Laertes privately of their plot to be rid of him.

The fencing match was fixed for the next day, to take place before the King and Queen. Hamlet had Horatio for his second, and Laertes a young courtier called Osric. All the King's murderous plans were followed carefully, and Osric knew enough of them to be sure that Hamlet did not get the poisoned and unbuttoned foil.

'I fear you will lose this match,' said Horatio to Hamlet.

'I do not think so,' was the answer. 'Since Laertes went away I have been practising constantly—but yet my heart is full of dread.'

'If you suspect anything, follow your intuition,' said Horatio. 'You can decline to fight, and lose no honour.'

'No, I defy augury,' said Hamlet. 'If the end is to be now, it will not be later—for all is pre-ordained by God. I will play this match.'

'Hamlet,' said the King, when all was ready. 'I have laid a heavy wager on your success. Each time you gain a point I'll drink to your health, and the trumpets shall sound, and the cannons speak, according to custom when Denmark's King drinks a health. Moreover, for each point you score I will fling a jewel into the cup as a gift to you. Now begin. And you two judges, Horatio and Osric, watch carefully.'

Hamlet was indeed a better fencer than Laertes, and scored two hits, one after the other, to each of which the King drank. Hamlet himself refused to drink, however, until the match was over.

'He's perspiring, and getting breathless,' said the Queen as they paused before the third round. 'Here, Hamlet, take my handkerchief to mop your brow. I drink to your success!'

So saying, she picked up the nearest cup and raised it in salutation.

'Gertrude, do not drink!' exclaimed the King, realizing suddenly that it was the poisoned cup.

'I will, my lord,' she insisted, and drank before he could do anything to stop her.

'My lord, I'll get him this time,' muttered Laertes. 'Yet it almost goes against my conscience.'

They engaged again, and this time Laertes struck Hamlet and, since the weapon was sharp, wounded him slightly. The moment he felt the pain, Hamlet realized that his suspicions of treachery were well founded—though he still had no idea that the sword was poisoned. He charged Laertes again, twisted the sword out of his hand, flung him his own foil and snatched up the sharp one. Then he sprang at him, beat aside his guard, and wounded him so seriously that he fell to the ground.

'They are both bleeding!' cried Horatio. 'How is this, my lord?'

'How are you, Laertes?' asked Osric, kneeling beside his friend.

'Why, I am caught in my own trap!' gasped Laertes. 'I am justly killed with my own treachery!'

'The Queen is ill!' exclaimed Hamlet.

'She faints at the sight of the blood!' said the King hastily.

'No!' shrieked the Queen, sinking to the ground. 'The drink! The drink! Oh, my dear Hamlet! The drink! I'm poisoned!' and she fell back dead.

'Treachery!' cried Hamlet. 'Lock the doors! Let no one escape.'

'Hamlet,' gasped Laertes. 'The treachery is here. Nothing can save you. You are a dead man. The sword in your hand is smeared with poison, and has no button. My own foul deed has turned on me. Your mother's poisoned . . . The King! The King's to blame!'

'The point poisoned too!' cried Hamlet. 'Then poison, do your work!' So saying, he whipped round and passed his weapon through the King's body.

'He's justly served,' gasped Laertes. 'Exchange forgiveness with me, noble Hamlet. My father's death and mine cannot be blamed on you—nor yours on me,' and so saying he too fell back dead.

Now the poison began to work on Hamlet, and he sank slowly to the ground, Horatio supporting him.

'I cannot tell you all that happened to bring this tragedy to pass,' he said in a broken voice to the courtiers and attendants who crowded round. 'Horatio, you yet live; tell all you know when I am gone.'

'Never believe it!' cried Horatio. 'I come with you—there's still some poison in the cup.'

'Let go! By Heaven, I'll have it!' Hamlet caught his friend suddenly by the arm and wrenched the cup from him. 'Dear Horatio,' he gasped, 'think what will be said of me if you too are dead, and cannot tell the truth of all that has happened. If ever you loved me, live on to tell my story.'

Now Osric came forward to say that young Prince Fortinbras of Norway had just arrived on his way back from his victorious invasion of Poland, and that ambassadors from England were with him.

'I cannot live long enough to hear the news from England,' whispered Hamlet, 'nor to greet Fortinbras. But I prophesy that the election falls on him. He has my dying vote as next King of Denmark. Tell him so; and tell him all you can of what has happened. . . . The rest is silence.'

'Now cracks a noble heart,' sobbed Horatio, as Hamlet sank back dead in his arms. 'Goodnight, sweet Prince, and flights of angels sing you to your rest.'

So Hamlet died, and Fortinbras gave him a soldier's funeral and paid all honour to his memory before taking his place as King of Denmark.

OTHELLO, THE MOOR OF VENICE

In the days when Venice was the chief sea power in the Mediterranean, the Turkish Empire, which had spread from Asia Minor into Greece, was a constant menace to Western civilization; and it was threatening the important islands of Rhodes and Cyprus, and with them the Venetians' rich trade with the East.

At the time of her direst peril, Venice found a leader for her fleets and a commander for her forces in a Moor of noble birth called Othello. He was a simple, straightforward soldier of great courage, and an expert in the art of war; and because he had done so much for the State and was still its main bulwark against further Turkish agression, Othello was very popular in Venice.

But there were a number of Venetians who were jealous of him—and none more so that his Ensign (or aide-de-camp), Iago, a man with a great reputation for honesty, which he was careful to cultivate. But Iago's honesty was only skin-deep. He used it as a means to an end, and was ready to employ the most shameless treachery or indeed cruelty if he could gain by it.

The longer he served Othello the more he was treated as a friend; and all the while his hidden hatred grew deeper. The time came when Othello failed to choose him as his Lieutenant and instead selected a certain Michael Cassio. Iago, who had risen from the ranks, particularly disliked Cassio who had little practical experience of battle, but had studied the art of war at the University, and was a noted mathemetician.

So Iago determined to discredit both Othello and Cassio—and if possible take the place of one or both of them himself. His jealousy and dislike of Othello grew to such an extent that it became an obsession—the Moor's every action seemed like an insult. Iago even began to suspect that Othello had been making love to his wife Emilia—and it was his own jealousy that at length suggested to him a way of ruining Othello's happiness.

The Moor, as the hero of Venice, was welcomed by all the great lords of the city. Among the wealthiest was one Brabantio who had a daughter, Desdemona, to whom many suitors came—but without success. Brabantio welcomed Othello to his house though never dreamt of him as a possible son-in-law. It hadn't even entered his head that his daughter, a shy and modest girl who so far had encouraged none of her suitors, would fall in love with a dark-skinned man—one, moreover, who would have been treated as inferior among the people of Venice had he not become so important to the State.

But when Othello told stirring tales of his past—of 'moving accidents by flood and field', of hair-breadth escapes, of sufferings when taken captive by the Turks, and adventures in escaping from them; of the strange places he had visited and the stranger things he had heard—Desdemona was enthralled. And she showed her love so plainly that Othello soon dared to hope that she might be his. But as it was obvious that Brabantio would never give his consent to their union, Desdemona suggested that she should slip away one night from her father's house and that they should be married in secret.

Now among her suitors was a wealthy young gentleman called Roderigo who had more money than brains, and had made friends with Iago whose help he sought in his suit. Iago saw how useful Roderigo might be, and promised to help him.

He was too late to prevent Desdemona's elopement with Othello, for he only discovered it on the actual night; so he explained to Roderigo that he himself could do nothing without showing that he hated Othello and was working against him.

'Go and rouse Brabantio,' he urged Roderigo. 'Even if it is too late to prevent the marriage, you can cause Othello a great deal of trouble. Under normal conditions, the Duke would probably rule that the marriage was not legal—but as things are, Othello is needed to save Cyprus from the Turks, and he can do no wrong. But you can depend on me. Together we'll ruin Othello, and Desdemona shall be yours in the end.'

Roderigo did as Iago suggested; and Brabantio, finding his daughter gone, raised the alarm and hastened to Othello's house with a band of followers. They met Othello already on his way to the Duke, having been summoned hastily on account of a reported Turkish invasion of Cyprus: and when they reached the Duke's presence, Brabantio claimed the right to speak first:

'My daughter has been stolen from me by a villain who has used drugs and magic and other forbidden means to win her!' he shouted. 'I claim the law against him for practising witchcraft!'

'If he has done so, and if you can prove such wickedness has been committed, he shall die—even if he were my own son,' said the Duke.

'I thank your Grace,' said Brabantio bowing. 'Then fulfill your word! Yonder Moor, with a heart even blacker than his skin, has bewitched my daughter.'

'What have you to say in your defence?' asked the Duke turning to Othello.

'He can answer nothing!' cried Brabantio. 'He has my daughter. That is proof enough.'

'Most grave and noble sirs,' said Othello bowing low, 'It is true that this gentleman's daughter is now my wife. For this very night I was married to her. Forgive me, I am a plain fighting man and have no gift of words. But with your permission I will tell you of my wooing—and of what magic I used to win the fair Desdemona.'

'It is impossible that he could have won her by any means other than magic or drugs!' insisted Brabantio.

'I beg you to send for Desdemona,' said Othello quietly. And when the Duke had given the order, Othello proceeded to tell how he had won her by his stirring tales of deeds he had done and of all his sufferings and escapes.

When Desdemona came into the court, Brabantio asked her:

'In all this noble company, lady, to whom do you owe the greatest obedience?'

'Dear father,' she answered, 'I seem to have a double duty. To you who have brought me up and educated me—a daughter's duty. But here is my husband, and just as my mother left her father to become your wife, so must I leave you and own that my first obedience is to my lord, Othello.'

'Then I have no more to say,' Brabantio exclaimed bitterly. 'Take her, Moor! I give her to you willingly, since you have her already. If you had not, I would have done everything in my power to prevent you getting her. . . . And now to the business of the State.'

'Messengers have just reached us,' said the Duke, 'bearing news that the Turks are sailing with a great fleet to attack Rhodes. We think that they are merely trying to deceive us, for Rhodes is so well fortified that they cannot hope to take it without a long siege. But Cyprus is undefended; and we believe that that is where the Turks really mean to attack. So we have sent for you, Othello, to bid you set sail at dawn in command of all our ships and go to Cyprus. We create you governor of the island, and give you full powers. Defeat the Turks at sea, if you can; and if not, defend Cyprus from them.'

'Good,' said Othello, 'I'll sail with the dawn—to seek the Turks. Let my Lieutenant, Michael Cassio command in Cyprus until I arrive. My Ensign, Iago, shall accompany him: his wife will go with him, and they can attend on Desdemona until I join her in Cyprus.'

'Let it be so,' said the Duke. 'Goodnight to all. Farewell, brave Othello. Be a good husband to Desdemona.'

'Take good care of her, Moor,' said Brabantio. 'Do not forget that she has already deceived her father. . . . She may yet deceive you.'

Iago had had exactly the same idea, and he suggested it so persuasively to Roderigo that the foolish young man filled his purse with money and embarked immediately for Cyprus.

'She'll grow weary of Othello,' Roderigo told himself—

repeating Iago's cunning insinuations. 'For a girl like Desdemona to get involved with a Moor and run away from her father only shows that she's out for a good time and doesn't care about how she behaves. To marry Othello is about the most unconventional thing she could do. The novelty will soon wear off, and she'll want fresh excitements. And anyhow, this Moor won't be faithful to her for long. He's the sort of man who'll leave her as soon as he gets tired of her.'

Iago knew better than to believe any such nonsense. 'Othello's an absolute innocent,' he thought. 'He's so honest himself that he believes everyone else is. And Desdemona's just the same. She'll never be false to him! But if I can make him *think* she's false . . .' Iago savoured the idea with great enjoyment.

'Yes,' he thought, 'and Michael Cassio's the man. Handsome, clever in his own foolish way—but almost as unsuspecting as Othello himself. If only I could make Othello believe he had reason to be jealous of Cassio. . . .'

Iago knew that this was not as difficult as it seemed. For Othello, being a Moor, and knowing that, were it not for his unusual position as commander of the Venetian forces and Governor of Cyprus, most of the men among whom he moved would consider him inferior, was very sensitive. He loved Desdemona and knew that she loved him; but if a man whom he trusted, such as Iago, were to suggest that she had suddenly fallen in love with a handsome young Venetian—he might really believe it.

Iago did not have long to wait for an opportunity to put his devilish scheme into effect.

Although Cassio's ship reached Cyprus first, with Desdemona, Iago and Emilia on board, Othello was not far behind. Trusting to his judgement and his knowledge of the enemy, Othello intercepted the Turkish fleet midway between Rhodes and Cyprus, and inflicted a crushing defeat on them. Then he sailed on to Cyprus, where he was greeted as a hero who had saved the island from cruel invaders.

On the very first night after he had landed, there was to be feasting and rejoicing—and Iago began his intrigues.

'All goes well,' he said to Roderigo. 'Desdemona and Cassio are already in love with one another. Have you not noticed how lovingly he greeted her when she landed? How his hand lingered in hers? Remember with what violence she first loved the Moor just because he boasted and told her impossible lies! Now she's tired of him, and has turned just as suddenly and violently towards Cassio. But don't worry: I see an excellent means of disgracing him and getting him out of your way. . . . Then your turn will come! You must quarrel with him tonight. I'll put you in command of the watch, and when he comes round, annoy him. He's very quick tempered, and gets drunk very easily; he'll strike you on the slightest provocation. Run to me for help; but make sure he's chasing you, and I'll see to it that he gets into trouble. Then you'll have your chance with Desdemona!'

At the end of the evening's banquet Othello bade Cassio a kindly goodnight, bidding him go the round of the guards before turning in.

'Iago knows what needs doing,' Cassio assured Othello, 'but none the less I'll certainly go the rounds as well.'

'Iago is a most honest and conscientious Ensign,' agreed Othello; and he and Desdemona went off, leaving Cassio in command.

Very soon Iago found him, and persuaded him to join in another drink before they inspected the watch.

'Not tonight, good Iago,' said Cassio. 'I have a very poor head for drinking, and have had quite enough already. It's a most unfortunate weakness, but I dare not risk taking any more.'

'You are right to be so careful,' cried Iago, slapping him on the back. 'But, my dear fellow, tonight is not an ordinary night. It is a night for revels, by the orders of our good General Othello who has sent the Turks scurrying away for shelter. No need to be over-scrupulous tonight! Come! I have a couple of friends waiting to join us in a nightcap.'

Cassio was already a little flushed with wine, and could not resist Iago's persuasions. So very soon he was drinking and joking with Iago and Montano, the commander of the garrison, and two or three other officers—Iago being careful to refill his cup whenever he got the chance.

It did not take long for the wine to go to Cassio's head, and he was soon so drunk that he could scarcely stand or speak. He did not quite forget his duties as Lieutenant, however, and at last he staggered to his feet, saying very indistinctly:

'Gentlemen, let's attend to our duties. Do not think, gentlemen, that I am drunk: this is my Ensign, this is my right hand, an' this is my left hand! I am not drunk now. I can stand or' right, an' speak or' right!'

'Excellently!' agreed everybody.

'Ver' well, then!' concluded Cassio, 'you mus' not think then, that I'm drunk!'

So saying Cassio went reeling and staggering away to inspect the guard on the battlements overlooking the harbor.

'Let's follow and make sure all's well with the watch,' said Montano. But Iago delayed him, and signalled secretly to Roderigo to go after Cassio.

'It's so sad,' said Iago with a deep sigh. 'Cassio would be as brave a soldier and as fine a commander as any in the world—were it not for this vice of his.'

'Is he often like this?' asked Montano.

'Every night,' said Iago promptly. 'Before he goes to bed.'

'It would be a good thing to tell Othello about it,' said Montano. 'There might be some disaster if Cassio were drunk at a vital moment. You should tell.'

'Not I, though my reward were all Cyprus!' exclaimed Iago indignantly. 'Cassio is my dearest friend, and I would do anything in my power to cure him of this habit . . . Listen! What's that?'

There were shouts for help, and Roderigo came dashing up to them with Cassio just behind him, striking at him.

'Help! Murder!' yelled Roderigo.

'You rogue, you rascal!' shouted Cassio. 'I'll beat you black and blue!'

'Good Lieutenant, hold your hand!' exclaimed Montano.

'Let go, or I'll thrash you too!' cried Cassio.

'Careful now, you're drunk——' began Montano.

'Drunk?' shouted Cassio. And with that he whipped out his sword and attacked Montano.

'Go quickly!' whispered Iago to Roderigo. 'Tell the garrison there's a mutiny! Ring the alarm bell!'

As soon as Roderigo had gone, Iago drew his sword too, and tried to beat down Cassio's weapon. The other officers joined in, and the fight became a real brawl, during which Cassio wounded Montano seriously.

Then the alarm bell began ringing; and Othello appeared just as Iago and the others succeeded in disarming Cassio.

The result was precisely as expected. Cassio was dismissed from the service on the spot, in spite of Iago's carefully worded attempts to excuse him—which in fact suggested that his behavior had been much worse than it was.

'Iago, I know your honesty, and your love for Cassio which leads you to make light of what has happened,' said Othello. 'Cassio, you are my dear friend; but never more can you be my officer. Some of you look after Montano and dress his wound. Iago, inspect the guard and see that all rumors of mutiny are contradicted. Then to bed, all.'

When all but Iago had gone, Cassio sank on a seat and buried his head in his hands.

'My dear Lieutenant!' exclaimed Iago, giving him the rank he had just lost, which he knew would hurt, 'Are you wounded? What's wrong?'

'Yes, wounded beyond cure!' sobbed Cassio. 'My reputation is blasted for ever. Oh God! That men should put an enemy in their mouths to steal away their brains!'

'You seem sober enough now,' said Iago.

'I think the devil called anger has driven out the other devil—drink,' said Cassio. 'Oh, what fools we are, that for a little enjoyment we turn ourselves into beasts! I am ruined for ever. If I asked Othello to give me my place again, he needs only to speak the one word "Drunkard" and there is nothing I can say.'

'Wine is a good friend, if used wisely,' said Iago. 'Any man may get drunk sometimes—and not be a drunkard. Look, Cassio, I'll plead for you with Othello, and tell him so. But by far your best chance is to get Desdemona to plead for you. Othello may be our General, but Desdemona rules him with her beauty. Come to see her in the morning and ask her help. I'll arrange that the Moor's out of the way so that you can be alone with her and beg her to help you. Goodnight, Lieutenant. I must go the rounds.'

'Goodnight, kind, honest Iago,' said Cassio, much encouraged.

'Who says I'm a villain?' thought Iago to himself with a grin as Cassio left him. 'What I suggest is simply good sense. The obvious way for Cassio to win his forgiveness is to get Desdemona to plead for him. . . . Ah, but I'll hint to Othello that Desdemona is only pleading for Cassio because she loves him. Then the more she tries to help Cassio, the more Othello will suspect her. In this way I'll use her kindness to damage her, and catch all my victims in the net of her very goodness!'

Desdemona's goodness was put to the test early the next morning when Cassio arrived to beg her help. She had already been told what to expect by Iago's wife, Emilia, who was her constant attendant. She welcomed him in the garden where he made his petition to her and then, kissing her hand warmly, slipped hurriedly away when he saw Othello coming.

'I don't like that!' muttered Iago, who was with him.

'What don't you like?' asked Othello, not paying much attention.

'The furtive manner in which Cassio left your wife when he saw you,' answered Iago.

Othello took little notice of what Iago said, but went forward to talk with Desdemona who, full of her mission to help poor Cassio, could talk of little else, and kept returning to the subject until the time when she and Emilia were sent by Othello into the house.

'Did Cassio know of your love when you wooed the Lady Desdemona?' asked Iago casually when the two men were alone.

'Yes, right from the start,' answered Othello. 'Why do you ask?'

'Just something I was thinking,' said Iago casually.

'What's troubling you?' asked the Moor, interested now.

'Oh, nothing,' answered Iago. 'I didn't know that he knew her then.'

'Certainly he did,' said Othello. 'He frequently carried messages between us.'

'Indeed!' muttered Iago, as if trying in vain to shut out a horrid suspicion.

'Indeed and indeed!' exclaimed Othello. 'What's wrong? Surely Cassio's honest?'

'Honest, my lord?' Iago panicked suddenly.

'Yes, honest! Honest!' exclaimed Othello impatiently—but now just a little worried.

'Yes . . . As far as I know . . .' Iago was almost overdoing it. But Othello was too honest himself ever to suspect dishonesty in another without a direct statement.

'Speak out, man!' he cried. 'If you are hinting at anything, tell me straight out!'

'I expect Cassio really is an honest man,' said Iago, 'and probably it's just my mind that always sees the slightest hint of wrongdoing . . . But honor means so much to me . . . Anyone who steals my purse, steals trash; but whoever robs me of my honor takes something which is of no value to him, though it leaves me poor indeed.'

Now at last Othello began to realize what Iago was hinting at—and Iago made haste to fan the flame by pretending he was trying to put it out.

'Oh, beware of jealousy, my lord!' he cried. 'It is the green-eyed monster that only grows hungrier by eating. Why, for example, the man whose wife is deceiving him and really loves someone else is perfectly happy so long as he doesn't know. But oh, what misery he endures once he begins to suspect.'

'No, Iago, I am not of the jealous type!' said Othello. 'I must see certain proof before I give way to jealousy.'

'I'm glad to hear that,' replied Iago. 'It shows that I can speak to you straightforwardly, like one man of the world to another. I've no proof at all yet, but only the vaguest suspicion—which you can easily prove or disprove by keeping an eye on your wife and Cassio. I'm really only warning you. After all, I know more about Italians than you do, and I know, alas, that in Venice to do wrong is not so great a sin as to be found out. . . . Venetian women are famous for their skill in deceit.'

'I didn't know that!' Othello seemed dazed.

'Well, look how easily and cleverly Desdemona deceived her father,' said Iago. 'He never had the slightest suspicion—until it was too late. . . . But forgive me, I am greatly to blame. I should not be causing you this uneasiness. Nothing but my great love for you made me do so.'

'I'm sure Desdemona's honest!' cried Othello.

'Long may she remain so!' echoed Iago. 'And long may you think so.'

'And yet she erred against nature when she married me,' mused Othello, thinking of the way Desdemona had misled her father.

'Yes, there's the point,' agreed Iago, purposely misunderstanding him. 'To turn down so many suitable young men of her own race and color . . . Heaven grant she never repents of her unusual choice.'

'Leave me now,' said Othello. 'But keep your eyes open, and tell your wife to do the same.'

Iago turned to go, but then hesitated:

'My lord, I beg you to think no more about this,' he said. 'Leave it for time to show. You'll be able to see by the way your wife behaves over Cassio's disgrace whether there's anything in my suspicions, which I truly hope—er—think is all they are.'

'He's a very honest man,' thought Othello, when Iago had gone, 'and he naturally understands his countrywomen better than I do. . . . Perhaps, because I'm black, and no longer young, it was only a passing love . . . But here she comes. If that loveliness is false, then heaven itself is too!'

Desdemona came only to tell Othello that it was lunchtime, but seeing that he looked worried, she asked what troubled him, if he were ill.

'I have a headache,' he admitted.

At once Desdemona, all tender care, tried to bind his head with her handkerchief, but it was too small and fell to the ground.

'Don't worry!' exclaimed Othello. 'Come! Let's go to lunch!'

'I'm so sorry you're not well!' murmured Desdemona, clinging to his arm as they went into the house, and quite forgetting her handkerchief which still lay where it had fallen.

Emilia, however, had noticed it, and she had just picked it up when Iago appeared once more.

'What are you doing here alone?' he asked suspiciously.

'You mustn't be cross,' she said. 'I found something for which you've often asked: the handkerchief that was the Moor's first gift to Desdemona.'

'Have you stolen it?' asked Iago.

'No,' answered Emilia. 'She dropped it, and forgot about it for the moment.'

'Give it me!' cried Iago eagerly, and he snatched it from her.

'What do you want it for?' asked Emilia anxiously. 'Poor lady, she'll go almost mad when she finds she's lost it.'

'Never mind,' said Iago shortly. 'I have a good use for it. Be sure not to say what has become of it.' And Emilia had such a well-founded fear of her husband that she stole away without another word.

But Iago was gloating over the handkerchief, which had come at the perfect moment for his wicked schemes. 'I'll drop it in Cassio's lodgings,' he decided. 'He'll find it there, and use it—and the Moor will see it in his hand. Mere trifles like this seem positive proofs when jealousy is really roused. And he's already poisoned through and through . . . Ah-ha! Here he comes! The poison's eating into his mind! Not poppy nor mandragora, nor any other cunning drug will give again the sweet sleep that he had last night!'

Sure enough Othello was by now almost raving; and a few more cruel shafts from Iago reduced him to such a frenzy that he was ready to kill Iago if he did not prove definitely that Desdemona had deceived him and was in love with Cassio.

With a tremendous pretence of sorrow and unwillingness, Iago proceeded to poison his mind still further by clever lies which suggested more than they said, but could not be proved—and Othello continued to rave.

'I'll tear her all to pieces!' he shouted.

But Iago hastened to soothe him. 'Be wise and careful,' he cautioned. 'We know nothing certain yet. She *may* be honest. Tell me this, however: Have you not sometimes seen your wife using an embroidered handkerchief—embroidered with strawberries, I think?'

'I gave her just such a handkerchief!' said Othello. 'It was my first gift to her.'

'Cassio was wiping his mouth with just such a handkerchief only today,' declared Iago. 'I'm sure it was your wife's.'

'Now I know it's true!' roared Othello. 'Now love has gone forever, and I have nothing left in me but hate! If only that devil Cassio had forty thousand lives for me to take! Here I vow before heaven to have my full revenge!'

'And I vow by the same holy oath to do all in my power to help you!' cried Iago, turning up his eyes piously. 'You have but to command, and I will obey in anything.'

'I thank you for your love,' said Othello grimly. 'And I'll put it to the test at once. Within these next three days come to me and say "Cassio is no longer alive!"'

'Then my friend dies,' said Iago. 'He dies at your request . . . But let *her* live.'

'Damn her, oh damn her, the lewd minx,' raved Othello. 'Come and help me find some swift means of killing this beautiful devil . . . And, here and now, I create you my Lieutenant.'

'I am yours forever!' exclaimed Iago enthusiastically.

Desdemona had so little suspicion of what was happening, that she was jesting with one of Othello's sergeants.

'Where does Lieutenant Cassio lie?' she asked him.

'I dare not say that he lies anywhere!' was the answer.

'Why, man?'

'To say that a soldier lies is to risk getting my throat cut,' answered the sergeant.

'Well then,' laughed Desdemona, 'tell me where he lodges.'

'To tell you where he lodges is the same as to tell you where I lie!' countered the sergeant.

'You are too witty for me!' smiled Desdemona.

'Quite simple,' was the answer. 'I should lie if I told you where he lodged—because I don't know!'

'Well, ask someone who does, and go and tell him to come here quickly,' commanded Desdemona; and the man saluted and went.

He had scarcely gone, when she saw Othello coming towards her: 'Ah,' exclaimed Desdemona to Emilia, 'now's my chance to persuade my husband to forgive Cassio and restore to him his rank.'

She at once began urging Othello to do so. But he cut her short by saying:

'I seem to be starting a cold. Lend me your handkerchief.'

'Here, my lord,' said Desdemona.

'Let me use that special one which was my first gift to you,' said Othello.

'I haven't got it with me,' answered Desdemona anxiously, for she had missed the handkerchief and had been searching everywhere for it.

When she admitted that she had not got it, Othello went into such a rage that Desdemona completely lost her head and dared not admit that she had simply lost it, but tried to change the subject. Unfortunately the first thought that came to her was to go on pleading Cassio's case—which seemed to Othello to prove beyond all doubt the lies which Iago had been feeding him. He still, however, did not accuse her of anything, but seemed so fierce and strange that she was quite upset.

'The man's jealous,' said Emilia, when Othello had gone.

'I never saw him like this before,' agreed Desdemona sadly. 'Even if the handkerchief had been a magic one, it's too little a thing to make such a fuss about. But I'm most unhappy at the loss of it.'

Emilia was too frightened of Iago to tell her what had become of it. But when Cassio arrived a few minutes later, Desdemona was forced to admit that she could not help him back into Othello's favor.

Othello was by now so mad with jealousy that all sense of judgement seemed to have left him, and Iago found it easy to make him believe anything on the slightest evidence.

Thoroughly enjoying his feeling of power, dangerous though he knew his position to be, Iago went on goading him to madness. He arranged for Othello to overhear a conversation in which Cassio was actually telling Iago about his own friend Bianca—but which Iago turned in such a way that Othello thought it was Desdemona whose love Cassio was treating so lightly. And later on he again arranged matters so that Othello should see Bianca with the handkerchief and think that Cassio prized Desdemona's love so lightly that he was even passing on her gifts.

Matters were brought to a head by the sudden arrival of messengers from Venice commanding Othello to set out immediately to lead a campaign in Mauritania, and to leave Cassio behind as Governor of Cyprus.

The messengers, Desdemona's uncle, Gratiano, and his kinsman Lord Ludovico, were much shocked at the change they observed in Othello. Iago, on being asked, hinted that the Moor was mad, that he could say more, but that loyalty kept him from doing so.

'We will go into this fully tomorrow,' said Ludovico; and Iago realized that all his schemes must reach their conclusion that very night—which was not difficult to bring about. For Othello was so beside himself with jealousy and he so lusted for revenge, that a very few more delicate barbs from Iago's clever tongue sealed both Desdemona's doom and Cassio's.

'Get me some poison,' Othello commanded him. 'I'll poison her tonight.'

'Don't do it with poison,' said Iago, anxious not to be involved. 'Strangle her in bed.'

'Good. I'll execute her tonight,' said Othello. 'And Cassio——'

'I'll look after him,' said Iago. 'He'll not live through the night either.'

Cassio's assassin was ready: the wretched Roderigo, who was no match for Iago's clever tempting, was easily persuaded to do the deed by specious lies about Desdemona being left behind in Cyprus when Othello set out for Mauritania.

Cassio was dining with his Bianca, and Iago posted Roderigo in a dark alley near Bianca's house, and himself waited a little further away.

'I must get Cassio out of the way,' thought Iago. 'At any moment Othello may accuse him to his face, and Cassio may be able to prove his innocence. . . . Then Othello will suspect me. As for Roderigo, if Cassio should kill him, I'm rid of a nuisance: for as I've kept all the gifts of jewels and money he's sent by me to Desdemona, I'm open to exposure there, too.'

Midnight had scarcely struck, when Cassio came out of Bianca's house, and Roderigo sprang on him, crying, 'Die, villain!' as he stabbed him.

'That thrust would have done for me, if I were not wearing armor under my jerkin!' cried Cassio, whipping out his sword. 'Let's see how good your armor is!'

He lunged at Roderigo, who fell wounded, gasping, 'Oh, I'm killed!'

Seeing what had happened, Iago stole up behind Cassio and slashed at his legs. Cassio fell, crying for help. Seeing lights, Iago fled into the shadows, still unrecognized.

A few minutes later Ludovico and Gratiano found Cassio; and while they were bending over him, Iago returned as if drawn by the shouts.

'It's Lieutenant Cassio!' exclaimed Iago. 'Oh, some murderous villains have done this!'

'Help me, I'm bleeding to death!' cried Roderigo, from the shadow of the alley.

'There's one of the murderers!' shouted Iago; and drawing his own sword, he silenced Roderigo forever.

But Cassio, though seriously wounded, was not dead, not even dying. And Iago had no chance to finish him off, now that Ludovico and Gratiano were there.

Emilia had joined them by now. While Cassio was being carried towards the castle, she ran on ahead to tell Othello what had happened. When she reached the bedroom door, she found it locked, and hammered on it, shouting to be let in as she had important news.

She was too late. Othello had gone to the bedroom already determined to strangle Desdemona. He had locked the door and now stood looking at her as she slept.

'It is the cause,' he said bitterly. 'Her very beauty is the cause. I cannot shed her blood, nor mar the whiteness of her skin. Yet she must die before she betrays more men. Put out the light—and then put out the light. If I quench the candle's flame, I can light it again when I wish. But if I put out *her* light, no earthly power can call it back again. Yet she must die. I'll kiss before I kill. When she is dead, I'll love her for her beauty: all that is evil dies with her.'

In kissing her, Othello woke Desdemona, who stretched out her arms to him.

'Have you said your prayers tonight?' asked Othello. 'If not, say them now, for I would not kill you unprepared.'

'You will not kill me?' gasped Desdemona. 'What have I done?'

'That handkerchief which I prized so highly,' said Othello. 'You gave it to Cassio—your lover.'

'No, by my soul!' cried Desdemona. 'I lost it. He must have found it. And I never loved him—nor any man but you.'

'You lie!' cried Othello. 'Cassio has confessed! And honest Iago is even now stopping his mouth forever.'

'Alas, he was betrayed by false accusations!' sobbed Desdemona, 'and now he cannot prove that what I say is true!'

'How, you weep for Cassio before my very face?' shouted Othello; and in his madness he seized Desdemona and smothered her in spite of all her cries and prayers for mercy.

Scarcely was she still when Emilia's knock sounded on the door, and at length Othello let her in.

'Here's murder done!' she cried. 'A young Venetian tried to murder Cassio, and he's dead.'

'Cassio's dead?' asked Othello.

'No, Cassio's not dead,' gasped Emilia.

'Not dead? Then murder's out of tune, and revenge is still to come,' cried Othello.

'Oh, falsely, falsely murdered!' It was Desdemona's voice, like a sigh of conscience.

'What's that?' cried Emilia, rushing to the bed. 'My lady! Help! Sweet Desdemona! Oh sweet mistress! Speak!'

'A guiltless death I die,' whispered Desdemona. 'Farewell, my dear Othello. He did not do it.'

Then, still thinking first of her husband, Desdemona sank back dead.

'There's a liar gone to burning Hell!' raved Othello. 'She was false and rotten. She loved Cassio. Your husband, honest Iago, proved it to me.'

'Did he say so?' cried Emilia. 'Then he's a liar, and may his wicked soul rot half a grain a day! He lies, I tell you! Oh wicked, foolish dolt to be so easily deceived! Help! Murder! Help!'

Emilia's cries brought Montano, Gratiano and Iago who were on their way to tell Othello about the attempted murder of Cassio. Iago tried to silence Emilia, but she would not obey him any longer. Instead, she told how she had found the handkerchief and how Iago had insisted on her giving it to him and saying nothing about it.

Now Iago realized that he was betrayed, and that the truth would come out. Suddenly mad with fear, he stabbed Emilia in a vain attempt to stop her tongue, and fled for his life.

But she repeated her accusations before she sank dead beside

Desdemona. And Othello realized that they were true, and that his wife was innocent.

By Gratiano's order, Othello was disarmed and held prisoner until Ludovico arrived, accompanied by men carrying the wounded Cassio in a chair, and others leading Iago with his hands bound.

Then all was made clear—except the reason for Iago's wickedness against three such innocent people as Othello, Desdemona and Cassio.

'Well, he shall die under torture,' said Ludovico grimly. 'Perhaps then he'll confess. As for you, Othello, what shall we say to the Duke; you who were once so good, but now have fallen a victim to this foul villain?'

'Speak of me as you will,' answered Othello, all the nobility of his true character returning to him in the moment of supreme tragedy. 'Call me an honorable murderer, if you will. For I did nothing in hate, but only for the sake of honour. I have done the State some service, so speak fairly of me. Make no excuses for me, but tell just the truth—say I was one who loved not wisely but too well; one not easily jealous but, being roused, one who was made mad and blinded by that evil passion. Call me one who, like the ignorant Indian, found a jewel more valuable than all his tribe—and threw it away thinking it was only a pebble.'

Othello paused, leaning back against the bed, and then suddenly cried out:

'Say also that once, in Aleppo, when fighting for Venice, I seized the very leader of the Turks, and stabbed him—thus!'

Before anyone could stop him, Othello snatched out a sword that had lain hidden among the bedclothes, and plunged it into his heart.

'I kissed before I killed,' he whispered. 'There is no way but this—to kill myself and die kissing the one I loved.'

And so he sank dead beside Desdemona: a great man despite his fatal fault of jealousy.

MACBETH

When King Duncan was growing old, a rebellion broke
out in his kingdom of Scotland led by a traitor called Macdonwald, who was aided by Sweno, King of Norway. Old though
he was, Duncan had good soldiers and generals. He gathered his
army and marched against the rebels who were defeated in a
series of battles in which the Scottish powers were led with
great distinction by their best general, Macbeth, the Thane of
Glamis, and his friend Banquo.

The two generals thought the war was ended, and were on
their way to report to Duncan, when the Norwegian King made
one last attempt. He was helped by a traitor, the Thane of Cawdor,
who suddenly changed sides during the battle. But, even though
Macbeth and Banquo were no longer with the army, the Scots
defeated the enemy and drove the Norwegians from the country.

When Duncan heard of all that had happened, he sent messengers with commands that the Thane of Cawdor should be
executed there and then, on the battlefield; and that the Thane of
Ross should find Macbeth and, in recognition of his great services,
should confer on him the title which the traitor had held.

Macbeth and Banquo knew nothing of these final developments. They were proceeding quietly across a lonely heath in the
direction of Duncan's camp, when a strange and unexpected
adventure befell them.

Three witches were waiting on the heath—women so evil that

they had sold their souls to the Devil to gain a little power beyond
that of ordinary mortals, and whom the Devil was now using.
Macbeth was already struggling against his ambition and had, in
his wife, a temptress whose lust for sovereignty was even greater
than his own. For both Macbeth and his wife knew that if Duncan
had had no sons, Macbeth would have been the most likely to
succeed him on the throne of Scotland. And now these three
witches greeted him suddenly in his hour of triumph:

'All hail, Macbeth, hail to you, Thane of Glamis!' cried the first.

'All hail, Macbeth, hail to you, Thane of Cawdor!' the second
cried; while the third addressed him with:

'All hail, Macbeth, that shall be King hereafter!'

Suddenly to hear his most secret thoughts put into words by
these strange creatures so staggered Macbeth that he was held
speechless.

'Why do you seem so surprised, and so afraid of a greeting
which appears on the face of it to promise you such honors to
come?' asked Banquo. And then, as Macbeth still seemed tongue-
tied, he turned to the witches and cried:

'In the name of truth, are you visions, or no more than you
appear to be? You greet my friend with prophecies of a royal
future that seem quite to have charmed his senses. If you can really
look into the future and see what will come to pass, speak to me.
I do not fear whether you tell me good or ill.'

'Hail, lesser than Macbeth and greater!' cried the first witch.

'Hail, not so happy, yet much happier!' cried the second.

'You shall be the forefather of kings, though you be none yourself,' cried the third.

Now Macbeth seemed to wake out of his trance, just as the
witches were moving away:

'Wait, you who suggested hidden things!' he exclaimed.
'Tell me more! I know I am Thane of Glamis, as I succeeded to
the title on my father's death. But how can I be Thane of Cawdor?
The Thane of Cawdor lives, a noble and distinguished gentleman.
And to be King is quite beyond the bounds of possibility. How
do you come to be here on this lonely heath greeting us so pro-
phetically? Speak, I command you!'

But the witches were nowhere to be seen: they might have sunk into the ground, or become air and mingled with the winds.

'Were they really here?' asked Banquo at last. 'They seem now more like a vision.'

'Your children shall be kings,' mused Macbeth, who was only too ready to believe in the witches' prophecy.

'You shall be king!' countered Banquo, meaning to discredit the whole thing.

'And Thane of Cawdor, too,' insisted Macbeth.

While they were still discussing their strange experience, the Thanes of Ross and Angus met them bearing warm greetings and congratulations from Duncan.

'And in token of the King's gratitude for all your valor and good leadership,' concluded Ross, 'he bade me greet you as Thane of Cawdor—which title and position is now yours.'

'What, can the devil speak true?' ejaculated Banquo under his breath.

'The Thane of Cawdor is alive and well!' cried Macbeth. 'Why do you give me another man's title?'

'He who was the Thane may still be alive,' explained Angus. 'But he is under sentence of death, and has been deprived of title, lands and everything. For he was in league with Macdonwald and the Norwegians, and has confessed all his treason.'

'Glamis—and Thane of Cawdor,' thought Macbeth. 'Then the greatest rank may still be mine! I thank you for the news,' he added aloud to Ross and Angus. Then aside to Banquo he said: 'Do you not hope that your children will be kings, since those who prophesied that I should be Thane of Cawdor promised it to them?'

'If you put too much trust in their words,' said Banquo warningly, 'you may be tempted to seek the crown—as well as being Thane of Cawdor. Remember that the powers of evil, trying to win us, often tell small truths to lure us into greater sins.'

Banquo turned to speak to Ross and Angus; but Macbeth still stood buried in thought. 'They told me two truths,' he mused, 'and surely these are but prologues to the third, greatest truth— the crown! But are these supernatural pryings good or bad? If they are bad, why have they begun by showing me the truth? I *am* Thane of Cawdor. . . . Yet if they are good, why am I seized by this horrible temptation to make myself king—No, I must not think such treacherous, murderous thoughts. If chance will have me king, why let chance crown me: and well it may, without my doing anything further.'

So Macbeth set out, with Banquo and the two Thanes, determined to do nothing to help the third prophecy come true.

Yet he could not put it from his mind. And when Duncan had greeted him, thanked him for what he had done, and bade him prepare to welcome him and the royal party at his own Castle of Inverness, Macbeth set off with his mind full again of evil thoughts. For Duncan had also created his eldest son, the young prince Malcolm, Duke of Cumberland—and this meant that Duncan considered Malcolm to be next in succession to the throne. At that time the throne did not necessarily pass from father to son, but the king was elected from among members of the Royal Family. Macbeth was related to Duncan, and might at least have stood some chance of succeeding the old king by honorable means, had Duncan not put forward Malcolm as his heir.

Directly after his meeting with the witches, Macbeth had sent a letter to his wife telling her the whole story. She was already planning how to get rid of Duncan—and how to persuade Macbeth to make some active move to seize the throne.

'Yet I am afraid of his nature,' she thought, 'He's too full of human kindness to take the obvious step. He's ambitious, but wants to win greatness only by lawful means. I shall need all my cunning before he attempts anything.'

While these thoughts were still uppermost in her mind, a messenger who had ridden ahead of Macbeth arrived to tell her that the King was coming to Inverness Castle that very night.

Lady Macbeth realized at once that if Duncan was to be killed, it must be done there and then; and she tried to screw up her courage to persuade Macbeth to murder Duncan in his sleep. She thought she might even help him do the horrid deed, and prayed to the powers of evil to stop her from feeling any pangs of remorse, but to fill her, instead, from top to toe with direst cruelty. Thus she was ready, when Macbeth arrived, to present him with the idea of murder as the obvious and expected course.

'My dearest love, Duncan comes here tonight!' began Macbeth.

'And when does he leave?' asked Lady Macbeth, putting the most sinister meaning she could into her voice.

'Tomorrow, so he intends,' answered Macbeth, falling into her snare.

'Never let the sun rise on his tomorrow!' she cried. 'Oh your face, dear Thane of Cawdor, is like a book in which I can read terrible things! You must learn to hide your thoughts. Look like the innocent flower, but be the serpent under it! Our royal visitor must be provided for . . . If you will only do as I tell you, what happens tonight will give us absolute power for the rest of our lives.'

'We will discuss this some other time,' prevaricated Macbeth.

'Then at least greet him with a happy look,' said Lady Macbeth. 'If you look gloomy and worried, he may suspect something. Leave all the rest to me.'

Duncan found nothing lacking in the loyalty and warmth of his reception at Inverness Castle, and his own natural nobility and honesty prevented him from having the very slightest suspicion of the brave general on whom he had heaped so many rewards and tokens of favor, or of his lady wife who seemed so solicitous for his comfort.

Although Macbeth himself was in a great state of worry and uncertainty, he managed to follow his wife's instructions and hide his guilty dreams under an innocent smile. Once during the evening's banquet he felt he could conceal his feelings no longer, and he slipped out for a few minutes of quiet thought by himself.

'If it's to be done at all, it must be done quickly,' he thought. 'If only his death would bring success, and no troubles or dangers, well—I'd risk it, and forget whatever punishment I might receive after my own death for so frightful a deed. But evil has a way of earning its own reward here on earth. Those who commit murder

are apt to set a bad example, and be murdered themselves. Justice
is very fair, and often pays us back in our own coin.

'And think how ghastly a crime it would be. He is my King
and my relative. To kill either is worse than an ordinary murder,
but in this case he is also my guest, and so should be as sacred to
me for that reason as for either of the others. Besides, there is no
excuse as there might be if he'd been a bad king. Duncan has
filled his office of God's viceroy on earth so well, and has been so
good and humble in his divine position, that his very virtues will
plead for him, as loudly as the angels, at the Day of Judgement.
Pity will make the deed even more loathsome to all who know
of it. No, I have no excuse, nor anything to urge me on, except
my vile ambition—and ambition may lure a man so high that he
can only fall.'

Fearing that he suffered from some such qualms of conscience,
Lady Macbeth had quickly found an excuse for leaving the
banquet-hall as soon as she could after seeing Macbeth go; and
now she hastened after him, exclaiming:

'The king has almost finished dinner. Don't you realize that he's
missed you already?'

'We'll go no further in this business!' exclaimed Macbeth firmly.
'He has honored me in many ways lately, and I have won golden
opinions from all sorts of people. They should be enjoyed now
while they are fresh and new, not thrown away so soon!'

'Then the hope of being King was merely drunken imagination!' cried Lady Macbeth. 'If so, I'll think your love for me is no
more real. Are you afraid to realize your ambition simply because
you daren't do the deed which will win it for you—like a silly cat
who won't catch the fish he wants because he's afraid of wetting
his feet?'

'Stop it!' shouted Macbeth. 'I dare to do anything a man should
do—who dares to do more ceases to be human.'

'What animal was it, then, that suggested this scheme to me?'
asked Lady Macbeth relentlessly. 'When you dared to do it, *then*
you were a man. To do more than you were then prepared to
do would show yourself even more of a man. When you first
suggested it, there seemed little chance of accomplishing that

for which we now have the perfect opportunity. Even I, a woman, would not withdraw. I know what it is to be a mother for I had a child by my first husband, but I would have taken my baby while it was smiling in my face and dashed its brains out—if I had sworn to do so as you have sworn to do this deed.'

'Suppose we fail?' Macbeth was weakening under her cunning mixture of taunts and half-truths.

'Then we fail,' she replied grandly. 'But screw up your courage so that it doesn't desert you again, and we won't fail. Listen! Duncan will sleep soundly after his long journey and good dinner. I shall make sure that the two servants who sleep in his room will have had so much to drink before retiring that they'll remember nothing of what happens during the night. Then, when they're sunk in swinish sleep, we can do what we like with the unguarded Duncan—and blame his drunken servants, who will be held guilty.'

'If we splash these two with blood, and use their own daggers, everyone will think they've done it!' cried Macbeth, quite won over by his wife's persuasions.

'No one will dare to think anything else,' she answered. 'And no one will be more shocked or grieved at his death than we will.'

'Then I'm decided,' said Macbeth firmly, 'and all my determination shall make me strong to perform this terrible act. Let us go back now, and pass the rest of the evening as innocently as we can. Our false smiles must hide the thoughts which fill our hearts.'

The smiles were successful, and Duncan retired to bed, having distributed largesse to all Macbeth's servants, and sent a diamond as a present to his 'most kind hostess.' Banquo was charged to deliver it, and he met Macbeth in the castle courtyard not long after midnight when he and his son Fleance had come out for a breath of air on their way to bed. Banquo was troubled, he hardly knew why, and was telling Fleance how he did not want to sleep, yet could not keep his eyes open. He too was somewhat subjected to the temptations put in his way by the witches, but was fighting virtuously against them, and praying that he might not even dream of them.

When he had delivered the jewel and the message to Macbeth, he said:

'I dreamt last night about the three weird women. They have certainly shown you some truth.'

'They haven't crossed my mind again,' lied Macbeth hastily. 'But let's discuss them when we have an hour or so to spare. If there is any truth in what they said, I may one day be in a position to advance you to great honors.'

'Always provided I lose no honor in the process,' said Banquo, 'but still remain loyal and honest.'

'Well, goodnight for now!' interrupted Macbeth.

'The same to you, and may you sleep well,' said Banquo as he and Fleance went off to bed.

'Tell your mistress to ring the bell for me when my drink is ready,' said Macbeth to his servant. 'Then off to bed with you.'

When he was alone Macbeth moved slowly towards the stairs leading to Duncan's apartment, and paused to fight his last losing battle against temptation. It seemed to him, as he passed slowly up the steps, that a ghostly dagger moved in front of his eyes, its handle towards his hand. He tried to clutch it, but touched nothing—only now as it moved ahead of him the blade and even the wooden handle dripped with blood. And as he went his mind became filled with evil. He thought of all the wickedness done at night when nature seems dead and terrible dreams come to torment and to tempt: of witches making their horrible sacrifices to Hecate, their Queen; of murder, as if it too had a demon of its own moving with stealthy pace, as the wolves howled to tell him it was time to strike his cowardly blow; of evil men like Tarquin creeping through the darkness to work their wicked will on poor, defenceless women. It seemed to him that the earth itself must hear his guilty steps, and he was half afraid that the very stones would tell tales and accuse him of the crime he was about to commit.

He hesitated; then Lady Macbeth's bell rang softly as if to remind him. With a curse, he straightened his back and stole quietly through the doorway towards Duncan's room. When he did not come for his drink which she had ready Lady Macbeth came out into the yard to look for him, and seeing the door of Duncan's apartment open, knew that he was doing the deed at that moment.

She was very much on edge, though she was well fortified with the same strong drink that had reduced Duncan's unfortunate servants to deepest slumber; but in her case it seemed to have filled her with fire and boldness. Yet she was almost unnerved by the sudden screech of an owl, and she completely broke down for a moment when a voice suddenly cried out from the direction of Duncan's room.

'Oh, I'm afraid they've wakened!' she gasped. 'Wakened too soon! The attempt rather than the actual deed will bring disaster on us.' She paused, and as there was no further sound, began to regain courage. 'I put their daggers ready,' she thought. 'He couldn't have missed them. I'd have stabbed Duncan myself —but he looked so like my father as he lay asleep.' There was a movement above which for a moment caused her to fear; then she saw that it was Macbeth.

'I have done the deed,' he mumbled, groping his way towards her. 'Did you hear a noise?'

'Only the owl screeching,' she answered. 'Did you call out?'

'Yes . . . Who's in the second room?' and then, scarcely waiting for an answer, he sobbed, looking at his hands, 'This is a dreadful sight!'

'A foolish thing to say,' she began. But Macbeth was quite unhinged for the moment, and broke out:

'Someone in the second room laughed in his sleep, and his companion cried out "Murder!", just as if he'd seen me with these slaughterer's hands. But they said their prayers and settled to sleep again. One said, "God bless us" and the other said, "Amen." Listening to them, I couldn't repeat "Amen"—and yet I had more need of blessing than either of them.'

'You must not give way to these feelings,' exclaimed Lady Macbeth. 'Such thoughts will drive us mad.'

'It seemed to me as if a voice cried, "Sleep no more!" he went on wildly. 'It seemed to say, "Macbeth is murdering sleep— Macbeth shall sleep no more!"'

'*Who* cried like that?' asked Lady Macbeth. Then, pulling herself together by a great effort, she went on hastily: 'My noble Thane, you do yourself an injustice by this behaviour. You must

get some water and wash the blood from your hands—Oh!' she
nearly shrieked as she suddenly saw the slip he had made which
might have betrayed them. 'Why have you brought their daggers
with you? They should have been left with the servants. Take
them back quickly, and smear the drunkards with blood.'

'I won't go in there again!' cried Macbeth hysterically. 'I'm

afraid even to think of what I've done—I certainly daren't look
at it again!'

'You coward!' taunted Lady Macbeth, striving to bring him to
his senses. 'Give me the daggers. The sleeping and the dead are
no more than pictures—and only children fear the picture of a
devil. If Duncan still bleeds, I'll gild the valets' faces with his
blood—for it has got to prove their guilt!' So saying, Lady Macbeth took the blood-stained daggers from her husband, and
hastened up the stairs to Duncan's apartments.

As Macbeth stood lost in a daze of fear and bitter self reproach
there came a sudden knocking at the Castle gate.

'What's that?' he cried. Then realizing what it was, he muttered desperately, 'I'm in such a state, every sound terrifies me.' Then his glance fell on his bloody hands, and he shook suddenly from head to foot. 'Oh these hands!' he gasped. 'The very look of them burns out my eyes! Will all great Neptune's ocean suffice to wash them clean? No. This hand of mine is more likely to turn the un-countable seas to blood—to redden all the green waters in the world.'

Now Lady Macbeth returned to him, exclaiming:

'Look, my hands are the same color as yours, but I would be ashamed to show your cowardice!' Another knock sounded hollowly through the sleeping Castle, and she went on: 'Some-one's knocking at the south gate. Let's go to bed quickly. A little water will wash away all traces of this deed. It will be so easy. Come! Put on your night-clothes, in case we should be needed—it would never do if we were found still up and about.'

'Wake Duncan with your knocking!' cried out Macbeth as he turned and followed her. 'I wish you could!'

But the first to wake was the Castle porter, whose job was to lock and unlock the doors, and see who was there if anyone knocked during the night. He came reeling dizzily out of his room at last, for like the rest of Macbeth's servants he had been feasting and drinking half the night in honor of the royal guest.

'Who's that knocking?' he hiccupped. 'If I were porter to the gate of Hell, I wouldn't be so bothered by visitors. I've never known so many as come here! You, whoever you are, wait a minute! Have a little thought for the wretched porter!'

When he finally got the gate unlocked and unbarred it was to admit Macduff the Thane of Fife, and the Thane of Lennox; and when they had finished joking with the still half-drunken porter, they entered to find Macbeth coming down to greet them, with a cloak over his night-clothes.

'Good morning, noble Thane,' said Macduff. 'Is the King up yet? He commanded me to call on him early.'

'I'll bring you to him,' said Macbeth. Then, afraid of being present at the discovery himself, he paused at the foot of the stairs and pointed, 'That's the door.'

'I'll make so bold as to call him,' said Macduff, 'for it is my appointed duty.'

While Macduff went to wake the King, Lennox chatted to Macbeth, telling him how stormy the night had been, and how the old people were prophesying some dreadful catastrophe to the country.

But Macbeth paid little attention: 'It was a rough night,' he agreed, his every nerve keyed to the cry which must come at any moment. . . .

'Oh, horror, horror, horror!' Macduff was at the top of the steps, his eyes wild with the dreadful sight he had seen, his tongue groping for words to express the enormity of what had happened. For this was not just a murder but the murder of a king. 'I cannot name it,' he cried. 'But come and look! This is terrible sacrilege—murder has struck at God's temple and stolen away the life. Come up and see: the sight will almost freeze you to stone with horror, as if it were another Gorgon.'

Then, while Lennox and Macbeth dashed past him into Duncan's room, Macduff let out his great voice until all the Castle came crowding to see what had happened; and soon the deep notes of the alarm-bell tolled with the terrible news.

No one was louder in his lamentations than Macbeth. But he overdid his grief and fury by killing the two valets who were supposed to be guilty, before they even had a chance to deny it. Many suspected Macbeth, but he was far too powerful to be accused—even by Banquo who had most reason for suspicion. As for Malcolm and Donalbain, Duncan's two sons, they fled at once fearing to share their father's fate; so Macbeth gave it out that they had plotted the murder, and had run away to escape punishment.

Under these circumstances, Macbeth was chosen King, and went to Scone to be crowned almost before Duncan's body was cold in its grave. Then he held court at Forres Castle, summoned his Thanes, and held a great feast at which the most honored guest was to be Banquo.

Macbeth was now at the pinnacle of his fortunes, and might to some extent have atoned for his crime by ruling well and justly.

But the murder of Duncan had blotted out all his finer feelings, and instead of bringing him peace of mind, had filled him with greater fears—though, as King, he had the power to safeguard himself. Moreover, having murdered a king, he felt that he was already damned, and that a few lesser murders could now make no difference.

'Merely to be King is nothing,' thought Macbeth. 'But to be safely King is everything. And there is Banquo. . . . When the witches prophesied that I should be King, he bade them speak to him; they told him that he should be the ancestor of a line of kings. If this is true, I've murdered Duncan and damned my soul to Hell so that Banquo's children shall be kings. But if I kill Banquo and his one son, Fleance, he *can't* have any descendants. And Banquo is dangerous. He's far too good a man to murder me as I did Duncan, but he's very likely to win the crown from me by honest means. . . . No, I must remove both him and Fleance, and at once.'

On the afternoon of the day for which the banquet was arranged Banquo and Fleance had gone out riding, and did not intend to be back at Forres until after dark. Here was Macbeth's chance. He hired two assassins to work for him, paying them well, and he persuaded them that they owed their lack of fortune to Banquo.

'Make sure that you kill Fleance as well,' he added. 'His absence is as necessary to me as his father's.'

Macbeth even sent a third murderer to help the two hired assassins, and they all hid in the park waiting for Banquo and Fleance to return. Having stabled their horses, the unsuspecting victims were finding their way towards the Castle with the aid of a single flaming torch, when the three murderers sprang out on them.

'Treachery!' cried Banquo. 'Fly, Fleance! Fly! You can revenge me!'

As Banquo fell, pierced through and through, he extinguished the torch on the ground, and in the sudden darkness Fleance got away unhurt.

Meanwhile, the feast was beginning in the Castle hall, and

Macbeth went among his guests welcoming each in turn. Presently he saw one of the assassins come in and stand by the door. As soon as he could, he went over and spoke to the man:

'There's blood on your face,' he said.

'It's Banquo's, then!' was the answer. 'He lies dead in a ditch, with twenty gaping wounds, each one enough to kill him.'

'You're a good cut-throat,' said Macbeth, with a grim chuckle. 'If you did the same for Fleance, you're best of them all.'

'Royal sir, Fleance escaped,' confessed the villain.

'Then I am still insecure!' exclaimed Macbeth. 'However, the full-grown serpent's destroyed, and there's time enough to deal with the worm that's fled.'

Feeling very much relieved that Banquo at least could trouble him no more, Macbeth returned to the table, and greeted his guests afresh, wishing them all health and happiness.

'And if only our dear Banquo were here,' he added, 'all the noblest and most important people in our country would be present tonight in my hall.'

'His absence breaks his promise,' said the Thane of Ross. 'And now may it please your majesty to join us at the table.'

'All the seats are full,' said Macbeth.

'There's one specially for you,' replied Lennox, pointing.

Macbeth took a step towards it, and saw that it was already occupied—by Banquo.

His first thought was of a trick. 'Which of you has done this?' he shouted.

'Done what?' several Thanes asked in surprise.

But now he saw that it was no trick—that it was Banquo's ghost wearing the likeness of his body still bleeding from the twenty hideous wounds that was each only too obviously fatal.

'You cannot say I did it!' cried Macbeth, staggering back in horror. 'Do not shake your blood-stained locks at me!'

'Gentlemen, rise! The King is ill!' exclaimed Ross.

'No, sit dear friends!' begged Lady Macbeth. 'My husband has these strange fits sometimes—he has had them all his life. They are momentary and are best ignored. He'll be all right again in a minute.'

Then she drew Macbeth aside, and tried to calm him. Neither she nor anyone else could see the ghost; but Macbeth could not believe that it was revealed only to himself and was invisible to others.

'This is no more than the air-drawn dagger that you saw on the night you killed Duncan,' she insisted. And as she spoke the ghost suddenly faded away, though Macbeth was still quite unnerved.

'Men have been murdered before now,' he muttered. 'But when their brains had been dashed out, they were dead, and that was the end of it. But now they rise from their graves, though they have twenty deadly wounds, and push us from our places.'

Realizing, however, that the ghost had gone and that the guests must be wondering at his strange behavior, Macbeth took a firm hold of himself and returned to the table.

'Do not be surprised, my good friends,' he said. 'This is a strange illness which comes on me suddenly from time to time— no more than that. Give me wine! I drink to you all—and to my dear friend Banquo, whom I miss sadly. I wish he was here!'

Scarcely had he spoken, when Banquo's ghost appeared once more sitting in his place. And again Macbeth lost all control:

'Go away!' he yelled. 'Leave my sight! You are dead! There is no blood in your veins, your flesh is cold—you cannot see out of those corpse-eyes with which you glare at me! Come in any other shape, and I'll not be afraid—the savage Russian bear, the Iranian tiger, the wild rhinoceros—none of them shall make me tremble! Or be alive again, and I'll fight you to the death!'

So he raved, until suddenly the ghost disappeared again, and with it went his terror. But now he could not believe that he alone had seen it, and spoke so wildly that in fear lest he should give himself away completely, Lady Macbeth begged the company to leave quickly.

Soon Macbeth sat alone at the banquet board; his wife stood beside him, drawn and haggard.

'Blood will have blood,' said Macbeth at last, for he realized that after what had happened that evening no one could again doubt his guilt. 'I've waded in so far that it would be harder to return than to go on. I'm fighting for myself now, and will consider nothing but my own advantage—I'll kill first, and think about right and wrong afterwards. But tomorrow I'll go and find the three witches: I ought to have gone sooner. They shall tell me more. By whatever means, I must know the worst.'

The three witches were ready for Macbeth. As, this time, they had to do more than merely tempt him with predictions—one true, and one for which he must do evil to fulfill—the Devil had sent Hecate, Queen of the Witches, to help them. With the aid of a charm that she brought from the further side of the moon— the home of unutterable wickedness—they would be able to show him false shapes and apparitions which could, if he believed them, lead him into the very depths of damnation.

When he reached their cave, they were already brewing charms in a great cauldron into which they threw a ghastly collection of ingredients which they themselves had collected. For Hecate saw to it that they should always be practising evil lest, if they paused even for a moment, their souls might be won back to salvation by the powers of good.

As they danced round the fire they chanted:

> 'Double, double toil and trouble;
> Fire, burn; and cauldron, bubble.'

Suddenly they paused, and one witch exclaimed exultantly:

> 'By the pricking of my thumbs,
> Something evil this way comes!'

The evil thing that came was Macbeth, and he demanded answers to his questions.

'You need not ask,' the witches told him. 'Those who will appear know before you speak. Listen to them, but say nothing!'

Then the thunder rumbled through the cave, the smoke and steam swirled up from the cauldron until all was filled with haze, and suddenly a head wearing a helmet seemed to rise up from

the seething Hell-broth, and spoke in deep, sepulchral tones:
'Macbeth! Macbeth! Macbeth! Beware Macduff. Beware the
Thane of Fife!'

As it faded slowly away into the fumes, Macbeth muttered to
himself:

'Whatever you are, your advice is good. I already distrusted
him, since he refused to come to my banquet at Forres.'

Then he was silent as there rose out of the cauldron the likeness
of a child dripping with blood:

'Macbeth! Macbeth! Macbeth!' it shrilled. 'Be bloodthirsty,
bold and resolute! Laugh at your enemies, for no one born of
woman shall harm you!'

'Then live, Macduff!' exclaimed Macbeth with a great sigh of
relief. 'But no, to make assurance double sure, you shall not live!'

Now the third apparition came into view, another child, but
holding a tree in its hand and chanting:

'Macbeth shall never vanquished be, until
Great Birnam Wood to high Dunsinane Hill
Shall come against him!'

'That can never happen!' cried Macbeth gleefully. 'No one can
tear up a whole forest and make it march against me like an
army! So I am safe. But one thing more troubles me. Will
Banquo's descendants ever reign in this kingdom?'

'Seek to know no more!' chanted the witches.

But Macbeth insisted; and there passed before him eight kings,
all looking like Banquo; and the last carried a mirror which
reflected yet more kings fading away into the distance. Last of all,
Banquo's ghost appeared, smiling triumphantly, and pointing
to the endless troop of his descendants.

Then the thunder roared once more, the smoke billowed out
until it filled the cave. And when it cleared, there was no sign of
the witches or their cauldron.

The very first news Macbeth heard when he left the cave
was that Macduff had fled to England. However, being now

absolutely merciless, he sent men to Macduff's castle in Fife to kill Lady Macduff and all her children, and with them every-one in the castle.

Now Scotland began to rebel against the tyrant Macbeth. In England, Macduff had joined Malcolm, Duncan's eldest son; and when the terrible news arrived from Fife, England's good and pious King, Edward the Confessor, whose very touch healed the sick, sent an army under Siward, Earl of Northumberland, to overthrow Macbeth and set Malcolm on the throne.

As his Thanes and their followers began to desert him, Macbeth withdrew into his strongest castle, that of Dunsinane, and fortified it as best he could. He still had an army—though most of his followers served him out of fear rather than love or even loyalty —and it was in fact larger than that of the liberators.

However, things were going very ill with him. Lady Macbeth had never been the same after the terrible banquet at which Banquo's ghost had been a guest; and her mind gradually gave way. She began walking in her sleep, and talking too: living over and over again the dreadful night on which she had helped Mac-beth to murder King Duncan, and trying in vain to wash imagin-ary blood from her hands.

At last, just as the invading forces drew near Dunsinane, her mind gave way completely, and she killed herself.

For a moment, Macbeth felt that nothing was worth living for, that life was a vain, empty mockery, a mere shadow without meaning. 'I have lived too long!' he thought bitterly. 'I am already growing old, but without the good things of age—love, honor, obedience, friends. Instead of these what have I? Curses, not loud but deep; honor that is no more than empty words that no one would utter if they weren't forced to by fear.'

Nevertheless, he rallied once more and made ready to sally out against the enemy, realizing that his whole future depended on this battle.

'Yet what does it matter?' he mused. 'No man born of woman can hurt me; nor can I be conquered till Birnam Wood comes to Dunsinane.'

Even while he bolstered himself with these prophecies, a

servant came stumbling down from the look-out tower of the castle, almost speechless with terror:

'Gracious my lord!' he gasped. 'I hardly dare to tell you what I've seen—no one could believe it!'

'Well?' barked Macbeth.

'As I stood on the tower and looked down the hill towards Birnam,' he said, 'the wood began to move!'

'Liar and slave!' hissed Macbeth. But the man stuck to his story.

'Kill me if it's not true! But come and see for yourself. The whole wood moves towards Dunsinane!'

'If you're lying, you shall hang on the nearest tree,' said Macbeth quietly. 'If you speak the truth, I shall hardly care if you do as much for me . . . I begin to doubt whether the Devil has not cheated me: "Do not fear till Birnam Wood comes to Dunsinane." And now a wood *is* moving towards Dunsinane. Well, at least I can die fighting! Ring the alarm-bell! Arm and out!'

The explanation of the moving wood was very simple. When Malcolm and the English army reached Birnam, very few of the Thanes who had revolted from Macbeth had yet joined him, and his forces seemed ridiculously small. But Earl Siward was a general of great cunning and long experience.

'Let every soldier cut a branch from the nearest tree,' he said, 'and march forward in open order, holding it up. That will make our army seem several times larger than it is.'

Only when Macbeth's forces poured out of the Castle against them did the English soldiers throw down their branches; then the last battle was joined with great fierceness—for Macbeth was still a brave warrior and a furious fighter.

'*You* were born of woman!' he cried exultantly as he slew Earl Siward's son. But he avoided Macduff who was raging through the battle seeking him, yearning to avenge the cruel slaughter of his wife and children.

Near the end of the day, when the battle was almost won, and Macbeth's wretched followers were going over to Malcolm in larger and larger numbers, Macduff came up with him.

'Turn, hell-hound, turn!' he shouted.

'Of all men, I have avoided you only,' said Macbeth. 'I have too much guilt for your blood on my head already.'

'I have nothing to say,' shouted Macduff, advancing upon him. 'My voice is in my sword—you bloodier villain than words can describe!'

They fought for a while without either wounding the other, lashing together with their broadswords so furiously that at last they paused for breath.

'This is all wasted labour,' panted Macbeth. 'I bear a charmed life which no one born of woman can take from me.'

'Then despair of your charm!' cried Macduff triumphantly. 'The devil whom you serve did not tell you that I was never born of woman. For my mother was dead before the surgeons took me from her body!'

'Accursed be the tongue that tells me so!' exclaimed Macbeth. 'For you have made a coward of me. Never again let these fiends be believed. They cheat us with double meanings, keeping their word, but breaking their promise. I'll not fight with you.'

'Then live!' taunted Macduff. 'Yield, coward, and we'll put you in a cage for people to stare at when they want to see what a tyrant looks like.'

'I will not live to kiss the ground before young Malcolm's feet!' cried Macbeth, some of his old courage returning to him. 'Though Birnam Wood has come to Dunsinane, and you were never born of woman, I'll fight you to the last! Lay on, Macduff; and let him be damned who first cries out for mercy.'

So Macbeth died fighting, and Macduff cut off his head and carried it in triumph to Malcolm, who was proclaimed King of Scotland there on the field of battle.

But though Malcolm reigned long and justly, and was much beloved by his subjects, the throne passed in time to Banquo's descendants. And one of them was James VI of Scotland who became James I of England, and is the ancestor of Queen Elizabeth II.

KING LEAR

Long ago there was a King in Britain called Lear. He had three daughters: Goneril, the eldest, was married to the Duke of Albany; Regan, the second, to the Duke of Cornwall. But the youngest, the most beautiful, and her father's favorite, was Cordelia who was unmarried but had two suitors, the King of France and the Duke of Burgundy.

When the time came for the successful suitor to be named, King Lear who was by now an old man announced his intention of resigning the throne and dividing his kingdom into three parts, to be ruled by his three daughters and their husbands.

As Lear had grown older, he had become more and more accustomed to being obeyed and flattered, and he had become less able to control his violent temper to which he gave way if crossed or annoyed by anything. It was high time for him to lay down his sceptre; but though he was prepared to admit this, and even announced his intention, he could not actually bring himself to do it. Indeed, to make up for the apparent loss of power which he was about to allow, he wanted to be flattered and treated almost as a god.

So he called his whole court together, summoned his three daughters, and declared his wishes:

'Let it be known to all!' he said impressively, 'we have divided in three our kingdom, and intend to shake ourselves free of all cares and business of State, and enjoy our ease during the last few years of life. Our son of Cornwall, and no less dear son of Albany, we propose to declare here and now what dowries we have settled on our daughters—here on this map to point out how we have divided our kingdom among them. And at this same time to choose whether the sovereigns of France or Burgundy shall wed our youngest daughter. Now tell me, my daughters'—Lear dropped the royal 'we' for a moment to point the fact that he spoke as their father as well as their king—'since now we propose to divest us of rule, of interest in territories and of the cares of State, which of you loves me most? Who loves most shall receive the largest share. Goneril, our eldest born, speak first.'

'Sir, I love you more than words can describe,' exclaimed Goneril flinging herself on her knees on the lowest steps leading up to the throne, and making her voice tremble to suggest the overwhelming power of her affection. 'You are dearer to me than the sight of my eyes, than liberty itself; you are beyond anything that can be valued, either for richness or rarity; you are no less than grace, health, beauty, honour—life itself. No child has ever loved a father as much as I love you. My love is so great that it makes breath poor and speech unable to express it. Yes, and I love you still more, even beyond all that I've tried to suggest.'

At all these extravagant words Cordelia shuddered, thinking to herself: 'My love would be desecrated by such words.' But Lear lapped up the flattery and adulation eagerly.

'Then you have deserved all these lands,' and he pointed them out to her and Albany on the map. 'And we give them to you now, and to your heirs forever. So. Now what has our second daughter, our beloved Regan to say?'

'I am made of the same pure metal as my sister,' she answered, kneeling before the besotted old King and raising her hands to him as if in worship. 'Her words have expressed all that is in my heart—only she falls short of the love that I bear to you. No other joy in life is equal to my joy in loving you.'

'Alas for me,' thought Cordelia. 'And yet I am not poor: I'm sure my love is richer than my tongue can ever be.'

'This is your third of the kingdom,' said Lear, almost purring with gratified vanity as he pointed out Regan's portion on the map. 'And we here and now make it yours and your heirs' forever. But now our joy: last, but not least—our youngest, for whose hand both France and Burgundy are contending. What can you say to win a richer third than either of your sisters?'

'Nothing, my lord,' said Cordelia quietly.

'Nothing!' exclaimed Lear in amazement.

'Nothing,' repeated Cordelia firmly.

'Nothing will come of nothing,' said Lear warningly. 'Speak again.'

'Then I am unfortunate,' said Cordelia, showing perhaps a little of her father's obstinacy in her refusal to pander to his vanity with fulsome lies like her sisters. 'I love your majesty as much as is right and proper, nor more nor less.'

'How's this, Cordelia?' Lear was keeping his temper with difficulty. 'Be careful what you say, or it will be the worse for you.'

'I love you, obey you, honor you as a daughter should,' said Cordelia. 'Why have my sisters husbands, if they say that all their love is yours? When I marry, surely my husband will receive half my love and duty. I shall certainly never marry if, like my sisters, I give all my love to my father.'

'Do you mean this?' asked Lear.

'Certainly I do,' replied Cordelia.

'So young, and so unnatural?' Lear seemed almost puzzled for a moment.

'So young, my lord, but true,' said Cordelia stoutly.

'So be it,' said Lear quietly, 'and let truth be your dowry. For—' and he suddenly burst out into a bellow of rage, 'by the radiance of the sun, by all the stars, I cut you off from me here and now. You are no longer my child. From now onwards and forever I look on you as a stranger; cannibals and savages shall be as near to my heart as you.'

At this the most faithful and honorable of his lords tried to interrupt; but Lear cut him short and went on working himself up into an ecstasy of rage and wounded vanity.

'Be quiet, Kent,' he raved. 'Do not come between the dragon and his anger. I loved her most, and looked forward to spending my old age with her. But now I'll give away all that I had kept for her. Cornwall and Albany, divide her dowry between you. Let pride, which she calls plain-speaking, be her portion. The sovreignty is now yours. All I retain is the name and reverence of King; and I will dwell with you, month and month about, with a hundred knights whom I retain to be my guards and companions, but whom you must keep and entertain. And as token of the power which I now hand over to you, take this my royal crown and divide it between you.'

'Royal Lear!' cried the Earl of Kent, breaking in at last. 'Let me speak! I have always honored you as my King, loved you as if you were my father, and served you faithfully. Forgive me for speaking bluntly. I must do so, since you are behaving as if you were mad. What are you doing, old man? Age is blinding you. Do not condemn your youngest daughter; she does not love you least—remember that empty vessels make the most sound.'

'No more, Kent, or your life's in danger!' shouted Lear.

'I never valued my life more than a pawn to be used against your enemies,' answered Kent stoutly. 'Nor do I fear to lose it, since you are running into fresh danger now. Cancel the sentence you have pronounced on Cordelia, and give her back her share of the kingdom. While I can still speak, it will be to tell you that what you are doing is wrong.'

'Since you have dared to try and make me break my vow— have tried to come between me and the exercise of my power—' cried Lear, 'I banish you from the kingdom. If in ten days' time you are still in the country, you die.'

'Then farewell, King,' said Kent, 'since freedom no longer dwells in your country. May the gods protect you, Cordelia, who only think as you should, and who have said what it was right to say. As for you,' he turned to Goneril and Regan, 'I hope that your words of love may lead to deeds as kind.'

Kent had scarcely gone, when the Earl of Gloster ushered in the King of France and the Duke of Burgundy.

Lear wasted very little time over them. 'If you will marry my daughter Cordelia for love, and take her without any dowry at all, she is yours. But you shall have nothing with her: she has forfeited my love.'

The Duke of Burgundy turned down the offer immediately, refusing even to think of marrying Cordelia without her third of the kingdom. But the King of France asked what she had done to forfeit Lear's love, for he felt that it must be some terrible crime to be punished so harshly. When he learnt what it was, and that even so, the Duke of Burgundy would have none of her, he broke out:

'Fairest Cordelia, who is most rich, being poor; most worthy to be chosen, being forsaken; and most lovable, since others despise you. If you will have me, I take you here and now. It is strange how, in your misfortune, my love grows all the stronger. King Lear, your dowerless daughter is now Queen of us, of all that is ours, of France itself. Bid your father and sisters farewell, Cordelia: you will find more kindliness across the sea.'

'Take her, France,' said Lear with an imperious wave of the hand. 'Let her be altogether yours. We have no such daughter— nor do we ever desire to see her face again.'

So Cordelia went away to become Queen of France, though with dread in her heart, for she knew how false and self-seeking her sisters were. She feared greatly that her father—whom she still loved dearly, in spite of his unkindness—would suffer bitter disappointment and neglect in their care, if nothing worse.

Sure enough, scarcely were they alone together, when Goneril and Regan fell to plotting how they could rob the King of his last vestiges of power, and deprive him even of the hundred knights who were to attend on him.

He was to spend the first month with Goneril, and she instructed her steward, Oswald, and the rest of her servants to be as rude as possible, and to pick any quarrels they could with the King's followers. Such behavior was all too easy; for Lear did not intend to play the humble guest. He still considered himself King, and expected every scrap of his former dignity to be observed. Everyone was still to cringe to him and leap to obey his smallest wish, just as in the days when he had absolute power of life and death.

But his circumstances were now very different; and indeed, before long he found that he had only two really faithful friends.

One of these was his Fool, a very wise man who hid his wisdom in his jests, and who, because official Jesters were allowed a measure of free speech, was the only man who dared to tell Lear the truth. The other was a new servant whose rough and bluff good humor and honesty attracted Lear, and had made him trust the man from the first. Though he did not know it, he was right in his judgement, since this downright, abrupt serving-man was none other than the banished Earl of Kent, disguised to serve the master whom he loved.

Lear was not an easy guest, and Goneril magnified every petty complaint and misunderstanding with gleeful malice. She soon decided to bring matters to a head, and therefore directed Oswald to tell the King when he returned from hunting that she was not feeling well, and could not see him.

'Be as offhand as you please,' she said, 'you and the rest of the servants. I want to upset him. Then if he's really angry, he'll storm out and go to my sister—who'll treat him just as I do. He's a silly old man, who still behaves as if he were King, even though he's given away all the power to enforce his will. He's in his second childhood, and must be treated accordingly. Remember what I have said, and see to it that his knights get even less courteous treatment. You understand?'

'Very well, madam,' smirked Oswald, who was the sort of man who delights in being rude to a superior if he can do so with impunity. And he had not long to wait; for the moment Lear came in from hunting, he sent his attendants scurrying in every direction to get his dinner ready and find his Fool.

When the immediate activity had ceased, Oswald strolled across in front of the King.

'You there, fellow,' called Lear. 'Where's my daughter?'

'Excuse me, sir,' replied Oswald, and strolled out as if he could not be bothered to answer.

'What does he say?' exploded Lear. 'Call the fat-head back! And send my Fool.'

One of his knights went after Oswald, and returned a moment later looking rather blank.

'Well?' demanded the King. 'Where's my daughter?'

'He says,' answered the knight, 'that your daughter isn't very well.'

'And why didn't that oaf come back to deliver the message himself?' shouted Lear.

'Sir,' replied the knight, 'he answered me in the rudest possible manner. He said he wouldn't.'

'He would not?' Lear seemed hardly to understand.

'My lord,' went on the knight, 'I don't know if I'm right, but it seems to me that these last few days your majesty has not been attended with the ceremony that is your due. Nor do we seem to have fared any better.'

'I too have noticed a good deal of slackness,' said Lear. 'I'll speak about it to my daughter. Now go and find my Fool.' Scarcely had the knight gone, when Oswald appeared again.

'Oh, you sir! Come here!' shouted the King. And when Oswald stood before him, he frowned and said with heavy irony: 'Who am I, sir?'

'You, oh my mistress's father,' replied Oswald offhandedly.

' "My mistress's father!", ' Lear mimicked Oswald's affected lisp. Then he roared: 'Your master's knave! You filthy bastard! You slave! You abject cur!'

'I'm none of these, my lord,' stammered Oswald, scared into good manners by Lear's rage. 'I beg your pardon.' But then, regretting his moment of courtesy, he grinned impudently at Lear, who immediately struck him with his whip.

'I won't stand being struck——' began Oswald. But Kent, who was standing by in his guise of Lear's new servant, sent him sprawling with a neat twist of the ankle.

'Nor being tripped either, you vile footballer!' cried Kent. 'Now then, up you get, and make yourself scarce—or I'll trip you again, and teach you your place!'

Oswald departed in a hurry, and Lear thanked his new servant, and then turned with delight to welcome his Fool.

But the Fool had only bitter jests for him which underlined the truths that he felt it his duty to make clear to his master—who was not altogether willing to hear them even from one with such special privileges.

'Please nuncle,' said the Fool at last, 'keep a schoolmaster that can teach your Fool to tell lies. I should like to learn how to lie.'

'If you do, I'll have you whipped,' said the King.

'It surprises me that you and your daughters are related,' the Fool remarked. 'They threaten to have me whipped for telling the truth, and you'll have me whipped for lying. And sometimes I'm whipped for saying nothing at all. I'd rather be any kind of thing than a Fool—and yet I wouldn't like to be you, nuncle. You've sharpened your wits on both sides—and left nothing in the middle. Here comes one of the sides you've cut away!'

It was Goneril, looking thoroughly annoyed, and Lear began at once:

'What's the meaning of this look? There have been too many frowns lately.'

'You were better off when you didn't need to care whether she frowned or not,' remarked the Fool. 'Now you're a zero sign with no figure in front of it to make it a number. I'm better off than you are: I'm a fool—but you're nothing. Yes, madam, I'll hold my tongue—for so your look bids me, though you don't say it.'

'It's not only this over-indulged Fool of yours who causes trouble,' said Goneril with carefully weighed insolence, 'but all the rest of your bad-mannered knights and servants. I thought that you would have kept them in better order; but now I see that you are encouraging them in their riotous behavior. If this be so, we will have to take steps in the interest of law and order, which without so good an excuse might seem hard on you, but which, under the circumstances, everyone will praise.'

'Remember the song, nuncle!' interrupted the Fool, while Lear stood speechless with amazement and rising fury:

' "The hedge-sparrow fed the cuckoo so long
   That it had its head bit off by its young."

'So out went the candle, and we were left in the dark.'

'Are you our daughter?' began Lear, working himself up into a royal rage. But Goneril cut in quickly:

'Be sensible, father: carrying on like this will get you nowhere.'

'Even a donkey can see when it's the cart that draws the horse,' remarked the Fool.

Lear was so taken aback for a moment he seemed lost:

'Who am I?' he asked. 'Am I not the King? Am I not Lear?'

'Only Lear's shadow,' muttered the Fool.

'This is just typical of your general behavior lately,' went on Goneril remorselessly. 'You are an old man, and should have more sense. Here you keep a hundred knights, men who are so ill-mannered and disorderly that they reduce this place to the level of a tavern. Such a shameful state of affairs calls for instant remedy, and I beg you to take steps immediately; otherwise I'll take the matter into my own hands. You don't need a hundred knights: choose out a number of the more sober and suitable, and dismiss the rest.'

Then Lear really lost control of himself. He stormed and raved, cursing Goneril in the most outrageous terms, and lamenting his treatment of Cordelia for so small a fault compared with Goneril's. The Duke of Albany, who had no part in Goneril's schemes, but was very much under his wife's thumb, tried to pacify Lear, but in vain. The almost demented King insisted on setting out immediately with all his followers to stay with Regan, whom he was sure would treat him properly and be thoroughly shocked by the unnatural behavior of her elder sister.

But scarcely had Lear left the house, when Goneril dispatched Oswald to Regan, with a letter warning her what Lear was doing, and reminding her how to treat him.

In order to prepare Regan and her husband, the Duke of Cornwall, for his coming, Lear sent his servant, the disguised Earl of Kent, in advance with letters, while he followed more slowly with his company and the Fool.

Kent had hardly reached the Duke of Cornwall's palace when Oswald arrived with his letter from Goneril. On reading this, Regan and her husband immediately left their own palace and travelled speedily to the Earl of Gloster's castle. They told Kent to follow them and wait for his answer.

Kent was annoyed by this; and, meeting Oswald outside the castle, he lost his temper and drew his sword on Goneril's impudent steward. The cowardly Oswald immediately screamed for help, and the Duke of Cornwall had Kent arrested and put in the stocks outside the castle gate.

There Kent sat all night until he was found next day by King Lear who arrived with only the Fool and a single one of his knights, having left the rest at Cornwall's palace in his haste to find Regan and be comforted and reassured by her.

'I can't understand how they came to leave home so suddenly,' Lear was saying. 'And they did not even send back my messenger.'

'They had no intention of leaving, until the last moment,' remarked the knight.

'Good morning, noble master!' cried Kent from the stocks.

'Hallo!' exclaimed the Fool. 'He's wearing a very uncomfortable pair of garters!'

'Who dared to put you there?' demanded Lear, and would hardly believe it when Kent told him that it was Regan and Cornwall. And when he heard how they had immediately left home on receiving the letter from Goneril, and that Kent had been stocked simply for beating Oswald, Lear's rage was such that he felt as if his mind might give way at any moment.

'Let me not go mad, dear God!' he cried. 'Not mad!'

When he found the Earl of Gloster, the whole business seemed to be even worse, for Gloster—who, though honest, liked to have his cake and eat it if he possibly could—only infuriated him further by making excuses for Cornwall and Regan:

'They are ill and tired, after travelling all night,' he said lamely. 'And how can I bring you a better answer? You know, sire, how fiery the Duke's temper is.'

'Vengeance! Plague! Death! Confusion!' foamed Lear. '*Fiery!* Gloster, I wish to speak with the Duke of Cornwall and his wife!'

'Well, I've informed them so,' hesitated poor old Gloster.

'Informed them!' raved the King. 'I don't inform, I command! Tell them to come out at once—and to release my servant from the stocks. This instant!'

'All I want is peace between you,' sighed Gloster as he hastened away.

But Regan did not bring any peace with her when at last she obeyed Lear's summons. Indeed she was even more insolent and callous than Goneril had been, and her husband backed her up in everything, being if anything crueller than she herself.

'You are old and foolish,' she ended. 'You should do what we think best, as we know much better than you do. So go back to my sister, and beg her pardon. You can't stay with me now, I'm not expecting you until the end of the month. And anyhow, I'm away from home until then.'

Lear had scarcely had time to realize what Regan was saying, when Goneril arrived and was warmly greeted by her sister, in spite of all that Lear had said about her bad behavior.

After that the two evil women seemed to vie with one another to see who could hurt the old man most and drive him into the greatest paroxysm of frenzy. Before they had finished, they had both declared themselves unwilling to shelter him so long as he was accompanied by even one of his knights, and had driven Lear to the very edge of madness.

'Oh you unnatural hags!' he raved. 'I'll have such revenges on you both that all the world shall—— I will do such things—— what they are, I don't yet know, but they'll be the terrors of the earth. You think I'll break down and weep. No, I'll never do that, though I have a hundred causes for tears. Oh, Fool, I shall go mad!'

And with his mind already failing, Lear turned suddenly and dashed away into the night, followed by Kent and the Fool.

'There's a storm coming up,' said Cornwall. 'Let's retire into the castle.'

'The King is out in it——' began Gloster.

'Let him stay out,' said Regan. 'Wilfull men must have their own way.'

'Shut the doors,' agreed Cornwall. 'It's a wild night, and Regan is right. Come in, out of the storm.'

But the Earl of Gloster, though weak, was not wicked. He could not bear to think of Lear out on the open moorland on such a night, and he decided to slip away quietly and help him—in spite of strict orders from Regan and the Duke of Cornwall, who even threatened him with death if he followed Lear.

Before setting out, Gloster told his son Edmund what he intended to do, since he required Edmund to hide the fact that he had gone and, if need be, to tell the Duke that he was ill and had retired to bed.

'I may tell you also,' Gloster confided to Edmund, 'that the King has friends who have heard how he is being treated, and intend to avenge his injuries. Only today I received a letter in secret saying that the King of France is on his way with an army: I've locked it away in my study, for it would be dangerous if the Duke were to see it.'

Edmund agreed readily to hide his father's absence, and the old Earl hurried out into the night, where a great storm was raging, in search of Lear.

But Lear was not the only father to be betrayed by his children. The King's inability to control his passions, and the calculating cruelty and viciousness of his two elder daughters, was mirrored in Gloster's own family. Edmund was his illegitimate son. His true son, Edgar had suffered even more severely than Cordelia. Edmund was completely wicked, but extremely cunning, while Edgar was the exact opposite: transparently honest and quite unsuspecting of any guile. At about the same time that Lear was disinheriting Cordelia, Edmund deceived Gloster into thinking that Edgar was plotting to murder him so as to become Earl; he then tricked Edgar into believing that he was in danger from unknown enemies. Edgar fled; and Edmund, after giving himself a trifling wound that would bleed convincingly, shouted for help, and swore that Edgar had tried to kill him for refusing to help murder Gloster. Consequently Edgar was proclaimed an outlaw whom anyone might kill on sight, and as he was not able to get out of the country, he disguised himself as a half-naked mad beggar—a Tom o' Bedlam. There were a number of these poor madmen wandering about the countryside, and living as tramps, in those days when there were no asylums for them.

Of course Gloster knew nothing of Edgar's plight. He disowned the son whom he thought had tried to murder him, and believed that Edmund, who had apparently saved his life, was everything that a virtuous and dutiful son should be.

Edmund, however, cared about nobody and nothing but himself. As soon as Gloster had gone out into the storm to look for Lear, he went to his father's study, found the letter, and took it to Cornwall and Regan.

'I would rather have my hand cut off than inform on my father like this,' he lied. 'But patriotism, and my loyalty to you, leave me no other choice. This letter shows that my father is a traitor conspiring against our country with its enemies.'

'You have done nobly,' said Cornwall, 'and I here and now create you Earl of Gloster, with all your father's lands and wealth. Go, seek him out, that he may be arrested and brought before us for punishment.'

'If I find him comforting the King, his perfidy will seem even more certain,' thought Edmund. 'I will obey your command,' he added aloud, 'though my heart aches at the prospect of doing anything against my father.'

Gloster took some time to find Lear, for the night was very dark, and a most tremendous storm was raging, with deluging rain, thunder, lightning and a tearing gale.

Kent and the Fool had done their best to help the poor old King. But owing to the cruel shocks which Goneril and Regan had given him, and the sudden change that had turned him from a rather pampered King into a beggar without a roof to cover his white head, Lear had gone completely out of his mind.

As if to make his extraordinary change of fortune even more acute, the wretched hut of sticks and clay where they at last found shelter, was occupied by Edgar, masquerading as a mad Tom o' Bedlam. And the more Edgar, who was pretending to be mad, raved and talked nonsense, the more Lear, who really was mad, insisted that he had at last found a truly wise man.

'Poor fellow,' said Lear pityingly, when he saw Edgar's condition. 'Have his daughters brought him to this? Could he save nothing?'

'Only a blanket,' muttered the Fool, through his chattering teeth. 'Otherwise he wouldn't have been fit to be seen.'

'All the plagues in the world fall on his daughters!' cried Lear.

'He has no daughters, sir,' said Kent, trying to bring the King to his senses.

'Confound you, traitor!' shouted Lear. 'Nothing would have reduced a man to such a state except unkind daughters.'

> 'Pillicock sat on Pillicock-Hill:
> Halloo, halloo, loo, loo!'

sang Edgar.

'Tonight will turn us all into fools or madmen, it's so cold,' sobbed the Fool.

It was in this condition that the Earl of Gloster found them, and tried to get Lear into proper shelter for the night.

'Come with me,' he urged. 'I'll take you to a farmhouse of mine. I cannot obey all your daughter's commands, though they told me to shut you out and let cold and wet do their worst to you. I've a fire and some food waiting for you.'

'First let me talk with this learned philosopher,' said Lear, pointing to Edgar.

'Good my lord, accept his offer and go to the house,' urged Kent.

'I'll talk with this Theban scholar,' insisted Lear. 'What is your special subject?'

'How to prevent the devils from tearing me!' shrieked Edgar, 'and how to catch vermin!'

'His mind is going,' said Kent sadly. 'It's no good asking him anything.'

'It's not surprising,' answered Gloster, shaking his head. 'His daughters hope he will die out in the cold tonight. Help me lead him to shelter.'

Between them, they got the old King into an empty farmhouse not far from the castle, and Gloster hastened away to bring food and cloaks. While he was gone, Lear, now quite mad, imagined he was conducting the trial of his two wicked daughters—and even Edgar was so moved to tears by the pathetic sight that he could hardly keep up his own Tom o' Bedlam act on which his life depended.

Even here, however, Lear was not to be left in peace. He had just fallen asleep when Gloster returned.

'Lift him up and bring him quickly!' he exclaimed. 'I've over-heard a plot to murder him. But I have a litter waiting, with men who'll carry him to Dover where he'll find friends.'

'If only he could have remained undisturbed now,' sighed Kent, 'the madness might have left him. Well, help me with him, Fool. You must not stay here either.'

'I'll go to bed at noon,' sobbed the Fool, who was completely worn out. He continued to do all he could for his beloved master, though he did not live to reach Dover with him.

When Lear had been smuggled away, with Kent and the Fool still attending on him, Edgar lurked behind as Mad Tom, and Gloster went back to his castle. There the cruel Duke of Cornwall was in charge; and when he heard that Gloster had returned, he had him seized and bound. He then sent Edmund with Goneril and Oswald to muster their forces, since news came that the French army was already landed at Dover.

When Cornwall and Regan had the poor old Earl of Gloster to themselves, their rage and cruelty knew no bounds. In revenge for rescuing Lear and giving him an escort to join the King of France and Cordelia at Dover, Cornwall blinded him with his own hands, while Regan stood by shrieking taunts—a deed so horrible that one of Cornwall's servants drew his sword and attacked his master in an attempt to prevent it. Regan stabbed the man from behind, and he died; but not before he had given Cornwall a fatal wound.

When Gloster was blind, Cornwall told his other servants to turn him out of the castle, and 'let him smell his way to Dover.' But these two were much more merciful than their fiendish master and did what they could to ease Gloster's pain by putting a bandage across his face and finding 'Mad Tom' to lead him.

So Edgar, still disguised, found himself in charge of his own father, whom he thought had tried to kill him, but was now blinded and dying. He tended the old man carefully, though he

did not reveal who he was for a long time. He led his father by
easy stages towards Dover, changing his disguise on the way
from Mad Tom to a poor countryman with a strong Somerset
accent. In this condition they were found by Oswald, who had
been sent with letters from Goneril to Edmund—and had also
been told to kill Gloster if he should happen to meet him.

Oswald prepared to obey these cruel orders, but Edgar defended the old man with his cudgel, even against Oswald's sword.

'Out of the way, you dunghill!' swore Oswald. 'Leave that
traitor, or I'll kill you too!'

'It be no matter for your saard!' cried Edgar. 'Us'll pick tha
teeth wi' this!' and he waved his cudgel.

Oswald promptly lunged at him with his sword, thinking that
a mere peasant would not be able to defend himself. But Edgar
parried the thrust and struck Oswald so hard a blow on his skull
that the villain was brought to a well-deserved end.

Oswald being dead, Edgar made so bold as to read the letter he was carrying, in which Goneril urged Edmund to murder her husband, the Duke of Albany, so as to marry her himself. Armed with this letter, Edgar led Gloster as near to the field of battle as he dared, and lay hidden under a tree, waiting to see what would happen.

Meanwhile the King of France was forced, by urgent matters of State, to return to his kingdom, but Cordelia remained to command the army. Her messengers found the mad King Lear wandering on the downs above Dover, and brought him to her camp. There medical aid and a long sleep more or less restored his wits, and her tender love and care began to make up for the inhuman cruelty of his other two daughters.

They, however, were not idle. Although Albany disapproved strongly of what Cornwall had done, and indeed of all that the two sisters were doing, he finally gathered his men together and marched to repel the invaders.

Edmund continued with his plots, becoming so deeply involved that he found himself secretly engaged to both Goneril and Regan. Feeling sure that one would remove the other sooner or later, Edmund went on his wicked way unconcerned. Albany did nothing to check him—he was too busy preparing for the battle. In this the British powers were successful, the French defeated and driven to their ships, and Lear and Cordelia captured and sent to Dover Castle.

Now events moved quickly. Edgar in disguise had given Albany Goneril's letter, and promised to produce a champion to fight Edmund after the battle. For it was held that in such a trial by combat, the guilty party would be sure to fall before the hand of justice.

As soon as the battle was over, Albany took charge, and arrested Edmund as a traitor. He had a furious quarrel with Goneril and Regan, but refused to obey either of them, and commanded the trumpet to sound.

At the third blast, Edgar appeared, wearing a helmet with a visor, and challenged Edmund, who denied the name of traitor, and agreed to fight it out. In their duel justice prevailed, and Edmund fell, mortally wounded. Only then did Edgar reveal who he was, and point out how Gloster's original weakness had cost him his eyes and subsequent death; and how Edmund's sheer wickedness had brought him no good, but a fatal sword-thrust after bringing misery and death on many others besides himself.

'What you say is true,' gasped Edmund, 'the wheel is come full circle.'

While Edgar was telling Albany all that had happened, and the disguised Kent was revealing who he was and how he had attended Lear throughout his sufferings, a servant rushed up to them, gasping with horror and carrying a blood-stained knife in his hand: Goneril had poisoned Regan out of jealousy; and when her plot to murder Albany had been discovered through the letter which Edgar had taken from Oswald, she had stabbed herself.

'I am dying,' gasped Edmund. 'But I'll do some good before I go, despite my nature. Send quickly to the Castle—run! Goneril and I gave orders for both Lear and Cordelia to be killed in the prison. The Captain of the Guard was instructed to hang Cordelia, and then pretend she'd committed suicide on her father's death.'

Edgar set off at full speed. But he was too late. He returned a few minutes later accompanying Lear who carried the dead body of Cordelia in his arms.

'Howl, howl, howl!' cried Lear. 'Oh you are men of stone! Weep with me! Weep!'

Lear laid Cordelia on the ground, and knelt beside her, while all stood round in stricken silence, and Edmund was carried away to die.

'She's not dead!' Lear insisted at first. 'See, this feather stirs on her lips!'

'Oh my dear master,' sobbed Kent, kneeling beside him.

'A plague upon you all, murderers, traitors!' cried Lear. 'I might have saved her, but now she's gone forever. Cordelia, Cordelia! Wait for me a little while.'

Now Albany knelt by the King and formally gave back to him all his powers for the rest of his life. But it was too late: Lear could scarcely even understand what was said to him.

'And my poor child is hanged,' he murmured. 'No life, no

life at all. Why should a dog, a horse, a rat have life, and Cordelia no breath at all? You'll come to me no more: never, never, never, never, never . . . Pray you, undo this button . . . Thank you sir . . . Look! Look! her lips—look there!'

Lear bent forward over Cordelia and was silent.

'He's fainted,' whispered Edgar.

'Break, heart, I beg you, break,' said Kent quietly.

'My lord, look up!' insisted Edgar.

'Do not trouble his parting soul,' whispered Kent, the tears streaming down his cheeks. 'It would be no kindness to wish him further torture in this cruel world.'

'He's gone indeed,' said Edgar.

'The wonder is that he endured so long,' muttered Kent.

'Our first duty is one of mourning for the King and his noble daughter,' proclaimed the Duke of Albany. 'Then to restore peace and order to this sadly ravaged land. Edgar—you are now Earl of Gloster—you and Kent, two friends of my soul, help me in this great task; it is our final duty to our King.'

Part III

THE ROMANCES

CYMBELINE

ONCE UPON A time, in the early years of our era, when Britain was part of the Roman Empire, there was a King called Cymbeline who had two sons and a daughter. While the boys, Guiderius and Arviragus, were still babies, they were stolen away from their home and never heard of again—though it was thought that the thief was a lord called Belarius who had recently been banished by King Cymbeline. But long and careful search through the whole island of Britain revealed no trace either of Belarius or of the two little princes.

Thus Cymbeline's one daughter Imogen became heir to his throne. She grew up clever and brave and beautiful, and many young men sought her hand in marriage. But the King would allow none of them to woo his daughter: he intended her for his step-son, Cloten.

Imogen's mother had died of sorrow not long after the loss of her sons, and when Imogen was just growing up, Cymbeline married again. His new Queen was a widow with a single son Cloten, who was to be Imogen's husband. But from the first she hated him—and so did most of the people at Cymbeline's court—for he was cruel and rough, and boorish, full of self-conceit, and wanting in honor.

The man Imogen loved was a brave young Roman called Posthumus Leonatus whom Cymbeline had adopted. His father had been killed before he was born, and his mother died when he was a small baby, and Cymbeline had brought him up to be a knight at court.

Posthumus and Imogen had loved one another from childhood. And when the King married again, and both he and her stepmother began to make Imogen's life a burden by forcing Cloten upon her, she and Posthumus were married in secret.

When it was discovered, Cymbeline's rage knew no bounds. The Queen pretended to be very sorry for Imogen and promised to influence the King to forgive Posthumus, though in fact she did exactly the opposite. But she could not persuade Cymbeline to kill him—only to banish the young Roman from Britain.

Posthumus and Imogen had no more than a few moments for leave-taking. The Queen found them together, and promised to keep the King away until they had made their farewells; instead however, she went straight to him, and told him that they were speaking together in complete disregard of his commands.

'Do not weep, my sweet lady,' Posthumus was begging Imogen. 'However long we are separated, I swear to remain true to you. Write to me whenever you can. I shall be in Rome with a friend of my father's called Philario.'

'Wear this ring, and think of me whenever you look on it,' sobbed Imogen. 'It belonged to my mother. Keep it, till you woo another wife—when I am dead.'

'You are the only wife that I shall ever have,' said Posthumus, taking the ring, 'even though I lose you today for ever. This ring will remain on my finger until I am dead—unless you claim it back when we are united once more. Now you shall wear this bracelet—a manacle of love, which I clasp round the wrist of my fair prisoner!'

Scarcely had they exchanged gifts when Cymbeline came bursting into the room in a royal rage:

'Go, you vile wretch!' he shouted as soon as he saw Posthumus. 'If you are seen ever again at my court, you die! Away, you are like poison to my blood!'

'May the good gods protect you, and bless your court!' said Posthumus, bowing to the angry king, as he turned and went.

'There cannot be any pang, even in death, more painful than this,' sobbed Imogen.

'You wicked, undutiful daughter,' stormed the King. 'Are you past all grace, past all obedience? Your disobedience has aged me by a year. And you might have had my Queen's only son for a husband!'

'Thank Heaven that I did not,' answered Imogen with spirit. 'I chose an eagle—and in so doing avoided a toad.'

'You took a beggar who would have made my throne a seat for baseness,' cried the King.

'No, he would have added lustre to it!' answered Imogen. 'Yet I wish I were but a farmer's daughter, and Posthumus our neighboring shepherd's son.

'Take her away!' shouted the King to the Queen. 'Look after her. Keep her locked up! We'll find a way to break her wicked obstinacy.'

So poor Imogen was kept in the palace, her only friend a servant of Posthumus's called Pisanio, who did his best to comfort her after he had seen Posthumus set sail for Rome. And she needed comfort, for she was constantly pestered by Cloten and urged both by the Queen and Cymbeline to forget that she had ever been married to Posthumus, whom she would never see again, and to wed the man her father and step-mother had chosen.

But Imogen would not waver in her faithful love and duty to Posthumus, and the Queen began to make other plans to accomplish her design of raising Cloten to the throne. She had great skill in preparing drugs and ointments and perfumes from herbs, and had learnt all she could of medicine from Cornelius, the court doctor. Now she began to experiment with poisons, and asked his help.

Cornelius did not trust the Queen, and suspected her of dark designs. So when she asked him for a deadly poison, with which she said she wanted to try experiments on animals, he gave her instead a drug which would cause only apparent death for a few hours.

Believing that it would prove fatal, she gave it to Pisanio, telling him it was a rare and valuable drug which would cure anyone who was ill.

'It has saved the King from death five times,' she assured him, 'and I give it to you now to prove that I am your friend and wish you well. And further, I will make sure that the King heaps riches and honors on you if you will help us to make Imogen forget Posthumus Leonatus and consent to marry my son.'

'That'll rob her of her last friend,' thought the Queen, when Pisanio had gone. 'And if she won't marry Cloten, I'll give her some of the same medicine and get rid of her altogether.'

All this was bad enough for poor Imogen. But worse was to follow—and Posthumus was largely to blame for it. He had been living in Rome for some time, where he never tired of praising his wife's virtues. The women of Italy were said to be not so virtuous, and one of the friends he made there, a clever and unscrupulous Italian called Iachimo, became annoyed at these constant praises of the absent Imogen.

One evening when he and Posthumus and several friends had all had a good deal to drink, Iachimo began to scoff at what Posthumus was always saying in praise of her.

'I'll bet you ten thousand ducats—and that jewel on your finger which you value so much—that I'll win your wife from you without any difficulty,' cried Iachimo. 'I'll set out for Britain at once. All I ask is that you give me letters telling her I'm your friend and am to be entertained kindly.'

Instead of having nothing to do with such an unworthy proposal, Posthumus accepted the wager, merely adding that if Iachimo failed he would challenge him to a duel for even suggesting that his wife might be false—to which, he added, he looked forward on Iachimo's return, as he had not the slightest doubt of Imogen's honor.

Posthumus was perfectly right, as Iachimo soon discovered when he reached Cymbeline's court. Imogen welcomed him eagerly as a friend of her husband, and was delighted to receive the letters from Posthumus. But Iachimo realized at once that she was very different from most women he had ever known.

'If her mind is as pure and beautiful as her looks,' he thought, 'she is the very Phoenix among women, and I have lost my wager!'

Nevertheless he began at once on his dishonorable task. praising her lavishly, and regretting that Posthumus was so unworthy of her. Imogen denied this, and Iachimo went on to tell her how badly Posthumus was behaving in Rome, and how he had forgotten her and all his oaths to her, and was having love affairs with any woman who would have him.

Honest Imogen believed every word, and was very upset to hear this, and begged Iachimo to say no more.

'But you cannot forgive him for such behaviour!' declared the sly Italian. 'It is your duty to seek revenge for the way in which he is dishonoring you.'

'Revenge?' asked Imogen. 'How can that be? All I can do is to weep for my husband's weakness.'

'But your revenge is easy and obvious,' said Iachimo softly. 'Pay him back in his own coin. If he is unfaithful to you, be unfaithful to him. He has new mistresses over there in Rome, you can easily find yourself a lover here in Britain—I ask no more than to take his place myself.'

Then Imogen turned on Iachimo with indignation and disgust:

'I condemn my very ears for listening to you,' she said. 'If you had been an honorable man, you would have told your tale simply in the interest of virtue. But now that I realize what you're after I don't believe a word you've said about my husband. The King my father shall hear about your disgraceful behavior and he'll have you driven out of his court.'

Seeing how mistaken he had been in thinking he could win Imogen to dishonor by these or any other means, Iachimo hastily changed his tune:

'Oh how fortunate Posthumus Leonatus is!' he cried. 'You are even more virtuous than he said! Forgive me, noble lady, for the lies I have told, and for what must indeed have seemed most dishonorable conduct. I could not believe in the virtues he never tires of describing, and so I tried this unworthy trick. It has confirmed both his opinion and your own wisdom in choosing so rare a husband.'

At this Imogen readily forgave him; and they talked of Posthumus and his devotion to his wife until Iachimo said:

'I must leave tomorrow, but tonight you can do me a great
service. Some dozen Roman lords, including your husband and
me, have pooled resources to give a present to the Emperor, Caesar
Augustus; I was commissioned to buy it while in Britain. It con-
sists of a chest full of silver plate, and I am in constant fear of it
being stolen. Will you guard it for me tonight?'

Suspecting no evil, Imogen replied readily: 'Indeed I will—
particularly as my husband has a part in it. So send it later in the
evening, and it shall be put in my bedroom for greater safety.'

'I'll bid my men bring the chest,' said Iachimo. 'If you wish to
write to your husband, do it now, for I must leave early tomorrow and will carry letters to Rome.'

So that night Iachimo's chest was put away in the corner of
Imogen's bedroom, and after reading Ovid until nearly midnight
Imogen said her prayers and went to sleep.

When all was quiet, the chest opened softly, and out stepped
Iachimo.

Imogen was asleep, and did not stir as he crept forward and
bent over her. One arm lay out over the coverlet, revealing the
bracelet which Posthumus had given her before he went into
exile. This Iachimo managed to unfasten and slip off without
waking Imogen; and at the same time he noticed a mole on her
breast.

'This will serve as proof positive when I tell Posthumus,'
he thought. 'If I describe the mole to him, besides giving him the
bracelet and telling him what pictures there are in the room and
how it is furnished, he'll believe that Imogen has let me take his
place and so is false to him.'

Then, thinking these wicked thoughts, Iachimo got back into
the chest which was carried out in the morning without anyone
suspecting what it contained.

Iachimo hastened back to Rome and claimed that he had won
the wager.

Posthumus was hard to persuade. Iachimo, he said, might have learnt what Imogen's bedroom was like, and even have bribed a servant to steal the bracelet. But when Iachimo, with a smirk of self-satisfaction, described the mole on her breast Posthumus gave way to rage and despair.

Having given the ring and the money to Iachimo, he rushed away declaring that he hated all women—and Imogen in particular. He must be revenged upon her for her treachery, he said, and sent letters of instruction to Pisanio. Then he joined the army which Caesar Augustus was gathering to send to Britain; but he did not make one of the embassy under Caius Lucius which preceded it.

Caius Lucius came to demand the annual tribute which Cymbeline had promised to Julius Caesar many years earlier, and which had always been paid until the previous year or two. He found Cloten and the Queen very much in power, with Cymbeline doing more or less what they said.

'There are many Caesars,' scoffed Cloten, 'but only one Julius. Anyhow, Britain is free, and owes nothing to Rome.'

The Queen joined Cloten, pointing out that Julius Caesar had never really conquered Britain, and together they persuaded Cymbeline to defy Rome and declare war on Augustus if he or his troops tried to collect the tribute.

All this time Cloten had been trying to win Imogen—bribing her waiting-women, paying minstrels to sing outside her window, and attempting to woo her in his own coarse fashion.

At last he became very angry: 'You cannot consider yourself married to Posthumus,' he said. 'He's a beggar, brought up by charity and fed on scraps thrown to him here at court; you are a Princess, and will be a Queen. You cannot sell the crown for brats and beggary: it is your duty to marry a prince, such as I, and not throw yourself away on a base slave, a mere servant who hasn't even got a livery—a dirty scullion.'

'You are an impudent blackguard!' cried Imogen, losing her temper at last. 'If Jupiter himself had been your father, you would be too base even to be my husband's servant. If Posthumus were King and made you assistant hangman the honor would be too great! Why, his meanest garment is dearer to me than your whole body.'

' "His meanest garment!" How the devil——' spluttered Cloten, who had a very high opinion of himself. ' "His meanest garment—" I'll tell the King!'

'Yes, and your mother too!' cried Imogen. 'She may think what she likes. I'll not be afraid to repeat my words!'

Cloten went off in a rage, and Imogen sought Pisanio. That faithful servant was sorely torn between two duties. He had just received letters from Posthumus accusing Imogen of adultery and treachery, and bidding him lure her out into the forest and kill her. Posthumus also enclosed a letter for Imogen that would make her leave the safety of the court and thus give Pisanio the opportunity to do as his master commanded.

'What false Italian with a poisonous tongue has deceived him?' thought Pisanio. 'Disloyal? Never! Why, she has been suffering all these months for her very faithfulness!'

When Imogen found him, Pisanio said nothing about his own letter, but gave her the enclosure from Posthumus. Imogen read it, and nearly died for joy.

'Oh for a horse with wings!' she cried. 'He is in Wales at this moment, near Milford Haven. How far is it? If the journey takes a week, I shall do it in a day! I must go to him at once! Help me, Pisanio. Get horses, and let us slip away unseen. Tell my women to pretend I'm ill—and get me a simple riding-costume, such as a country girl would wear.'

'You had better consider the dangers——' began Pisanio.

'Consider!' cried Imogen. 'When my husband is so near? No, I can think of nothing else. Away! Make haste! We'll go to Milford!'

Very soon they were on their way. But Pisanio did no more than accompany Imogen into a wooded valley among the Welsh mountains. Leaving the horses, he led her still deeper into the solitude until they came to a lonely glade. Then he turned and silently held out to her a letter.

Imogen read it slowly—the letter from Posthumus to Pisanio accusing her of adultery, and commanding him to kill her and send a token of her death. When she had read it all, Imogen sank slowly to the ground in a faint.

'I need not even draw my sword,' exclaimed Pisanio bitterly. 'The letter itself has killed her. No, I'll never believe it. She is pure and innocent; my master's ear has been abused and deceived by a villain.'

'False, false to Posthumus?' sobbed Imogen, when she recovered consciousness. 'What is it to be false? To lie in bed and think only of him, weeping his absence and counting the clocks? And sleeping, to dream of him and cry myself awake? That Italian who came—Iachimo: he must have spoken the truth. My husband has grown tired of me and wants to be free to marry some scheming painted hussy. . . . Well, Pisanio, do your duty. See, I draw the sword for you myself. Plunge it into my heart as you are commanded. Fear not, my heart is empty of all things but grief— you'll not even find your master there anymore.'

But Pisanio flung aside the sword and said, with tears in his eyes:

'Madam, I *know* that my master has been deceived. Some clever and malicious villain has done both of you this wrong—and I cannot imagine why.'

'Some cunning Roman wench,' said Imogen sadly.

'No, on my life!' exclaimed Pisanio. 'He's as true to you as you are to him.'

'What shall I do then?' asked Imogen. 'Why have you brought me so far towards Milford, if not to kill me in this lonely place?'

'I'll pretend to have obeyed your husband's orders, and send him a token,' said Pisanio. 'But you must disguise yourself as a boy: I've brought clothes for you in this bundle. The truth will come out sooner or later; and when your husband has been punished enough by grief and remorse, you can reveal yourself.'

'But where can I hide?' asked Imogen. 'Nothing will induce me to return to my father's court, and to Cloten whose love-suit has been as fearful to me as a siege.'

'Go on towards Milford,' answered Pisanio. 'There you'll find Caius Lucius on his way back to Rome with your father's defiance of Caesar Augustus. Go with him, and you can easily find employment as a page, and see your husband without him knowing you.'

Imogen agreed to this, and Pisanio gave her the clothes, and with them the drug which the Queen had given him.

'This is a precious remedy for all sickness,' he said. 'Take it, and use it if perhaps you are ill at sea. I must hasten back to the court as fast as I can, so as not to be missed. Otherwise I shall be suspected of having helped you to run away.'

Pisanio only just reached the court in time, for having bidden farewell to Caius Lucius and seen him off, Cymbeline suddenly realized that it was several days since he had seen his daughter. Cloten was sent to fetch her—but he found her door shut, and her room empty.

While the Queen was pretending to soothe the King's anger, but really fanning it in hope that he would have a fit and die, Cloten found Pisanio.

'You villain!' he cried, catching hold of him and shaking him.

'Where is Imogen? I'm sure you know. Tell me at once, or I'll break your worthless neck.'

'Do not be so violent, my lord,' gasped Pisanio. 'All that I know is contained in this letter,' and so saying he handed over the false letter which Posthumus had written to lure Imogen into the forest so that Pisanio could kill her.

'It's from that villain, the outlawed Posthumus!' shouted Cloten. 'She's gone to meet him at Milford Haven! I'll go there myself immediately, kill him, and bring her back. Then she shall be mine by force! I'll dress myself as Posthumus—if it doesn't help, it will certainly distress her—and I mean to be as harsh with her as she deserves. You there, slave! Fetch me a suit belonging to Posthumus, and be quick about it.'

Before long Cloten was dressed in a suit which Posthumus had left behind, and was riding for Milford Haven as hard as he could go, while Pisanio laughing to himself, thought that Posthumus was still in Rome and Imogen already on her way to seek him.

But Imogen, now dressed as a boy with the assumed name of Fidele, had never reached Milford Haven. For after Pisanio left her, she strayed from the path, and lost her way in the forest which covered most of South Wales at that time. Twice she met wandering beggars who directed her and told her she 'could not miss the way,' but after two nights and days she was still lost, and beginning to feel faint with hunger.

At last she found a path which led between rocks to a large cave at the side of a pleasant green glade hidden among trees. The cave was obviously inhabited and well used, but no one was there.

After calling once or twice, Imogen ventured inside where she found it to be deep and dry, well furnished, and stored with food. As there was no one to ask, and she was dying of hunger, Imogen began to help herself, deciding that whoever lived there must be gentle and civilized to arrange their cave with such order and neatness and refinement.

Presently the owners came back from hunting: an old man called Morgan and his two handsome sons in their early twenties, Polydore and Cadwal.

Imogen was very frightened when she saw them, and begged their forgiveness with some agitation.

'I called out before I came in,' she exclaimed. 'I'll pay for all I've eaten. See, here's gold. It was only hunger that made me help myself and not wait for you.'

However, Polydore and Cadwal soon reassured her, for both of them were delighted with this handsome boy, and Morgan made Fidele welcome as if he had been a great lord in a castle and not an outlaw living in a cave.

So Fidele took up his abode in the cave, where Polydore and Cadwal treated him as a brother. Each day they and Morgan went hunting, while Fidele cleaned and tidied the cave and had a meal ready for them when they returned.

But this happy life lasted only for a few days. Fidele fell sick one morning, and lay resting in the cave, while Morgan and his two sons, having done all they could for him, went off hunting.

Left to herself, Imogen suddenly remembered the precious drug which Pisanio had given her. 'I am sick—heartsick too,' she sobbed. 'I'll take the drug, and perhaps it will cure me.' She did so, and presently fell into a deep sleep that seemed like death.

Meanwhile, as they returned to the cave, Morgan and his sons met Cloten who was still searching for Posthumus and Imogen.

'It's Cloten, the Queen's son,' muttered Morgan. 'Let us hide: he may think we are robbers, and be leading a band of men to catch us.

'He's alone,' said Polydore. 'You and Cadwal go and see if anyone's near. I'll speak to him and prevent him from entering the cave and disturbing Fidele.'

'What are you?' shouted Cloten when he saw Polydore. 'Some wild man of the mountains? Yield, slave! You are a robber and a villain.'

'Why should I yield to you?' asked Polydore scornfully.

'You'll quake with fear when I tell you,' answered Cloten. 'I am none other than the Queen's son. I am Prince Cloten!'

'I laugh at fools, not fear them!' jeered Polydore.

'Then die the death!' shouted Cloten drawing his sword. 'I'll kill you, and cut off your head—and the heads of those other two who ran off when they saw me. And I'll set all your heads in a row on the gates of London!'

Polydore drew his sword to defend himself. They fought; and before long it was not Polydore but Cloten who lacked a head.

When Morgan returned, having found no sign that Cloten had any companions, he was much upset by what had happened.

'This will not be forgiven,' he said. 'They'll scour the woods to avenge the death of the Queen's son. You should not have killed him.'

'It was my life or his,' answered Polydore. 'And he called me a slave and a wildman of the mountains. But I'll throw his head into the stream, and the current will bear it down to the sea. He can tell the fishes he's the Queen's son, the terrible Cloten!'

'Well, it's done,' said Morgan with a sigh, 'and I suppose it couldn't be avoided. Cadwal, you prepare our dinner if Fidele's not well enough to help.'

But it seemed that Fidele would help them no more. When he went back into the cave, Cadwal found him lying on the floor, his right cheek resting on a cushion and a smile on his lips. At first he thought him asleep, and took off his shoes so as not to disturb him. But at last he realized that it was more than sleep, and carried his body sadly out of the cave, where Morgan and Polydore both agreed that he was dead. So they mourned their newly-found, swiftly-lost brother, and laid his body in a cleft of the rocks nearby, and covered it with leaves.

'While summer lasts and I live here, Fidele, I'll sweeten your sad grave with fairest flowers,' said Cadwal. 'You shall not lack pale primroses, nor the blue harebell, nor the eglantine. And when winter comes, the rich green moss shall take the place of flowers.'

Then they sang a dirge over him:

'Fear no more the heat o' the sun,
    Nor the furious winter's rages;
Thou thy worldly task hast done,
    Home art gone, and ta'en thy wages:
Golden lads and girls all must,
As chimney-sweepers, come to dust. . . .'

Not long after Morgan, Polydore and Cadwal had left, Imogen awoke from the effects of the drug and sat up pushing the leaves away with ease, and then climbed out of the cleft in which she had been laid.

The drug had cured her of her sickness, but her mind was confused, for she could not remember whether or not her days in the cave had been a dream.

'I was on the way to Milford Haven,' she thought. 'I must have slept and dreamt here by the wayside.' Then she saw the body of Cloten, and cried out in agony of mind—for, the head being gone, she thought from the clothes that it was Posthumus.

'Pisanio must be in league with Cloten,' she thought. 'He gave me a drug and said it was only a cordial. He must have murdered my dear Posthumus while I slept. Oh, let me die, here by the man I love.'

Imogen flung herself down beside the body, and there she was found by the Roman general, Caius Lucius, on his way to Milford. Once more the boy Fidele, she became his page and went with him to the Roman camp. For the ships had already arrived and the legion had landed to punish the Britons for refusing to pay tribute.

With the Roman army came Posthumus Leonatus: a false message and a bloodstained handkerchief awaited him from Pisanio. Believing that his orders had been carried out and that Imogen was dead, his grief knew no bounds.

As soon as he could slip away from the Roman forces, he disguised himself as a British peasant, meaning to join Cymbeline's army and die fighting for Imogen's country.

The battle commenced not far from Morgan's cave in the forest, and Morgan and his two sons soon found themselves engaged in it. At first the Romans were victorious, and the Britons fled. But Morgan with the help of Polydore and Cadwal defended a narrow ravine, where the disguised Posthumus joined them, and the four held the whole Roman army while Cymbeline's forces reformed behind them, and turned the fortune of the day, capturing Lucius and most of his men.

After the battle, Posthumus, still wishing only for death,

changed back into his Roman garb and gave himself up to the Britons. He was brought before Cymbeline who promptly condemned him to be hanged, and sent him to join the other Romans in prison.

Next morning, Cymbeline held court in his tent to bestow rewards on the victors and deal with the vanquished.

Foremost among them were Morgan, Polydore and Cadwal—but continuous search had failed to find the brave peasant who had stood with them and turned the tide of battle.

'Stand by my side,' said Cymbeline, 'you whom the gods have made the preservers of my throne. And say whether there is any news of the peasant who stood beside you in the battle, and should stand with you now.'

'He has been sought for among the living and the dead,' reported Pisanio, 'but he cannot be found.'

'His reward shall be great if he appears,' said Cymbeline. 'Meanwhile, kneel down you three, and arise my Knights of the Battle. Henceforth be in attendance on me, and you shall have lands and wealth to suit your new rank.'

Now Cornelius the doctor drew near, accompanied by the Queen's attendants.

'Hail, great king!' he cried. 'To sour your happiness, I must report that the Queen is dead.'

'How did she die?' asked Cymbeline.

'Cruelly and with horror, as she lived,' said Cornelius solemnly. 'These ladies were with her, and can testify to my words. For before she died the Queen made confession: she hated your daughter, Imogen, and would have poisoned her if she had not run away. But worst of all she hated you, whom she married only to gain the throne. She had a poison ready for you also, which would have caused you to suffer a cruel and lingering death during which she would have tended you with great show of love and sorrow.'

'All can, at least, bear witness she was beautiful,' said Cymbeline. 'That blinded me to the rest. But I am sorry that she swayed my mind against my daughter.'

At this moment the Roman prisoners were brought before the

King, headed by Caius Lucius and Iachimo, with Imogen (still disguised as Fidele) behind them, and Posthumus in the rear.

'Well, Caius, you do not come now to demand tribute!' exclaimed Cymbeline.

'No, my lord,' answered Lucius. 'Yet it is but the fortune of war, and whatever you may do to me, you still have Rome to deal with. But I do ask one thing: spare this page of mine, Fidele, who is a Briton born. Though he served me, a Roman, well and truly, he has done no Briton harm.'

'I grant your request,' answered Cymbeline. 'Boy, you are now my page. And moreover, for I like you strangely, I grant you one request whatever it is—even the life of the greatest,' he added with a significant glance towards Caius Lucius.

'I do not beg my life, good lad,' said Lucius, 'and yet I know that is what you will ask.'

'Alas,' said Fidele, 'I must betray you—and ask another boon. My lord king, bid yonder Roman answer me truly all I ask!' and she pointed to Iachimo.

'I swear he shall,' said Cymbeline in surprise, 'or torture shall wring the truth from him!'

'Let him tell how he got that ring!' cried Fidele, pointing to the diamond on Iachimo's finger which Imogen had given to Posthumus and Iachimo had won from him.

'I am glad to be forced to tell the truth at last,' said Iachimo, 'for the torment of concealing it has grown worse day by day. Yet it will torture you to hear it, for it concerns your daughter.'

With that, Iachimo proceeded to tell the tale of the bet with Posthumus and by what lying and underhand means he had won it.

When he heard the truth, Posthumus, who was awaiting execution with the other Roman prisoners, pushed forward crying:

'Italian fiend! King, I am worse still! Torture me! Kill me! I am Posthumus Leonatus who believed this devil, and killed your daughter by the hands of that lesser devil, Pisanio there. . . . Oh Imogen, my queen, my wife, my life! Oh Imogen, Imogen, Imogen!'

It seemed as if Posthumus would die of grief and self-loathing, and Imogen sprang to him exclaiming: 'Peace my lord. Listen to me!'

'You saucy page, would you mock me?' cried Posthumus, and struck Fidele, who fell to the ground.

'Help! Oh my lord Posthumus, you never killed Imogen until this moment!' cried Pisanio bending over Fidele whom he had recognized at once.

'Does the world go round?' cried Cymbeline in bewilderment.

'Am I mad?' echoed Posthumus.

'How are you, my dear mistress?' asked Pisanio as Imogen sat up slowly.

'Oh not you! You gave me poison!' cried Imogen, seeing Pisanio.

But Cornelius was soon able to explain how he had put a sleeping drug in place of the poison which Pisanio had believed to be a precious medicine.

Then Morgan told all he knew of Fidele, who had seemed to die in the cave, and Imogen turned to Posthumus with full forgiveness. A moment later they were in each other's arms, and Cymbeline was blessing them, pardoning all that was passed and begging their forgiveness.

But this happy reunion reminded him that Cloten had disappeared, leaving no trace. A few questions revealed how the Prince had forced Pisanio to give him a suit belonging to Posthumus. And then Polydore described how he had killed him and cut off his head in the forest.

'I am sorry to hear this,' said Cymbeline sadly. 'You have killed a man of higher rank than yourself, and by the law you must die.'

At this old Morgan flung himself at the King's feet and cried:

'And I declare that the killer's rank was higher than that of the dead Cloten! These two boys, Polydore and Cadwal, are your sons Guiderius and Arviragus, whom I stole away when they were babies. For I, Morgan, am not their father, but the Lord Belarius whom you unjustly exiled, and who took his revenge by stealing them.'

Then indeed there was rejoicing in Cymbeline's court. The King at once forgave Belarius and made him his chief adviser, while Imogen rejoiced that 'Cadwal' and 'Polydore,' whom she had loved as brothers were her brothers indeed, and had no regrets at losing her place as heir to the kingdom.

'I will be merciful to all my prisoners,' cried Cymbeline. 'But my joy is still incomplete, since I cannot find that soldier who stood with Belarius and my sons in the battle.'

'I am the man, sir,' said Posthumus. 'And Iachimo can prove my words. For I had him at my mercy in the fight, and spared his life.'

'That is true,' said Iachimo, kneeling to Posthumus. 'I am down again, and await the punishment I deserve.'

'I forgive you everything,' said Posthumus. 'Live— and deal better with others.'

'Nobly done!' cried Cymbeline. 'Pardon's the word to all. Caius Lucius, although I am the victor, we submit to Caesar. Go free, all of you, and return to Rome bearing the tribute, which we will pay faithfully each year. Our wicked Queen, who is now dead, dissuaded us from paying it before. Now I proclaim peace and forgiveness to all. Follow me to the temple, there to thank the gods who have given me my sons, and brought happiness to my daughter and her husband.'

And so they all trooped away to the thanksgiving, headed by Cymbeline with Guiderius and Arviragus, followed by Imogen and Posthumus Leonatus with their arms round one another. And they all lived happily ever after.

THE WINTER'S TALE

WHEN LEONTES, KING of Sicily, was already middle-aged he married a young wife, the beautiful Hermione, daughter of the Emperor of Russia. They had one child, a boy called Mamillius, and it seemed to Leontes and Hermione that their happiness was complete.

Only one thing was lacking, and that Leontes made haste to supply. When he was a boy, his closest friend had been Polixenes who was now King of Bohemia. Indeed the two had only parted when fortune called each to his throne and gave him a land which took all his care and attention. But now both countries were prosperous and at peace, and Polixenes needed no urging to visit the Sicilian Court and stay for a long time.

Polixenes had been in Sicily for more than nine months when he decided that he must return to Bohemia. Leontes begged him to stay longer, but Polixenes was firm in his determination to go and fixed a day for his voyage.

'I must leave tomorrow,' he said. 'Bohemia has been without a king far too long—my country needs me.'

'If I cannot persuade you to stay longer,' said Leontes, 'perhaps my wife can. Hermione, won't you try?'

'I have still not heard all the tales of your childhood and youth!' she exclaimed, taking Polixenes by the arm. 'Stay and tell me. You and my husband must have been fine young fellows.'

'We were, fair Queen,' answered Polixenes. 'Two lads who had no thought for the future other than that each golden day would be repeated in the next; we thought we should stay boys forever!'

So, cunningly, Hermione lured Polixenes on to tell of his boyhood, and at last persuaded him to extend his visit a little.

But her success brought disaster where no one expected it. Hermione's easy conquest of Polixenes in this matter where all his own endeavors had failed, triggered off a sudden flood of hidden jealousy in Leontes. It seemed like a madness that had come upon him from nowhere and with no cause: in a moment he was possessed by it entirely—a jealousy that would hear no argument and see no reason. And the great tragedy was that, as King, he had absolute power of life and death, and no one could control him but himself: and he had had his own way too long to be able to do so, or even to see that there was need for reason and self-control.

Within a day his friendship for Polixenes turned to hatred. He was convinced that Polixenes and Hermione were lovers, and had been deceiving him during the whole visit. Now if they spoke or drew near to one another he saw double-meanings and guilty secrets in all they said and did.

Soon he could bear it no longer, and sent for his most faithful lord, Camillo.

'Are you blind?' he asked, 'or are you pretending not to see? Are you shutting your ears to what everyone at court must be whispering? Why have you not told me? It's perfectly obvious that my wife's an adulteress!'

'If it were anyone but you who slandered the Queen like this,' cried Camillo, 'my sword would be out to ram the lie down his throat!'

'The lie?' cried Leontes. 'It is you that lie. I say you are a liar, or a blind fool. For I tell you that the Queen has betrayed me: she is in love with my false friend Polixenes of Bohemia!'

Camillo did his best to reason Leontes out of his terrible delusion, but all his words were in vain.

'I know it to be true!' cried Leontes. 'I command you to kill Polixenes. Poison him, cunningly, so that everyone may think he has died a natural death.'

'If I do so,' said Camillo, 'will you treat your Queen as if nothing had happened? You owe it to your son Mamillius—and to the second child whom she is likely to bear you before this month is out.'

'You advise me just as I had planned,' said Leontes. 'Kill Polixenes, and the Queen shall not know that I even suspected her guilty secret.'

So Camillo promised to do the king's bidding. But as soon as he was able he went to Polixenes and told him everything. Polixenes was shocked and horrified, for the very idea of behaving in such a disgraceful manner to his friend had never crossed his mind. But he agreed with Camillo that the King's delusion was dangerous, and that words would not cure it.

'My ships are ready to sail,' he said. 'For I was prepared to leave two days ago, before the Queen persuaded me to stay at the King's bidding. You will come with me to Bohemia: Sicily will not be safe for you any longer. You shall be my most trusted friend and adviser.'

'We must go tonight,' said Camillo. 'It will not be difficult, since I have the keys to all the gates, and know all the passwords.'

So Polixenes escaped, and with him went Camillo thinking that he had also saved the Queen. But his flight seemed only to prove Leontes's suspicions.

'No wonder Camillo pretended to be so surprised!' he shouted, when he heard of their escape. 'He is Polixenes's ally and must have known all along what was going on. Hermione's guilt is unmistakable. I will show her no mercy.'

But to be quite sure, Leontes sent messengers to Delphi, to enquire of Apollo's oracle, and bring back certain proof—for the oracle could not lie.

'With Apollo's divine word to prove it,' he thought, 'no one in Sicily or elsewhere will oppose me when the Queen is tried and punished.'

Poor Hermione still knew nothing of what was happening. She and her ladies were sitting happily with little Mamillius who was joking pertly with them.

'Come and sit down,' said Hermione at last, 'and tell us a story.'

'Shall it be merry or sad?' asked Mamillius eagerly.

'As merry as you can make it,' begged Hermione.

'A sad tale's best for winter,' declared Mamillius. 'I know one about sprites and goblins.'

'Then tell it to us!' smiled Hermione. 'Come and sit here, and see if you can frighten us with your goblins.'

'Once upon a time there was a man who dwelt beside a church-yard——' began Mamillius.

But at that moment Leontes and his attendants came storming into the room.

'There's a plot against my life—against my crown!' he raved. 'Camillo is in it with Polixenes! Guards, take the boy! He must not remain with this tainted creature who is about to bear Polixenes's child!'

'What strange mistake is this?' cried poor, bewildered Hermione. 'Coming from anyone else, I would have called it wicked-ness and villainy.'

'There's no mistake!' shouted Leontes. 'Or if there is, it is you who have mistaken Polixenes for me. You are an adulteress and a traitor. You are in league with Camillo, and helped him and that villain Polixenes to escape.' He spoke to his attendants: 'Away with her to prison.'

'Farewell, my lord,' said Hermione quietly, as she turned to go. 'I never wished to see you sorry; now I hope I shall.'

When she was gone, his lords and advisers tried to persuade Leontes that he was mistaken. Foremost among them was Antigonus who persuaded the King to give Hermione a trial in court as soon as his messengers, Cleomenes and Dion, returned from Delphi with Apollo's oracle.

Meanwhile, Hermione remained in prison, where a daughter was born to her, comforting her grief a little.

When she heard of it, Paulina, wife of Antigonus, who was a close and true friend of the Queen, went to the prison and sug-gested that she should take the baby and show it to Leontes.

'We do not know how he may soften at the sight of the child,' she said. 'The silence of pure innocence often persuades where speaking fails.'

But Leontes was becoming more and more insane with jealousy and lack of sleep. Although Mamillius was ill with grief, both at being separated from his mother, and at knowing of the false accusations that had been made against her, Leontes insisted on believing that it was sorrow and horror at her wickedness that was upsetting the boy so much—and blamed her for that too.

Paulina was a lady with a strong, honest character who spoke her mind without fear or hesitation, and could be curbed neither by her King nor her husband when doing what she thought was right.

Now she came straight into the King's presence, though the guards tried to keep her out, and told him that he was a wicked tyrant, and that she, a loyal servant and obedient counsellor, had come to plead the cause of his 'good Queen.'

'Good Queen!' sneered Leontes.

'Good Queen, my lord, good Queen!' cried Paulina. 'And if I were a man, I'd challenge anyone who said she was not!'

'Throw her out!' commanded the King.

'Let that man try who wants to lose his eyes!' exclaimed Paulina fiercely, crooking her fingers like claws. 'I'll go of my own accord as soon as I've done my errand. The good Queen— for she is good—has born you a daughter: I have brought her here to receive your blessing.'

'This child is none of mine!' shouted Leontes, when he saw the baby. 'Polixenes was its father!'

'It is yours, as anyone can see,' retorted Paulina, 'and all the worse for looking like such a father!'

'Silence, hag!' thundered Leontes. 'Antigonus, you deserve to be hanged for not being able to keep your wife quiet.'

'If you hanged all the husbands who couldn't do that, you'd leave yourself very few subjects,' murmured Antigonus.

'I'll have you burnt!' roared Leontes.

'I don't care,' retorted Paulina. 'The heretic is he who makes the fire, not he who burns in it. I'll not call you a tyrant—yet. But your behavior to your Queen, without any more proof than your own brain-sick fancies, is well on the way to tyranny, and the world will hold your conduct scandalous.'

'Throw her out!' repeated Leontes. 'If I were a tyrant, she would be dead by now.'

'There's no need to push me,' said Paulina with dignity. 'I am going now. Look after your child, my lord, for it is certainly yours. And as for the rest of you, you'd be far better employed in correcting the King's follies than in shoving me about!'

When Paulina had gone, Leontes turned once more on Antigonus and accused him of being a traitor and of having encouraged his wife to insult him. Antigonus denied it strenuously, and he and all the other lords begged Leontes on their knees not to carry out his cruel purpose of killing the child with her mother.

Leontes granted their request, but he called Antigonus to him and said:

'To save your own life, and perhaps this infant's, obey my commands. Take it up and carry it to some desert place well away from my kingdom, and leave it there. Someone may find and rear it; if not, our hands will be clean of its blood if it dies or is eaten by wild beasts.'

Antigonus was forced to do as Leontes bade him; and he set out at once by ship, carrying the baby with him.

Hardly had he gone when Cleomenes and Dion returned from Delphi bearing the words of the Oracle in a sealed scroll. Leontes at once summoned the court to assemble for the trial of Hermione, and accused her of adultery with Polixenes and of a conspiracy against his life, aided by Camillo who had fled.

Hermione denied it all in the strongest terms:

'I confess that I loved Polixenes,' she said, 'but only so much as you commanded me to do—as your dearest friend in whose praise you had spoken so often. I loved him as honor required, and as such a lady as I might without shame, but no more. As for this plot against you, I know nothing of it, nor why Camillo fled. Your accusations are on the level of your dreams, and I do not understand them.'

'Your actions are my dreams,' answered Leontes. 'The child

was a dream. . . . Well, as it has been cast out to die, so shall you die as you deserve to do.'

'Sir, spare your threats,' answered Hermione calmly. 'The thing with which you try to frighten me is what I seek. Life has no more sweetness for me, since I have lost all that made life happy: your love, my son who is kept from me, and now our daughter. Tell me what I have to live for, since even my good name has been taken from me? Yet, that I would see cleared before I die. For I am innocent, and am being condemned on false charges suggested by your jealousy. I set my trust in the Oracle. Let Apollo be my judge!'

So Dion and Cleomenes were summoned into the court, and having sworn solemnly that they had received the scroll direct from the Oracle at Delphi, and had not so much as broken the seal or looked at the contents, it was opened and read aloud:

'Hermione is pure; Polixenes blameless; Camillo a true subject; Leontes a jealous tyrant; the innocent babe truly his; and the King shall live without an heir, if that which is lost be not found.'

There was a great sigh of relief throughout the court, and Hermione murmured: 'Praised be Apollo.'

'Have you read what is written?' asked Leontes in a strained voice.

'Even as it is set down here,' answered the officer.

'There is no truth in the Oracle!' shouted Leontes. 'Let the trial proceed.'

Scarcely had he spoken when an attendant rushed into the court crying:

'My lord, the prince your son is dead of grief for his mother!'

There was a stunned silence.

'Apollo is angry,' murmured Leontes, in a broken voice. 'The gods smite me for my injustice.'

Even as he spoke these words Hermione slipped to the ground and lay still.

'This news has proved a mortal blow to the Queen,' said Paulina.

'Carry her carefully to her room,' begged Leontes. 'She has only fainted, and will recover.'

When Paulina and the other ladies had borne Hermione away, Leontes wept.

'Pardon me, Apollo, for doubting your Oracle,' he cried. 'I was carried away by my madness. I'll be reconciled to Polixenes, recall Camillo, and woo my Queen afresh!'

He was confessing all the wicked thoughts and deeds that his mad jealousy had led him into, when Paulina rushed back into the court.

'The Queen is dead!' she screamed at him. 'Your tyranny and your jealousy—your stupid jealousy—have been too much for her. Her death lies on you alone—and the deaths of your son and daughter.'

'I am altogether to blame,' moaned Leontes. 'And on their tomb shall be written a full account of my guilt so that all the world shall know me for what I am. Now, until death releases me, I'll spend some part of every day doing penance in the chapel where they lie—and you shall be my conscience and lash me daily with your tongue to remind me how I have caused the deaths of all I love: my wife, my son, my daughter.'

While Leontes was beginning his long penance, Antigonus was still sailing across the sea carrying the baby girl. Each night he was troubled with strange dreams in which Hermione appeared to him and told him to place the child on the shore of Bohemia, with jewels and tokens and a letter saying that her name was Perdita, 'that which is lost.'

'The Queen must be dead,' he thought, 'and this is her ghost telling me to place the child in its father's kingdom. For the Queen must have been guilty after all, and Leontes will have had her burnt to death.'

And so, never thinking that it could be Hermione's wraith and not her ghost, Antigonus landed at the nearest point in Bohemia and left the child not far from the shore in a little cradle containing gold and jewels, as well as a letter giving her name, but no more.

Antigonus was not to return home, however. On the way back to the ship he was caught and killed by a bear. The ship itself was wrecked trying to put out from the mysterious coast of Bohemia, and all her crew perished.

But Perdita was found by a shepherd and his son who took her to their cottage, and brought her up as if she were the shepherd's daughter. She grew into so beautiful a girl that the shepherds more than half believed that she was a changeling left by the fairies, and that the treasure left with her was fairy gold.

They were not the only Bohemians who thought that she was of more than mortal loveliness. King Polixenes had a son, Prince Florizel, who happened to see her one day and fell in love with her. So he dressed himself as a shepherd and began to spend more and more time at the cottage where she lived. Like called to like, and the Princess of Sicily loved the Prince of Bohemia as truly as he loved her—though each thought the other no more than a shepherd and shepherdess.

Presently Polixenes began to notice how often Florizel was absent from court and soon discovered where he was spending his time.

So he decided to go in disguise to the old shepherd's cottage, and to take Camillo, who was still his most valued adviser, with him. To avoid exciting suspicion, they went on the day of a sheep-shearing festival that was being held there.

Many others were preparing to go to the festival, and among them was a merry rogue who described himself as 'a snapper-up of unconsidered trifles'. He called himself Autolycus after the grandfather of Odysseus who was a famous Master Thief.

He met the shepherd's son on the day before the festival, hastening to market to buy provisions for the feast, and at once scented game.

'Oh, oh!' yelled Autolycus, rolling on the ground and tearing at the rags he was wearing. 'Help me pluck off these horrors. Then I shall die!'

'What's the matter with you?' asked the shepherd bending over him.

'I've been robbed and beaten by villains!' wailed Autolycus. 'They left me these filthy rags and took my decent garments. But help me up, and support me for a little. I'll soon recover enough to hobble along to a friend who lives near here. He'll give me clothes and money.'

So the shepherd helped Autolycus to his feet and supported him along the road. Autolycus recovered remarkably soon—particularly after he had picked the shepherd's pocket—and was soon able to walk alone. Then the young shepherd hastened off towards the market, while Autolycus skipped merrily away across the fields, singing:

'Jog on, jog on, the foolpath way,
And merrily hent the stile-a;
A merry heart goes all the day,
Your sad tires in a mile-a.'

With the stolen money Autolycus was able to buy clothes so that he could attend the sheep-shearing next day disguised as a pedlar selling ribbons and gloves and handkerchiefs and the like for the shepherds to buy as presents for the shepherdesses of their choice.

Florizel arrived early at the festival, in his rôle of the shepherd Doricles, though by now he had confessed to Perdita who he really was. She feared what the King would do if he discovered—and that then Florizel would leave her. But the Prince vowed again and again that he loved only Perdita and would marry her whatever happened, and she was comforted.

As the old shepherd's wife had long been dead, Perdita, whom everyone supposed to be his daughter, was in charge of the feast. She welcomed all the guests and gave flowers to each of them.

Before long Polixenes and Camillo arrived, so cleverly disguised that even Florizel had no suspicion of who they were, and, as strangers, Perdita greeted them with special attentions.

'For you, sir, there's rosemary and rue,' she said to Camillo. 'These keep green and scented throughout the winter, and best suit your time of life.'

'Fair shepherdess, you fit our ages well with flowers of winter,' said Polixenes.

'These are for you,' she said, curtsying to him. 'Hot lavender, mints, savory, marjoram; the marigold that goes to bed with the sun, and rises with him, a tear of dew in its eye: for these are flowers of middle summer, and are given to men of middle age.'

'And what for me?' asked Florizel with a smile.

'My fairest friend,' she answered, 'I wish I had some spring flowers to suit your time of day—and for all these other friends who are still young. Oh Proserpina, if only I had some of those flowers that you let fall in fright when Pluto captured you: daffodils that come before the swallow dares, and catch the winds of March with beauty; dim violets, sweeter than the lids of Juno's eyes or the sweet breath of Venus; pale primroses that die un-married before they can behold the sun-god in his midday strength; oxlips and fritillaries, and lilies of all kinds. But these I lack to make you garlands with, my sweetest friend.'

'When you speak, my love, I'd have you go on forever,' said Florizel tenderly. 'When you sing, I wish you bought and sold in song, prayed in song, sang in all you did. When you dance I wish you were a wave of the sea that you would dance so forever. Everything you do crowns you the queen of each.'

'Dear Doricles, you praise me too highly,' said Perdita, taking his hand.

'Come now, my Perdita, our dance,' he answered; and away they went together. Presently Autolycus came, singing gay songs and selling his wares to the young shepherds, his former victim among them; and then there were other dances, and masques and entertainments, with plenty of food and drink.

Later, Polixenes and Camillo found Florizel and Perdita together, still hand in hand.

'How's this?' asked Polixenes. 'Are you not buying your lady-love rings and gloves and knick-knacks? At your age I would have ransacked the pedlar's treasury to buy fairings for my love.'

'I shall have more to offer her when we are married,' said Florizel. 'But now, ancient sir, since it seems that you have known what love is, listen to my pledge of faith to Perdita—here, before her father.'

With that Florizel poured out his heart in words of true love and eternal constancy:

'If I were crowned the monarch of the world,' he ended, 'If I were the handsomest of men, and had more knowledge than the wisest sage, I would prize them as nothing compared with the love of this maiden; I would employ them all in her service, give up all for her.'

'My daughter, do you say the same?' asked the old shepherd.

'I cannot speak so well as he does,' answered Perdita, 'but what he says exactly tells what I would say.'

'Then that's a bargain!' cried the old shepherd. 'Take hands on it before these worthy strangers. There, I give you my daughter; take her hand.'

'A moment, shepherd,' said Polixenes to Florizel. 'Have you no father to set your hand in hers? Does he know of this compact of true love?'

'He neither does nor shall,' said Florizel.

'At the betrothal of his son, a father is surely the guest most worthy to be there,' said Polixenes. 'If he is alive and hale and in his right mind, he should be here.'

'He has his health, and greater strength than many of his age,' answered Florizel. 'But there are special reasons why I cannot tell my father of this business.'

'Tell him, my son,' begged the old shepherd. 'He will have nothing to grieve over when he sees your choice.'

'No, he must not,' said Florizel firmly. 'Now mark our contract.'

'Mark your divorce, rather,' said Polixenes sternly, throwing off his disguise. 'Base and unworthy son, who would exchange a sceptre for a crook! If ever you see this girl again—if ever you so much as sigh for her, I'll bar you from the succession to the throne. This once the girl and her father shall go free.' He turned towards them, 'but if ever, after today, you receive him here again, or speak with the Prince, I'll devise the cruelest possible death for you.'

Polixenes went storming off and Perdita sobbed:

'We are undone and ruined. Yet once or twice while he was speaking I was about to tell him plainly that the same sun which shines upon his court, shines also on our cottage. As for you, my Prince, think of your royal state, and go. This has been a dream, and I am now awake.'

'I am only sorry, not afraid,' said Florizel. 'Why do you look at me like that? I am not altered, and what I said before, I mean now.'

Then Camillo tried to persuade Florizel to give up Perdita. But when he found that nothing he could say would shake him, he asked what he intended to do.

'I will not break my oath to Perdita. No, not for all Bohemia,' declared Florizel. 'So, noble friend, tell my father that I have put to sea with the girl of my choice to seek our fortune wheresoever we can find it. I have a ship ready to sail—though I did not think to be sailing in her myself.'

Seeing that he was determined, Camillo decided to help Florizel—and also to further a plan of his own.

'Go to Sicily,' he said. 'I'll give you letters to Leontes. You know the story of his mad jealousy, and how for the last sixteen years he has been begging your father to visit him again and witness his penitence. You have but to say that you have come as an ambassador from King Polixenes, and Leontes will welcome you as if you two were his son and daughter. And meanwhile I'll do all I can to soothe your father. I am sure he'll forgive in the end and welcome this maiden as your wife; and when he does, I'll be ready to tell him where you may be found.'

Florizel agreed. Autolycus appeared conveniently at that moment, so Camillo paid him to change clothes with Florizel who could then get on board the ship unnoticed in the pedlar's rough garments.

As soon as the change was made, and Florizel, Perdita and Camillo had gone, Autolycus who had overheard a little and guessed more, began to make his own plans. The old shepherd and his son, in terror of their lives, had decided to go to Polixenes with the letter and jewels that had been found with Perdita and tell him she was no relation of theirs, so that they could not in justice suffer for what she had done.

Autolycus put them in a great fright by telling them of the terrible tortures which Polixenes was preparing for them, and so lured them on board Florizel's ship. He intended to leave them there and tell Polixenes where the fugitives were going. But as the ship sailed while he was still on board, he found himself on the way to Sicily, and so had to change his plans.

As it happened, he would have gained nothing by reporting to the King, since Camillo had already told him where Florizel and Perdita had gone. For Camillo knew that Polixenes would pursue them, and this was his only means of getting back to Sicily without losing the friendship of Polixenes. But he had great hopes that once there Leontes would persuade Polixenes to forgive Florizel.

At his court in Sicily, Leontes was still doing daily penance for the mad jealousy which had caused the loss of his wife, his son and his daughter; and Paulina, still his faithful conscience, was reminding him daily of what he had done, and so helping him to become more and more truly penitent.

He was surprised, when Florizel and his Princess were announced, that they had come so unexpectedly and with so few attendants—but he welcomed them warmly.

'If I were still twenty-one,' he said to Florizel, 'I'd call you brother, as I did your father at that age—you are so like him. And your fair princess-goddess . . . Alas, by my own folly I lost a son and daughter who might have stood there just as you do—and just as much admired. It was through my same wicked stupidity that, at the same time, I lost me your father's love; but my greatest desire is to see him again before I die.'

Florizel began to tell a feigned tale of how Polixenes had bidden him visit Sicily on a return voyage from Libya, when he was interrupted by the sudden appearance of the Sicilian lord Cleomenes to announce that Polixenes had just arrived in Sicily:

'He greets you by me, says he will attend upon you shortly, and charges you to arrest his son who, in rank disobedience, has fled with a shepherd's daughter. The King would be here now, but has just met the father and brother of this seeming lady.'

'Camillo has betrayed us!' exclaimed Florizel.

'He is with your father,' said Cleomenes. 'I have spoken with him. He is at present questioning this old shepherd and his son.'

'Is this girl then not a king's daughter?' asked Leontes.

'She will be when she is my wife,' answered Florizel, 'and I beg you help me. Implore my father to let us marry. He'll refuse you nothing.'

'I'll do the best I can for you,' said Leontes. 'I'll go at once to greet my old friend, and beg him to be kind to you. Come, follow me.'

But Leontes had no need to urge Polixenes to allow the marriage. When he reached the ship, it was to find that the old shepherd and his son had told their tale of the finding of Perdita, the death of Antigonus and the wreck of the Sicilian ship. They produced the jewels they had found with Perdita, the cloak in which she had been wrapped, and a letter in the handwriting of Antigonus begging whoever found her to tend her carefully, name her Perdita, and take the gold for themselves but keep the jewels and the cloak for her when she grew up.

When Leontes realized that his daughter had been found, he was beside himself with joy. There was now no more objection to Perdita marrying Florizel: both their fathers wished for nothing better—and both loaded the old shepherd and his son with thanks and rewards, while Leontes gave him lands in Sicily where he settled down as a gentleman-farmer, and was able to employ Autolycus as his bailiff.

When the first transports of their rejoicings were over, Paulina invited Leontes and Polixenes, Florizel and Perdita, and the faithful Camillo, to visit her house to see a wonderful statue of Hermione which, she said, had just been completed by the leading sculptor of the day.

Paulina led them to the alcove where the statue stood, and slowly drew back the curtain which hid it. There was a little gasp of wonder as they all stood looking at its marvellous workmanship.

'I like your silence,' said Paulina at last, 'it shows your wonder. But speak, my liege, and tell me if it is like your lost Queen?'

'How natural she looks!' murmured Leontes. 'But Paulina, Hermione was not so wrinkled nor so much older as this statue makes her seem.'

'So much more excellent is the sculptor's work,' said Paulina. 'He has made her as she would appear if she were still alive—sixteen years after you last saw her.'

'Yes, so she might have looked if she had lived,' said Leontes.

'And now she would have brought me comfort—but her image pierces me to the soul. She stood just so when first I wooed her. I am ashamed: the stone rebukes me for being even harder than itself.'

'Do not think me superstitious if I kneel to ask her blessing,' whispered Perdita. 'Lady, dear Queen, that ended when I began, give me that hand of yours to kiss.'

'Be careful not to touch it,' cautioned Paulina. 'It's only just finished, and the colors are not yet dry.'

Leontes was overwhelmed at the sight of Hermione's statue; Camillo and Polixenes tried to comfort him.

'Dear brother,' said the latter, 'let me, that was the innocent cause, have power to take from you some little part of your grief.'

'Indeed, I would not have shown it to you, my lord,' said Paulina, 'if I had known it would affect you so strongly. I'll draw the curtain: you are so much upset that presently you'll think it moves.'

'Sweet Paulina, make me think so twenty years together,' begged Leontes.

'And I could also stand and look for just as long a time,' said Perdita.

'Either let me draw the curtain, or prepare for a greater marvel,' said Paulina. 'If you can bear it, I'll make the statue move and take you by the hand. But you must not think I am assisted by evil magic if I do.'

'Do all you can!' gasped Leontes.

'It is required that you call up all your faith,' said Paulina, 'and remain still. Music, play! . . . Now it is time: descend, be stone no more. Come, I'll fill your grave up, give death your numbness, for your husband calls you back to life.'

Slowly Hermione stepped down from the pedestal, advanced to Leontes and put her arms round him.

'How warm she is,' whispered Leontes. 'If this is magic, let it be a lawful art!'

'She hangs about his neck!' exclaimed Camillo. 'If she is alive, let her speak too.'

'Yes, and tell us where she has lived, and how she was stolen from the grave,' added Polixenes.

'She is alive,' said Paulina solemnly. 'Turn, good lady, your lost Perdita is found!'

'You gods look down and pour your blessings on her head,' said Hermione. 'Tell me how you have lived and where? For I have dwelt here, waiting for the day of your return since I knew from the Oracle, of which Paulina told me, that you *would* be found, and that I had a purpose to live for.'

So Hermione's long vigil in the house of Paulina came to an end, and with it the penance which had purged the evil from the heart of Leontes. All ended in happiness: Leontes and Hermione were reconciled; Polixenes became again their dearest friend; Paulina and Camillo, to whom they owed so much, were happily united in the quiet marriage of old age; and joyously they all celebrated the wedding of Florizel, Prince of Bohemia, to his beloved shepherdess, Perdita, the Princess of Sicily.

THE TEMPEST

Prospero, Duke of Milan, spent most of his time in study and became so learned in the hidden secrets of nature that he earned the reputation of being a magician—a white wizard whose art was altogether pure, and owed nothing to the Powers of Evil. As a result of being so absorbed in his books, he left most of the work of government to his brother Antonio, a man of small intelligence and great ambition.

Prospero was much loved by his subjects, but Antonio was able to promote several of his own traitorous followers to places of importance in the government. And when he had accumulated enough power, he entered into a secret alliance with Alonzo, King of Naples, promising him homage and an annual tribute, and with his aid seized control of Milan. He dared not kill Prospero, who was so beloved by his subjects, and, in any case, he hesitated to raise his hand directly against his divinely appointed lord, who was also his brother; but he caused Prospero to be hurried aboard a ship at dead of night and carried far away from Milan.

Prospero, who was a widower, had an only child, a three-year-old daughter called Miranda. She was taken with him, and far out at sea they were both placed in an open boat, without sail, oars or rudder, and cast adrift. Thus Antonio's hands were technically clean of royal and kindred blood, but Prospero and Miranda were given up to an almost certain fate. Antonio had intended that they should be set adrift without food or water; but old Gonzalo, a noble of Naples, who was in command of the ship, was more merciful than the cruel usurper. He furnished the boat not only with the necessities of life, but also with rich garments, linens and other useful articles, and added to these certain volumes from Prospero's library which he prized above his dukedom.

The castaways' sorry plight lasted for several days until they came to an uninhabited island rich with trees and fruits, and blessed with a warm and pleasant climate.

Here Prospero settled comfortably enough, making his home in a suitable cave; and here Miranda grew up, knowing no other human being than her father until she was about sixteen.

Meanwhile Prospero had continued with his studies in natural science and white magic, and had turned them to good use. Before his arrival, there had been only one inhabitant of the island, a foul old witch called Sycorax. She had barely escaped trial by fire and had also been marooned there. The island had many good but invisible spirits dwelling upon it, and Sycorax had tried to make Ariel, the chief of these, into her servant. But Ariel refused to do any evil, and Sycorax confined him in a pine-tree where he suffered grievously until Prospero discovered him and set him free. In return, Ariel became Prospero's servant, but with the promise of absolute freedom as soon as his services were no longer needed.

Sycorax had died before Prospero and Miranda reached the island, but she left behind her a son called Caliban who was half-human and half-animal. Prospero tamed him, taught him to speak, and tried to civilize him. But Caliban showed little sign of becoming truly human and finding his soul, so at last Prospero gave him up in despair and set him to do such menial tasks as hewing wood and drawing water. Ariel saw he performed these tasks which he would only do when forced to them by constant punishments: he was pinched, or tripped into the brambles, by the invisible Ariel for his smaller rebellions; and wracked with cramp or ague by Prospero for more serious ill-doings.

At last the day came when fortune offered Prospero the chance of taking revenge on all his enemies. A ship came past the island, far out to sea but still visible. In it, Prospero learnt by his magic arts, sailed Alonzo, King of Naples, with his brother Sebastian and his son Ferdinand; and with them went Antonio, Prospero's wicked brother who was now the usurping Duke of Milan, besides several other lords including good old Gonzalo.

Then Prospero set to work in earnest: by his art he conjured up a terrible tempest which struck the ship and seemed about to dash it to pieces on the rocky coast of the island.

When all was over, and the sea was calm again, Ariel reported to his master to whom alone he was visible:

'At the height of the tempest, when it seemed that the ship must split at any moment, I drove them even madder with fear by making myself seem one of those balls of fire which appear in the direst storms. Sometimes I burnt on the deck, sometimes in the waist of the ship; sometimes I even divided myself in two and blazed on the mast and the bowsprit at the same moment. And all the time I saw to it that the thunder roared and the lightning flashed terribly enough to cow the very bravest.'

'Was anyone unshaken by these horrors?' asked Prospero.

'Not a single person,' answered Ariel. 'The King's son, Ferdinand, was the first to plunge into the sea, crying that all hell was let loose on the ship; and the rest followed him.'

'This was near to shore?' asked Prospero.

'Yes,' nodded Ariel, 'and I have obeyed your orders exactly. Not a hair of one of them is harmed, nor have even their garments suffered. The King's son is alone in one part of the island, believing himself to be the sole survivor of the wreck; the King and his party are in another, believing that all have perished except themselves. But the ship is safely anchored in the hidden bay, with all the sailors comfortably asleep below decks. Only two of the crew are on the island, the butler Stephano and Trinculo the Jester, as you instructed me. And the rest of the fleet, from which I had separated the King's ship, has turned back sadly to Naples, thinking they saw him go down with all hands.'

'Why, that's my dainty spirit!' cried Prospero. 'But there's more work for you!'

'Am I never to be free?' lamented Ariel.

'Remember the torments I freed you from,' Prospero reminded

him sternly. 'Have you forgotten Sycorax and the torture you endured shut up in the pine-tree? Be careful, lest I split an oak and leave you to howl there for a dozen years. But I know that such a punishment will be unnecessary. Your freedom is near. After today I shall have no more commands for you, and you may go where you will.'

'That's my noble master!' cried Ariel gleefully. 'Now what shall I do? Say what—what shall I do?'

'First bring Prince Ferdinand hither,' commanded Prospero, and in an instant Ariel was gone.

When he found the Prince, he floated before him invisible, playing seductively beautiful music, and singing:

'Full fathom five thy father lies;
　Of his bones are coral made;
Those are pearls that were his eyes;
　Nothing of him that doth fade
But doth suffer a sea-change
Into something rich and strange.
　Sea-nymphs hourly ring his knell:
Hark! Now I hear them!—Ding, dong, bell!'

The music continued, and Ferdinand followed it as if in a dream until it drew him near to Prospero's cell.

Miranda and her father were standing inside, and Prospero said to her:

'Look out and tell me what you see.'

'What is it?' gasped Miranda. 'A spirit? Oh, it's a handsome one—but it must be a spirit.'

'No, girl, it's a human being, as we are,' smiled Prospero. 'He was in the wreck. Except that he is a little marred with grief, you might describe him as a fine young man.'

'I would call him a thing divine!' exclaimed Miranda. 'Surely no natural creature could look so noble!'

Now Ferdinand saw Miranda, who was advancing from the cave, and he was as struck by her beauty as she had been by his:

'This must be the goddess of the island,' he exclaimed. 'What can I say to you? Sweet wonder, tell me if you are a maid or not?'

'No wonder, sir, but an ordinary maid,' she answered.

'At first sight they've fallen in love,' thought Prospero. 'This is just what I hoped would happen.'

'Sweet maid,' cried Ferdinand, 'if you will have me, I'll make you Queen of Naples!'

'They are both in each other's thrall,' thought Prospero. 'But too easy a wooing may make the prize seem light'. 'Listen, young man! I don't believe you are the King of Naples, as you suggest— I think you are a spy come to win this island from me. Follow me, traitor. Come; you shall be tied up in my cave, and only let out to do hard labor.'

'I'll resist such entertainment until my enemy has more power!' cried Ferdinand drawing his sword.

But Prospero merely raised his wand and Ferdinand's arm fell powerless to his side.

'Oh my dear father,' cried Miranda. 'Do not put him to such trials. I'm sure he's true and noble.'

But Prospero pretended to be angry with her, and using his magic, led Ferdinand away to a great pile of logs which he commanded the young man to carry to the cave.

While Ferdinand was laboring as a woodcutter to win his princess, the King of Naples and the rest of his party had settled themselves on the other side of the island. Alonzo was brokenhearted at the supposed death of his son, and even Gonzalo could do little to cheer him up. The good old man did his best by starting a spirited discussion on the best forms of government with Sebastian, Alonzo's brother, and Antonio, Prospero's brother.

But even on Prospero's enchanted island the evil at the hearts of evil men could not rest. At Prospero's command, Ariel caused all the company, except Antonio and Sebastian, to fall asleep; and these two villains began at once to plot the murder of King Alonzo and the faithful Gonzalo, in order to make Sebastian King of Naples.

When the two conspirators had actually drawn their swords to do the deed, Ariel wakened Alonzo and Gonzalo; and the two villains tried to explain their naked weapons by a lame and muddled excuse which, in their fright, they gave as the bellowing of lions and the roaring of bulls.

Nevertheless, they decided to continue their murderous design when the chance came.

Prospero, who had been watching, now caused Ariel to spread a wonderful banquet before the party just when they were hungriest—and then to snatch it away in the form of a Harpy who reminded Alonzo, Antonio and Sebastian of their crime against Prospero. The words of this supernatural monster—a creature with wings and claws, but with the head and breast of a woman—filled the three guilty men with such fear and shame that they went out of their minds, and their companions led them forlornly about the island hoping that they would soon recover.

Two other survivors from the ship were wandering on the island, thinking themselves the only ones left alive; and neither of them was in complete control of his senses. These were Stephano the butler and Trinculo the jester. Trinculo was a little off his head with fear, and when he found Caliban lying under a cloak—trying to hide from his latest punishment for disobedience to Prospero—he took him for a dead islander, and hid under the cloak with him, thinking another storm was about to break.

Stephano, who had swum ashore on a barrel of sack and had drunk a good deal of it since he landed, was so fuddled in his wits that he took the strange object under the cloak for a monster with four legs and two voices.

When he discovered his mistake, he gave Trinculo and Caliban liberal doses of sack which worked marvels on them.

Caliban assumed that Stephano and Trinculo were gods, and swore to worship and serve them. The drunken Stephano proclaimed himself king of the island, and when Caliban told him about Prospero and Miranda, decided to go and murder Prospero and take Miranda as his wife and queen.

While these two strange parties of conspirators were moving round the island under Ariel's secret guidance, and never catching up with each other, Ferdinand was still laboring at his logs.

'Some sports are painful,' he thought, 'and some base employments can be endured because they have noble causes. This mean task would be odious to me, a prince, did not the lady for whom I labor turn it into pleasure. Thinking of her refreshes me in my hard work, and makes it a delight.'

Miranda herself was so much in love with Ferdinand that she could not stay away from him for long. At first she hid in the cave and watched him; but when he came staggering past with a heavy log on his shoulder, she could bear it no more, and ran out to him, exclaiming:

'Please do not work so hard, you'll hurt yourself. I wish the lightning had burnt up all those wretched logs! Put that one down and rest. My father is deep in his books and not likely to leave them for a good three hours.'

'But dearest, he's given me a certain number to move, and it will be dark before I've shifted them all,' protested Ferdinand sadly.

'Sit down and rest for a little while,' begged Miranda. 'I'll carry that log for you.'

'No, precious creature,' answered Ferdinand firmly. 'I'd rather crack my sinews and break my back than let you do such menial work while I sit by idly.'

'It would be no more shame for me to carry it than you,' said Miranda. 'Indeed, I'd do it better, for I'd do it because I wanted to, and you are carrying logs against your will. Moreover, from the way you speak I know that you are exhausted.'

'Not when you are near me,' he cried. 'For you come to me like fresh morning to the night. But please tell me your name, so that I may set it foremost in my prayers.'

'Miranda,' she answered; and then with a little gasp: 'Oh, I've disobeyed my father. He commanded me not to tell you.'

'Lovely Miranda,' said Ferdinand setting down the log. 'I have looked on many ladies, and listened to their sweet voices; I have liked several of them for different virtues, but have found some defect in them all. You, however, are quite perfect, as if created from the best in each woman.'

'I have never seen another woman,' murmured Miranda, 'nor any men except my father and yourself. But I could not wish for any companion in the world but you, nor can I imagine any shape which I could like as I do yours.'

'Miranda, I am a prince; perhaps by now a king, as I think my father's drowned,' said Ferdinand. 'And as such I would never endure my present slavery, except for your sake. Hear my soul speak: the very instant I saw you, my heart flew to your service, and there it dwells—and makes me a patient log-man.'

'Do you love me?' whispered Miranda.

'Heaven and earth bear witness that I do!' cried Ferdinand fervently. 'Beyond anything else in the world I love, prize and honor you.'

'I'm silly to weep at what makes me so happy,' sobbed Miranda. 'But it is at my unworthiness. I am your wife if you will marry me. If not, I'll die your maid—to serve you forever, if I cannot be your equal.'

'My beloved mistress, I it is who am ever in your service,' said Ferdinand, kneeling to her.

'My husband then?' she asked.

'Yes, with all my heart,' he answered, 'and here's my hand in pledge of it.'

'And mine with my heart too,' said Miranda. 'But now,' she continued, 'I must leave you for a while; you to carry your logs, and I to do what my father has bidden me.'

When they had each gone their separate ways, Prospero stepped forward smiling happily to himself. 'I cannot be so delighted as they are,' he thought, 'for to them their love is a joyful surprise; yet there is nothing in the world that can make me happier. But I must return to my magic book, for I've much more to do this day if all is to end as I intend it shall.'

He spent the next hour or so passing invisibly about the island to see how well Ariel was managing his various victims. The royal party he found penned by invisible barriers into a grove of trees not far from his cell. But the courtiers showed little desire to wander, for Alonzo, Sebastian and Antonio were raving mad; and it took Gonzalo and the other lords, Adrian and Francisco, all their time to prevent them from doing themselves or each other some injury.

Caliban was still trying to lead Stephano and Trinculo towards the cell, begging them to keep quiet and hurry so as to arrive while Prospero was taking his afternoon nap.

'You must creep in and sieze his magic wand and book,' Caliban kept explaining. 'Without them he is powerless, and we can drive a peg through his head, or whatever we like.'

'Then I shall be King Stephano!' hiccupped the butler, who had finished up his flaskful of sack, and was more drunk than ever. 'An' I'll have his daughter as my queen, an' we'll have an eee-normous family, an' people all the island with subjects for me to rule.'

Once or twice Trinculo began a song, and Stephano joined in. But when they sang, Ariel caught up the tune, and the wild music moaning through the trees terrified the drunken butler and jester until they were ready to run away.

'Don't be afraid,' Caliban urged them again and again, 'the isle is full of noises: the sounds and sweet tunes are most pleasant and do no harm. Sometimes a whole concert of instruments seems to be playing all round me; and sometimes voices so sweet that I fall asleep through listening to them. And when I do such wonderful dreams come to me; sometimes the clouds seem to open and shower riches on me—so that when I wake I cry to dream again.'

'This will turn out a marvellous kingdom,' cried Stephano. 'I'll get my music for nothing!'

'But not until Prospero is destroyed,' growled Caliban.

'All right, monster, lead on!' said Stephano, and they continued on their unsteady course, drawing slowly nearer and nearer to Prospero's cave.

There was still a little time before his schemes were due to reach their climax, and Prospero returned to his cell. He found that Ferdinand had finished carting his quota of logs.

Now Prospero appeared in quite another guise from the stern taskmaster, and was ready to let Ferdinand marry Miranda.

'All my harshness was but to try you,' he said, 'and I have found you worthy. And so, before Heaven, I give you my daughter to be your wife. But you must swear solemnly that you will treat her as if she were your sister or some virgin priestess until you can be married to her by the full and holy rites of religion.'

'As I hope for quiet days, a happy family and long life, I promise this,' said Ferdinand solemnly. 'My love is so true and pure that no temptation shall prompt the worser part of my nature to gain control and turn love into lust.'

'Nobly and honorably sworn,' said Prospero. 'Now take Miranda by the hand and sit with her here. We have a little time to spare, and I will show you what my magic arts can do. The spirits whom I rule can take on whatever shapes I wish, and speak words suitable to their form. Now they shall assume the likenesses of the goddesses of old—who were themselves the spirits of the powers of nature—and bring suitable gifts in the form of blessings on your betrothal.'

Sweet music began to play, and as the young couple sat entranced, the lovely shimmering form of Iris the Messenger, whose path from Olympus is down the arch of the rainbow, came gliding into sight.

When she reached earth she turned to summon the goddesses who were to bring gifts. And the first of these was Ceres (as the Romans called Demeter), the goddess of fruitfulness.

'Come, Ceres, bounteous lady of rich crops and meadow lands!' she cried; and very soon the dignified goddess stood before them, crowned with her emblems of the golden harvest: wheat, rye, barley, oats and the rest.

'Hail, many-colored messenger!' she cried. 'Why have you summoned me hither?'

'To celebrate a contract of true love,' answered Iris, 'and make some gift to these happy lovers. But now great Juno comes!'

Then the Queen of the Immortals, the Greek Hera whom the Romans named Juno, came into sight in her chariot drawn by peacocks, and spoke to Ceres:

'Come with me, my generous sister, and bless this pair of lovers so that they may have all wealth and happiness, and be fortunate in their children.'

Then the two goddesses drew near to Ferdinand and Miranda, and Juno began to chant:

> 'Honor, riches, marriage-blessing,
> Long continuance and increasing,
> Hourly joys be still upon you!
> Juno sings her blessings on you.'

Then Ceres took up the hymn:

> 'Earth's increase, and harvest plenty,
> Barns and garners never empty . . .
> Scarcity and want shall shun you:
> Ceres' blessing so is on you.'

Then, at a word from Juno and Ceres, Iris chanted her summons:

> 'You nymphs, called Naiades, of the wandering brooks,
> With your sedged crowns and ever-harmless looks!
> Come, temperate nymphs, and help to celebrate
> A contract of true love; be not too late!'

At her words a great concourse of nymphs appeared; and after them came reapers. All then performed an intricate dance about the three goddesses. The evening sun flashed on their bright garments and glittering jewels, on the golden crowns of Ceres and Juno, on Iris's rainbow train, and on the shining eyes in the tails of Juno's peacocks.

Suddenly Prospero remembered the other parties on the island. He waved his wand, and all the bright pageant faded away and was gone like a whisp of mist touched by the glory of the sunset.

'Do not be troubled,' said Prospero with a smile at Ferdinand who had sprung to his feet in surprise. 'Our revels are now ended, and these actors who, as I told you, were spirits, have melted into thin air. Take this, if you will, as a lesson: all this world of ours, and the cloud-capped towers, the gorgeous palaces and the solemn temples—yes, and we ourselves—shall fade one day as these have done, and leave no trace behind.

'You must forgive me for sending the spirits away so suddenly,' he continued. 'I have a tiresome business to attend to. You and Miranda go into my cell; I'll join you later.'

So Ferdinand and Miranda drew the curtain across the entrance and sat down to play chess, while Prospero directed Ariel to hang gorgeous robes and crowns on the bushes nearby. Scarcely had he done so, when Caliban came creeping along, followed by Stephano and Trinculo.

'There is the cave!' whispered Caliban. 'Go softly in and do the deed which will make you king of this island.'

Stephano drew his knife and began to advance cautiously towards the cave. But suddenly he and Trinculo saw the glittering robes hanging on the bushes, and at once they forgot all else and began to handle them and put them on.

In vain Caliban begged them to forget such trash and kill Prospero before he woke and turned them all into barnacles or apes: they could think of nothing but the rich booty that they had discovered. And when Stephano and Trinculo had put on as many robes and crowns as they could wear, they loaded up Caliban with the rest and bade him carry them to the cave by the seashore where the barrel of sack was hidden.

But they had not gone very far when a great troupe of spirits in the shape of hounds broke upon them and sent them flying with screams of terror.

'Have them hunted soundly!' directed Prospero, 'but let them be ready to appear when the time comes. When you have seen to this, come back, for my schemes are nearly complete. The sun is low, and all must be ended with the day.'

As soon as Ariel returned, Prospero bade him bring King Alonzo and his party to the cave. 'Where have you left the courtiers?' he asked.

'Where you told me to,' answered Ariel, 'among those trees over there. They are in a very sorry state, the three mad and the rest mourning over them. The saddest of all is the old man you call "the good Gonzalo", whose tears run down his beard like rain from thatched eaves. If you saw them you would be truly sorry for them.'

'Do you think so?' asked Prospero.

'I know I should if I were human,' answered Ariel as he sped away to fetch them.

'My own purpose is for mercy, forgiveness and reconciliation,' mused Prospero. 'I have no use or wish for vengeance. All shall end in happiness—and to this end only have I directed my magic powers. But once I leave the island, I'll use them no more. I'll break my wand and bury it deep in the earth, while my books of spells shall sink further into the sea than sounding-lead has ever gone.'

Presently the woeful party arrived, and for a little while stood as if dazed while the magic music sounded and the madness slowly faded away from the brains of Alonzo, Sebastian and Antonio.

'Now Ariel,' said Prospero before the charm had quite passed from them, 'hasten to where the ship lies and fetch the captain and the boatswain. Swiftly!'

'I am gone!' cried Ariel, and was away at the speed of light.

In a few moments the royal party was completely free from the enchantment; they were staring in amazement at Prospero, who spoke to them, saying:

'Behold, my lord King, here is the much-wronged Duke of

Milan, Prospero. And here is my hand to prove that I am he, a living man, and no ghost.'

'There has been a strange madness on my spirits,' said Alonzo. 'Yet I think you are real, though I do not know how you can be Prospero. But whether you are real or not, I herewith resign my sovereignty over your dukedom, and beg you to pardon me for the wrong I did you.'

'First let me embrace the friend to whom I owe so much,' said Prospero, clasping old Gonzalo. Then he turned to the others and greeted them all; but to Sebastian and Antonio he said in a low voice which no one else could hear:

'As for you two, you tried to murder the King. If I wished it I could denounce you as traitors; but for the moment I'll tell no tales.'

'The devil speaks through his mouth!' gasped Sebastian.

'Not so,' said Prospero; and turning to Antonio he went on: 'You, most wicked of men—I will not infect my mouth by calling you brother—I forgive you all your faults, and ask only that you return my dukedom to me. I think you will, in any case, be forced to restore it.'

'If you are indeed Prospero,' said King Alonzo, 'tell me how you were saved. How did you come to be on this island? We were wrecked on your shores scarcely three hours ago; I lost my dear son Ferdinand in the catastrophe.'

'I can share your grief,' said Prospero. 'For in that same tempest I lost my own child, my daughter Miranda.'

'A daughter!' exclaimed Alonzo. 'I wish to Heaven they were both alive, in Naples, and as king and queen! I'd give up my throne for that; I'd even change places with my son in the oozy bed where he now rests.'

'Let me repeat,' said Prospero, 'that I am the very man who was Duke of Milan and who was dethroned by my brother Antonio, and set adrift. How I came here and what has happened since I landed, I'll tell you later. But now welcome to my cell. And you, my lord King, since you have given me back my dukedom, I'll give you a gift yet more rich. Draw back that curtain and you'll see.'

Alonzo did so, wondering, and there sat Ferdinand and Miranda playing chess.

'Sweet lord, you cheated!' exclaimed Miranda.

'No, my dearest love, I would not for the world!' said Ferdinand. Then he saw Alonzo and sprang up, to kneel before him, saying:

'Dearest father, the seas are merciful and I have cursed them without cause.'

'Oh wonders!' exclaimed Miranda, seeing the King and his followers. 'What a lot of lovely creatures are here! How beautiful mankind is! Oh brave new world, that has such people in it!'

'It is all new to you!' smiled Prospero.

'Who is this maid with whom you were playing?' asked Alonzo. 'You cannot have known her for more than three hours! Is she the goddess of this island, who has separated us and brought us together again?'

'Sir, she is mortal,' answered Ferdinand, 'but by the will of immortal Providence, she's mine. I chose her when I could not ask my father for his advice, nor indeed thought I had one. She is the daughter of this famous Duke of Milan, Prospero, of whom I have so often heard. From him I have received a second life, and this lady makes him a second father to me.'

'And I will be a second father to her,' said Alonzo. 'But how oddly it will sound when I begin by asking my new daughter for forgiveness.'

'Speak no more of that, sir,' said Prospero. 'All are forgiven. Let us forget past injuries.'

'Give me your hands,' said Alonzo to Ferdinand and Miranda; and he joined them, and blessed them ending with the words:

'Let grief and sorrow still wring the heart of anyone who does not wish you joy!'

'Be it so. Amen,' said old Gonzalo solemnly.

At this moment the captain and boatswain appeared, shepherded by the unseen Ariel, and told the King the joyful tidings that his ship was safe in harbor with all hands on board.

While they were rejoicing over this unexpected good news,

Trinculo and Stephano appeared in their stolen robes, all scratched and torn, followed by Caliban. Prospero told the King what his two drunken servants had been up to; but forgiveness was in the air that day, and they were let off with scarcely even a reprimand.

But Prospero spoke more sternly to Caliban:

'Go to my cave,' he said, 'take these two companions of yours with you, and see that they work hard making all ready for my guests. If all is done well, I'll forgive you your plot against my life.'

'That I will indeed!' exclaimed Caliban, 'and I'll be wise after this, and try to live as you have taught me. But oh what a thrice-double ass I was to mistake this drunkard for a god!'

So that night Prospero entertained the whole party in his cave, and next day they all set sail for Naples, leaving Caliban in possession of the island.

'One last command, sweet Ariel,' said Prospero. 'See that we have calm seas and following winds to take us safely to Naples—to the wedding of Prince Ferdinand and my daughter Miranda. After that, you may go where you will and mingle with the elements to which you belong.'

Ariel did as he was bidden; and then with a glad cry of farewell to Prospero, he was away into the wide world, singing:

> 'Where the bee sucks, there suck I:
> In a cowslip's bell I lie;
> There I couch when owls do cry.
> On the bat's back I do fly
> After summer merrily.
> Merrily, merrily shall I live now
> Under the blossom that hangs on the bough.'

Roger Lancelyn Green

has been a professional actor, an antiquarian book-
seller, and the deputy librarian of Merton College,
Oxford. But he is best known as the author of splendid
versions of Ancient Greek and Norse legends and for
his retellings of the King Arthur and Robin Hood
stories. He has also written biography, literary criticism, and original books for children. He is a graduate
of Merton College, Oxford, with both a B.Litt. and
an M.A. His home is at Poulton-Lancelyn and Lower
Bebington, where he is hereditary Lord of the Manors.